'With well-rou[nded ... te]rific sense of time and place and masterful pl[ot ... police] procedural is a 24-carat holiday read' *Guardian*

'Vivid and compelling, with great evocation of the 1980s period' Peter James

'Authenticity in spades' crimefictionlover.com

'A top read' *Sunday Sport*

'Astringent and ambitious' *Financial Times*

'A fast-moving thriller ... strong characters, dark humour and a terrific sense of place. I was totally absorbed' Elly Griffiths

'A masterclass in place and landscape' Christie Watson

'This is old-style policing set in an interesting period' Geoffrey Wansell, *Daily Mail*

'Brilliantly engineered police procedural' *Daily Mirror*

'Taut, atmospheric' Simon Kernick

'Perfectly structured . . . a new Essex reimagined as a noir landscape' Lawrence Osborne

YELLOWHAMMER

James Henry

riverrun

First published in Great Britain in 2018 by riverrun
This paperback edition published in 2020 by

riverrun

an imprint of

Quercus Editions Ltd
Carmelite House
50 Victoria Embankment
London EC4Y 0DZ

An Hachette UK company

A CIP catalogue record for this book is available
from the British Library

PB ISBN 978 1 78087 984 0
EBOOK ISBN 978 1 84866 916 1

10 9 8 7 6 5 4 3 2 1

Typeset by CC Book Production
Printed and bound in Great Britain by Clays Ltd, Elcograf S.p.A.

Papers used by Quercus are from well-managed forests and other responsible sources.

For the six in Fuerteventura many years ago.

'A happy home of sunshine, flowers and streams.
Yet in the sweetest places cometh ill'

The Yellowhammer's Nest, John Clare

Come she come say
Ride on the night

Soolaimon, Neil Diamond

PROLOGUE

8.05 a.m., 25th July 1983

Hide and seek.

Alan was twelve. It should be girls, pop music and maybe cigarettes, yet he loved it out here on the farm, where nobody from school could see him play these childish games with his cousins. All three were girls – the youngest, Emma, was only six, the same age as his brother, Darren – but the other two were older than Alan; Alice by a year, and Lucy by three. This made it okay – even they couldn't resist the thrill of hiding out in the meadow over the summer holidays. They all set off through the towering poplars beyond the farmhouse, the rooks cawing above them, and headed straight for the ageless great oak in the middle of the pasture. The ancient tree with its unfathomably huge trunk marked the starting place for their game. From the oak to the woods that bordered the railway line was a two-hundred-yard sprint through the tall grass; or they could double-back through the poplars and hide in one of the farm buildings (but this was unwise since Uncle Christopher had angrily ordered them to go outside and leave him in peace). Emma was 'it'. Small, with short, unruly tomboy hair, she stood on one side of the gnarled trunk, facing towards the house. The rest of them, Alan included, stood on the other side. As soon as Emma began the count, they all dashed for cover.

Alan hurtled towards the dense green woodland and made for an entrance point leading to the tracks and paths he knew by heart. The count to one hundred grew distant, as did the cries of the others as they fanned out across the field. He darted nimbly into the darkest part of the woods. He resisted the obvious place – the giant rhododendron with the huge pink flowers and strong branches that could easily support the weight of a small boy. Instead he carried on through and beyond the thick holly where the ground began to rise. The railway track. Had he come that far? Yes, as the trees fell away he could see the overhead lines.

He scampered up the embankment. After quickly looking left and right, in Green Cross Code fashion, he climbed up and stood on the tracks, hand on hips. With a deep breath, he took in the distance he had covered. Out beyond the woods he could see the oak.

A flash of orange caught his eye on the nearside track; he turned cautiously knowing it to be a fox. The animal, about twenty yards away, looked up at him then returned its attention to tugging and playing with something on the gravel near the track. It looked like a sack, a dark blue colour. A rubbish sack? Coal sack, maybe . . . no, wait . . . oh, no . . .

Just then a sound reached him from the farmhouse, sending the rooks in the poplars skywards. He turned back towards the fox but the animal, having a natural fear of shotguns, had fled.

Part 1

THE ACCOUNTANT

Monday 25th July

8.30 a.m., East Street, Coggeshall, ten miles west of Colchester

'What a quaint place,' WPC Gabriel remarked as the police car ground to a halt.

'Hmm, I don't know about that.' WPC Fletcher yanked up the Allegro handbrake. 'Funny goings-on's all I hear.' Fletcher was Gabriel's senior by five years and she was a lot more guarded in her attitude.

'That pub next to the church back there can't have changed since Shakespeare's time, and just look at those little pink cottages. I'd love to live here,' Gabriel said brightly.

'Used to be a noisy old place,' said Fletcher. 'Traffic that thunders down here, I'm amazed half these building are still standing.' The two policewomen walked down a street lined with Grade II listed buildings. 'They just put in a bypass north of here at Great Tey, expect it'll quieten down a bit now. You'd be closer to Lowry if you did move.'

Gabriel pulled a face. The thought of bumping into the

taciturn CID inspector on her days off was, she had to admit, a definite downer.

'Right, where are we.' Fletcher checked the house numbers and pulled out her pocketbook. 'Disturbances, disturbances.'

None of the houses were detached but each one was individually crafted, no two the same. Plaques on several of them cited years of construction, ranging from 1566 to 1640, but the house they were to call at was undated. Orange in colour, it was distinctive for being set back from the street more so than the others, forming an indent along the row, like a wonky tooth.

A grey-haired woman opened the timber door.

'Mrs Harris?' Fletcher asked.

'You've come! Thank you, so much.' She stepped back from the threshold to allow them to enter her home.

Gabriel blinked, her eyes adjusting to the darkness after the bright July morning outside. An air of claustrophobia hit her, a quality born of something other than just the gloom and low ceilings.

'Excuse the mess,' the lady said.

Gabriel surveyed the room. It was, to her mind, perfectly tidy, if one excluded the books – all shapes and sizes on the shelves and stacked in neat piles on the floor.

'How can we be of assistance, Mrs Harris?' Fletcher asked stiffly.

Mrs Harris' deep blue eyes darted between Fletcher and Gabriel, back and forth in their sunken sockets.

'It's the noises,' she said sharply.

'Noises? Where?'

The woman gingerly pointed up.

'Upstairs?'

Mrs Harris did not answer. Instead she turned and made towards the staircase. The two policewomen had no option but to follow. The stairs creaked as the old lady slowly ascended. On reaching a tiny landing, she once again pointed her crooked forefinger at the roof.

The ceiling height here was even lower than downstairs, and Gabriel was forced to stoop. 'What sort of noise is it that's bothering you, Mrs Harris?'

'Crying.' Her head gestured slowly towards a hatch in the ceiling.

Fletcher, the shorter of the two, stood firm, pulling a face. 'As in, human tears?'

'No doubt about it.'

'Excuse me, madam, your call was –' she consulted her pocketbook – 'in relation to a disturbance?'

'Yes, well. It is a disturbance; it's disturbed my sleep.'

Gabriel was unsure what to say, but her kindness took over. 'We can take a quick look, would that be helpful? Have you any steps, and a torch?' Mrs Harris nodded. Moments later she was back with both.

Gabriel was tall enough to dislodge the roof hatch without aid. Standing on a footstool, half in and half out of the roof, Gabriel darted the torch beam around. She was not sure what she was seeking. In truth it was merely a gesture. All she could see was brickwork and dust.

'Do you use the roof for storage?' she called down.

'As you can see, there's not much room for more than a couple of spiders up there,' came the reply. 'Oh, and maybe some old seventy-eights.'

Sure enough, wedged over in the far corner was a cardboard box of vinyls in yellowing record sleeves. But certainly no evidence of human occupation.

'I can't see anything, Mrs Harris,' Gabriel said as she stepped down.

Mrs Harris shook her head doubtfully. 'It'll be there again tonight.'

They all filed back down into the front room in silence. Mrs Harris stood beside a fireplace so large it dominated the entire room. A Tudor beam festooned with horse brasses ran at shoulder height across the chimney breast.

'Have you noticed anything else unusual?' Gabriel asked, not wishing to leave just yet.

'Him.' Mrs Harris turned and pointed towards the floor-to-ceiling bookshelves. 'He moves.'

Puzzled, the two policewomen looked across the room. The 'him' Mrs Harris was referring to was in fact a wooden figurine of a rather rotund Buddha, sitting cross-legged and laughing. Fletcher rolled her eyes.

Gabriel took a step closer. 'May I?'

She picked up the ornament. On closer inspection, she

noticed extraordinary detail in the crafting. The intricacy was impressive; from the braiding on his open jacket revealing the smooth shine of his belly, to his grinning mouth and eyes. She wondered where it had come from. Suddenly Fletcher snatched it away from her.

'Not motorised, is it?' she sniffed, holding it upside down. 'Or maybe you've a draft. Do you leave the window open?' Fletcher always got snarky when she lost patience and felt someone was wasting her time.

Gabriel heard a siren approaching fast outside. In seconds a police car shot past, the noise amplified, bouncing off the old buildings in the narrow street, leaving a ringing in her ears.

'Come on,' Fletcher urged, placing the Buddha back down. 'We're done here.'

Gabriel gave the old woman her card and smiled apologetically. There really was nothing they could do to help.

'Do call if, if anything strange . . . anything happens again,' she said, not knowing in truth what 'anything' might mean.

9.15 a.m., Fox Farm

The police were called at 8.25 a.m. to Fox Farm, a three-acre small holding between the village of Kelvedon and Silver End, twelve miles west of Colchester. A 53-year-old man had killed himself with a shotgun. Less than half a mile away, on the railway line that borders the property to the south, a second body had been found.

The parish of Kelvedon sat on the old London Road, sandwiched between the A12 motorway and the railway line; the main arteries from the capital to the east coast. Although London was slowly extending its sprawl into the home counties, this far out – fifty-five miles to the north-east – the sleepy rural towns of Essex remained much the same as they had been at the beginning of the century. The only real progress had come with the Victorians, visible in the stout, red-brick buildings made possible with the advancing railroad. Yes, the Second World War had brought the U.S. Airforce and numerous army bases to the fields of Essex, but after they left, the rich boulder clay soil was reclaimed by arable farmers and the topography soon reverted. As the decades rolled on, progress bypassed the region rather than came to it. Heavy articulated trucks and freight trains chuntered straight through and beyond, to Harwich and the rapidly expanding port of Felixstowe.

This morning, however, the train line was silent.

Detective Constable Daniel Kenton of Colchester CID and a uniformed officer stood outside the farmhouse gate with a broad woman in her thirties from the cottage on Fox Lane. Her hair was in disarray, having overslept and been woken by the phone call. Her face was freckled, lightly sun-kissed on the forehead and nose, and if pressed, Kenton would have described her complexion as rather more 'rural' than 'ruddy'.

'Mrs Everett, why do you think the girl telephoned you first, and not the police?' The uniformed officer was a local bobby from Kelvedon station.

'It's "Miss". The children are terrified. They need the comfort of a person they know and trust. The police are ...' She couldn't think of a word.

'To be feared?' Kenton offered.

'I wouldn't put it as strongly as that, but along those lines, yes. Seeing their father like that ... Scarred for life.' They both looked over at the five children standing together in the shade of the ambulances near the farmhouse. WPCs Gabriel and Fletcher were with them. Kenton watched the taller WPC comfort the two older girls who were wailing uncontrollably, while the medics moved from one child to the next.

'Remind me – the boys are not the deceased's children?' Kenton said.

'No. Alan and Darren Ward are his nephews, the girls' cousins. The boys' parents, Suzanne's sister and her husband, have gone to Greece. They dropped them here yesterday evening.'

The brothers stood silently, in shock most probably. The youngest Ward boy, Darren, had only just been found, thinking the game of hide and seek still ongoing.

'Why ... ?' she repeated. 'Why shoot himself? Those poor children.'

Kenton wasn't really listening; his attention was on Jane Gabriel – he'd seen quite a bit of her lately and she had indicated she would come to the beach with him one day. He prayed the weather would hold. There was talk of a sea breeze.

'It's a great shame,' Kenton said eventually, without much

conviction. In truth he didn't have much sympathy with suicides. The man on the train track could well be a suicide, too, jumping from a moving train. His position on the embankment could lead one to that conclusion, though usually they chose the bridge.

The crunch of tyres on gravel behind him heralded Inspector Lowry's arrival. Kenton turned and frowned at the smashed headlight and the crease running from the wheel arch to the driver door that had yet to be repaired. In a small way, this upset the junior officer. He wished his boss would have it fixed; it was a constant reminder that Lowry occasionally had too many and drove. The Saab had been in sharp contact with a pub sign pole near his home and the car door squealed as he emerged.

'Morning, guv,' Kenton nodded.

'What have we got?'

'Two bodies, both male – one inside the building and another on the railway line half a mile away, beyond those trees. This lady found the one in the kitchen and made the call to the constable here, who waited for my arrival.' Lowry started towards the house. 'Er . . . we've been asked to examine the body on the track first, sir.'

'By who?'

'The chief. Folk at Felixstowe getting in a fluster with the line being down – cargo trains delayed, not to mention the commuters.'

Lowry's broad frame continued towards the house, in his unchanging grey suit.

'Not to mention the heat, flies and so forth,' Kenton persisted. 'There was even a fox at the body when the boy found it.'

'Boy?' Lowry paused in his tracks.

'Alan Ward, twelve years old.'

'I see.' Lowry paused to acknowledge the children by the ambulance.

'Have we identified either of the bodies?'

'Only the one in the house: Christopher Cliff, who lives here.'

To Lowry's mind the unidentified man took priority.

'All right, Dan, lead on.'

2

9.45 a.m., Fox Farm

The man in charge was a detective. He was not in uniform but Alan reckoned he was in charge because all the uniformed police, and another man in shirtsleeves with wavy hair, all had to talk to him urgently. He was a big man, tall and wide, and despite the hot weather he wore a pale grey suit and black tie, like Napoleon Solo out of *The Man From U.N.C.L.E.* Some uniformed police had recently returned from the pasture, having been up to see the mess Alan had found.

The group parted and the man in the suit walked slowly towards Alan. He even smiled slightly as he grew closer. Alan's knees went weak; maybe they thought he had something to do with it? The thing on the train track, not what had happened to Uncle Christopher.

'Hello, Alan,' he said in a friendly way. 'My name is Detective Inspector Lowry. You can call me Nick. Don't worry, you'll be able to go home soon. Shall we get away from here a bit? Maybe walk over to the tree, in the shade?'

'Yes, sir.' He sipped the rest of the Coke a kind police lady had given him, placing the can on the ground by the ambulance wheel. His brother stood nearby holding Emma's hand, watching. The game of hide and seek seemed a long time ago.

'Come on,' said the detective. 'Let's go.'

'Thank you, sir,' Alan said without thinking, and they set off in the direction of the meadow.

'What school do you go to? One in Colchester?'

Alan told him.

'I know it. It's a good school.'

The detective picked a piece of long grass and put it between his teeth, like all the bigger boys did.

'Tell me as slowly or as quickly as you like what happened from the time you arrived at your uncle's house.'

'What, from last night? What about the train track?'

'We'll get to that. You see, I need your help with your uncle, too. Your cousins are very, very upset and can't really remember what happened. Losing their dad, it's a terrible shock.'

'"Losing"? Saying it like that, doesn't sound like someone dying,' Alan said, looking up at him as they reached the tree.'

'This is a big old tree,' Lowry said, patting it. 'I wonder how old it is.' He turned to Alan, taking the grass from his mouth and said, 'I reckon you're big enough to talk about what happened, right?'

Alan agreed keenly.

'That noise you heard when you were out on the track

was a shotgun. Your uncle took his own life. You know that, right?'

'Uh-huh.'

'Now,' Lowry placed his hands on the boy's tiny narrow shoulders, 'I want you to tell me everything you remember since arriving here last night. Think you can do that?'

Alan quickly nodded and told him everything he could think of, from being dropped at the farm after tea, and then Auntie and Uncle leaving them alone to go to the pub, to watching the cowboy film . . .

Lowry let the kid gabble on. It was like floodgates – the sheer relief of talking to someone, anyone. It made sense to view the body on the track first – not because it remained unidentified but because Lowry wished to see the two deaths in reverse order to Kenton and Uniform. The instincts are dulled by repetition, even in dealing with death. He listened to the lad as they walked slowly through the long grass. The boy and his younger brother had arrived yesterday evening; they played outside with their cousins, had tea, and later the grown-ups had gone to the local pub, leaving the kids to their own devices. This morning, the boy's aunt had left home before breakfast for an appointment, leaving her husband in charge. There had been shouting, an argument between the children after her departure.

'Uncle Christopher got very cross.'

'Oh, why was that?'

'He was trying to work, but the girls were fighting.'

Lowry turned to Alan Ward, who was pink in the face now. 'Fighting about what?'

He shrugged. 'I don't know . . . girl stuff. Anyway, he wanted us all outside, and that's why we ended up playing hide and seek.'

Two constables greeted them at the path into the woodland.

'Thank you for the chat, Alan. You've been really helpful. You can go back to your brother now; I'll go on alone from here.'

'Sir?' said Alan. 'There's just one more thing.'

'Yes, lad?'

'I remember exactly the time the gun went.'

'You do?'

'8.15. I have a new digital watch, see.' He proudly presented his wrist and the silver Casio.

'That's very useful to know, thank you.'

The boy nodded. 'Can I go home now?'

Lowry patted the lad on the shoulder.

'Soon enough.'

Lowry gestured to one of the two Uniforms to take the boy back to the farmhouse, before following the other on through the trees.

On reaching the railway track, he stood and looked and listened. The view of patchwork fields – some green, some yellow, some brown – spread out as far as the eye could see underneath a ceaseless blue sky. There was not so much as a breath of wind. The sound of a shotgun would easily travel.

To the north, the cawing of rooks in the poplars; to the south, the faint sound of a skylark high over the field, and crickets in the surrounding grass. He walked slowly towards the body, heat shimmering on the track, white in the sunlight. Dr Sutton, the Scene of Crimes doctor and a man of agitated disposition, waited to one side. Sergeant Barnes's head appeared from the south side of the embankment.

'Morning, Inspector,' he puffed.

'Sergeant.'

'There is no access to the track from this side.'

Lowry knelt down beside the body, which lay face down, diagonally, six feet from the track. The body could have rolled; they were on an incline. He was not immediately visible from the track – the boy's attention had initially been drawn by a fox. Blood soaked the back of a navy cotton shirt. The head was pointing north towards the farmhouse, cheek down in the grass. A blade of coarse sedge grass touched the eyeball.

'If he was hit by a train, he wouldn't be on the rails,' Barnes said. 'Locomotive would've sent him flying, like this distance. Maybe he jumped.'

'The driver would have seen a man on the track. And reported it.' Lowry looked back the way he'd come. 'Why jump here, though? Surely the bridge would be the obvious.'

The sergeant grunted. 'Maybe he missed his stop.' Lowry recognised Barnes's cynicism.

The dead body appeared to be largely undamaged. A large

fly explored a well-manicured hand. Sunlight caught the case of a silver wristwatch, which poked out from a shirt sleeve. Lowry resisted the temptation to root around for ID – he had to let the doctor continue his work, then get forensics in. Lowry didn't believe the man had been struck by a train. The trains ground to a halt if they hit a small deer; a grown man would not have gone unnoticed unless the driver was asleep. He batted the flies away and knelt closer. Hard to see, but there it was – a tiny hole in the shirt, less than half a centimetre beneath the left shoulder blade. A puncture wound? He stood up, wincing as a twinge from his morning run caught his knee.

Dr Sutton – bald with an unruly peppery beard – paced back and forth in the heat. As difficult as he could sometimes be, the fellow was one of the best and would quickly have a professional theory. Lowry looked up and down the track. The buzz of flies was increasingly urgent now, as Kenton predicted, slowly overshadowing the noise from the rooks in the poplars beyond. You didn't need to be an expert to work out this man had died sometime the previous day: Lowry reckoned on twelve hours.

He scanned the immediate vicinity of the body.

'No sign of bleeding anywhere,' Barnes said.

'Comb the woods,' Lowry said.

'Eh? That'll take all bloody morning.'

'Call in a dog unit.'

Barnes didn't question the inspector's orders further; they'd worked together for years. The sergeant nodded and left. Lowry rose and climbed back to the track, nodding to the forensics men, who hurried up the embankment. Lowry surveyed the farmhouse; this man may well have come from there. The red tile roof and bleached yellow rendering stood proud amid a cluster of vehicles in the sunlight and, if he was not mistaken, Colchester's police chief Sparks was just visible emerging from the back seat of a pale blue panda.

'All done, inspector?' He turned to meet Sutton's nervous eyes.

'Busy day, eh, doc?'

'Quite,' he said sharply. 'Excuse me.'

'Come find me in the house when you're finished.' If the doctor heard he didn't let on; he was already on the ground flapping angrily at the flies around the body's head.

3

10 a.m., Fox Farm

Lowry was up at the railway track when Colchester police chief Stephen Sparks arrived on the scene – meaning Kenton was in the firing line. A situation Kenton was usually careful to avoid. This morning, however, the chief had hardly uttered a word.

'Nasty,' was his only remark, after peering cursorily at the body by the fireplace.

Kenton was surprised by the chief's apparent lack of interest. He obviously considered the actual investigation to be beneath him. He seemed more interested in the farmhouse kitchen's décor. To be fair, it was an impressive set-up. The large spacious room was a tasteful combination of old farmhouse charm (wooden table and chairs before an open hearth), and the latest, smartest gadgets and appliances. It was the tech that had piqued Sparks's interest. He examined the expensive Bosch fridge-freezer, the state-of-the-art washer/dryer and the window-fronted dishwasher, all integrated with a granite work surface. The owners were not short of a bob or two. The chief eyed up a neat display of cookware on a tripod rack next to an Aga. He picked up an orange saucepan, weighing it curiously in his hand.

'Le Creuset,' Kenton said. His mother had the same posh French utensils at the family home in Godalming.

'That so.' Sparks sniffed, placed the pan back on the rack without further comment and continued his perusal of the room.

Why exactly was Sparks even *here*? The man famously didn't care for nuts-and-bolts police work, he displayed little or no concern for the deceased, and he was evidently preoccupied with other matters. The chief tutted in what Kenton thought a satisfied way. Suddenly a silhouette appeared at the stable-style kitchen door, casting a shadow across the grey slate floor.

'Nick,' said Sparks. 'About time. Right,' he said, suddenly animated. 'I'll be outside having a smoke.' And with that he bolted from the room.

Lowry said nothing in reply.

Sparks and Lowry went back years and their relationship was impossible to fathom. Kenton watched Lowry expectantly. Where the chief had seemed taciturn, he knew his boss would take an interest in the scene.

Other men Kenton had worked with would make straight for the body at a crime scene. (Indeed, Kenton had to admit, he'd done exactly that this morning.) Not so Lowry. Lowry stood in the middle of the kitchen, absorbing the feel of the room, taking his time, taking it all in before heading over to the huge, silver fridge-freezer. Attached to the side was a calendar, the cheap sort card shops become littered with at Christmas. Lowry lifted the page of the calendar and glanced at it, then walked across the kitchen and stood under the low, blood-splattered ceiling near the fireplace.

'To me, it looks as if he sat down on the chair, stuck the barrel in his mouth and pulled the trigger,' Kenton said, as calmly as possible. 'There's a case of cartridges on the side with a cloth and cleaning fluid.'

Lowry turned from the plump man's body to consider a glass vase of flowers on the kitchen table, his brogues mere millimetres away from the pooled blood.

'Freshly cut,' he said quietly to himself.

Kenton cleared his throat and spoke again. 'There is a gun cabinet, unlocked in the next room, containing painting materials – an easel and canvases.'

'Who found the body?' Lowry glanced across the room as if noticing him for the first time.

'One of the children, the middle daughter, Alice, thirteen years old. The eldest, Lucy, then telephoned a neighbour, a Kate Everett, who knows the family well. The dead man is identified as Christopher Cliff, a historian . . .'

'Where is the mother?'

'Not been able to locate her. The children are in too much shock to be very helpful – something about her leaving early for an art exhibition.' Kenton consulted his pocketbook.

'Christopher Cliff and his wife Suzanne have three daughters. The two boys are cousins come to stay.'

'Rather inconsiderate to leave all these children running around unsupervised, don't you think.' He said it as a statement, not a question.

'Why care if you're going to blow your brains out?'

'Even if a man considers his own life worthless, that doesn't mean he wouldn't care for his children. Or anyone else's, for that matter.'

Kenton, at twenty-five, was reminded of his relative immaturity. Being a single male without children, he would never have made the observation Lowry just had.

'If he was in his right mind, then perhaps he would have considered a more suitable venue, out of the way, but I guess he wasn't thinking too clearly . . .' Kenton reasoned.

Lowry glanced at him with a wry smile. 'True, Daniel, true.' Then added, 'Did he leave a note?'

Kenton shook his head.

Lowry pulled what appeared to be a tape measure from his pocket then bent down towards the shotgun, the butt of which rested on the deceased's ankle. A forensics man stood expectantly, waiting for the detective to let him do his job.

'Who can tell the state of a man's mind when he reaches this level of despair.'

'So you do think it a suicide, then?'

Lowry nodded. 'Unless he was sat here waiting for someone

he knew to come in and blow his brains out – there's no sign of a struggle.'

'What are you doing, then?'

'Admiring the weapon. It's eighteenth century.' With that, his boss proceeded to measure the gun's barrel.

10.20 a.m., Fox Farm

Sparks stood smoking by the panda car in a check sports jacket and plus fours. It looked for all the world as if he was about to go for a stroll in the country, not mount a major police investigation. The chief grew increasingly eccentric but at least he was actually *here* rather than presiding over law and order from his Queen Street garret. So that was something. Lowry hadn't bothered to enquire as to why he'd decided to flout expectation by turning up at the crime scene. He put it down to the fact that the railway line was still shut: like it or not, these two deaths would make the morning news cycle, and Sparks was probably under pressure to clear the track so the network could get back to business as usual.

Lowry and the chief strolled round the perimeter of the farmhouse. As they walked, Lowry described the scene out on the railway line, how he'd found the body largely unscathed, the small puncture wound. He was keen to ascertain whether the man on the track had set out from the Cliff residence, and therefore whether a link may exist between the two deaths.

Evidently this place had long ceased to be a working farm.

Cavernous barns, where one might expect to find agricultural machinery, lay empty with the exception of a few scuttling chickens and a lazy cat sunning itself on a bench. A brick outbuilding with fire-engine-red doors housed a bright red Alfa Romeo Spyder and a motorcycle under canvas. There was certainly plenty of space out here for a family. It seemed a country idyll, so perhaps the dead man had felt comfortable with five kids running amok after all. Apart from the neighbour, Miss Everett, further up the lane towards Silver End, there was not another dwelling between here and the village of Kelvedon, nearly three miles back towards Colchester. As they finished the loop of the house, Lowry found the chief reluctant to be drawn on either death. In fact he'd not said a word.

'We're trying to track down the wife, who left early to go to an art exhibition.'

'Hmm.' He wasn't paying attention.

'And as I said, the chap on the track has not been identified yet.'

Lowry had braced himself for an earful about keeping the line closed during rush hour, yet it didn't come.

'He's a jumper, no doubt,' Sparks muttered, absent-mindedly.

'Did you not hear what I said? I think we'll find he was stabbed. Anyhow, it's a raised embankment – there's nowhere he could have jumped *from*.'

Sparks stopped suddenly and sniffed the air. 'Do you have any idea what we are dealing with here? Do you know who's lying dead in there?' he said, nodding towards the farm-house.

Lowry shrugged. 'No.'

'So the name Christopher Cliff really means nothing to you?'

'Doesn't ring a bell.'

'Christopher Cliff! The famous academic on the telly? Professor of the Romantic period?'

'Professor of . . . ?'

'History,' Sparks repeated, missing the specific. Lowry knew Sparks well enough to know he had no more interest in history than he did in arable farming.

'Right. Famous, you say.'

'On the telly and everything.'

Well. This explained what Sparks was doing here. The man in the kitchen was a celebrity: *this* death was newsworthy.

'Oh. So what's a man like Professor Cliff doing out on a farm in Essex?'

'Living here.'

'A country retreat? No wonder there's not so much as a chicken.'

'What were you saying about the chap on the line? Sorry, my mind was travelling.' Travelling? Wherever his mind was, it clearly wasn't on the case.

'That there's no evidence so far to suggest that the man on the tracks set out from down here. No car, for instance. The red sports car in the barn is layered in dust.'

Sparks engaged at last. 'The children, you'll need to talk

to all five. Are they old enough to know what's happened, what we're doing here?'

The question was at least genuine. Sparks did not know how to deal with children. He didn't have kids of his own and, at fifty-four years of age – rough-hewn and barrel-chested – he was one of those men it was somehow impossible to imagine ever having been a child himself.

'They're never easy to talk to,' Lowry said, and left it at that.

– 4 –

10.45 a.m., Hollesley Bay Borstal, Suffolk,
thirty-five miles north-east of Colchester

Edward's expression was hard to read. No. Not that, exactly. He was expressionless. His complexion was one of outstanding health, though; bronzed from working the fruit fields, clear eyes – no hint of alcohol or drugs. His lean frame had filled out, too; labouring on the facility's farm plus regular gym sessions had changed him physically. The cliché was true: he had gone in a boy and would come out a man. After Suzanne had updated him on all her news and the girls, there was little left to say, apart from the obvious – Edward's living arrangements when he was released. It was a conversation they both seemed eager to avoid but she knew they could not delay it much longer; he was released in under a fortnight. She had argued it at length with Christopher last night before driving up this morning and had failed to reach an agreement. Her husband was nothing short of a bastard when it came to her beloved boy. Christopher was adamant: it was time Teddy moved out for good. Edward's year here would make it impossible to readjust to family life. Realistic as this may appear, he would never dream of it were Edward his own flesh and blood.

'It's hard to believe you're finally getting out,' his mother said, without any real enthusiasm. In truth, his time here had done him the power of good; the future held only uncertainty and worry, and she could not hide it. 'Have you thought any more about what I said?'

'The army,' he said, in the surly tone she was familiar with. 'Always, the army.'

'Yes.' Suzanne was tense, her fingers laced on the gun-metal tabletop, orange nail varnish jarring and adding to her discomfort.

'You don't want me anywhere near you, do you?' The bridge of his nose crinkled the way it always had, since he was a little boy.

'It's not that, Edward. You'd excel in that environment. Grandpa would be so proud.' What she actually meant was *you need the discipline* but she tried to put a better spin on it. 'Think of the travel; you'll see the world. You hated being stuck out on the farm, bored out of your brain. Look where that got you.' She opened her hands in a half-hearted gesture towards the present situation. She had his best interest at heart.

'Huh, see the world – and end up a grunt in Northern Ireland, like Mike.'

Despite his aversion towards the army, Edward really did admire his older cousin and she couldn't help think that counted for something.

'Michael's completed his tour,' she said. 'He's back in Colchester.'

'I didn't know that.'

Colchester was a major garrison town. Soldiers had been based there since the Romans. Suzanne's father had grown up there. He was an army colonel who saw action in Suez and when he retired they stayed close to home – he had lived out his final years in a cottage near East Bergholt. Her nephew Michael was the only one of the younger generation to follow in her father's footsteps, but he'd had a less than glamorous start to his career. Too young for the Falklands, Michael had ended up in Ireland, where he spent most of his tour driving armoured cars – 'pigs' as they were known (hence the term 'grunt') – through the streets of Londonderry. Nevertheless, Suzanne's mother was pleased as punch when Michael had signed up for his first tour of duty. She had passed away peacefully the previous November, content in the knowledge that her grandson was upholding family tradition.

Suzanne regarded her son, who'd lapsed into a thoughtful silence.

'Yes, he's back.'

'In Hyderabad Barracks? Mersea Road?'

This she didn't know for sure. According to her sister, Mike was on leave while seeking permission to live off-barracks, but the IRA threat had increased and spread to the mainland, making such applications less likely to be granted.

'I don't know exactly where he is. I'm sure you'll see him when you get out.' She smiled.

A man in shirtsleeves and tie was talking to the guard. The warden – she'd had occasion to meet him once before, when there was trouble. Suzanne could feel the men staring. So could Edward, who flinched in discomfort.

'Don't pay them any attention,' he said.

'Why? You haven't done anything wrong, have you? God, Teddy, you're out in two weeks . . .' The warden left the room. He wanted to talk to her, she could sense it. She reached down for her handbag, feeling silly when she remembered she'd handed it over to security.

'Did Dad sort the bike? I'm buggered without that.'

'Yes, of course, the battery is connected and there's a full tank of petrol waiting. Anyway. I have to go now.' The guard, motionless in navy blue, stood as if part of the furniture. Suzanne glanced at him nervously as she rose. 'Same time next week?'

Edward scraped back his chair as he stood. She so wanted to hug him but knew that was unacceptable – even a ruffle of his hair would upset him and cause abuse from other inmates. Her son sloped off.

As she expected, the guard collared her as she tried to leave. He guided her down a passageway where a colleague took over. Nobody exchanged a word during the transition between the visiting hall and the warden's office.

'Ah, Mrs Cliff,' the warden exclaimed, as if hers were a wholly unexpected arrival. 'Do please take a seat.'

His office was like a different country after the severe visiting hall. Behind the warden's large, leather-clad desk, an enormous oil painting of the building as it stood a century ago hung on the wood-panelled wall in all its colonial glory.

'Two things,' the warden started. Suzanne felt her pulse quicken. 'I have Edward's best interests at heart, you understand that, before we go on?' The warden had a small, round face. Suzanne nodded.

'We believe that Edward may have left the establishment last night, returning this morning.'

'He got *out*?' Suzanne said, aghast.

'It's possible.'

'How?'

He smiled. 'This isn't Wormwood Scrubs, Mrs Cliff. As a progressive correction facility, it's quite open. Public perception is quite wrong. That film *Scum* has a lot to answer for. Nevertheless, the borstal system is in the process of being abolished; as a consequence of the Criminal Justice Act passed last year, we are evolving, Mrs Cliff, into a youth custody centre.'

'I see.' Suzanne had heard of this reform and remembered thinking that her son's detention under the new label may not sound so bad. She sat, not knowing how to respond. 'Does that mean he's not in trouble?'

'Usually he would be. However, leniency in a period of

transition is no bad thing, and it hasn't escaped my attention that Edward is due for release in a fortnight. So the question I'm left asking myself is, why? Why would a young man jeopardise that so carelessly?'

'Careless, how so?'

'He was missing until 10 a.m., Mrs Cliff.'

'Where could he have gone?'

The warden shrugged. '*Where* isn't really the point . . .'

'No?'

'No. Mrs Cliff, may I be frank? In my experience, teenagers that default so close to release do so with reason. And most often, that reason is they do not want to leave.'

Suzanne fidgeted in her chair. 'Maybe he was seeing a girl in a village.'

The warden was unimpressed. 'That is highly unlikely; this is not a boarding school. No, this is far more likely to have been a deliberate gesture. It is hard to avoid the conclusion that Edward wished his absence to be noticed. Are you with me, Mrs Cliff?'

'Yes, yes . . . I am. So is he in trouble or not?'

'No. My concern, as I said, is why he did it. What awaits him on the outside that he might be at pains to avoid? What could be making him so anxious?'

Suzanne was unsure how much the man knew, but she had the distinct impression that it was she, not Edward, who was under scrutiny.

'I'm afraid I don't know what you're getting at, but please

be assured, I know my son. I think it far more likely that he is impatient for his freedom, not that he wants to avoid it. I appreciate that his absence last night was not a smart move, but it hardly strikes me as behaviour that should put his release in jeopardy. He has done his time, and what he chooses to do with his freedom when he has it is naturally up to him. He is a grown man.'

'Almost. But Edward needs security, Mrs Cliff. He needs support to keep on the straight and narrow.'

'He's had every chance a boy could have – it's the "security" that he is rebelling against. I thought that much was obvious. Look, I don't have time for this. I'm sure he's fine.' Honestly, the warden was more institutionalised than the boys under his jurisdiction. 'Now I have to go. My husband will be wondering where I am.' Besides, some of her paintings had been on sale in Dedham town hall last weekend – she had stopped by to drop a new one off on her way to the borstal, but now she wanted to return and see how the rest had fared; maybe rearranging them would help.

10.45 a.m., Fox Farm

It was important to get as much out of the children as possible today, now, before their recollections started to dull or skew. Mrs Cliff was still unaccounted for, but at least this bought a bit more time – her point of view would certainly influence her children's. They *had* managed to reach the two boys' parents in Athens through the travel agent, but it would obviously take some time for them to return home. Yes, Lowry could certainly use the parents' absence to his advantage.

He had enlisted Kenton and Gabriel to help with the first round of interviewing. Already it was proving to be a lengthy and unsatisfactory endeavour. The primary aim of their questioning was to gain a general impression of the previous day – anything unusual, arguments or so forth. The secondary aim was to find out if any strangers or visitors had been at the farm. Two hours since arriving at the scene, they had yet to make any progress on either point. All five children were minors, the eldest only fifteen, and Lowry had underestimated the effect of such a trauma on the children – notably the girls, whose stories were garbled and confused. The two cousins, Alan and his brother, fared slightly better, speaking quietly and evenly. Kenton believed the boys would say anything to be away from this place but their evidence seemed considerably more trustworthy than that of the deceased's own children. In addition, at this stage, Alan Ward was the only witness with any knowledge of the man who had been found on the track. His cousins were too engrossed in their own personal tragedy to register what he had seen and paid him no heed.

The middle daughter, Alice, a pretty girl with long blonde hair, had been the unfortunate one who found her father's body. They had not been able to get much out of her beyond wild exclamations. They pieced together that she was the first one out in the game of hide and seek and had skulked back to the kitchen in a strop for something to eat, where – confronted with her father's body – she had fled back out to the meadow and found her big sister.

The eldest, Lucy, was not much better – too distressed to handle anything more than the most basic questioning. With a neat fringe, acne and spectacles, she was a teenager in earnest; one intent on stepping out into the world, only to have the rug pulled viciously away. It was she who had telephoned their nearest neighbour, Kate Everett, moments after seeing her sister's distress.

Now they were chatting to Emma, the youngest girl, in the spacious farmhouse front room. And 'chatting' was the operative word; they had to tread carefully with the younger child. At six years of age, Emma held a paradoxical position: she was closest to her mother, yet her very age limited the value of her statement. Lowry allowed Kenton to lead the questioning. The younger detective had a kind face, which encouraged the little girl to open up. So far they had elicited that the mother, Suzanne, had left the house early, to her youngest daughter's huge consternation.

'How was mummy dressed?' Kenton asked.

Emma, with short, untidy urchin hair, a wild country child dragged into a very serious adult world, sat neatly on a chintz sofa bathed in sunlight from the large bay window, clutching a straw figure. She frowned.

'Err . . .' she placed a tiny finger to her mouth, her eyes darting thoughtfully from left to right, conveying what her young mind considered deep thought. 'Purple. Big purple flowers.'

'Good, good,' he encouraged. 'Was it a special dress?'

The girl took time to consider. According to the police's chat with the neighbour, Suzanne Cliff was an academic with an obsessive penchant for art, as was evidenced by the room put aside for her hobby on the ground floor. The one thing they had learnt early on was that the mother had gone to an art show – but whether it was to view or exhibit was unclear.

'I liked it, it was pretty – but she was grumpy,' Emma said frowning.

'Why? Had there been an argument?' He wanted to say *with your father*.

'No, Daddy was with his books as always. She didn't want to be late and she couldn't find something.' The stress was on *late*. The girl spoke clearly, and was to Kenton's mind well brought up.

'What couldn't she find?' Gabriel asked.

'Oh, I don't know. Something she needed to go out to a gallery. She's a painter.' As if this explained everything.

'When did she leave? Were you dressed – had you had breakfast?'

'Seven-thirty. I'm not a baby, you know. I can tell the time.' Kenton couldn't help a small laugh.

'And no, I wasn't dressed. I got my own breakfast – Frosties, if you must know. Then Daddy shouted and we had to go outside. I'm hungry now. Can I have something to eat, please?'

That was at least consistent with what the middle girl had said – the father had raised his voice. 'Of course, let me see what we can rustle up.' Kenton rose. 'Stay here.' He winked at Lowry at the window sill. That the child had an appetite was encouraging. He headed for the kitchen.

'What's that you're holding?' Lowry turned to ask the girl.

'My dolly.'

'Can I have a look?' The child clutched the object tighter.

'Please,' he smiled, 'I won't hurt her.'

'All right then,' she said and thrust out her arm. 'Be careful though, she's very fragile.'

Lowry examined the doll. It wasn't a doll as such; more of a hoop formed from braided spirals of dried grass with wheatsheafs protruding from beneath.

'It's very beautiful,' Lowry said. 'Where did you get it?' On closer inspection he realised he'd seen one somewhere before.

'We made her.'

Kenton returned with ham sandwiches that the neighbour had made. Kate Everett had kindly stayed at the farm to support the children. Lowry handed the doll back.

'So,' Kenton said, taking a sandwich for himself and biting, 'what happened after you said goodbye to your mummy?'

'Daddy told us off, and to go play outside.'

'Were you misbehaving?'

The child pouted. 'We were arguing ... being noisy,' she huffed. 'I wanted the cream on my breakfast, Alice wouldn't let me . . . we were taking too long and Daddy wanted us out of the way before the man came. He was angry with us.'

Here, Emma stopped talking and tucked into her sandwich.

'A man coming?' Lowry rose from the window. The child nodded, cheeks full, all her attention on her food. 'Do you know who he was? Did you see anyone?'

'Uh-uh, no. Daddy just wanted us out the way, I told you.'

5

Alan watched through the crack in the door. Emma spoke differently when talking to the policeman; like he imagined she behaved at the posh school the girls attended. Politely, and in no way resembling the little tearaway he witnessed during the school holidays. And nothing like the way she bossed him and his brother around yesterday evening when they had risked poking their heads into Alice's bedroom looking for their cousins. *'Weren't you taught to knock before entering a lady's room?'* Emma had yelled sharply from the bed, looking up from the book she was reading. For a six-year-old, she was quite the little madam. The two older girls had been sitting on the floor playing a board game and his middle cousin Alice had jumped to her feet to greet them, grabbing Darren's hand and leading them both back out to the landing. Soon enough their aunt had ushered them all to go and play outside while it was still light.

He had not heard his aunt and uncle get back from the pub; he and Darren were asleep in the attic, far out of earshot.

He pressed his face hard against the cool door hinge. The policewoman with the wavy hair spoke softly and he couldn't make out her questions. No, the Emma over there was not the Emma he knew; smiling coyly like butter wouldn't melt, her expression flicking back and forth in an instant, now surprise, now horror. It was all an act for the police, to impress them, make her seem older, like her sisters ... To be fair, Darren, who was the same age, would not have been able to give an account of himself like this without bursting into tears and calling for their mother.

A tap on the shoulder caused Alan to shoot backwards in alarm.

'I'm pretty sure you shouldn't be here.' A WPC towered over him, but she was smiling.

The lure of a sandwich and orange juice had failed to produce any further details from Emma Cliff on this 'man' her father had been expecting, so Lowry called for a break and went to wander round the house.

The only thing they knew for certain was that Christopher Cliff had pulled the trigger on himself at 8.15 a.m. Alan Ward, acting on reflex, had checked the time when he heard the gunshot; Kate Everett had corroborated his statement – she had received the telephone call within minutes. The previous evening had passed without event, though Lowry thought it odd that the couple had strolled off to the local boozer just hours after Suzanne Cliff's sister, Clare Ward, had deposited the boys. The parents didn't spend long on goodbyes before jetting off on their holiday – this seemed a little unusual to him, too, but then what did he know? Perhaps this was acceptable behaviour these days. He wondered what Kenton or Gabriel made of it.

Lowry spent the most time in what Kenton had labelled the 'Hobby Room', where various artist's materials and the gun cabinet lay. The incongruity of two disparate interests of two people none of them had actually met was, Lowry had to admit, one of the fascinations of policework. The paintings were garish and unappealling, and the room was littered with squeezed paint tubes and random brushes, lending an air, to Lowry's untrained eye, of authenticity of intent at least.

In the corner of the room was the gun cabinet: austere in dark wood, holding three weapons, neatly aligned vertically. The glass door was unlocked, as Kenton had said it was. There were two shotguns and a .22 rifle, no ammunition. The weapon Cliff had turned on himself Lowry believed to be an antique hunting gun. Firearm ownership in rural England was governed under laws of a bygone age, predicated on the need to shoot animals, which continued century after century and decade after decade, occasionally standing up to scrutiny in times of tragedy, such as this, only to continue unchanged as the years rolled by. Lowry left the room untouched and ventured upstairs.

He reckoned Fox Farm was seventeenth century. The flag-stone throughout the ground floor was possibly original.

Upstairs was a spacious landing with beige emulsion on the walls, durable weave carpet and a large bookcase on which stood some moth-eaten taxidermy encased in glass bulbs. A sparrowhawk and a young tawny owl. East Anglians had a penchant for stuffed wildlife – pubs, libraries, town halls, village halls – the county was awash with the stuff. Lowry found the whole idea distasteful, even repellant. He stepped closer to the sparrowhawk, a bird dear to his heart since childhood; even now when one hurtled wildly through the garden after a tit or pigeon, his pulse quickened. The thing before him – awkwardly perched, dead-eyed, dulled and tatty with the decades – bore no resemblance to that magnificent bird.

The books beneath were an eclectic array of natural history, novels, a row of Penguins, classical history, folklore, and books on plants, the weather, astronomy and art. Indicative of a well-read family. The house was quite a size. There were five rooms on this floor alone. The floorboards eased as he sought out the master bedroom. The first thing that struck him was the décor – Mrs Cliff's aesthetics clearly took precedence in here. Her own paintings – a gaudy expressionism – were hung on the walls. None struck him as familiar. Among her own work was one framed print he *did* know: Klimt's 'Lady in Gold', bright, loud. On the dresser there were framed pictures of the couple and the three girls. Also a photo of a broody young boy he didn't recognise, in flared jeans astride a Chopper bicycle in an urban street.

The children's rooms were untidy in the way of most children's dwellings. Dolls in one, astrological charts in another, wildlife posters and knick-knacks including a bird's nest in a third. The final room he came to was the father's study. Academic texts, papers, a typewriter; books on art, English mainly, and some artists he'd heard of and some he hadn't, Turner, Stubbs, Grimshaw and Constable. On the wall was an array of small prints, landscape paintings mainly. It was a world Lowry knew nothing about and on the face of things it struck him as a very comfortable existence. He peered out of a narrow window overlooking the courtyard below and out across the meadow. It was a scene worthy of any painter. English summer in all its glory.

The familiar bark of Stephen Sparks interrupted his thoughts. '*Where are you?* C'mon, stop poncing about up there; we've company. There's something you need to know.'

Sparks was put out. This was all he needed to add to his worries this summer: a mate of Merrydown's blowing his brains out after breakfast and a dead bloke not half a mile away on the train track bordering the property. Sparks and Lowry waited outside the house puffing on Lowry's Players while the ACC finished addressing her driver. Sparks smiled broadly at his boss. She acknowledged their presence. As Merrydown moved towards them and away from the car, her white cotton skirt caught tantalisingly in the late afternoon sun.

'Not bad, not bad at all,' Sparks remarked.

'That's the first compliment you've ever paid her,' Lowry said.

'Credit where credit's due.' The chief puffed keenly on the Players. 'She's a decent pair of pins on her.'

'So she knew Cliff. I'm guessing that's why she's here?'

'At Cambridge together,' he sniffed. She'd been on the blower first thing.

'Right,' Lowry said, unimpressed.

'Didn't mention it before, didn't want it to cloud your judgement.'

'Opting instead to turn up yourself to oversee proceedings, trussed up like a country squire.'

'You know how it is with these university types, so judge-mental . . .'

'No, I don't,' Lowry said quickly.

Sparks marched off to meet his commanding officer.

Poor bugger. It was tragically clear that he'd chosen his ridiculous outfit especially for Merrydown. This was his idea of fashion befitting a man in his position, a man of standing. As a result, he looked like a fool.

Sparks greeted Merrydown graciously, complimenting her on her tan. This was fatuous toadying: the County Supremo was going on holiday at the end of the week and station gossip had it she'd been using a sunbed. According to his wife, they were all the rage in Chelmsford. The chief summed up the situation with authority and aired the facts as they presently knew them – suicide, tragic for the kids, etc. – but he was cagey about the second body.

'Another dead body, *here*?'

'No, no, not here, exactly. Over the way by the railway line.' He nodded towards the horizon.

Merrydown's eyebrows converged into her Carreras. 'That's what, half a mile away?'

'About that.'

'Cause of death?'

'Unconfirmed, ma'am,' Lowry spoke for the first time.

'Update me soonest. In the meantime, show me the body.'

'Ma'am?' Sparks was taken aback.

'I haven't come all this way to chat with you – I want to see Christopher.'

6

Lowry watched Sparks climb into the back of Merrydown's Jaguar after viewing the body. It didn't matter to him whether the ACC wished to see the dead man and it struck him as peculiar that Sparks seemed taken aback by her request. No matter what they thought of her professionally, she was only human; even the high and mighty experience grief.

Merrydown's interest in a celebrity death clearly bothered the chief, but it couldn't account for his distraction. If that were the case he would have been paying full attention, rather than drifting around the place barely even acknowledging the presence of a man with his brains blown out. The chief's mind was somewhere else – but where?

A cloud of dust flew up as the Jaguar pulled away.

Lowry moved slowly back towards the house to resume talking to the children. The sniffer dogs were here now, straining and pulling in all directions. The first sweep had yielded nothing but they would be fed and watered and then sent back out again. If they couldn't link the fellow on the track with the farmhouse, what was his next line of enquiry? He parked that thought as WPC Fletcher approached to advise him that the oldest daughter, Lucy, was now much calmer, possibly due to tiredness. He found her in the front room, sitting on a sofa with Kenton and a WPC. She watched him closely as he walked in and joined them.

'Go back to last night.'

The neatness of Lucy's dead-straight fringe was at odds with her skin, troubled by pimples, themselves exacerbated by bouts of weeping and now coalesced into angry red patches across her forehead and cheeks. She sighed. 'Alan and Darren were dropped off by Aunty Clare after supper. We played outside for a bit then came in and watched television.'

'What did you watch?'

'Some cowboy thing.'

He could check the listings. It matched what Alan had told him. 'Were your parents with you?'

'No, they were out.'

'Where?'

'The Angel. It's the pub in the village.'

'Who saw you to bed?' He knew the answer from her cousin already.

'We're big enough to do that ourselves,' she said indignantly.

'Of course, I'm sorry . . . Is that usual, for them to go to the pub on a Sunday night?'

'Hmm. No, it's *un*usual,' she said thoughtfully. Then, sadly,

'They used to take us sometimes, but we're too big and and noisy now.'

'I'm sure that's not the case. Did you hear them come in from the pub?'

Lucy shook her head vigorously. 'Sound asleep.'

'Moving on to this morning, how did the day start?'

She described her mother's early departure; that they knew already. Her father was in his study on the first floor, as he was every morning. Lowry asked if his routine would have been any different had her mother not been off to the gallery. No, she told him, he worked religiously from five-thirty to seven each morning before stopping for breakfast.

'The only difference was that, as the boys were here, he didn't come down until he'd had enough of us. We were being quite loud and he doesn't like noise.'

'So he came down to tell you ... to play outside?'

'Yes.' She adjusted her glasses. He wondered if she took after the mother or father. None of the girls exhibited any likeness to one another, unlike the boys, who were obviously brothers. He cleared his throat and continued. 'So this morning, your mum leaves, your father is in his study when you guys get up and—'

'I'm sure you heard this from the others,' she interrupted him. 'There was a bit of a to-do between Emma and Alice this morning. Daddy was expecting a man to come, and lost his temper.'

'Go on.'

Lucy perked up at the opportunity to bemoan her sisters. 'They're always antsy when Mum goes to the gallery. It's so tiresome, attention-seeking.'

'Hmm. This man your father was expecting, who was he?'

She shook her head. 'I don't know. He wouldn't tell us.'

'But a friend or someone from work, television people, maybe?'

'Err . . .' she paused. 'Work, I would guess . . . if it were a friend, why was he so ratty?'

Whoever he was, he would have been the last person to see Mr Cliff alive. The wife would know. He changed tack.

'Can you tell me what your sisters were arguing over, exactly?'

'Alan.'

'Alan, your cousin Alan?'

'Yes, they both have a crush on him.'

'Oh really,' Lowry said. 'And does he know this?' He tried not to smile. Of course the boy wouldn't know a thing about it.

'No. I doubt it. And what would he care? Emma squealing like a baby.' She was evidently unimpressed.

'And did the argument disturb your dad?'

'He's usually immune to . . .' She heard herself use the present tense and stopped abruptly as the reality of her father's death hit her like an aftershock.

'I'm sorry,' Lowry said. 'I have to ask these questions.'

She nodded profusely, but he could see the tears.

'Who won?' he said gently.

'What?'

'Alan's heart.'

She snuffled. 'Oh, neither. It all blew over.'

'Your sister Emma said the row was over who had the top of the milk?'

Her eyes narrowed. 'Well, she's hardly going to tell *you* it's over a *boy*.'

'Fair enough.' He suppressed a smile. 'Please, go on.'

'So Father ordered us out – like I said, he was expecting someone and wanted us to clear off. So we went to play hide and seek just to amuse the boys.'

'Are you too old for that yourself now? What age are you?'

She gave him a withering glance. 'Fifteen. Yes, I've better things to do with my time. But it was lovely out this morning.' She warmed to being the eldest and her role as boss over the other children (even if it was only to tell Lowry how she marched them out to the oak tree, and told them the rules of the game: count to thirty and no going back to the house). Lucy was a pleasant girl, and the more animated she grew, the sadder he became for her loss.

Kenton watched the girl be led out by WPC Fletcher to join her sisters. Lowry remained on the chintz sofa.

'How'd it go?' he asked Lowry.

'She's young. They're all very young.'

'No clue as to who the visitor might be?'

'Nope.'

Lowry struck him as sad and drained. It had been a long morning. Kenton felt it himself – just being around children, one had to be on guard. Taking care not to frighten, upset or scare them took a whole lot of extra energy. The inspector rose and pulled out his cigarettes.

'I can't imagine losing a parent at such a young age,' Lowry said eventually. He had moved to the sun-bleached window and lit a Players. 'The years in front of them without guidance.'

Smoke curled above Lowry's head as he drew deeply on the cigarette. 'Anyway, I think the kids are pretty much exhausted. We don't want them to flake out before their mother rolls in; they'll need a rest. In the meantime, let's see what these chaps have found out.'

Kenton stepped forward to the window and realised Lowry was watching Sutton and two men in whites approach across the dusty track.

7

11.15 a.m., Stanway Road

Sparks was in the back of the ACC's Jag. It was the first time he'd travelled in it. They sat together on the oxblood uphol-stery as Merrydown's driver filtered out onto the A12. Sparks thought he could do with a chauffeur himself.

Her voice dropped, 'I've never seen a body like that, of someone I knew.'

'Tragic,' he muttered, not sure what to say; he had seen several in his time.

His boss changed the subject. 'I want this to be the very definition of a model investigation,' she said, without looking at him.

'Very good, ma'am. I've my best men on it.'

'Yes.' She clicked her tongue. 'Lowry. How's the new bod settling in at West Mersea? Maybe bring him in to help?'

'Sergeant Finlay? No need, we have it covered. Besides, he's still finding his feet,' he said, then added, 'slowly.'

'Oh?' She turned to face him. 'He's very bright.'

'I'm sure, ma'am, but he's a bit lacking in hands-on experience.'

'He was fast-tracked through Hendon, having achieved a double first,' she continued, ignoring his remark, staring out the window. Sparks couldn't deny the bloke's education: the man was just an arsepot. Merrydown had pressured him into 'diversifying' his recruits. This was the second graduate in as many years; the first having arrived in the shape of Kenton.

'Not everyone we employ needs to be a boxer, Stephen,' she said with a smile.

'Good job, too,' he muttered. 'This one couldn't fight his way out of a paper bag.'

'And Jane, how is Jane?'

ACC Merrydown's niece, a constant niggle.

'She's doing just grand.'

'And how's her progress in CID?'

'I'm not really sure she's up for it,' he said, swerving the fact he'd not assigned her yet.

'Nonsense. She needs to use her brain. Not everyone needs to tramp the beat for a decade like you and Lowry . . .'

12 p.m., Fox Farm

Lowry had set up Incident HQ in one of the farm's outbuildings. The investigation had picked up pace with the identification of the man on the track.

Forensics had examined his wristwatch; it was engraved

To Peter, All My Love X. There was only one jeweller on the high street that sold watches of this quality. Lowry used the telephone in the study and called the shop himself, struck gold. A watch of that description had been in for repair. It belonged to one Peter Darnell, an accountant with a Lexden address. A second phone call to Darnell, Cross & Bingley in the town connected Darnell directly to Mr Cliff: he had been Cliff's accountant.

This slice of good fortune marked excellent progress and they had to keep giving their full effort – it was vital to learn as much as they could before the sun set and night drew a veil over whatever evidence remained lying on the surface.

The rioting in Brixton had left the Colchester force short of men and resources, so there was to be no running back and forth from Queen Street. Lowry needed all his men on the ground now. If nothing else, Merrydown's appearance had given the investigation clout and galvanised Sparks to return solo to HQ to marshal their forces. Lowry stood before the assembled team in the makeshift room, addressing them to determine the next steps.

'At this stage, it seems permissible to think this man's death was connected with Cliff's suicide. Blackmail is the obvious grievance; perhaps Darnell discovered some irregularity in Cliff's finances and tried to squeeze, knowing him to be in the public eye. Having killed Darnell in anger, Cliff then takes his own life the following morning. The missing link is the wife, of course. For now we only have the statements of the children in the house and they have no knowledge of a visitor the previous evening, which suggests Peter Darnell returned later with the Cliffs from the Angel public house in Kelvedon. Note that Lucy and Emma both said that Cliff was expecting a visitor in the *morning*. We need to find whoever that was.'

At this point Barnes entered, red-faced. Lowry paused for the sergeant to catch his breath and report.

'Nothing,' he said eventually. 'I need some water.'

Gabriel passed him a bottle from an icebox.

'Nothing?'

He shook his head. PC Parker stood to one side in short sleeves, perspiring heavily.

'Did you try every route? Had the man been stabbed in the back? No blood anywhere?'

They both responded in the negative, shaking their heads in unison.

'And the dogs?'

'Same.' Lowry found this hard to believe. If Professor Cliff had indeed taken the man's life, which was their working theory, the location of Darnell's body was unusual, to put it lightly.

'Search the track.'

'You wha—?'

'A mile either side,' Lowry ignored their protests, 'while DC Kenton and WPC Gabriel return to town. The rest of you: if Mrs Cliff returns, do not mention Peter Darnell. All we have discussed thus far is supposition and confidential; the fact that one was the other's bookkeeper is circumstantial. As far as the outside world is concerned, this man's murder is unrelated to her husband's death until we find evidence to the contrary. Is that clear?'

A response of nods and murmurs came back from the hot and probably uncomfortable assembly.

Lowry conferred with Kenton outside the barn. He could see Kate Everett out of the corner of his eye, studying the fish pond in the full glare of the sun at the front of the property. Further off, under the shade of a row of poplars, WPC Gabriel was waiting for Kenton. The two of them were tasked with visiting Darnell, Cross & Bingley – Peter Darnell's accountancy firm in Crouch Street. They were going to meet with Miss Juliet Bingley, who worked there, continuing in the family trade. After they were done there, they would pay their respects to Darnell's wife, Elizabeth, who had been informed of her husband's death.

'I did a business paper at uni,' Kenton informed him.

'Hardly makes you an accountant, does it,' said Lowry. 'You shoot back to town – ask the Bingley daughter if there were any irregularities with Cliff's finances. Poor people kill themselves for love and the rich over money and ruin.'

'Is that true?' Kenton flicked back his hair and considered his boss in earnest.

'How many people on the dole shoot themselves over

financial ruin? Go on, get out of here. I'll stay here, speak with Miss Everett and wait for Mrs Cliff to return.'

Kenton had already taken a statement from Kate Everett. Her words correlated with Alan Ward's, allowing them to place the time of the gunshot at 8.15 a.m. exactly. Everett's house was on Fox Lane, further on towards Silver End. Miss Everett looked up from the fish pond on hearing their voices and came forward to meet him.

'Sorry to keep you,' Lowry said, offering his hand. He placed her in her mid-thirties.

'Not at all.' She smiled hesitantly; her grip was firm yet soft. Wearing a pale blue dress open at the neck, tanned and freckled with sharp green eyes partly obscured under heavy lids, Kate Everett struck him as charming in a whimsical, old-fashioned way. After thanking her for her assistance throughout the day with the children, Lowry asked if she minded a short stroll.

As they walked up the driveway, he began to relax for the first time that day, now in the company of an adult. He passed her a cigarette and his lighter.

'Tell me, Miss Everett, when was the last time you saw either Suzanne or Christopher?'

'Not for a while. They both lead very busy, hectic lives. I see much more of their children. I'm a teacher, you see, and out here on my own most of the summer.' Her movement was slow and leisurely. It was she, not he, that set the pace.

'Hence why they telephoned you this morning?'

'Yes.'

'They are lucky to have you to hand, Miss Everett . . . where exactly is your cottage? West towards Silver End, I gather?'

'Yes, if you continue along Fox Lane as it dips down round towards the Silver End Road, my cottage is there after a mile.'

'My colleague says the telephone call woke you?'

'That's right.'

'You didn't hear the gun then?'

She shook her head. 'No, but I'd not think anything of it if I had. This is the country, inspector, everyone has a gun.'

'Do you, Miss Everett?'

'Hah, no, I don't, but then I'm the exception to the rule.' They stopped where the driveway met the road.

'So a fifteen, twenty-minute walk to your house?' Lowry stepped out onto the tarmac. The narrow lane, a tractor's-width only, hedged either side, soon curved off from view.

'On the road, yes, or cut across the fields; there's a bridleway takes about ten minutes. I usually go on my bicycle. I might drop in on the way to Kelvedon, to the village store.'

'You wouldn't walk down the railway track?'

'Good heavens, no!'

'I'm glad to hear it. Though I am sorry to say, Miss Everett, that another body has been found, near the track past Fox Farm towards Kelvedon.'

'I daresay it's possible, the level crossing is at the church . . .' She spoke before his words fully sank in; Lowry gave her a moment for them to register. He studied her features as they flexed in surprise: she was healthy in appearance with a complexion more akin to a farmer's wife than a schoolteacher. Her bearing was earthy and could be found seductive.

'Gosh,' she said finally.

'Miss Everett,' Lowry's voice was growing hoarse, 'were you aware of any visitors at the farm last night or this morning?'

'No, I was not . . .' she mumbled quietly. 'How dreadful . . . this will take me time to comprehend.' She turned her head, eyes wide. 'Sorry, inspector.'

Lowry uncharacteristically touched her gently on the elbow and together they walked back to the farmhouse in silence. He too needed time to digest what had happenened out here, turning this most tranquil part of the countryside upside down.

8

1 p.m., Crouch Street, Colchester

The young accountant showed them out onto the street.

'Sorry not to have been of more help. As I say, the man was in rude health financially; nothing from our records shows any problems. Any recent transactions you'll need to check with the bank.' She shrugged in apology.

'And Mr Cross the senior partner is back tomorrow?'

'Yes, Mr Cross knew him well; I've only been here three months. Poor Mr Darnell. His poor wife. Peter seemed so happy last time he was here.'

'Happy, how so?'

'Humming, singing quietly to himself, cheerfully.'

'Was that unusual, then?'

'I'd not heard it before.'

'Paying respects' to Mrs Darnell, as Lowry put it, was a formality more than anything – letting her know CID were doing everything they could. It wasn't that Kenton was expecting it to be fruitful, exactly, but he had imagined it would be at least a little moving. In fact, he had found the experience to be altogether empty.

Putting it politely, Mrs Darnell was simply not with it. Kenton could only assume she was in shock, or medicated, or both. A short woman with greying hair wearing a cardigan despite the hot weather, Elizabeth Darnell appeared far older than her years.

On the subject of her husband's whereabouts Sunday night she had no answer. Was he working that day? It was a valid question – Mr Darnell had been wearing a blue M&S shirt and tie at the time of his death – but her reply made it sound as if it were a preposterous suggestion.

'On a Sunday? Are you serious.'

Kenton let it slide.

'Mrs Darnell, is your car still here?'

'We have a blue Volvo estate ... I've actually not looked to see whether or not it's outside. I don't drive,' she added.

'Would you say your husband was a happy man?' Gabriel spoke for the first time.

'Happy?' The word tapped into something. 'I've never thought of Peter as happy ... or sad for that matter. He's an accountant, or was ... content was as good as it gets. That's why I married him.'

'Sorry, I'm not with you,' Kenton said.

'Safe, you mean?' said Gabriel.

65

She nodded, her gaze returning to the mid-distance. 'Yes, safe. You always knew where you were with Peter.'

As they were leaving, Kenton nodded to the officer on the doorstep. He made a point of acknowledging Uniform whenever it was possible; he needed to work on his relationships within the force. He noted that Gabriel, in uniform herself, ignored the man completely.

'You were good in there,' he said as they reached their car. She opened the door and smiled faintly across the roof in acknowledgement. He stood on the other side, and paused while he checked up and down the neat Georgian road. No sign of a blue Volvo. 'Let's hope Mrs Cliff is a tad more engaged than Mrs Darnell when she finally puts in an appearance,' he mumbled under his breath, and climbed in.

2.30 p.m., Fox Farm

The railway line had finally reopened but only after Barnes and an officer had marched for a mile in both directions, and covered the pathways through the woods. The investigative team had gathered in the disused barn for an update. Lowry, leaning on a wooden support, gestured for Barnes to start.

'The floor's yours.'

Barnes cleared his throat to begin.

'After a slow start, we eventually came across blood on the tracks.'

'Great record,' Kenton said without thinking. All eyes turned on him, forcing an explanation. 'Dylan,' he said, embarrassed.

'If that's to be the level of your contribution, don't bother,' Sparks snapped, muttering, 'Long-haired layabout.'

Lowry was unsure to whom the chief was referring; the detective or the singer. The banter would be amusing in different circumstances, but now was not the time. Sparks had returned and an OS map was now tacked to the barn wall.

'Sergeant Barnes,' Lowry said, wearily. 'Please continue.'

'There was blood on the wooden sleepers, but not much of it. Odd spot or two, a couple of hundred feet apart in the direction of Kelvedon. Weren't much blood to speak of with the body, either – as the inspector saw himself this morning. Not like the mess with the other fellow,' he added.

The room fell quiet, all thinking the same; a fatal wound would produce more blood than that . . . Lowry looked over to Sutton, who seemed eager to speak.

'As the crow flies, the train track is the quickest way to the farm from the village,' Barnes continued. 'Up through the meadow, thirty feet o' trees then walk along the railway line straight into Kelvedon. More direct than by car, where there are two routes.' He squiggled a thick finger across the yellowing map to show the winding roads. 'Either up this way, from the high street on to Church Street, then Hollow Lane, across over to Fox Lane, or carry on down the high street along the old London Road and then up looping over the railway line on to the Silver End Road, where Fox Lane joins it, right down here. If you were walking, though, the quickest route on foot to the farm is half a mile along the track here, at the crossing by St Mary's Church.'

'Or coming *from* the farm to the village – the blood on the sleepers means Darnell was staggering from Kelvedon *towards* Fox Farm, not away from it,' Lowry muttered, addressing his feet. This was a fundamental blow to their theory that Darnell was escaping from the farm, having been attacked by Cliff. Why would he be heading towards Fox Farm with a fatal wound?

'Thank you, sergeant. Doc, any theories on the lack of blood?' Lowry asked.

'The left lung has been punctured by an instrument or knife with a diameter of approximately five millimetres. Such a narrow entry would not allow for much bleeding. What there was would be absorbed by the material of the deceased's shirt. As is the case.'

'The wound was big enough to kill him, though?' Sparks said from the back.

'Yes, I would hazard one of two possibilities. He may have drowned – blood filling the lung, preventing oxygen entering the bloodstream – but the other lung should have been able to function. Or – and this is my favoured view – the puncture would have caused air to leak into the pleural cavity sur- rounding the lung, compressing internal organs and leading to the lung itself collapsing.' He paused to collect his thoughts.

'And that killed him?' Kenton said.

'Not necessarily – an autopsy is required, you understand,'

he said sternly towards Sparks. 'No, it's more likely that compression on the heart led to a cardiac arrest. That's my theory, anyway.'

'How long would that take to kill him?'

'There is no exact answer, depending on the fellow's general health and so forth, but, as a guide, between thirty minutes and one hour of receiving the wound.'

'Thank you very much,' Lowry said, moving to the front. 'All right, let's get on it. Search the surrounding area starting with Kelvedon itself – Mrs Darnell confirmed the family car, a pale blue Volvo 343, is missing . . . unless, chief, you've anything to add on Cliff?' Lowry looked expectantly towards Sparks.

Sparks stepped forward and began a largely fawning account of Cliff's celebrity status, seeming to think it would inspire the room of tired, sweat-drenched coppers. His speech, needless to say, fell flat. The only one impressed with the glow of stardom was the chief himself.

9

3 p.m., Kelvedon

Uniform had found the accountant's car straight away. The pale blue Volvo estate was parked behind the Angel pub, on the knee of the bend, where Church Street joins the high street, and where the Cliffs had been the previous evening. The road itself was the old London Road, the main carriageway east before the A12, and the pub dated back to the sixteenth century where it would have served as a coach station.

The pub, a wide-fronted detached building that sat back from the road, wasn't open. Lowry banged on the door using the huge knocker. Kenton stood next to him in aviator sunglasses and an open shirt, the second button now undone.

'Funny, isn't it?' said Kenton.

'What is?' The inspector stepped aside to let an old boy with a terrier pass on the narrow pavement, cuffing a geranium hanging outside the low doorway.

'That the pubs are shut on a summer's afternoon like this. In France – '

'We're not in France,' said Lowry, cutting him off, 'and they don't have pubs over there, they have bars. It's not the same thing at all. Open the saloon all day over here and the country would grind to a halt.' He banged again; he was not in any mood for chat. He put his colleague's good mood down to some positive development in his love life; the usual explanation, a hidden excitement.

The old oak door eventually opened and they ducked into the dark interior. The landlord had obviously been roused from an afternoon nap, unruly grey hair poking up in all directions.

'Inspector,' he said. 'No lock-in here!'

Lowry smiled half-heartedly at the lame joke. He knew the pub – its low beams had always posed a problem – and the man was familiar.

'Last night,' Lowry said. 'Many in?'

'The usual.' The bar lights flicked on. The landlord reached for the tumblers overhead, and rammed them one after the other under the Famous Grouse optics.

'Regulars? No one you didn't recognise?' Lowry suggested.

Lowry took the drink he'd been offered and stepped away from the bar. Dust motes danced in the sunbeams that leaked through the thick, yellowing windows. Across the street was St Mary's Church and less than five hundred yards up the road, the level crossing and the rail link to London. Kenton shook his head, prompting the proprietor to take the second himself.

'Pretty much.'

Lowry laid two photographs side by side on a beer mat. One of the Cliffs and the other of Darnell, the accountant.

'These two? And this one?'

'They were here,' he said, pointing at the Cliffs. 'Don't know 'im, though.' He grimaced as he downed the Scotch.

'Are you sure?' Kenton asked. 'Maybe you'd not noticed.'

The landlord rolled his eyes. 'Look, it's big old boozer, I grant you, but never full; I can see every table from behind these pumps, even those by them windows.'

'But his – ' Lowry placed his hand on Kenton's forearm to shut him up.

'Tell me about the Cliffs,' said Lowry.

The man patted his hair down, as if he'd only just become aware he had company. 'Not much to say, they come most Sundays now the girls are older. Sometimes they bring 'em along, sometimes not. He'll have a couple pints o' best, and she'll have gin and tonic, or sherry in the winter.' He was evidently proud of his knowledge of his customers. 'It was him, this morning, was it?'

Lowry nodded, gravely. 'Anything different about last night?'

The landlord tugged an earlobe. 'Been thinking a lot about it, since the panda cars flashed by . . . But, sorry to say, I'd not really noticed them.'

Lowry shook out a Players. He was not giving up. He could live with Darnell not having been in here, though that was odd, given the Volvo was right outside . . . But he couldn't quite accept that nothing had seemed out of character between the couple. He turned to survey the pub. It was not as small as the landlord made out, though the bar at the centre did give a panoptic view.

'Where were they sitting?'

'In that bay in front of you.'

A worn bench seat.

'Don't suppose you know whether the Cliffs walked or drove?'

'Drove. Always drives. He's not much of a walker, more of a talker, saves 'is energy for that. If you'd met him you'd know what I mean.'

'Car?'

'A silver Lancia.'

'Nice,' Kenton said, unnecessarily.

'He drives down and she back. 'E likes a drink. Come to think of it, they were subdued . . . on the whole, she's very lively, being all arty-farty and that, maybe that's why I didn't notice them much . . .'

'Maybe they'd had a row?'

'Maybe.' Then after a pause, 'He still put away a few, though. Wait . . .'

'What?'

'He's got a tab as long as your arm.' His fissured face moved from one to the other. 'Who's gonna settle that?'

They exited the pub through the rear to the tarmac car park. Two forensics had already arrived and were examining

Darnell's car. A Volvo 343 DL; solid, dependable and accountant-like.

'There all alone, who'd notice a Volvo in the corner of a car park?' Kenton said

'No one, clearly,' Lowry replied, though it would draw a crowd now, what with all its doors open and forensics clambering all over it.

'It don't mean the fella drank here,' the landlord appeared behind them, 'there ain't nowhere else to park this end of the high street.' He pointed to a painted PATRONS ONLY sign. 'And people don't pay *that* any bother.'

'True,' Lowry acknowledged, 'but where else is there to go in Kelvedon on a Sunday evening?'

'The Labour club? Or the Institute?'

'But both have parking,' observed Lowry, moving towards the car. One of the forensics was handling a green canvas bag.

'What's that?' he asked.

'A tent. Lying on the back seat.'

'Anything else?'

'A receipt from a camping store in town in the glove box and a pack of Murray Mints.'

'Not much,' Kenton muttered.

'It is something, though.' Lowry's interest in this case was growing; the odder the circumstances, the less the puzzle pieces fit together, the more intriguing. He felt a surge of excitement. At times like this, he did love the job.

3.30 p.m., Fox Farm

The telephone rang. Alan looked up. His cousins and brother continued watching the television.

'Someone get that!' barked Sparks, causing a great galumphing around the house as police in heavy boots tried to find the phone.

'Where the hell . . .'

'Sir,' called the tall policewoman with blonde hair from the hallway, 'I have it!'

Her bad-tempered boss was standing right in front of the screen now, obscuring their view. Alan was a little scared of the man but Alice glared at him daggers drawn, entirely unafraid, and he instantly moved to one side. A minute later he was called to the door.

'Sir, that was Mrs Cliff.'

'About bloody time too,' he said loudly. 'And . . . ?'

'I thought it unwise to relay precise details of the situation here,' she said softly, 'only urge that she should return home immediately.'

'Where the devil is she?' he said, annoyed.

'At an art exhibition in Dedham – her own, it seems.'

Alan eavesdropped as they continued to discuss his aunt. As he listened, he looked at his cousins. It was hard to believe their father was dead, as they all sat here now peacefully in the front room, watching *Catweazle* on telly. Emma, the youngest, was the only one visibly engaged with the show, a faint smile on her face as a close-up filled the screen with the wizard confiding a spell to his toad. The others were just as distracted as he was.

The grumpy policeman raised his voice again, still talking to the police lady – Alan was pretty sure they were discussing him and Darren now. He felt the man watching him but pretended not to notice. Miss Everett's name was mentioned.

'Wait until Mrs Cliff shows. I doubt she'll want the responsibility now – they'll have to go somewhere, I suppose, and we can't chuck everyone in a hotel. Is she still here?'

Alan felt a pang in his chest. He wasn't keen on Miss Everett. She wasn't comfortable around them and it made him feel awkward. According to Lucy, she'd had a child of her own once but it had died. Lucy moved to switch channels and, as if on cue, Miss Everett appeared in the hallway.

'So the boys will be down later, about six?'

That was that then; it had been decided. On the television, the cartoon was finished and the credits were rolling. It was nearly time for the news. Alan wondered whether they'd be featured but the police lady turned the set off before they could find out.

'I'll be outside, okay?' she said. They all nodded in unison. 'Your mother is expected back very soon.'

The second after she had left, Emma rose and marched out of the room, signalling for him to follow.

*

Gabriel took in the balmy summer air. Martins shot past, gorging on the insect haze. She wandered a little way, disturbing rabbits by the outbuildings and watching them scamper off. In the distance a train rattled along. She could see it through the trees, a perfect, horizontal sunlight catching the carriage. It was a beautiful summer afternoon. Hard to imagine the dead body now. The human brain always found ways to paint over the stains.

A swarm of insects hung thickly over a low brick wall. As she approached she realised it was a pond, reeds growing tall all around. What a wonderful place to grow up. She was from Derby. As a child she would go walking in the Peak District with her father, and though lovely, she could only ever remember it raining. Essex really had its moments; funny, she thought, how one notices beauty at the most unexpected times. Her ruminations stopped abruptly, however, with the return of Lowry and his Saab.

10

4.30 p.m., Fox Farm

When Suzanne Cliff arrived at the farm, Lowry was waiting. He and Gabriel stood outside on the porch. Conscious of his cigarette, he flicked it discreetly into a lavender bush. The woman knew immediately something was very wrong as she stepped out of the Lancia.

They moved to greet her, but she did not stop to hear them, instead pushing through into the house to find her children. Lowry nodded to Gabriel to follow inside. Suzanne Cliff heard of her husband's fate from her two eldest children.

Mrs Cliff clutched her middle child and sobbed. The youngest could be heard shouting from the top of the stairs, 'Mummy, Mummy!' before stampeding down to clutch her. Gabriel found it difficult to take and hung back by the cool stone wall of the porch; Lowry was in command. Soon all four Cliffs were in a tight scrum. The two cousins loitered at the bottom of the stairs, not sure what to do with themselves. Alan caught Gabriel's eye and she moved over to comfort him. She felt for the boys, adrift in this house, not theirs, filled with death and grief. They would spend the night with Kate Everett while awaiting their parents' return from Athens the following morning. After a suitable interval had elapsed, Lowry signalled to two WPCs to remove the children. Suzanne Cliff faced Lowry. Her face was distorted, wild-eyed and desperate: *Tell me it isn't true.* Lowry's serious expression gave her no reason to doubt her children.

'I'm very sorry, Mrs Cliff,' he said.

'Where?' Mrs Cliff could barely manage that single word. Lowry beckoned the woman to sit with him on the sofa. Gabriel gently ushered the boys out to join their cousins. Suzanne sat down, her sobs drowning out Lowry's voice, which had dropped to little more than a whisper. Gabriel stood close by, still and soft and silent, both reaching out and holding back: compassionate but professional. After several minutes, Lowry lifted his gaze towards her and raised his eyebrows ever so slightly, prompting her to ask, 'Can I fetch you a cup of tea?'

Suzanne Cliff nodded imperceptibly.

It felt like an awkward question to ask the widow in her own home. The kitchen remained sealed off until the police had finished so instead Gabriel entered the scullery, which they'd been using all day. The family would be relocated to the George Hotel on the high street for the night to give the police another twenty-four hours.

She stood over the sink and filled the kettle. A huge pile

of laundry was to the side. Her husband's shirts on the top no doubt.

'I should help you.'

Startled, Gabriel turned round to face Mrs Cliff.

'Don't worry,' Mrs Cliff added hastily, 'I understand the kitchen is out of bounds . . . Ah, good, you've made yourselves at home.' There was not a hint of rebuke as she noted the police's plastic cups littering her work surface.

Gabriel didn't know what to say. She looked properly at Mrs Cliff for the first time. She was in her early forties, her hair tied back. Her clothes were understated and expensive. Her skin was clear and gently tanned. *Money*, thought Gabriel.

'May I ask where Christopher is now?'

'He has been transferred to the hospital in Colchester,' Gabriel replied hesitantly. Where was Lowry?

'Then why must we stay in town? It won't do the children any good.'

In truth Gabriel wasn't sure.

'We just need to make sure we haven't missed anything, Mrs Cliff. There are tests . . .'

'Tests?' The woman's manner switched unexpectedly. 'He blew his brains out. Surely you don't need to run tests to confirm that?'

'Just for a night,' Lowry said from the doorway. 'While we inspect the kitchen carefully one final time, if that's okay, Mrs Cliff? And I'm afraid you'll need to identify your husband's body.' He stood calmly and expressionless, which Gabriel admired, as it must be the only way to deal with such a situation, though at the same time she found it creepy.

Lowry watched Suzanne Cliff. She leant against the garden wall smoking a Consulate through thin lips. Her hair was tied back neatly, in a businesslike fashion, into a bun. She wore a white dress with purple flowers and a wide red gloss belt. He assumed that her frosty, distant manner was a kind of defense mechanism.

'You probably won't believe me,' she exhaled, 'but I have absolutely no idea why he's done this.'

Lowry stood next to her against the crumbling waist-high wall.

'Actually, I do,' he said. Two of the children were watching them from an upstairs window. He couldn't work out which two, due to sunlight falling on the glass. 'Who can tell what's going on inside any man's head.' He tapped his pocketbook on his thumb.

'There is no question, that it was . . .'

'Someone else?'

'What? No, no . . .' she said, confused. 'An accident.'

'Oh. We're investigating the possibility . . .' he let the word linger. 'It is rare that people handling firearms have an *accident*. Unless it's a misfire. The gun is old, that much is true.'

'He's handled guns all his life, since a boy.' She said this to herself; a strand of hair came free in the light wind.

'He wouldn't have cartridges out if he was just cleaning it. Usually, I mean,' Lowry said gently.

'I haven't the faintest idea, inspector; perhaps he planned to sound off a few rounds.'

Lowry didn't comment.

'How long will it be before we can use the house?'

'Tomorrow.'

'I don't want you to think me callous; it's just the children . . .'

'Of course.'

Lowry was used to people mistaking observation for judgement. And she did appear remarkably contained.

'They're not all his, you know.'

'No, I didn't.'

'Only Emma. Who happened by accident.' She sighed. 'I lived in London with my first husband but when that marriage failed, I moved back to be with my family in Colchester. I took up teaching again and met Christopher when he was here making a programme about Constable. The painter,' she added as an afterthought.

Lowry wasn't an educated man, but university had nothing to do with it: you couldn't grow up round here and not know the region's most famous son. 'Born in Dedham Vale, wasn't he, or . . . Flatford?'

'Yes, East Bergholt, to be precise. His father was a corn merchant, owned Flatford Mill. But Christopher and I met in Essex, just the other side of Colchester, at the university . . .'

'When was that, '77?' he asked, thinking of the youngest child.

'Seven years ago, May 1976. It was the bicentenary of Constable's birth, he was filming for *Arena*, and I ran the arts faculty. Christopher teaches, sorry, *taught* there ...'

Lowry was impressed; he had watched *Arena* on and off over the years. He remembered episodes with William Burroughs and Nico ... so Sparks hadn't been kidding, this Cliff guy really was famous.

'Forgive me for asking at a time like this, but, to your knowledge, did you and your husband suffer from any financial difficulties?'

Suzanne Cliff turned sharply. 'No, we did not. I understand why you ask, but no.'

'You'd be surprised at how many people live beyond their means; no matter how rich those means are. Did your husband have any expensive habits? Cards, horses?'

'My husband may have been in the media, but he was an academic presenter, not a celebrity. He spent most of his time in university lecturing.'

'Of course.' Lowry made a show of consulting his pocket-book, not that she saw – her gaze was now on the pasture before them. 'Your accountant, a Mr Darnell.'

'Yes.'

'Was he close?'

'Our accountant?'

'Yes.'

'No, he does the books.' Her surprise at the question seemed genuine. 'Why would he be a friend?'

'Oh, many people with complicated finances form close relationships with their advisors. I appreciate it's painful at this time –'

'Inspector Lowry, I fear you are under some illusion about the lifestyle we shared out here. Christopher was little more than an academic who occasionally appeared on TV and radio. He was not a popstar; he did not receive royalties, he was on a salary, or paid per commission, and had no need for an "advisor", as you put it. Yes, he had an accountant, who periodically visited the house – *not* to secrete funds in some offshore account, you understand, but rather to sort my husband's affairs. Christopher was appalling with paperwork and Darnell found it easier to keep track of things from here. Furthermore, my husband neither bet on horses nor gambled on cards. Now if you'll excuse me, I'll need to pack the children's overnight things.'

'Sure, I'm sorry, just a couple more questions. Last night. You and your husband went to the Angel public house, correct?'

'Yes . . .' her brow arched.

'What time did you arrive home?'

'About ten. Why is this relevant? The children are quite all right to be left home alone. Lucy is fifteen.'

Lowry thought it prudent not to mention her sister's children for fear she might take it as an accusation of neglect.

'It's routine, I'm sorry. Bear with me: so it was just you and your husband?'

'Yes . . .'

'How was he then?'

'If you're asking was he in the frame of mind to blow his brains out, no, he was not. We quite often go to the Angel on Sundays to round off the weekend.'

'And nobody came back to the house that evening, after hours, for a nightcap?'

'No. Is this routine, too?'

'I'm sorry.'

'No. Nobody came back – why would they? But we had had a row –' She drew hard on her cigeratte, which emphasised her cheekbones. 'Not about money, before you ask, but about the children.'

'Oh?'

'Yes. The only person Christopher cared about, other than himself, was Emma, his daughter; everybody else could go hang.'

Lowry was surprised at the venom in her voice. He could see she was starting to fray as the full import of what had come to pass slowly began to dawn; nevertheless, he let her continue.

'How about this morning, were you expecting anyone to visit this morning?'

'No . . . and I was at Dedham today.'

'An exhibition?'

'Correct. And Christopher was finishing a paper he was due to deliver this afternoon to a workshop at the university.'

'What time did you leave for Dedham?'

'Around eight . . . maybe just before.'

'And Mr Cliff's university lecture, where was that?'

'Wivenhoe. Where we met.' Her eyes glassed over, she blinked in the sunlight. Lowry scribbled details down then folded his pocketbook away.

'Your eldest daughter thought Christopher might have been expecting a visitor this morning – do you recall him mentioning anything?'

Suzanne Cliff massaged her eyebrows with thumb and forefinger then took a breath and said in a measured tone, 'I don't know, not that I can think of – might you give me some time?'

'Yes, of course. Thank you for your patience, and again,' he said quietly, 'I'm so very sorry for your loss.' She nodded as the tears began to flow. Lowry watched her return to the house. The Cliffs' marriage was not, it seemed, a happy one, but at this stage he could not diffuse the emotion from shock. A WPC waiting by the front door took charge of her and signalled towards the waiting Rover. Lowry decided to call it a day on the farm and return to Queen Street.

11

5.15 p.m., Sweet Pea Cottage, Fox Lane

Alan and Darren sat at the kitchen table in silence.

It seemed unfair. His cousins got to stay in a big hotel in town and they had to stay with Miss Everett. Alan didn't mind her – she reminded him of his French teacher, who wore open blouses in the summer term – just the house was boring and there was nothing to do, and they were forever being told not to touch things.

A bowl of stew was steaming away in front of him. Who had rabbit stew in July? It was boiling outside still; at home they'd be having salad for sure. He glanced at Darren shovelling it away. He wouldn't be so keen if he knew it was rabbit. Alan didn't care about that – there were hundreds of them in the fields round here; he just wasn't remotely hungry.

'Alan, eat it before it gets cold,' she called over her shoulder, as she reached for a jar from one of the shelves that lined the cottage kitchen.

'Please, can I have some water, Miss Everett?' She was

wider than his mother, and a lot wider than Mrs Cliff. But she did have bigger bosoms, which he couldn't help peeking at. He gawped now as she stretched overhead again for a glass tumbler, at the curve in her dress. The cat stirred from her observation post by the window, her big orange eyes catching him staring at her mistress's body, and Alan returned to his stew.

'There you go.' She placed it neatly on the coaster. He didn't see why: the table was badly marked.

'I expect you're both tired after such a long day.'

Darren carried on eating. He didn't know what was going on at the farm; he hadn't seen anything terrible and nobody would tell him when he asked what the fuss was all about.

'Not really. I just wonder who that man was up by the train track.'

'I don't think you need worry about that, Alan. You really shouldn't play up there. It's incredibly dangerous.'

'Was for that man. Should've told *him* that.' Darren slurped from his spoon. Kate glared at him in astonishment, triggering a snigger from Alan. She then turned on Alan.

'Your mother would be furious, to hear that you would be so *stupid*.' He noticed her knuckles clenched on the wooden table. Why was she cross at them?

'Well, if they cared at all, they wouldn't go on holiday without us. Then we wouldn't be stuck on a farm surrounded by dead people.'

Darren's face fell. What was funny a second ago lost all its comedy at the mention of the word 'dead', and became real, brutal life. Alan gulped; he'd pushed it too far. He didn't want to upset his little brother, especially out here alone – he'd even managed to spook himself. Knowing Miss Everett's eyes were on him, he blushed and stared into his bowl, wishing his mum would come and take them home.

Not until the detectives had all finally left the premises could Suzanne Cliff catch her breath. Only then did the enormity of the situation fully engulf her: Christopher had killed himself. She placed her hands flat on the window sill and pressed hard until her fingers went white. *Why?* The single word over and over. *The selfish bastard.* Despite what she'd said to the policeman, she now thought Christopher must have done something spectacularly stupid, financially probably, and taking his own life seemed the only, the easiest, solution. Oh, God, what sort of mess had he left them in? These last two years she had really started to loath her husband. All that business with Edward – only then did the scales fall; his only concern was himself and his career. She and the children were a nuisance. It was true Emma, his only biological daughter, got a look in, but even that was only because he could forget about her most of the time, packing her off to that ridiculously expensive school ... but did she hate him enough to want him dead? She had immersed herself in art – at first only to distract herself from Christopher's all-consuming career – but recently her own creativity had flourished. Selling paintings had given her great confidence. There was a photo of the pair of them by her hand on the sill, taken by Kate when they first moved here. They were leaning by the oak tree; they were so in love then. Another decade. Christopher with his wide-collared shirt, unruly lambchop sideburns and moustache . . . hirsute, unkempt, but a rakishly attractive, aspiring TV historian. She felt hands on her waist, and a head press between her shoulder blades. Suzanne turned to embrace her eldest daughter, Lucy.

'I'm so sorry, Mummy, so so sorry.'

'It's not your fault, honey.' She raised the girl's chin with her forefinger.

'We should have looked after him while you were out.'

5.45 p.m., Queen Street HQ

The traffic noise outside had now eased off, rush hour over, and a light breeze gently fluttered loose papers on his desk. The air temperature had fallen. Kenton knew that on the coast a sea breeze had kicked in, rising from the hot earth and strafing the north-eastern Essex peninsula of Walton, then Frinton, curving round Clacton and filling the Blackwater; too much for small dinghys off West Mersea but just right for the new sport he'd discovered . . . Kenton was desperate to get to the beach. The tides were right. But he had to get the statements typed for Lowry this evening. .

The children's statements took time. They were muddled and littered with non-sequiturs. Roughly translated, they amounted to not a great deal; suffice to say nobody had seen Peter Darnell arrive at the farm and nobody had come forward about Cliff following an appeal for information on local and national radio that morning. What did it matter, if the chap blew his brains out, anyway? What the children were all up to before the shooting was anyone's guess; tearing around fighting and squabbling before the father had ordered them to play outside. He took a sip of water. There had been an argument between two of the girls; Lucy and Alan had mentioned it, and so had Emma . . .

'Solved the case yet?'

Kenton turned round. Lowry had silently entered the office.

'Guv, what a day, eh.'

'How about you put that university education to some use and call on the faculty up at Wivenhoe. You speak their lingo. Cliff taught there from time to time – find out who his colleagues were, see if any of them were due to pay him a visit this morning, enquire into his state of mind.'

'Right now?'

Lowry snorted a laugh. 'The chances of anyone being there now are nil. I know you university types – all a bit part-time, knocking off mid-afternoon and so forth.' He slipped out of his suit jacket and loosened his tie.

'Well, if it can wait until tomorrow,' said Kenton, 'I might knock off then . . .'

He slowly stood up as Lowry sat down and put his feet up on the desk, apparently not hearing him.

'This one really gets under the skin . . . the circumstances are too strange. We must be missing something obvious.' He gestured at the witness statements. 'Anything in there?'

'Nothing as yet . . . Uniform are house to house this evening for sightings of Darnell in the Kelvedon area; we should hear later on that. Somebody must have seen him, surely.'

'It's not a big place, the old high street and a couple of side roads. And it would have been light when he died.' Lowry pulled out a bottle of J&B. Kenton didn't like this new habit and glanced down at the typewriter. 'Bright sunny day like this, someone will have seen him. And if not . . .'

Lowry poured generously into a crystal tumbler that Kenton could only imagine he'd brought from home. He then took half the measure straight down, grimaced slightly and lit a Players. The breeze carried the smoke towards Kenton. Lowry sat back, savouring the whisky and cigarette and gazing out of the open window to Queen Street below.

'And if not . . . what?' Kenton prompted.

The inspector sat up abruptly. 'If not, then he'll have been sneaking around, up to something he shouldn't.'

Lowry held the bottle out, gesturing for Kenton to join him. Kenton weighed his options: if he accepted, he could give up any hope of getting out on the water while the wind was up, but if he declined it would niggle, and his evening would not be enjoyable. He drained the water glass and nodded. His boss faced a comeback fight in the boxing ring, so why was he drinking and smoking so much? Hardly the right sort of preparation, if he was taking it seriously. Kenton knew, of course, that Lowry's marriage had hit the buffers, and where Jacqui was was anyone's guess. Lowry, being very private, had said nothing. Even when Kenton had visited the house, the inspector's behaviour was just as it had always been. Kenton held out a glass and watched the Scotch pour; he wondered what, if anything, went through the man's head when not on the job.

12

7.15 p.m., Colchester General Hospital, morgue

Lowry had kicked Kenton out at six – the younger man was itching to be elsewhere; there was a woman in play. Shortly after Kenton left, the pathologist Robinson called to confirm Sutton's theory of cardiac arrest and now Lowry stood between two bodies, Darnell and Cliff, laid out on gurneys in the morgue. Robinson stood, hands folded behind his back, at the head of Darnell's gurney.

'What sort of a weapon we after then? A knife?'

'No . . . something more akin to a skewer.' Robinson wore thick glasses, which always left Lowry with the illusion that he saw things to a degree of magnification.

'A skewer?'

'As in, meat skewer; as in kebabs on the grill, or outside over a fire or cooking contraption. The wound was dead straight, four inches deep. On the railway line, I read.'

'Yes. Doesn't immediately grab you as a place for a barbecue.'

'What was he doing out there?'

'If only we knew.' He pulled a glum face and turned to the next trolley. 'Now then, you mentioned on the phone Cliff's reach?'

'Ah yes, the length of his arms is significant when considering a gun with a barrel this long.'

Lowry watched the pathologist measure the dead man's arm. Cliff had great presence on television, but in fact he was a short man and paunchy; five foot three with a sizeable pot belly rising formidably from the gurney. The doctor consulted his pad. 'The barrel alone is thirty-four inches, as you know, before allowing for further length to include the stock and trigger . . .'

'Well?' Lowry said.

'This gentleman's reach would make the angle prohibitive.'

'Meaning?'

The man placed the pencil in the front pocket of his white coat. 'A short, chubby fellow like this would not get the leverage to shoot himself in the head. Has he been touched or cleaned?'

'No, of course not.'

Robinson removed his glasses, and rubbed his eyes, which were noticeably smaller naked. 'There's no gunpowder residue on either hand. That in itself is not conclusive, given the distance from the hammer and trigger – we'd have to test it.'

'Are you telling me this isn't suicide?'

The doctor replaced his glasses, his eyes resuming their usual size. 'It's certainly a consideration, Inspector.'

10.15 p.m., Creffield Road, Lexden

'And that will have to stop,' his wife remarked as he topped up his Scotch from the drinks cabinet.

'I'm sorry?' Although Sparks had been thinking about Antonia's condition, he hadn't actually been listening to a word she had said for the last ten minutes.

'Drinking.'

'Stop drinking? What on earth for?' He slumped into the recliner. The TV was on low, drowned out by the infernal wailing of Maria Callas on the turntable. Where had Antonia picked up this habit of playing opera of an evening? (He'd rather she'd stuck to Neil Diamond – he wasn't a fan but at least the Jewish Elvis kept his vocal range within the limits of decency.) He'd made a point of watching the ten o'clock news, to see if any of the local goings-on had caught Trevor McDonald's attention.

'The doctor said one shouldn't drink during pregnancy,' said Antonia, brushing past him in a lurid kaftan clutching a large glass of orange juice.

'And? What the hell has that got to do with me?' Sparks said, without looking up from the TV screen.

'Latest research says the baby could get drunk.'

He finally looked at his wife, trailing cigarette smoke as she paced the room. He still couldn't fully bring himself to believe this was happening. Had she for one moment considered whether or not he wanted a child? For that matter, had he? It had been on his mind ever since she'd dropped the bombshell on him at the weekend. Sparks had been married before – twice – but had always managed to dodge that particular bullet. And now here he was, fifty-four years old and a prospective father. It was all rather ... disconcerting.

'We don't want our child to be born an alcoholic, darling.' She had curled up on the wing-back chair and was staring at him with one raised eyebrow. '*Do* we, hmmm?'

'That's as may well be but still, I fail to see what it has to do with me and my Scotch.' The soprano screeched interminably. 'Can we wind the music down a tad? I've had a helluva day.'

Then something on the screen caught his eye and he jolted upright, his drink sloshing into his lap. Merrydown's face, outside Chelmsford HQ, followed seconds later by footage of Christopher Cliff.

'Look!' He raised the crystal tumbler towards the earnest academic. 'Him. Dead.'

'Oh my. *Him*. Christ, Stephen, that *is* news. He's famous as hell.' Antonia bounced up from the chair. The news item was playing a clip from one of Cliff's programmes. Nobody at Queen Street had a clue who this guy was. Sparks glowed inwardly, proud he'd married someone with an inkling of culture in their bones. There he was, this famous historian, standing, hands folded, in front of a manor house. 'Hey, I know that place ... where the hell is it?'

'Of course you do, we've had supper there countless times – that's Wivenhoe House.' Sparks rose, cut the music, and slid the volume up on the television. The elegant red brickwork building, with white cornice and window frames, was set in a landscaped park with a lake. The picture switched to an oil painting. Antonia started twittering on about the artist. Sparks had no interest whatsoever and shushed her sharply. The report returned to Merrydown, commenting upon how terrible a tragedy it was, and a loss to the nation. Naturally she didn't mention what old chums they were ... Darnell didn't get a mention. A mere civilian, rather than a celebrity, he would wait until tomorrow. Sparks had scheduled a press conference first thing. He took another slug of his drink.

The telephone rang.

'Bloody hell,' he muttered. Why couldn't people wait until the morning? He snatched up the receiver. 'Sparks.'

'Stephen?' A voice he knew but he'd not heard in a while.

'Speaking. Who's this, please?'

'Stephen, it's Jacqui.'

Of course. Lowry's wife. His face must have registered some surprise as Antonia mouthed, *'Who?'*

He shook his head and waved his wife way. A moment's pause. He took a deep breath.

'What do you want?'

1 a.m., Fox Farm

His beam caught the gateposts; the gate itself lay wide open onto the black night and the shingle driveway. Sloppy. Uniform ought to have shut the bloody thing. That there was no police tape out here was understandable. Until now it had been treated as a suicide.

Lowry had gone home after the morgue, but he couldn't rest. He wasn't a good sleeper at the best of times, but Robinson's earlier verdict was keeping him wide awake. After much tossing and turning, he had abandoned the effort, compelled instead to come out to the farm. The working hypothesis – that Cliff had murdered Darnell – may have been hampered by lack of evidence, but it would have been a convenient solution. However, in light of Robinson's findings, that seemed increasingly unlikely. What if Cliff was also murdered? Were they searching for one killer – or two?

He parked outside the farmhouse and dimmed the car lights. The dark night was absolute. He sat inside the Saab waiting for his eyes to adjust. There had been no street lighting since he left Kelvedon High Street and it was easy to miss turnings in the hedgerows, which he had done twice. Lowry took a quick sip from a hip flask then pulled the torch from the glove box and pushed open the car door. The ensuing groan caused something to rustle in the bushes.

The air was damp; fresh farmland earth and summer grass. The land he now saw was also illuminated by a soft grey from the gibbous moon. He stood motionless next to the car, leaving the torch in his hand switched off. The farmhouse loomed up in silence before him, austere and seemingly larger than it had appeared during the day. The yellow rendering had turned an off-white in the moonlight, lifting the building out of the night, casting an austere presence out in the landscape. Bats smudged along the pale walls, orbiting the roof in a long low oval as he approached the back door. He experienced the isolation of the house keenly, and smiled as he lifted the latch on the kitchen door.

The forensics team had long since gone and he'd cancelled the cleaners who were due the following morning. But Cliff's family were only booked in at the George for one night so there was bound to be disruption tomorrow, and he wanted a chance to examine the scene alone.

He flicked a switch. Fluorescent tube lighting stuttered into life, momentarily causing him to wince. He wasn't expecting to find anything obvious here. Forensics had worked through every inch of the kitchen and hadn't unearthed much. He started upstairs where his earlier search had been inter-rupted by Sparks. Turning all the lights on, he wandered from room to room; it was a chaotic place inhabited by a large family, untidy with dust on many surfaces. He won-dered if there was something he wasn't seeing through all the clutter.

It was a different story as he returned back downstairs: tastefully decorated, if verging on twee, but comparatively tidy – a thoroughfare for an army of busy feet. The kitchen was the most streamlined and state-of-the-art room in the home. One piece of furniture sat incongruously: a dresser to the right of the fireplace. Lowry was no expert but he knew it to be from another century, by virtue of its size and ornate curves. It would have blended in better with the stuffed birds upstairs. He walked over and touched the varnished surface. Dust. Broken only by sprays of blood. He turned and stood where Christopher Cliff's body had lain earlier, looking as if through the dying man's eyes: his last sight. The cartridge box had been placed on the dresser along with a cleaning cloth. Had he really had his own gun turned on him?

Lowry walked along the narrow hallway towards the front door, turning the lights on as he went. A visitor would have come in through the front entrance. The heavy door sat back in a recess of the porch and held a basket for post. He studied the area for signs of disturbance; winter coats, assorted wellingtons and cane sticks sat to the sides, unused for months, caked in crud from the spring. He thought he could smell damp. He made to open the door, which had a stiff latch. After a tug it eventually gave.

Lowry jolted back in surprise.

'Good evening.'

'Miss Everett, you gave me a fright.'

'Inspector,' said Kate Everett, standing pale before him. 'I thought Suzanne had returned. I saw the light and hopped on my bicycle.'

'I'm afraid not ... it's just me.' He stepped back to allow her over the threshold. 'Coffee? Since you're here.'

The woman remained on the threshold. Her eyes were bright, pupils dilated from the dark. He could see her calculating what to do. It must have seemed odd to find him here in the middle of the night, but he offered no explanation.

'I really ought not to – the children,' her face turned grim. 'It might be illegal to leave them on their own?'

'Ah, I see, yes, you've the Ward boys. You'll be able to see the light, should they wake, as you did here?' he offered.

'Ah, quick thinking. No wonder you're a detective. All the same, I'd be uncomfortable. They're not my children and I'd hate their mother to hear I'd left them alone. I best be off.'

'Are you a night owl, Miss Everett?'

'I'm sorry? Oh, no. Just having trouble sleeping, what with all that's gone on . . . I really ought to get back. I'm sure I'll see her tomorrow. Poor loves. I'm not sure what I thought had happened when I saw the lights on.' Her face lifted towards him. For the middle of the night, she struck him as lively and alert, not weary from lack of sleep. 'Thank you and good evening.'

'Good evening, Miss Everett,' he said and shut the door. Such an excursion at this hour was, he thought, odd; it wasn't as if she was just nipping across the street on a housing estate, either. He would pay her a visit soon. There was something curious about her.

He went straight to the first-floor landing window to watch her depart and get a sense of the distance between the homes. The rear light of her bicycle bobbed along, like some sprite in the night. Soon she disappeared behind a hedge. When he stepped back from the window, he noticed a football sitting at the far end of the landing. *The boys*. It occurred to him that he had never seen the attic where they had slept that night. In fact, in all their investigations yesterday, they had missed the attic entirely. It was concealed, accessible through a ceiling entrance via a set of stairs one drew down manually using a hooked pole that hung on the wall.

Lowry climbed up the steps and emerged into the attic. He'd expected to need a torch, but the room was well lit by the moon shining through a skylight. There was a small bed to one side and next to it a sleeping bag, both indicating they'd been slept in. Other than that, it appeared to be used for storage. An array of boxes were piled up on the floorboards. Lowry peered inside one and found it to be full of LPs. He pulled one out at random: Joy Division, *Unknown Pleasures*. This was unexpected; he wouldn't have had the Cliffs down as fans of that maudlin bunch of Mancunians. Lowry made a dim connection – didn't the lead singer kill himself? – but even so ... He foraged deeper. The Fall, Talking Heads and the Sex Pistols' *Never Mind the Bollocks*. You didn't need to be a detective to work out that these didn't belong to Christopher Cliff. This was a teenage boy's record collection if ever he'd seen one.

Part 2

ANTIQUES

Tuesday 26th July

13

6.45 a.m., America Road, between Coggeshall and Earl's Colne

Blood pounded in his ears in time with his stride. He increased his pace, pushing through from a jog to a run. Now on the home leg, fully warmed up and with a healthy sheen of perspiration, Lowry felt as good as he would feel all day.

The kestrel on top of the telegraph pole in front of him took flight with a lethargic flap, moving ahead down the country road and gently settling on the next post to wait for the man to catch up, as it had often done before.

Lowry had resumed running regularly in the spring, but had increased the frequency following his decision to return to the boxing ring. His decision was not entirely made to appease Sparks – though the chief had not been happy about him quitting the team back in January. In fact, it came down to the seasons. Lowry's new passion, birdwatching, had grown less active in high summer. He had enjoyed a full and successful spring devoting hours of his free time to watching the skies, as birds returned for the summer months: starting in

March with chiffchaffs, followed by ring ouzels, then came nightingales and April. All of this was new and rewarding – thrilling, even – but the action had peaked in the first week of May with three hobbies coming through over pastures in Ramsholt, Suffolk. Nothing could cap the raw excitement of seeing those most graceful of raptors, arching over the banks of the River Deben. The very recollection now, months later, brought a smile . . . After that, he'd tried once more to find the cuckoo in the fields behind his house, but time and again it evaded him. Lowry had not bothered to raise the Leicas since. Now the house was empty, save for Pushkin the cat, when he deigned to come in, which was not often in this weather . . . Lowry was a man who needed diversions. So boxing and running it would have to be.

He reached the next telegraph pole, but this time the kestrel stayed where she was. Her black eyes watched him as he approached below, a breeze ruffling her bared breast feathers as she adjusted her stance, head moving sharply. Lowry passed by, head tilted but holding the bird's gaze as he went. For several months now, the only birds he'd seen were those on his morning run. On the seven-mile circular from Great Tey, he would see three or four kestrels, often keeping him company as this one had, for up to a mile at a time. But birds were not uppermost in his mind as he ran; he generally used the time to reflect on work – something about movement and fresh air made his thoughts lively in new ways.

The situation at Fox Farm was extraordinary. Christopher

Cliff was murdered? And his accountant, before him? Rigor mortis had still been in progress and Robinson estimated the time of death in Darnell's case at ten p.m. Ten hours before Cliff … He felt a slight twinge in his left knee as the road started to climb back to Great Tey and the home stretch. He couldn't slow down now, and it took deeper, longer breaths to allow his core to propel him up the hill. What had happened to Cliff? What and who?

The exercise had unclogged his mind, leaving him renewed and clear like morning itself, with last night now out of his system. He'd reached a decision on his run: he would keep quiet about the switch from suicide to murder in the Cliff case – he'd have to tell Sparks, of course, but that was all, and Robinson would say nothing. He wanted the murderer to think they'd got away with it.

The two women, though not suspects yet, interested him most: Kate Everett living alone remotely, and Cliff's wife, Suzanne. His first move was to understand the wife. Could she have hated him that much? Her alibi should prove easy to confirm. And if clean, he'd need her confidence. Then there was the question of Darnell.

8.05 a.m., Creffield Road, Lexden

Sparks stood admiring himself in the full-length bedroom mirror and adjusted the knot of his tie. It was of paramount importance to appear immaculate for a press conference.

He would, however, go without tunic given the heat; one could still command respect from the rabble in shirtsleeves. Antonia emerged from the en suite amid a cloud of steam as the phone began to trill. Maybe it was Jacqui, maybe she'd changed her mind. He really, really did not fancy meeting her later today as he'd agreed to last night in a bid to get her off the line. They had sporadically kept in touch since she had split up with Nick. Sparks had been caught in the crossfire after that idiot doctor had chosen to confess his undying love for Staff Nurse Jacqui Lowry in the chief's very own office in Queen Street back in January. It had not been his finest hour. Sparks had mastered his surprise and bundled the blubbing medic out the back door, strongly urging him to keep a lid on all ideas of a confrontation with the nurse's husband. Then – and in hindsight this may have been unwise – he had immediately called Staff Nurse Lowry and relayed what had occurred, recommending her crazy lover have his head seen to.

Lowry and his wife had subsequently split up, of course. Sparks was not party to any details, and wished to keep it that way. He was a very private man, and indeed it was not until recently that Lowry had discovered the doctor had sought him out, that Sparks even admitted he had met the man in question. However, now, seven months later, he could not escape a sense of collusion with the wife, which troubled him, especially when she contacted him. Obviously he should tell

Lowry, especially if she was going to pester him and there was no sign of a reunion. He would.

Wrapped in only a towel, Antonia sat on the bed to answer the phone resting on Sparks's bedside cabinet. Someone she knew, it seemed – whoever it was, she was urging them round for drinks in the week. He did wish she wouldn't do that without checking with him. It was annoying to arrive home to find her posh friends lounging around the place. Seconds later, however, she held the plastic handset over her head – 'It's Nick, Stephen.'

'Ey?' he said, surprised as she dropped the receiver onto the duvet and strolled off towelling her hair.

'Nick, what was all that about?'

'I'm invited for drinks week after next.'

'That's rich, given nobody's supposed to be drinking.'

'What?'

'Never mind, what's up?'

Lowry proceeded to detail the pathologist's report. Sparks readily accepted that Darnell had been murdered; they'd suspected as much at the scene and they would keep that to themselves for now as far as the press were concerned. Time was needed with the immediate family to ascertain the deceased's last movements. What the chief wasn't prepared for, though, was the possibility that Cliff too had been murdered.

'Are you sure?'

Lowry explained how it was physically impossible for a man of Cliff's short rotund build to shoot himself through the roof of the mouth given the dimensions of the gun's barrel.

'Maybe he used something to reach down? That would also explain the lack of residue.'

Lowry thought not.

'What does that mean – who the hell was out there?'

'Anyone could creep in and out of that place and nobody would know. The kids were all out in the fields.'

They agreed to remain schtum, at least for the press release. Why was nothing ever straightforward?

14

9.00 a.m., Queen Street HQ

WPC Gabriel sat waiting for Chief Sparks in the latter's garret office. She felt uneasy, or exposed was perhaps more accurate, here in civilian clothes. She wore jeans, even though it was too hot, and a white long-sleeved top. There would be only one reason she had been summoned out of uniform. Uncomfortable, she took in the chief's office.

The walls were adorned with old black and white photographs of sparring bare-chested men. In the corner rested a cricket bat and pads, and behind the desk a trophy cabinet with assorted cups. The office was the very picture of alpha manliness. Beside an ornate teapot lazily emitting steam on the desk, was a photo frame. Curiosity prompted her to reach forward and turn it round to take a closer look. She expected a wedding photo – Sparks was recently married, much fuss was made of Antonia in the station – but found herself looking at a boxer posing, fists at the ready ... the chief himself, possibly. At the sound of a heavy footstep on the old wooden staircase, she swiftly let go of the frame and tried to steady her nerves.

'Ah, Gabriel, good to see you.'

'Chief.' She made to rise, he dismissed the gesture.

'Tactical surveillance.'

'I'm sorry?'

'Watching people, undercover. I think you'd be well suited to this sort of operation.'

He reached to pour his tea, left for him by Granger, as was the tradition (there was no second cup for her), and picked up a digestive.

'Not in uniform, then?' she asked.

'Correct; plain clothes. That is the nature of CID.' He slurped his tea noisily, then dunked his biscuit. 'But nothing too frilly, you know.'

It was useless to argue.

'And what will I be doing?' she said, with more edge in her than she'd intended.

'Whatever arises. We can't predict crime, can we? For now I just need you to help Inspector Lowry and your friend Kenton. They're massively overstretched. With a high-profile case like Cliff, they'll need all the help they can get and you were on the scene. Toddle off now to Crouch Street, they're over at Darnell's office.'

'Is it with immediate effect?'

'Yes, but so we're clear, this is a temporary secondment

due to staffing levels; anything beyond that and you'll have to do the exams like everyone else.'

'I would much prefer to remain in uniform.'

'Well, we can't all have what we want, can we?'

Sparks watched Gabriel leave his office. She was thin as a rake, lacking Merrydown's shapely figure. But tricky, tricky. Did the girl really think he'd tolerate such backchat if it wasn't for her aunt at County? Why the bloody hell Merrydown wanted her in CID was beyond him; she was not interested – nor was she cut out for it. She was wet. He considered the digestive. 'A limp biscuit if ever there was one.' Nevertheless, if the ACC insisted, so be it. In the meantime he had the press statement to run over ... now, where were his notes ... 'Bugger.' The digestive had broken wetly into his tea.

9.30 a.m., Crouch Street, Colchester

Neville Cross, senior partner at Darnell, Cross & Bingley Chartered Accountants, heard the news of his colleague's death in silence. After a few moments' grace to absorb what had been imparted, he removed his glasses, rubbed his rheumy eyes, then blew his nose loudly and looked up at Lowry.

'I'm not sure what help I'll be,' he sniffed solemnly. Located above a butcher's shop, these offices were of the same vintage as those on Queen Street; dusty and Dickensian. The twentieth century had yet to impede upon men of columns and ledgers, round here at least. Were it not for the lack of quill and ink, it could have just as easily been 1883 as 1983.

'You worked with Peter for over fifteen years,' said Lowry. 'We are trying to build a picture of the deceased's frame of mind. Had you noticed any behavioral changes over the last week? Was he depressed, happy, sad, worried?'

'He kept himself to himself, as ever. Assiduous about his work ... funny you should mention, though – there was something of a spring in his step of late, which was very unlike Peter, if you knew him.'

Lowry and Kenton waited for more.

Cross released his clenched fist and a handkerchief appeared. They all watched, silently, as it slowly unfurled in his palm.

'Yes, he was rather buoyant,' Cross mused, stroking his grey moustache.

'Any idea what brought that on? Your colleague the other day mentioned he was singing cheerfully.'

'Impending holiday?' He sniffed abruptly. 'Lake Garda. September. But then they've been going for donkey's years and Peter never grew excited before.' The gentleman paused. 'He had taken on the Figaro's account; maybe that explains it?'

'What's that?' Kenton asked.

'Figaro – the record shop in Eld Lane, you mean?' said Lowry. 'Was he a classical enthusiast?'

'Not that I'm aware of, no, but who knows? He may have

developed a taste. You'd be surprised what you can gain a passion for when it's paying the bills.'

'A singing accountant? Do me a favour,' Kenton said as the pair stood outside the practice on Crouch Street. A delivery van was unloading vegetables for the grocer next door. 'Sounds like a Monty Python sketch.'

Lowry didn't answer.

'Lake Garda,' he said eventually, 'are there campsites in Lake Garda?'

'Beg your pardon?' Kenton asked.

'Cross said Darnell was going to Lake Garda in September. There was a tent in the back of the Volvo. With my limited travelling, I've no clue as to what one does in Italy.'

Jane Gabriel stood across the street, in the shadow of the Bull. She wasn't in uniform but her slender figure was unmistakable. She looked entirely out of place outside the imposing boozer and she flinched at the noise of barrels trundling past.

'There she is, ready for action,' Kenton said – he'd noticed her as well. 'Do you think CID is best for her?'

'I'm not sure it's best for anyone.'

Lowry was not convinced this was a good idea. He waited to see if she noticed them watching. He turned to Kenton, whose eyes were still fixed on Gabriel. Romantic interest? Christ, Lowry thought, not again.

'Stop your gawping and get over to the university.'

'The chap's not free until noon,' Kenton said, pulling himself into check.

'Well then, if you have time on your hands, get some holiday brochures for the Italian lakes. Perhaps he was going to jazz it up a bit this year, camping out under the stars? And drop into the George on your way and check Mrs Cliff and the children are comfortable. I'll be there around eleven.'

'What about you?'

'Mrs Darnell awaits us. She didn't mention any holiday plans yesterday, did she?'

He frowned, recollecting the day before. 'No. But she didn't say very much at all.'

Lowry crossed the road and greeted Gabriel.

'We can walk,' he said.

'Where to?' Gabriel was baffled.

'Cambridge Road, to see Mrs Darnell.'

'Aren't you going to ask why I'm here?'

He had already started off towards Head Street. She didn't like his abruptness, finding it rude.

'Sparks told me.'

'I was at the farm yesterday, you know.'

They stood waiting for a gap in the traffic. Maybe she was paranoid; she never knew how anyone felt about her, her aunt being who she was. She was sure they all thought she was some entitled brat. Worse – an entitled *female* brat. The brightness of the sun was too much, even at this hour – coupled with buses trundling up to the high street, she was sure she'd have a headache before long.

'Here.' Lowry held out his sunglasses. '*Here*,' he repeated.

She took them without asking how he knew the sun affected her. They crossed the road and made their way down to the Southway underpass. Once up the other side and out of the town in the quiet of Maldon Road, with Lowry's wrap-arounds on, she felt better. They walked quickly, only the sound of their footsteps marking the silence. By now she knew the town well enough; Southway marked the boundary between the military area of town and the residential area. Maldon Road marked a further line between the working-class houses and the more aspirational homes in Lexden, where she herself hoped to live one day.

'You live near Coggeshall, sir?' She knew where he lived, of course, but sought to make conversation, feeling self-conscious.

'I do,' was the short answer.

'I was there yesterday morning on a call before Fox Farm. It's very quaint, but sort of . . .' She couldn't put a finger on it.

'Sort of what?'

'Oh, I don't know. All the houses are old and brightly-coloured, chocolate-boxy. You'd imagine they were quaint and happy, but they aren't. There's something strange about them . . . what I mean is . . . Oh, it's stupid, probably because of the quirky nature . . .' Gabriel found herself fumbling to explain what she meant.

They turned right onto Creffield Road.

'What were you doing there?'

'An old lady thought she heard noises,' she said, dubiously, 'as in . . .'

'Ghosts?' Lowry offered.

'It's foolish. But at the time, the woman was clearly scared, and who's she going to call?'

Lowry didn't laugh as she'd expected. 'It's a funny village. Notorious for strange goings-on.'

'That's what Fletcher said. Why?'

'They say it's on account of ley lines, or channels of natural "energy", which are said to cross in the village and create unusual happenings.'

'You don't believe that, though?'

He smiled lightly. 'I believe others believe it . . . everyone loves things that can't be explained.'

'Even policemen?'

'Especially policemen.'

'Nick!' A high-pitched female voice called from a double-fronted Georgian house. Lowry stopped abruptly and raised a hand. The woman, a short blonde in sunglasses and headscarf, waved back holding secateurs, and jogged over. 'How are you? It's been an age! And to think we just spoke on the phone this morning.'

'I'm good, thanks, Antonia; you're looking well.'

'Blooming, I hope, as one does!'

'Yeah . . .' he said uncertainly. 'This is WPC Gabriel.'

'Hi!' Antonia beamed, holding out a gloved hand. Jane

hesitated. 'Sorry, just doing the baskets.' The woman had tanned skin and a broad white smile. 'What brings you down here?'

'Routine,' he said evasively.

She stepped closer. Jane thought she caught a lilac fragrance, as Antonia said conspiratorially, 'Here, it's not about the historian on the television last night? Gosh, how dreadful.' Her perfect mouth made a perfect 'O'.

Lowry held up his hands and backed away. 'Hey, you know I can't say. We better go.'

The woman relaxed, and taunted Lowry with her secateurs, 'Ever the pro, Nick. Suit and tie, too, in this heat.'

They parted company and Antonia sauntered back to tend her plants.

Jane watched her go, perplexed. 'Who—?'

'Ooh,' Antonia spun round, 'and Nick, tell Himself to cut the drinking down. It's just not fair. See you next week! Toodle-oo!'

Suddenly it dawned on her. '*She's* Sparks's other half?'

'Certainly is.' He smiled thinly.

'But how?' she said incredulously. 'She's young, posh and beautiful – like, like an English Marilyn Monroe.'

'It's a mystery. He must have something.'

She quickened her step to keep up. 'What was she on about? I couldn't make head nor tail.'

'Who knows. Maybe he's keeping something from us. Never mind.' But he appeared genuinely puzzled.

15

10.25 a.m., The George Hotel, High Street, Colchester

The hotel lounge was a dusty quiet, and not the sort of environment to contain a lady of any determination. Mrs Cliff wore a paisley neck scarf that looked a little too tight and a yellow, figure-hugging T-shirt.

'Quite frankly, I didn't expect to find out that our accountant was lying dead at the bottom of my own bloody garden via a telephone call picked up by his blasted secretary.' Suzanne Cliff was furious. Kenton wasn't sure what to say. The police had not released details of the man.

'I—'

Kenton found her quite formidable. She had dark rings under her eyes from lack of sleep, lending her a haunted appearance.

'Inspector Lowry has good reason.' It was all he could think to say.

'Has he? Has he indeed. Well, I think it high time I brought in my lawyers.'

'Of course . . .'

'Well? What are his reasons for not advising me that Peter Darnell was found dead at the foot of our field?'

Kenton bit the bottom of his lip. 'Err . . . he was trying to shield you,' he lied. 'Give you room to grieve for your husband. The shock.'

The woman held her hand to her forehead in disbelief.

'What on earth happened to him? Peter wouldn't hurt a fly.'

'We don't know yet, honestly. Our investigations are ongoing.'

She sighed. 'When will we be allowed home? The children are bored shitless cooped up in here.' She waved abstractly towards a darkened corner, where two kids sat on a bar stool propped up close to a fruit machine.

'Very soon, I'm sure,' he replied, based on nothing.

10.30 a.m., Cambridge Road, Lexden

Lowry would play it straight with Mrs Darnell. Her husband's death was a murder. She needed to be aware of the situation. Kenton had dismissively said she wasn't the full deck; absent-minded.

'Here we go,' he said to Gabriel.

The door opened.

'Mrs Darnell, I apologise to call again at such at time,' he said politely. 'May we . . . ?'

He stopped short. The person at the door was not

Elizabeth Darnell, but introduced herself as her sister. Sarah Bowles had arrived overnight, and it was she who ushered them in.

'Peter was *so* well thought of,' she said, drifting into the drawing room. The room overlooked a narrow but well-kept back garden. Elizabeth Darnell was staring out of the window. The house was deep in an uneasy silence but Lowry had long since ceased to feel self-conscious in such situations.

They all remained standing.

'Elizabeth? The police are here,' the woman said softly.

'Mrs Darnell, would you mind if I asked you a couple of direct questions? I apologise in advance if we appear insensitive, but there are things only you would know.' He'd guess her to be older than her late husband. He moved closer. Her complexion was pallid and her pupils were dilated, despite the sunshine from the window, with a yellowing of the eyes, redolent of tranquilliser addiction.

'Of course.'

'You said to my colleague here that Peter would not have been working on Sunday. But what if the client was important – might he meet them on a Sunday evening?'

'Oh yes, if it was important.' Her focus was somewhere outside the house. A female blackbird paraded noisily on the tiny lawn, but he doubted she noticed.

'And I guess that's why he was wearing a tie,' Lowry said.

'Yes . . . he was.'

'Do you remember?'

'I can see him now, he kissed me – here.' She pointed to her cheek. 'He said he had business to attend to.'

'Did he ever discuss business?' Gabriel asked.

'Rarely . . .' she seemed thoughtful and distant at the same time.

'So, it would not be unusual for him to leave without telling you where he was going or for what purpose.'

'It wouldn't mean anything to me if he did, just names . . .'

'Not even when dealing with particularly difficult clients?'

She angled her head. 'It isn't that sort of profession, Inspector. And Peter was very gentle . . . not prone to losing his temper, even under stress. His clients held him in high regard. I was never aware of any difficulties.'

'Were you familiar with the Cliff family, out on Fox Farm?'

'Oh, yes, he was the chappy on the television.'

'Quite. Might Peter have mentioned that he had a meeting with Christopher Cliff?'

Mrs Darnell considered the question.

'Yes, he might . . .'

'So it might be unusual that he went to visit Mr Cliff and didn't mention it . . . ?'

Lowry waited. Mrs Darnell frowned.

'Tell me,' he said, convinced by now that she was heavily medicated, 'and this isn't a trick . . . you didn't report your husband missing when he failed to return last night.'

'I—'

She looked nervously from Lowry to her sister.

'I have difficulties sleeping.'

She crumpled in an armchair, her body convulsing in violent sobs. Lowry was taken aback; her emotional breakdown so at odds with her previous composure.

Gabriel rushed to sooth her while Lowry took a breather and stepped onto the front porch. He lit a cigarette.

'She's not been too good lately.' Sarah Bowles, not dissimilar in appearance to Mrs Darnell, appeared at his side. 'She's not well. Not well at all.'

'Could you define "not too good" for me?'

'Ladies' things,' she said quietly. 'A certain age.'

'Oh. Is she on tranquillisers?'

The woman nodded. 'Has been for years. The dosage has been increased to accommodate, you know . . . and she's not really been the same since.'

'How do you mean?'

'I live in Norwich and see my sister infrequently. She was not like this when I saw her last in March. I had a sneak at her prescription, and the dose would stupor an elephant; she wouldn't know whether Peter was here or not, most likely, and if she had at the time, she would be unlikely to remember now. The fact that she recalled things today that she did not yesterday is not a surprise.'

Mother's little helper, Lowry thought. GPs dished out millions of Valium each year to women, like sweets. Many became addicted as the dose increased. Come to think of it, Jacqui had some at home; he might pop one himself just to get a solid sleep. Lowry flicked his cigarette over the low wall.

'Anything else?'

'A dicky tummy,' Sarah Bowles's expression said more of the unpleasant suffering than her words, 'and complaints of a dry mouth.'

'That'll be the medication. You'll look after her, though?'

The sister nodded rapidly. 'Yes. Actually I was planning to take Elizabeth to see our mother in Canterbury next weekend. Lord knows what'll happen now. Probably finish the old duck off.'

When Lowry re-entered the drawing room, the widow Darnell had regained composure and was drinking a glass of water.

'Sir,' Gabriel said. 'Elizabeth was just saying she may go to Italy, anyway; perhaps her sister might join her.'

'Yes, Lake Garda, I believe.' He could imagine her driving there. 'We'll get your car and tent back soonest.'

'Tent?'

'In the car.'

She turned her attention from the window for the first time and glanced around the room, confused. 'We do not own a tent.'

'You husband recently bought one?'

'We always take a chalet on the lakes . . .'

'Perhaps it was for a stopover on the way down?'

'I really can't see Elizabeth in a tent, Inspector, can you?' her sister said disdainfully. She had a point.

'All that fresh air might do her good,' he said with all seriousness. The front doorbell rang.

11.00 a.m., The George Hotel, High Street, Colchester

Suzanne had calmed down by the time Lowry found her in the hotel lounge. She felt bad for giving the younger policeman such a hard time. She didn't give a fiddler's about the accountant. She'd been riled up before he arrived, having spent an exasperating morning on the phone to Christopher's father. How dare that old bastard insinuate she was too absorbed in her art. She realised she would need to employ a lawyer. For the first time in a long while, she really missed her mother – she had been a stalwart with the girls when they had all the bother with Edward last year.

'Mrs Cliff, my apologies.' The inspector was wearing identical clothes as the previous day, despite the weather being a good few degrees hotter. Light grey suit, white shirt and black tie.

'Inspector Lowry, your young colleague explained your rationale, but all the same.'

'My rationale?' He removed his sunglasses.

'For keeping Peter Darnell's death from me.'

He sat down opposite, lightly adjusting the knees of his suit trousers as he did so, the way the elderly do. 'Oh, good,' he said, clearly not wishing to take the matter further. 'I wanted to touch on the sequence of events leading up to your husband's death.'

A woman stood loitering by the concierge, striking and blonde, casting the occasional glance their way. Suzanne jutted her chin in her direction. 'Is she with you?'

'Yes, but what I wish to discuss concerns only you and me.'

'Yes, what precisely do you wish to know?'

'Was your husband expecting anyone yesterday morning?'

'I told you yesterday, not that I was aware.'

'Yes, I just wondered whether anything might have come to mind overnight.'

He offered her a cigarette.

'You mean like Peter Darnell? Forgive me, but I'm growing familiar with your oblique style of questioning – perhaps you think he was being blackmailed, or something equally unpleasant that might explain a suicidal reaction. Or perhaps you think that someone murdered him. Which is it?'

Inspector Lowry sat very still. The ancient lobby grandfather clock measured the heavy passing of time in a steadfast way. 'Mrs Cliff, we have reason to believe your husband may not have taken his own life.'

'Murder?'

He gave a slight nod.

Lowry's face blurred as her gaze dilated to the middle-distance. Two Japanese tourists came down the hotel stairs, slowly examining the wattle and daub wall as they did so. *Murder*. It was a word that had no meaning in her world. Her mind explored the idea as the fingers of the tourists did the ancient wall, delicately, tentatively. Christopher was dead; there could be no greater shock, but by another's hand . . . who could have loathed such a useless man as much as her – enough to kill him? She realised Lowry was talking at her.

'Am I a suspect?' she blurted out.

The corners of his mouth turned up ever so slightly, as if in a light smile. 'We will need to authenticate your story as a matter of procedure.'

'The children saw me leave, is that not good enough? Or are you supposing I crept round the house, after they ran off to play.'

'Just think, Mrs Cliff, who at the art gallery might vouch for you, please? Meanwhile, as I was saying, we know to the minute when Christopher died. Your nephew checked the time when he heard the gunshot – eight-fifteen. Whoever entered the property may have lain in wait for the children to leave the house. Your husband shouted at them to go outside, when two of the children were arguing and distracting him from his work . . .'

She listened intently as the inspector calmly detailed her husband's last minutes alive; Suzanne heard him at a remove – as if he was describing another family's morning, not her own.

'The only person in the vicinity at the time that we are aware of was Miss Everett.'

'The children, Inspector.' She leant down to the low table for her cigarettes. 'Which two were arguing?'

The policeman consulted his pocketbook. 'Alice and Emma.'

'Are you sure?' It was normally Alice and Lucy who rowed, being closest in age.

'Yes, over what they had for breakfast, apparently.' He didn't see the point in mentioning it might've been over Alan. 'Why do you ask?'

'No reason.' What a triviality. He held her gaze then made a mark in his notebook. She was about to ask what he was recording, then stopped herself.

'Miss Everett,' he continued, 'lives not far away?'

'Quite so, Sweet Pea Cottage, which once belonged to the owners of Fox Farm, many years ago.'

'Sweet Pea . . .'

'After the climbing flower. Fox Farm was a seed farm from the 1880s and cottages housed the workers up until the outbreak of the First World War. The area is well known for it since the turn of the century; the Victorians who arrived with the railway discovered the land perfect for seeds.' She heard herself reel off these facts Christopher had told her, facts he churned out at every dinner party they had at the house; she felt as if her own voice belonged to someone else. She stopped abruptly.

'And Miss Everett arrived when?'

'The farmer sold off most of the crop-producing fields to a multinational but they kept the farm and cottage. Kate has been there donkey's years.'

'A good friend?'

'Very.'

'If she heard the gun – would that cause alarm?'

'This is the country, Inspector. Good heavens, you live not five miles from here yourself; if you heard a shotgun, would it surprise you?'

'No, I guess not. Except perhaps for the early hour. What has Miss Everett said to you?'

'Nothing, I haven't had a chance to see her . . .'

A silence ensued.

'He was due to see an antiques dealer,' she said.

'When?'

'I'm not sure precisely . . . it might have been yesterday. I found a card in his wallet. I went through it last night, searching . . .' Searching for a reason for him to be doing this to them all. She rummaged through her handbag. 'Here.'

Lowry glanced at the card then pocketed it. 'Anything in particular, the antique dealer's visit?'

She sighed. 'Yes. A Welsh dresser. I had been haranguing him for ages to get rid of it . . .'

'In the kitchen, next to the fireplace?'

She nodded.

'Valuable?'

'That's what he intended to find out, Inspector,' she said tersely. 'Is that all?'

He rose.

'For now, yes. You'll be able to return home this evening,'

Lowry said. She stood and held out her hand. 'One thing, though; I'd be grateful if you kept what I just told you to yourself for now.'

'If it will help, of course,' she said, her hand still lost in his huge grasp.

16

11 a.m., Queen Street HQ

Sparks marched into CID. Kenton was sitting in Lowry's chair next to the open sash window, engrossed in a magazine.

'What the bloody hell you doing, Sonny Jim?' Kenton gave a start. 'You haven't got time to browse through holiday brochures!'

'I'm not . . .'

'C'mon. Press are waiting. All of Fleet Street down for this one, it'll be standing room only. Town hall as befits. Pronto.'

Kenton folded the magazines up and rose.

'Did you see her ladyship on the news last night?' Sparks said.

Merrydown's appearance on TV had unsettled him and he'd slept badly as a result. They were cut from very different cloth, him and the ACC, a fact that became magnified under the public glare. Sparks and Kenton rattled down the stairs towards the foyer. He knew some of his habits rubbed her up the wrong way, and he did not have any of the airs and graces she possessed, but he was no clown and he knew how to run a murder enquiry.

'Jesus,' Sparks winced as they approached the foyer. The place was thronging. The hubbub rose a notch on their appearance. Why the bloody hell hadn't Granger, his desk sergeant, herded them into the town hall as instructed?

The chief drew to an abrupt halt on the bottom step. Kenton walked straight into his back. Kenton knew it had been decided that Sparks would deliver his statement to the press in the town hall on the high street, but it seemed that clod Granger had failed to pass on the message to the swathes of hacks jostling before them. Kenton switched his mind to the holiday brochures.

Lowry had instructed him to call on various travel agents in the town, to ascertain whether camping was an option at Lake Garda. Thrilling policework it was not, yet he had diligently researched the short breaks on offer in the Italian lakes in September. Not a great deal, it transpired. Good air but that was about it. Lake Garda was not a particularly popular camping destination as it turned out – which was not to say it wasn't possible to pitch a tent there, just that few seemed to want to do so. However, he had just discovered there was a windsurfing centre there; a photo in the brochure of a chap powering across under the mountains had caught his eye and he made a mental note.

Sparks was barking disagreeably at the assembled hacks.

This was going to be a fiasco. Eventually several Uniform wedged themselves between the chief and the crowd, and forced them out onto the street. It appeared Sparks was to deliver his statement from the station steps.

Kenton stood back and observed without listening. He knew what was being said, anyway – one suicide, one death in suspicious circumstances. No mention of any connection between the two beyond the proximity of the bodies. Nothing new to be heard. The chief's balding pate was sunburned, he noticed. When it was finally over, Kenton slipped away to Wivenhoe. He had been daydreaming when the chief shouted at him; Jane and windsurfing at Lake Garda, heaven . . .

Suzanne Cliff stepped out into the sunlight. There were people milling around on the pavement. The high street was unusually busy for a weekday. Then again, it was the holidays. And when was the last time she came into town? She turned left and ambled down towards the castle to find the children.

Christopher . . . She had fallen out of love with him, but she had never wished him dead. That he may have been murdered seemed preposterous.

The police were obtuse and difficult to read, especially Inspector Lowry, which was maybe why something in her prevented her telling him her whereabouts at the time of Christopher's death. They had asked the children – who had told them what they knew: that she had gone to an exhibition. What she had *not* told them – and what the police therefore could not know – was that she had also gone to the Suffolk borstal. Was she witholding information? Was she a suspect?

She should of course tell Lowry about Edward. Edward. She hadn't given him a second's thought since arriving home yesterday afternoon. She wondered how Lowry would take the news that her son was currently in borstal. Without comment, in all likelihood; certainly without expression. Out of nowhere she thought of L.S. Lowry, his dour matchstick daubs. It seemed fitting that the inspector shared his name. Christopher would have seen the humour in this; he loathed Lowry's work, and no more considered him an artist than he did Rothko or Pollock. She tried to smile.

She turned into the castle grounds, and was greeted with a dazzling array of colours from the flower beds. The roses reminded her of Kate Everett's garden. The way Lowry had questioned her about her friend had made her feel uneasy. As if Kate were a suspect.

12 p.m., University of Essex campus, Wivenhoe, east of Colchester

The campus was less than two miles from the centre of town, set in two hundred acres of sculptured park. The landscape was designated as an area of outstanding natural beauty, in spite of the incongruous university buildings. The stark grey brutalist slabs amid carefully tended greenery reminded him of *Fahrenheit 451*.

Kenton made for Wivenhoe House, once the manor house, now the university's administration centre. Kenton had read that *Wivenhoe Park* was one of Constable's most famous paintings. The building before him was once the property of a general with a passion for trees, who, on his return from the Peninsular Wars, designed the impressive park that surrounded the house. Kenton found this local history fascinating. Leaving his Ford Capri on the gravel forecourt, he stood for a moment to admire the impressive red-brick building framed in cream architrave before hurrying in to find Cliff's colleague.

Tim Pine was head of the faculty and a long-time friend and colleague of Cliff's. His office on the first floor overlooked the park.

'Fantastic mind, simply fantastic,' he said, puffing thoughtfully on a pipe. 'What Cliff didn't know about art wasn't worth knowing.'

'How long have you been acquainted with Mr Cliff?'

Pine released a cloud of fragrant smoke. 'Twenty years. More.'

'Would you say he was a happy man?'

'Like all academics, he preferred to spend time alone. Especially as he grew older.' He removed the pipe from his mouth and poked the smoke cloud with its tip. 'We have less energy to spread ourselves around. Are you with me?'

Kenton wasn't. 'So, you're saying he *wasn't* happy?'

'The children wore him out, poor blighter. He grew vexed.

It was often a relief for him to come on campus – gave him a respite, you know.'

'Yes. According to our investigations, he was due to host an event here yesterday afternoon. Can you tell me what that was exactly?'

'Summer school for art students – the majority being Open University – for a lecture on the Romantic period.'

'Including John Constable, who painted this place?'

'Indeed. Constable was himself self-taught. Always proves popular with the autodidact.'

'A favourite of Mr Cliff's, too. I gather he met his wife out here, filming a documentary on the man's life and work?'

'Yes. Suzanne used to teach here.'

'A formidable lady.'

'Army stock for you: from a long line. Her father was one Colonel Hoare. Her grandfather was top rank too, and his father before him. Suzanne's actually related to the chap who originally built Wivenhoe House and commissioned Constable to paint it. See, comes full circle.'

The army were in the very fabric of the town, even where you least expected it. 'Christopher Cliff had no military background?'

'Not to my knowledge. At the time Christopher and Suzanne met, he lived in London. It was a big undertaking – her and three kids and then, ahem, a fourth on the way. But *gee whiz, she was stunner; girl with the sun in her hair.*'

'I'm sorry . . .'

'Hair ad in the sixties, before your time – '

'No, you misunderstand. You said four children? Three girls . . .'

'And the boy, Edward.' He puffed mischievously. 'Though I very much doubt you've come across him yet . . .'

17

12.45 p.m., Coggeshall, ten miles west of Colchester

Lowry parked in the heart of the village, underneath a blue weatherboarded clock tower. He picked up the radio handset from his lap and took a call from Queen Street.

'Uh-huh. Good. Thanks.'

'News?' asked Gabriel. The inspector was not what one might call a natural sharer.

'Forensics report is in from the farm,' said Lowry, placing the receiver on the dash. 'So here we are, the place you're fascinated with – spooks, and on this occasion, antiques.'

Gabriel was interested in forensics – all that evidence at a crime scene, invisible to all but the experts – but Lowry seemed reluctant to say more. She guessed she had some work to do to gain his confidence. Perhaps it would come with time – it was only her first official day out of uniform, after all.

On the drive over he had delivered a long-winded lecture on his working methods. It was vital to work exhaustively in the first few days after a major crime, he said. Covering all possibilities and leads in those early days offered the best chance of solving the case.

'The present is imperative when the scent is still warm and the tracks may not yet be covered,' he told her.

She found the whole speech patronising and wondered if he had difficulty communicating with women in general.

They got out of the car and stood on the pavement outside an antiques shop – there were a number of them along this street. Gilded picture frames of varying dimensions were propped alongside an array of ceramic pots on a bookcase with flaking paintwork. In the window were clocks of all ages and description; a brass telescope sat upon a worn chessboard. An empty birdcage hung from an ornate fascia.

They crossed over the triangular village centre and walked along the pavement for a stretch. Road workers stood outside a fish and chip shop opposite. A bypass had opened this month and the village was enjoying its quietest period in many years. They passed three windows – antiques galore, but nothing as enticing as the first shop they'd seen. A table or a row of poorly upholstered chairs. No colour, or frippery, or indeed signage.

Suddenly, Lowry stopped. Reaching into his pocket, he retrieved the business card that Suzanne Cliff had given him and, apparently satisfied this was the place, ducked inside. Gabriel followed. The low-ceilinged room was musty and filled with large items of dark furniture. Gabriel didn't know a thing about antiques, but to her mind the word 'antique' meant 'dainty and attractive' and this heavy oak farmhouse furniture did not qualify. She couldn't even fathom how they'd got them through the front door in the first place. The showroom was devoid of customers. They delved deeper, squeezing past a huge dresser, and eventually discovered two men sitting in deck chairs in a solitary square of sunlight beyond some French doors, smoking and reading the paper. Hushed voices emerged from a portable radio.

'Busy, gents?' said Lowry.

If the men were surprised to see them, they did not show it.

'Do I detect the faint aroma of rozzer?' said one of the men from behind his newspaper.

'One's a babe,' said the other, as he rose to his feet holding a mug of tea.

'Where's Derrick?' Lowry asked as they stepped out into the sunlight. The back of the building opened up onto a leafy yard. Assorted wooden furniture lay about the place, noticeably a wardrobe surreally under the shade of a willow tree.

'He's busy.' The man turned a page in his paper, unfazed by the intrusion. He wore a ratty ponytail.

'His card was found in a dead man's wallet not far from here.'

That caught the man's attention. 'How far?'

'Kelvedon. A Welsh dresser. Ring any bells?'

The man scratched his jaw lazily. 'Yep, Fox Farm. Called yesterday – geezer weren't in.'

'You're savvy with the news,' said Lowry, nodding at the newspaper. 'Why not come forward?'

'Never saw him.'

'Did you call in person, or the boss?'

'Who says I ain't the boss?'

'What's your business called?'

'Ya what?'

'What's it say above the shop window?'

The man shifted his posture in the chair uneasily. There was no signage. Lowry pulled out his own card and held it out between index and middle finger.

'Make sure Roger calls Queen Street before the end of the day, and I won't arrest you for wasting police time.' The man's jaw dropped, as Lowry stepped back inside.

Lowry knew Roger Derrick of old – a fancy entrepreneur; a property, art and antique dealer, and occasional fencer of stolen goods and money launderer. Essex was particularly popular with launderers; a wealthy county close to London, enjoying a roaring cash trade in caravans and Chippendale furniture, depending on the class of villain. Roger dealt more at the Chippendale end of things than the caravan – Chippendale, rugs, crockery, clocks, art – and, on occasion, antique guns.

The forensic report had revealed fingerprints not belonging to Cliff on the shotgun. Maybe they belonged to Derrick or one of his people?

'They're not doing a roaring trade,' said Gabriel once they were outside.

'No. But then again, they are not primarily in antiques.'

'How do you mean?' She blinked in the dust as a bulldozer drove past.

'Antiques are a way of laundering money. The shop's a front, or storeroom. Buying and selling cash. This place, Coggeshall, is renowned for it – laundering and haunting, their two claims to fame.' They walked back to the car. 'Of course there are genuine antiques places in the village centre, but often the shadier shops down the side streets are little more than masquerades.'

'So why would someone like Christopher Cliff call on a place like that? How would he even know of its existence, and why are we even here?'

Lowry frowned as yet another lorry trundled down the narrow street raising a cloud of dust. 'Because, if you met Derrick in the street, you wouldn't connect him with what you saw back there. He's the complete opposite – colourful, flamboyant, even entertaining . . . Cliff must have had something they were interested in.'

'Start from the beginning, please.'

As they made their way back to Colchester, Lowry explained the thriving black economy. He and Sparks had seen money laundering in the county grow exponentially since the sixties, as it was, by and large, victimless. Lowry explained how the average East End thief, having blagged a bank in Whitechapel, would catch a train out of London, jump off at Colchester, and hail a cab to Point Clear clutching a supermarket bag of used notes, ready to buy any number of 'holiday homes' to let short-term, thus fuelling the local community with no questions asked. At the other end of the scale was the more aspiring thug; a successful villain, established, where social status was as high a priority as the next job, who was prepared to pay over the odds for a decent piece of aged timber to add a certain refinement to his home. This is where Roger had been known to step in, and very lucrative it was for him, too. Antiques were one of the few items it was more expensive to buy with cash than credit. A trader, such as Roger, inflated his price by a margin, to cover his risk. The customer, a well-heeled crook, was only too willing to pay. A staggering price must mean staggering authenticity. (For that reason, even the most hardened criminal was reluctant to steal something for himself; leaving him with a nagging doubt he'd risked his neck for a pile of junk).

'And there is no reason not to assume that the occasional rare or valuable firearm might become highly desirable,' he concluded as they swung onto Queen Street.

18

2.30 p.m., Queen Street HQ

'How was the press conference?' Lowry settled in a rickety visitor's chair opposite the chief, tapping a Manila file gently on the desk. Gabriel sat beside him.

'A fiasco,' Sparks shrugged. 'At least it was mercifully short and we haven't fucked anything up yet as far as I'm aware, so there was nothing to criticise. What's that you've got there?'

A small fan whirred in the background. Sparks was on edge, fidgeting in his seat.

'You all right?' Lowry ventured, ignoring the question.

'Me?' He glared at his inspector. 'Of course I'm all right, why wouldn't I be all right? *You* better be right about Cliff being a murder case now. I don't want any grief on that front.'

Lowry sensed Sparks was troubled. Maybe Gabriel's presence had vexed him – if something *was* up, Sparks would never confess it in front of her. Lowry decided to let it go, and made to open the file.

'What's that?' Sparks repeated.

Lowry pulled out the top sheet of paper. 'Forensics report.'

'And?'

'There are fingerprints on the gun that are not Cliff's.' He slid the report across the desk.

Sparks leant forward, snatching the paper. 'You're having me on. Why the fuck didn't you say?'

'On the barrel and stock.' Lowry felt Gabriel staring at him. The file had been waiting on his desk when he got back to the office.

'Hmm –' Sparks pushed himself back in his chair – 'anything else?'

'The eldest and youngest girls mentioned her father was expecting a visitor. Suzanne Cliff corroborated this,' Lowry said. 'An antiques dealer from Coggeshall was there in the morning around the time Cliff was shot.' He paused. 'To view a Welsh dresser, apparently. Story is they rang the doorbell and knocked several times.'

On cue, there was a rap at Sparks's door. Kenton poked his head round and gingerly crept in.

'Do you believe them?' said Sparks, ignoring the newcomer.

'I'm not sure.'

'Bloody careless getting shot over a piece of kitchen furniture. What was it? A Welsh dresser?' Sparks asked.

'For plates,' said Lowry.

'Murdered?' said Kenton, suddenly catching up. 'Nobody gets murdered over a—'

Sparks silenced him with a sharp glance. Lowry rose and lit a cigarette.

'We need to match the prints before getting too excited,' he said. 'We've sent an expert to value the dresser – a chap from the auction place in Head Street. Taking a look at the gun too.'

'Very good. Ahh, Coggeshall, Coggeshall,' Sparks ruminated. 'Never was so pretty a place cursed with so much trouble. I'd find it hard to believe someone of Cliff's intellect would be hoodwinked by one of those chancers. Anyone we know?'

'Roger Derrick.'

'Christ! The Feering Fairy! Hahaha!' Sparks broke out in laughter. 'That old woofter wouldn't know which way to hold a gun.'

'He just might, especially a valuable one. Or maybe it was an accident ... We won't know until we have a chat with him. He wasn't there when we called by his shop, only came across a couple of his goons, too suspicious to speak without their gaffer there.'

Lowry rested his elbows on the small garret window. The sky outside was so blue it seemed unreal, as if from a child's paint palette. His initial reaction to the news of the fingerprints was indeed just that – an accident; a disagreement over a price perhaps.

'Maybe Cliff did have money troubles after all,' Sparks said over his shoulder. 'Roger would be attracted to a fancy fellow like him, and from Cliff's point of view, dealing with someone like Roger would certainly be quicker than going through, say, the auctioneer in the town. And the accountant – maybe he's mixed up in all this too?'

'No connection so far . . .'

'Christopher Cliff was murdered?' Kenton interrupted again. 'Nobody told me!'

'Sit down, for Christ's sake,' Sparks snapped.

He meekly pulled out a wooden chair and continued. 'I learnt something very interesting at the university this morning.'

Sparks raised a contemptuous eyebrow towards the young detective. Lowry was never sure whether the chief's antipathy towards the lad was genuine.

'Go on then,' Sparks said sarcastically, 'do tell.'

'Suzanne Cliff had three children before she married Cliff, not just the two girls. There is an older son in borstal in Suffolk. Edward Hoare. Hoare is her maiden name. He was arrested for theft, first in '81, then again last June, and was subsequently locked up.'

'What was he stealing?' Lowry said, tuning in.

'Antiques. Jewellery mainly, from a place in Kelvedon.'

The room fell quiet.

'Well, laddy,' Sparks rubbed his hands together. 'For once your presence has achieved more than cluttering up my office space. I think we have just discovered the proverbial skeleton in the Cliff closet . . .'

3 p.m., Fox Farm

Suzanne arrived home late afternoon with her children.

At least the night at the George had shaken off the press. Although no one was waiting for her at the farm, the phone rang constantly and she left it off the hook. There was no relief from Christopher's affairs. Perhaps once finished with this, she'd sell the blasted farm and get as far away from here as possible. The children would thank her for it and the London art scene would be more beneficial for her career; these parochial exhibitions were all very well, but ultimately for amateurs.

Once she had the children settled, she jumped back in the Lancia and headed down the road to Sweet Pea Cottage. To hell with it, she wanted to see Kate.

Kate was genuinely pleased to see her. Despite her best efforts to put on a brave face, her friend looked disturbingly drawn and gaunt and had clearly not slept a wink last night. She had an enviable beauty; no foundation and powder for her. Suzanne was shocked and wondered how she herself looked to others.

'You caught me having a nap!' Kate said when Suzanne expressed her concern. Suzanne's eye was drawn to some herbs on the chopping board, which indicated activity to the contrary.

'Oh that, that's from yesterday,' said the other, catching her gaze. Kate was a keen exponent on nature's kitchen and herbal remedies; the children were forever coming back with old wives tales and nonsense that used to drive Christopher crazy. Her dead husband, a man steeped in dates and historic facts, had no time for Kate and what he called her "country bunkum".

'What are you cooking up?' Suzanne asked, noticing the pan on the range. 'I could do with a sleeping draught myself ... Oh, Kate!' She flung her arms around her friend's neck. She truly was exhausted. 'Oh, that selfish bastard! Making me miserable even when he's dead!'

After tears and a hug, they moved outside to sit on iron chairs on the back patio. They sat a long time in silence until, without thinking, Suzanne spoke.

'The police believe Christopher was murdered.'

Kate was aghast. 'What the hell?' She placed her cup of lemon tea on the garden table.

'I've no idea.' Suzanne shook her head.

'The police telephoned to check I'd be in later today,' said Kate. 'I guess they need to question me some more. They'll be all over the place if they suspect it's murder. Do the police know about Edward?'

Suzanne shot her a sharp glance. The question was unexpected.

'No, why? Should it matter?'

'Sorry; I thought ...'

Suzanne felt her face become red. 'I don't see what he has got to do with anything at all. Edward's in Suffolk.'

After a while, Kate spoke. 'Christopher and Edward didn't get on . . . did they?' The sentence hung in the air.

Suddenly, the Ward boys appeared at the back of the garden from the gate that led out to the fields. Suzanne was grateful Kate had offered to take the two lads. It was generous and kind of her and the thought made her regret speaking sharply.

'I'm not keeping Edward from them. Or anyone,' she said, more calmly now. 'I saw him yesterday, as it happens, he's getting out in two weeks . . . though admittedly if they believe Christopher was murdered, it changes the situation.'

'If they think you've been withholding information, it won't do you any favours, Suze . . . they play their cards close to their chest.'

'I know,' she agreed. 'I meant to tell them yesterday, but couldn't . . . I know I'm over protective; I just want Edward kept as far away from all this as possible.'

'He was up at the house last night, you know.'

'Who was?'

'The inspector. Lowry.' Kate sipped her tea and stared across the garden.

'At the farm?'

Was that why he wanted her out of the house; to creep about in the middle of the night? Suzanne felt events slipping out of control.

19

3.30 p.m., Kelvedon High Street

Roger Derrick was not to be found at his family home – a manor house by the river on the Feering Road. One police Cortina remained outside in case he returned, while another peeled off up towards Coggeshall to wait at Derrick's shop. Gabriel and Kenton, meanwhile, followed Lowry down through Feering village. Police records showed Suzanne Cliff's son Edward had worked briefly in an antique shop there.

'There appears to be nothing new to be had in the area; everything is very much second-hand,' Gabriel commented, as they passed a reclamation yard with a banner advertising vintage railway sleepers for sale. She wondered what defined junk from antiques.

'Here we go,' said Kenton, pulling up outside the Cliff boy's former place of work. Lowry's Saab continued on to Fox Farm.

A huge round clock hung beneath the merchant's sign. Kenton pushed the shop door open, tripping a small bell. 'This looks promising,' he said.

Gabriel crossed the threshold. The shop was pokey. Clocks sat displayed along each wall, many similar in size to the one outside. A small man wearing spectacles appeared behind the glass counter, expectant of some business.

'Hello,' he beamed, 'what a lovely couple, feel free to browse.'

'Err,' Kenton stuttered, 'do you sell ...'

'Clocks?'

'Antiques,' said Gabriel.

'These are antiques, depending on your description – there's nothing later than Edwardian, most Victorian. From the railways.'

'Really?' Gabriel asked politely.

'Railway clocks, from India,' he said proudly.

Kenton shrugged, and pulled his badge. 'So we're making enquiries into one Christopher Cliff. Ring any bells?'

The man's face fell.

'Yes, lived out on the farm towards Silver End. Shot himself.'

Kenton shook his head. 'Awful business. We're trying to piece together his last movements, and making enquiries locally. Did you know the man yourself?'

'Personally no, but by sight, yes ...' The shopkeeper hesitated. 'But his son worked here for a spell. I presume that's why you're here?'

They both smiled, showing him a grainy mugshot of Edward Hoare faxed over from Woodbridge.

'There's not much to say.'

'You caught him stealing from you?'

'Yes, more than once.'

'Oh, so you didn't notify the police straight away?'

He glanced from one to the other. 'Do you know who owns this shop?'

'Not you?'

The man shifted uneasily. 'Mr Derrick.'

'The dealer in Coggeshall?' Gabriel said.

He pulled an expression, which she took to be a yes.

'Yes, I told him straight away of my suspicions.' He drew himself up straight to convey authority. 'I run the store, but Mr Derrick likes to know who's behind the till, it being his money.'

'And what did he do, the first time?'

'Nothing.'

'He gave him the benefit of the doubt then?' Gabriel asked.

The man shrugged. 'It happened two, three times.'

'So what did it take for Mr Derrick to finally call the police?'

'I don't know, you'll have to ask him. It was Mr Derrick that gave him the job, you see. He had a bit of a soft spot for the lad. Eddie was nice enough – quiet, well spoken. Generally well mannered as you'd expect, if it weren't for the stealing. But eventually they did come, took a statement off me, but not for anything gawn missing from here – he'd been caught shoplifting over the road, at the off-licence, that was what he was done for in the end.'

Gabriel nudged Kenton lightly at the elbow. It was time to leave.

'That's very useful, thank you.' The shopkeeper was surprised that the interview was at an end, but Gabriel was more than satisfied. She pulled the shop door open for Kenton.

'How do you know so much about dodgy antiques?' Kenton asked as they walked back to the car.

'Pick things up as we go, you know.' She smiled; Gabriel just knew that Derrick's connection to Edward Hoare was vital. How, she didn't know. For the first time since her secondment to CID she understood the intrinsic thrill of detective work – she really felt the adrenaline rush of following a lead. She couldn't wait to tell Lowry.

3.35 p.m., Sweet Pea Cottage, Fox Lane

Lowry took a circuitous route to Fox Farm, to check again on the distance from Kate Everett's cottage to the Cliff place. Not that he doubted the woman's word but he was surprised by the swiftness of her arrival last night. Instead of turning right up Church Lane and crossing the railway line, he had stayed on Kelvedon High Street, which dog-legged at the Angel pub and became the old London road, and taking a winding route over the old stone bridge, arrived at the cottage from the Silver End side of Fox Lane.

He drove slowly, unsure where precisely Miss Everett's cottage was, as the open fields gave way to brambles and hedgerow, impairing his visibility. Unexpectedly, after rounding a bend, he spotted the rear end of a silver car protruding from a hedge in the road ahead. It had to be Sweet Pea Cottage. He pulled up and took out his binoculars to get a better look. It was a Lancia Beta. Didn't see many of those round here. Before he could decide what to do, whether to approach or hang back, the car abruptly reversed out.

He watched Suzanne Cliff pull away. Her absent son was a curiosity. There was no reason she should have told the police of his existence yesterday, but now Cliff's death was seen as murder they would delve into the family background. To be fair, they'd not given her any chance to explain herself. Edward Hoare (he had chosen not to take Cliff's name) was currently detained in the borstal at Hollesley Bay. It was originally built by the Victorians as a holding pen to house convicts before shipping them off to Australia. Not secure enough for hardened adult offenders, but suitable for teenage malcontents. Edward had been there almost a year, and was due for release soon. His crime was habitual theft; the file Lowry had on the seat of the Saab from Queen Street records indicated his stepfather had been responsible for bringing him to account.

Lowry gave it five minutes before slowly moving his own vehicle forward. Kate Everett's house was half a mile west from Fox Farm on the OS map, out towards Silver End as the crow flies; an easy walk during the day along a public bridleway, but by night it would be safer to use the road as Everett had done.

If Lowry had not seen the Lancia pull away, he'd have driven straight past the concealed entrance. The cottage was shielded by dense blackthorn, its grey mesh blending seamlessly with the thatch of the roof above. There was a small front gate that had succumbed to the virulent hedge, and hadn't been used in years. He shut the car door. The front garden was tiny and the entrance itself may not be in use; the path leading to the door was overgrown with weeds, some waist height. Lowry opted to venture round the back.

To his surprise, the rear of the house was a complete contrast. Entering via a fragrant rose arbour in full bloom, he was met by a stunning array of colour and foliage with an immaculate lawn in the centre. He moved along the path, peering through the cottage windows as he went. Kate Everett would be expecting him. Lowry had said jokingly on the phone that, following on from their late-night meeting, perhaps she might have time for coffee during the day? Notionally he was hoping she may enlighten him to the Cliffs and her relationship, but the underlying reason was his interest had been piqued by *her*, creeping around the countryside in the middle of the night. The interior was too dark to see what lay within; however, she had clearly seen out, appearing at the back door to welcome him. 'Mind your head.'

The cottage was low-ceilinged and traditional in décor, with a rocking chair and wood burner at one end of a long and narrow kitchen across the back of the house. The walls were lined with shelves stacked with an assortment of pots, jars and knick-knacks; the very opposite of the Cliff's kitchen with its twentieth century modernity. 'Come through,' she beckoned, and resumed washing the dishes. The kitchen sink overlooked the wide back garden with its immaculate lawn.

'Last night, Inspector. You didn't mention that Christopher was murdered?'

Lowry continued to admire the garden, at the end of which, in the middle of a well-cared-for hedge, was a gate leading into the fields and bridleway beyond.

'Ah, nothing concrete, Miss Everett; covering our bases, as it were. And as point of fact, I was wondering whether you might be able to see comings and goings to the farm from over here. I see that traffic passes directly?'

'From a certain direction, yes, the road runs right past the cottage in the direction of Silver End or Witham.'

'How long did it take you to cycle last night?' He moved next to her.

'Oh, a matter of minutes.'

'Who cuts your grass? It's very neat.' Lowry in all his years as a homeowner had never managed a striped lawn; there was an art to it. He was all the more impressed to see one out here, where the grass must be blighted by weeds and pests from the neighbouring fields.

'A dear old chap, from Silver End. But the rest is my own work. Nature is a wonderful thing, don't you think? Though I doubt you've come all the way from Colchester for gardening tips.'

'No, I'm afraid not.' Turning from the window, his eye fell

on a piece of straw craftwork such as Emma Cliff had held yesterday, resting next to a pickling jar.

'I was wondering what you can tell me of the Cliff family. You and Suzanne are friends, correct?' Lowry continued, 'Did she confide in you about their marriage?'

'Yes,' she said glumly, 'oh, it's very sad to think from the outside they had it all, the perfect life, yet Suzanne has come to hate Christopher over the years.'

'How so?'

'Christopher had only love for Christopher, and time only for what interested him. He was charming and clever at first – unfortunately, as Suzanne was soon to learn, that's where it stopped. She has been cursing herself bitterly for falling for it in the first place, blaming herself for being gullible and stupid.'

'Do you agree?'

'Most definitely, she was on the rebound from her ex. If it was not for Emma, I doubt they would have married.'

'Ah yes, the children. You mentioned yesterday you saw a lot of them?' He moved to pick up the straw model.

'I have none of my own, you see, but I love children – that's why I'm a teacher.' She smiled warmly.

'Emma Cliff has one very similar to this, what is it?' he said, interrupting and holding up the straw object.

'Oh, she made it here – I taught them all a piece of traditional handicraft made at this time of year with the passing of the harvest.'

'Cute,' Lowry said, replacing it carefully. The harvest festival. That's where he'd seen one, when Matthew was in the cub scouts – at the harvest festival in St Mary's Church in Kelvedon.

'I must thank you again, Miss Evervett, for taking care of the Ward boys, something I failed to do last night. We will speak to social services, given the Wards' parents are unable to return until later in the week. It was very generous of you to step in there.'

'Think nothing of it,' though her features softened with the compliment, 'but you could have done that over the phone, and in fact, you've just missed Suzanne. She took the boys back with her; they are her nephews, after all.' Kate Everett moved a kettle from the range. 'Have you time for that coffee?'

'I shouldn't put you to any bother.'

'Not at all.'

Lowry graciously accepted. Having her on side might prove useful.

'It has been such a shock; Suzanne has yet to come to terms with the fact Chris is dead, let alone murdered. Then there's the accountant, found at the bottom of the pasture. Dreadful business. Do you think their deaths are connected?'

'No, I would say not,' he said honestly; 'though it's a small world and I reckon there will be a piece of twine tying them in some way.'

'Oh? What makes you say that?'

'He was the Cliffs' accountant. Whatever brought him out here may be known to Suzanne, whether she realises it or not. In general, there's an explanation for most crimes. It's just a matter of time.'

'Oh, you do sound world-weary, Inspector. Won't you sit down?'

'Thanks,' he said and pulled out a kitchen chair.

20

4 p.m., Crouch Street, Colchester

Sparks waited at the front bar of the Hospital Arms. The place was teeming with medical staff; she could've picked a more discreet venue. He glanced at his watch. Jacqui was on an early shift, meaning she'd have finished by two, also meaning they could have met anywhere – rather than in the pub directly opposite her workplace.

A pair of nurses entered. Not her. They walked over to the bar and stood next to him. He'd walked here past the Colne Lodge, the large establishment at the end of Crouch Street. When she showed up, maybe he'd suggest they go there – four bars and video screens everywhere, there'd be plenty of room this time of day. A police uniform would not be so welcome at the Lodge as it was in here. They'd been raided again at the weekend; the kids would flee like rats. He caught his reflection in the mirrored bar, and adjusted his stance, puffed out his chest . . . wait – a figure in the corner by the window caught his eye.

'Well, well,' Sparks said to himself, and strode over to a slender, jowly man with an advanced receding hairline wearing a cravat and a pink shirt, talking to a short fat man with a flat face. 'Roger!'

Derrick gave a start. 'Mr Sparks,' he said, with the affected affair Sparks associated with the swindler. 'I had no idea you consorted with the medical profession.'

'I could say the same for you,' said Sparks. 'What are you doing in here?' As pubs went, this was not a crook's haven, but as safe as any to conduct a shady conversation. 'Date with a nurse?' He nodded towards the flat-faced man.

'I've been to the auctions up on Head Street. Just wetting my whistle with my good friend here before heading home. How about you, all alone at the bar. Are you hopeful? I hear about these 999 parties . . .' He nudged his companion, whose face remained blank.

'Never you mind. We've been searching all over Essex for you.'

'Oh, and why might that be?' Derrick held his cigarette palm up, in an affected way.

'I'm led to believe a couple of your monkeys had paid a call to Fox Farm recently. They say nobody was at home. I reckon they were fobbing us off and it was *you* that went over there?'

'It was indeed me. I called to price up an item for the gentleman who lives there, what of it?'

'The man in question is now dead, you might have heard?'

Derrick shrugged non-committally.

Sparks felt a tug at his uniform sleeve.

'Ooh look,' said Derrick. 'He *has* got a date.'

'Hello, Stephen.' Sparks turned to see Jacqui. He did a double-take; she'd bleached her hair.

'I'm not finished with you, Roger.' Sparks poked the man in the chest. 'Wait right there.'

'Friend of yours?' said Jacqui laconically, as he followed her to the bar.

'Roger Derrick is the worst kind of crook.'

'What's that?'

'One that doesn't think he is a crook.'

She ordered a rum and coke and another Guinness for him. He hastily fumbled for some cash; Sparks was of a generation of men who felt uneasy with the notion of a woman paying for her own drinks. They sat down at a side table at the back of the pub, which was empty. Sparks's unease with their meeting was heightened by his encounter with Derrick. After exchanging pleasantries, he cut to the chase.

'So, Jacqui, what exactly can I do for you?' he said through a forced smile.

'How is he?' she said, eyes trained on her drink.

'Who? Oh, Nick, he's fine.' He nodded enthusiastically. She shot him a glance, which lingered questioningly before returning her eyes to the rum. He sensed she too found this awkward – not that it made him feel any easier. He cleared his throat and said, 'Nick and I don't really talk about, you know, what happened.'

'No, of course not.' She had very long eyelashes. He'd never noticed that about a woman before. He wondered if he was staring too hard. He looked around the pub shiftily. 'It's just that . . . just that he doesn't communicate with me . . .'

Sparks frowned. 'I'm sorry, luv, but what are you expecting?' He leant forward and hissed, 'Some bloke turned up at the nick, in my bloody office, professing to be in love with you.'

'I don't need reminding of *that*,' she said curtly and lit a cigarette, unembarrassed. 'Nobody knows other than you.'

'That is hardly the point.' Sparks sat back in the wooden chair and pulled out his No.1s. 'I've never known anything like it.'

'The situation was out of control, I accept that.'

'Everyone knows you are separated now.'

'It wasn't my fault.'

'Then whose was it?'

'I mean . . .'

'Look, I've got things to do – what is it you want?' he said, getting annoyed. Irritation was now overriding his discomfort.

'How is Nick? I mean, really?'

'He's absolutely fine,' Sparks said with unfounded authority.

'Will you just tell him I was asking about him?'

'Where are you living? In the Dutch quarter still with your

pal?' He asked, dodging the request, though he knew that to be the case, as Lowry had ceased going to the snooker evenings down George Street for fear of running into his wife. 'Is there anything else?'

She lifted her gaze. Jacqui Lowry, though still pretty, was washed out, her appearance so drained that he thought she might be ill. 'Just tell him, please?'

He drained his drink in anticipation of leaving. Sparks was still baffled as to why she had suggested they meet. What a waste of time.

'Wait.' She reached across and touched the back of his hand lightly.

'Yes?'

'There's a spot of bother at work.'

He sat there determined not to make it easy for her.

'I broke up with Paul . . .'

'Oh dear, I'm sorry to hear *that*,' he said sarcastically.

'He took it badly,' she continued, 'wouldn't let go . . . so I sort of saw him for a bit longer just to stop him moping and making life difficult. It was easier, you see, just the odd occasion.' Her eyes met his, seeking understanding where there was none. 'Anyway, I dragged it out, making it less frequent until the message finally sunk in after six weeks since we last . . .'

'Why are you telling *me* this?' he hissed sharply, causing Jacqui to flinch.

'And then last week he makes a complaint. At work. Says I'm incompetent – a liability on the ward.'

Sparks sat back. 'I see. Is it being taken seriously?'

She nodded.

'Still, the question remains, why are you telling me?'

'You know people,' she said conspiratorially. 'Nick always gave me the impression that you and he ... *knew people*.' Her voice was barely more than a whisper. 'Men who had sway – who could make people reconsider their choices.'

So. Now he understood. He understood clear as crystal.

'Well,' he said. 'It wouldn't take much to apply a little pressure to a wet blanket like that. I'll think about it.'

The two nurses from earlier passed by with a man he took to be a doctor. They sat down at the next table. Maybe Jacqui had picked the hospital boozer deliberately – being seen with Colchester's senior policeman might afford her some protection and prove that she still had friends in high places.

Sparks watched her walk out through the pub's rear entrance. He couldn't help but wonder what he'd do if the tables were turned. Imagine if he caught Antonia at it with some yachty twat friend of hers? Not that there'd be any takers right now, not in her current state ... But then, years down the line maybe. What about the sprog – would she swan off, leaving him to deal with that? A potential minefield. He suddenly remembered Derrick, and hurried back round to the front bar. He had long gone, of course. Sparks ordered himself a large Scotch. There was no rush – a car was waiting for Derrick at his home. Give it half an hour and his boys in blue would have him at Queen Street ... He nursed his drink, deep in contemplation of life's complexities. If only everything were as straightforward as police work.

21

4.30 p.m., Fox Lane, towards Kelvedon

Lowry sat in the Saab along a grass verge used by oncoming vehicles to pass from the opposite direction. He pushed in the car's cigarette lighter, having misplaced his Ronson. The car was parallel to a field gate, and with the window rolled down, he watched two horses shake their manes, listlessly troubled by insects. Having checked in with Queen Street, where Gabriel had called through excitedly about Derrick's connection to Edward Hoare, he now sat collecting his thoughts as to how best to question Suzanne again.

A bird flitted past, settling on the hedgerow adjoining the gate. He craned over the steering wheel to catch a glimpse. The hawthorn was cropped at a height of about seven or eight feet, so he could just make the bird out from inside the car – right at the top. But the sun was directly behind it, making identification impossible. Could be anything: bunting, lark, even finch. He sighed and lit a cigarette.

Kate Everett had given him pause for thought. She had not

mentioned Edward Hoare, and he hadn't asked. An explanation from the mother first; in the meantime, he could pardon a friend's loyalty. Regardless, Lowry had enjoyed chatting to the woman about rural living. Lowry was familiar with much of it himself, living as a boy out at Fingringhoe; even now at Great Tey, he was remote. They had talked of the passing of the seasons, something – despite his upbringing – he'd not considered properly until he took up birdwatching. They had, Kate said, much common ground. (She even had a black cat, like his own Pushkin.) He drew on the cigarette, watching the bird still atop the hedge, and wondered if he'd enjoyed their coffee together a bit too much. He was in the middle of a double murder investigation, after all, and one in which she was closely connected. The bird suddenly flew off. Lowry ground his cigarette out unfinished in the ashtray and made his way slowly to the farm.

4.35 p.m., Fox Farm

Alan Ward wasn't entirely sure about being back at his aunt's farm; it was better than being at the cottage with Miss Everett, but not as good as being back home. The house seemed larger without his uncle there. He had never thought of Uncle Christopher taking up so much space. His little brother Darren, on the other hand, was overjoyed; he was intrigued by the girls and when not playing games with them, spent all his time spying on them: twice he'd been caught with one eye pressed hard against the toilet keyhole. Alan himself found his cousins unpredictable and moody, best friends one minute, unbelievably spiteful and mean the next.

He was abruptly disturbed from his book by a commotion on the floor below. Somebody was here. Carefully placing *Vets Might Fly* to one side, he climbed down the ladder, to find his youngest cousin Emma whimpering.

Lucy met him as he reached the bottom rung.

'What's up?' he asked.

'That policeman is here again.'

'Oh, maybe they've caught who did it.'

She rolled her eyes. 'Don't be silly. I just hope he doesn't upset Mummy again.'

'I quite fancy him, he's cute,' her sister Alice appeared at her side, tying her hair back.

'You fancy everyone.' She shot Alan an angry stare, which made him blush.

'What's the matter with Emma?' he asked, trying to change the subject.

'Your brother keeps pestering her to play doctors and nurses.'

'I think I'll go back up and read,' he said, starting to climb the ladder.

'No, come outside with me,'Alice grabbed his hand and dragged him across the landing to the stairs, 'let's see if the tadpoles have lost their tails. There's nothing cuter than a froglet.'

Alice was behaving oddly. Cute was not a word he'd heard her use before; now it was applied liberally to frogs and policemen alike. She made him nervous. Her obsession with watching the frogs mate over the Easter break was scary – they had sat there for hours. His aunt was showing the policeman in as they passed.

'Don't worry,' Alice smiled at Alan, 'Edward will be home soon and everything will be all right.'

Throughout all this, he had not given his elder cousin a thought. Edward was practically a man before he got sent away; the prospect of him returning from prison was positively terrifying.

'What, today?' he uttered nervously.

'No, silly. But soon, very soon.'

He followed her out to the pond with trepidation. Never had he wished the school holidays over before. Never had the return to school seemed so attractive.

5 p.m., Queen Street HQ

'Roger! Didn't I tell you to wait for me?' Sparks entered the interview room clutching the auctioneer's estimate that Lowry had asked for. With everybody out, it fell to him to brace the suspect. Sparks was warming to the task. The two uniformed officers stood aside as the chief closed the door.

'Chief Sparks, I thought you were teasing me. Besides, how was I to know how long you'd be entertaining the young lady?'

Sparks bristled at the reference to Jacqui, especially in front of two of his men. Derrick thought himself the comedian; that foolishness would soon be shaken out of him.

'Never mind, you're here now, and that's all that counts,' he said in the tone of welcoming a lost relative back to the family fold.

'The pleasure's all mine but, please illuminate, why am I here?'

'Fox Farm. Yesterday morning . . . ? We've been through this.'

The man crossed his legs, dabbed his forefinger with his tongue then ran it along the creases of his beige, pressed trousers. If there was one thing Sparks had no time for it was effeminate men – in particular those that preened themselves in public such as this one. He took a deep breath and circled his subject; he must be controlled. Merrydown had berated him on more than one occasion for his inability to adjust to modern trends, the acceptance of gay culture; if only she knew. He'd seen plenty – you couldn't tell the boys from the birds in the Colne Lodge, more mascara than an Avon catalogue. There was, however, nothing revolutionary in this fellow's persona; quite the contrary. This type of dandy had been around for decades. Derrick was more Quentin Crisp than, say, Boy George. Besides, this was Colchester, and this was not Merrydown's patch.

'Sorry, am I supposed to do the talking?' Derrick yawned.

'Yes, get the ball rolling. C'mon, walk me through yesterday and how you happened to be out there the morning Cliff shot himself.'

'Very well. I received a phone call last week from Mister Cliff asking would I care to inspect a family heirloom, a Welsh dresser, Queen Anne, to which I agreed.'

'Why, Rog, and no disrespect intended,' Sparks bent down and spoke within inches of the man's ear, 'why would a respectable upstanding citizen, an academic, a television presenter, an *intelligent* man pick up the dog and give you a bell?'

Derrick dabbed the corner of his mouth with a fancy handkerchief. 'None taken, Superintendent.' He turned to meet the chief's eye, recoiling at the proximity. 'I don't know, and of course I may be wrong, but might it be that I was local and to hand?'

Sparks stood up straight and arched his back. 'Bollocks. Seems that even the most erudite of men can be taken in by your flowery guff.' Sparks didn't wish to offend the dead, but suppose Cliff had mistakenly believed Derrick's articulate banter indicated expertise and honesty?

'I turned up at the appointed time . . .'

'Which was?'

'Eight o'clock. I appraised the article, and left.'

'Why then did your goons tell my people you'd found the place empty?'

'Oh, come now, they're not paid to think. Your chaps turn up, I'm out, they know better than to consort with the constabulary.'

'Even when there's been a murder?' Though Sparks found this easy to believe, he suspected them of hiding something. Standing behind Derrick, Sparks could see the man dyed his rapidly thinning hair. Derrick had less hair than he did, why draw attention to it? Such vanity.

'What do you mean, murder? You said he shot himself. Besides, all the more reason, wouldn't you say . . . however, here I am at your disposal.'

Sparks grabbed the man's shoulder and pulled him backwards on the chair. Roger Derrick's eyes rolled to the back of his head and stared directly up Sparks's overgrown nostrils. The PC on the door shifted on his feet.

'We had a car waiting outside your front door. Of course you're here at my disposal. Now let's start over. When did you receive the invitation to Fox Farm?'

'Last week, I bumped into him in the village.'

'In that dodgy shop of yours?'

'There is nothing "dodgy" about the shop, Chief Inspector, it is simply a holding site for furniture acquired at house sales. The area is replete with fine country houses, Coggeshall is central to North Essex – Bures and Long Melford to the North, Maldon to the South, and Colchester to the Ea—'

'Yes, yes, spare me the geography lesson. Get to the point – he came in the shop . . .'

'No, he did not come into the shop,' he said emphatically, 'and if he did, would not have found me there – I spend most of my time at the gallery or in the auction house in Colchester.

We met at the clock tower, entirely by chance. We'd met once before many years ago, you see.'

'And Mrs Cliff will confirm this?'

'Mrs Cliff, I have no idea, I hardly know the woman.'

This man was remarkably composed. 'Walk me through your brief visit, every second, from the moment you arrived to the minute you left.'

'There's really not a lot to say; I went through to the kitchen, took a gander at the item and left.'

'What was Mr Cliff doing when you called?'

'What was he doing? I've no idea, he led me through to the kitchen to see the furniture . . .'

'And what did you make of it?'

'A fine example, well preserved. Early Queen Anne, pre-dating Chippendale, French, possibly from court, I'd place it at around £6,000 – indeed I will offer, as soon as it feels appropriate.'

The Head Street auctioneer had valued it at seven – enough to buy a brand-new, top-spec Ford Granada. 'What did he say to that?'

'He thought it was in that region, and would discuss with his wife. Apparently she was the one insisting on its sale. He was rather fond of it himself.' Derrick took a sip of water.

'Anything else?'

He shook his head.

No mention of the gun. The value of that was a grand. He was lying.

'Can I go now?'

'Soon. Let me fetch you some more water.' Sparks grinned and delicately lifted the glass by the rim. If Roger's prints matched the barrel, he wasn't going anywhere.

The desk sergeant had advised Gabriel of Derrick's detention and told her that the chief was personally conducting proceedings in interview room one. Sparks was anathema to her; aggression simmering barely below the surface. He loathed women, she was sure of it. In uniform it wasn't quite so bad, he just ignored WPCs, but in plain clothes he had no choice but to consider his female colleagues as people.

As she made her way lightly up the flight of stairs she wondered whom he hated more, women or criminals. Arresting wrongdoers may be his job but it evidently brought him no satisfaction – they were merely irritants, wasting his time. The social committee – something she had absolutely no interest in – was the be all and end all, from what she could see . . .

The chief was in the process of bumping the door open with his rear while holding two glasses of water.

'Sir, sir!'

Annoyance crossed his features.

'I have some useful information that you might like to hear.'

He stepped away from the interview room door. 'What?'

'Derrick employed Edward Hoare, Suzanne Cliff's son . . . he was caught thieving.'

Instead of answering, the chief winked at her in an unsettling manner and continued into the interview room, leaving her standing in the corridor like a spare part.

22

5.30 p.m., Fox Farm

'Your son.'

Suzanne's conversation with Kate had prepared her for this. She checked the library door was shut although she had done so only seconds earlier, and invited Lowry to take a seat. His demeanour was different to earlier in the day; though not untidy, he was ruffled in some way.

'Yes. I'm not hiding anything from you, Inspector. I have a son, Edward, who is currently in borstal. I visited him yesterday morning before going to Dedham,' she said candidly. 'I felt you should know this. Not that Christopher's death has anything to do with Edward.'

They sat in the two wicker chairs opposite Christopher's large desk. She felt her husband's presence, watching them, presiding from his worn leather chair.

'Did you know your son worked for Roger Derrick?'

'Who's he?'

The inspector crossed his legs, which signalled to her that he had no intention of going anywhere soon. 'He is the antiques dealer who was here on Monday, shortly before your husband was killed.'

'The antiques dealer.' She worked to try to place the man. 'And is he a suspect?'

'We are questioning him closely, yes.'

'And Edward worked for this man? The shop in Kelvedon High Street, I remember, after he left school?'

'For several months,' Lowry confirmed. 'Edward stole from him, I'm sure you must be familiar with that?'

She glared at him furiously. 'Are you calling me a liar? That was rumoured but never proved; it was certainly not what landed him in Hollesley Bay. My son was caught shoplifting, taking cider from the off-licence.'

'My apologies, I didn't mean to upset you.'

'You didn't upset me, Inspector,' she groaned wearily. 'Why he even got caught in Kelvedon is beyond me; by then Edward spent more time in Colchester than anywhere. He held down that job, as you say, less than three months. He was just a shop boy. I doubt he came into contact with anyone important in the antiques business, above board or not.' She waited, hoping this would be the end of it.

'It's good of you to come forward with this information. I don't think your son was involved directly, but his relationship with this man Derrick may be significant.'

May be significant, she repeated to herself. Not knowing what

182

to say, but keen to move the conversation away from Edward, she reiterated her position regarding the antiques dealer.

'I didn't arrange for the dresser to be valued – that was Christopher, as I told you – but it was done at my request.'

'Of course, but you can see the link. To the best of our knowledge, the last man to see your husband alive is an antiques dealer known to the police as possessing a certain reputation – to use your words, not entirely "above board", shall we say? Furthermore, it transpires, this man at one time employed your son. So, it's important to our investigation that you think whether you might have run into this man before.'

'I appreciate that, Inspector, but no. He was someone my husband had run into before.'

He pulled out a pack of cigarettes. 'Do you mind?'

She shook her head.

'Cast your mind back to yesterday. You called your accountant, why was that?' Suzanne was confused by the change in tack.

'Christopher had died, it was a natural enquiry; there's a large mortgage on this place.'

'Who else did you contact?'

Where was this leading? He knew, she was sure; she had no option but to say, 'The bank.'

'The bank,' he repeated.

'Please, Inspector, can you be clearer in your questioning? First you ask about my son, then who I telephone after finding my husband dead. Must you be so elliptical?'

'Sorry if you find me so – I try to be careful, more than elliptical; these are difficult questions, I know. I wonder if there are things, little things, that you are not telling us, maybe because you assign no importance to them.'

She started to protest, but he continued, waving his cigarette gently.

'In fairness, not twelve hours has elapsed since a revision in the circumstances of your husband's death, so perhaps I'm being unfair.'

His tone had eased to contain an air of apology.

'Mrs Cliff. Is there anything you wish to say that might help us catch the person who killed your husband?' he said, with utmost courtesy. 'I can't put it any plainer than that.'

Suzanne stood up and cleared her throat. The library was at the rear of the house and it was often the coolest room in which to work in the height of summer; by now, on a normal day if he was not at the university, Christopher would have moved all his notes and papers from his study, which would have grown stuffy, back here to continue into the evening. Outside she could see Alice and Alan on the other side of the drive by the pond. She smiled as she watched them. The shadow of the farmhouse just reached the water, and the sun caught her middle daughter's hair, a gold bulb in amongst the tall white reeds.

'I think, but I don't know, that Christopher was up to something – he was grumbling about what a bore it was to draw cash. I didn't think anything of it at the time – he was always moaning about one inconvenience or another. One of "the joys of living in the country". So, I called the bank.' She sighed. 'They confirmed a sum of two thousand pounds had been withdrawn on Friday but there's no trace of it in the house. I searched high and low.'

'Do you think he was being blackmailed?' he asked calmly, as if asking whether she took sugar in her tea.

'I have no idea, Inspector. You're asking me to think of possible motives for his murder, when I am having difficulty accepting the fact that he is dead – only yesterday you told me it was suicide.'

'I appreciate that, Mrs Cliff, and I apologise.'

She met his eyes, and thought how kind they seemed, the creases of age framing them favourably. She stared perhaps for a second too long, forcing him to rise. As she showed him to the door, grief and something new – a crushing fear – bore down upon her, rendering her limbs heavy and difficult to move.

'Inspector,' she said weakly. 'Please leave Edward be. Whoever it was he worked for, he was only a boy, barely sixteen. He'll be out in two weeks' time; isn't it important to give him a chance? Christopher didn't.'

'Of course. And call if you need anything. Or your friend, Kate – she has been a great help these past two days.'

'Kate's a dream, yes.'

The policeman considered this, then asked, 'Why do you think she has never settled down?'

'It's not for the lack of suitors. She has men friends from

time to time though, just not the marrying kind, I guess. Kate's a free spirit.'

'Really?' Lowry seemed surprised.

'Yes. I think she's seeing someone now.'

'What makes you say that?'

'Just a hunch. I'd not seen her in ages, that usually means she's otherwise engaged . . .'

'Good day, Mrs Cliff,' he said finally, and left.

Lowry opened the car door. He had assured her that he would do his best to keep her son as far removed from the investigation as possible. He told her he would be in touch soon; she was at the end of her tether and had three girls and her nephews to care for, out here all alone. She was in need of support. He would not trouble Edward, but rather keep a close eye on him when he was released. He caught a movement in the corner of his eye, then remembered the kids were ferreting around in the pond reeds catching frogs. He turned on the ignition and looked back at the farmhouse, where he noticed heavy cloud moving in from the west. The fine weather would break tonight, he thought. Suzanne Cliff had a lot to contend with. He sensed she was sifting through the ramifications of what had happened, processing the possible consequences for her, for her family. It made her appear to be both reserved and vulnerable. She had seemed calm, almost analytical, up until he was leaving, when something had hit her emotionally, almost pushed her over the edge.

He lit another cigarette. She had a complicated mind; but a murderer? No, he didn't figure so. In any case, the facts didn't fit – she was in Dedham by nine o'clock yesterday morning, and that ruled her out.

As for the two thousand pounds, Lowry too had searched the house and not found any money. It would be somewhere, though. He drove slowly back down Fox Lane, knowing he would be returning to the farm very soon, but not towards Kelvedon; it'd be in the direction of Silver End – he had one last question to ask Kate Everett. For all the pleasantries they had exchanged earlier, he had not once asked whether she herself had any visitors at the time in question.

6.25 p.m., Sweet Pea Cottage, Fox Lane

Lowry caught Kate Everett in the far corner of the garden with a basket. He called out to attract her attention. She beckoned him through the arbour. He explained he'd forgotten to size up the distance between her cottage and Fox Farm and asked if he may have a look from an upstairs window.

The first floor of the cottage was cramped, with a low ceiling and, though he could indeed see the farm far off through the pokey window, he did not feel comfortable questioning her about visitors at such close quarters.

'Would you mind showing me the bridleway? Then I promise I will leave you in peace.'

Outside he engaged her in conversation. The garden was

of a similar size to his own, but whereas his was currently overgrown and uncared for, before him lay a vision to make *Gardener's World* proud.

The patio was as neat as the lawn it lined. Colourful plants burst forth from pots and the garden was bordered on all sides by rose bushes. The distant rumble of a train could be faintly heard. He stepped onto the lawn and, shielding his eyes, looked to the horizon. Sure enough, in the distance was a thin line of Rail Blue rolling through the countryside. They started to walk down the garden towards the gate at the end.

'Forgive me for asking – this is just a formality – did you yourself have any visitors Sunday night, or Monday morning?'

'Are you asking whether I had anyone sleep over?' she said archly. That thought, even after Suzanne's remark, had not actually occurred to him.

'No,' he said evenly, 'there were two deaths, one in the evening and the other the following morning . . . I am simply wondering whether we have overlooked anyone.'

'Through here.' She pushed open the gate. 'If I had, I would have told you. I do realise how important that sort of information is.'

The field in which they now stood held animals – Lowry could smell dung; he grew oddly nauseous.

'Of course. Apologies.'

Kate Everett proceeded to point out the footpath to Fox Farm, but he was only half-listening. A strong urge to flee her had come over Lowry. Despite her denial, his suspicions were now aroused and somehow here, under the early evening sun, he had an acute sense of danger. He asked if he might have a glass of water before leaving.

Back inside the garden he stopped in the middle of the lawn and turned to look back at the cottage as Kate emerged from the kitchen door with a tray. He smiled and spread his arms, as if in appreciation of the lawn. He gave a thumbs up to indicate how impressed he was. Now within the cottage perimeter, the sense he'd experienced beyond the hedge had left him, and he felt better. He rubbed his neck which was stiffening and looked to the ground. Suddenly, something caught his eye. An anomaly amid the perfection. A patch of grass to his left, the size of a large rug, was lighter than the rest. Strolling casually over to that side of the garden as if to admire the roses, he surreptitiously examined the turf: if he was not much mistaken, the patch had been deprived of sunlight.

He smiled and took the glass. 'Ah thank you, I needed that,' he said genuinely, gulping the water down. 'Thank you, Miss Everett, Kate, I'll detain you no further.'

Lowry detected doubt flicker aross her face. She sensed something was not right. He chose not to linger and placed the tumbler back on the tray. At the arbour underneath a crimson rose, he turned and said, 'Thank you, it's been a pleasure to meet you properly today.'

She remained on the lawn holding the tray, uncertainty on her face.

*

'We're to assemble a tent,' Gabriel had announced and within fifteen minutes they were outside the Angel pub in Kelvedon. Darnell's Volvo was in exactly the same place where Barnes had discovered it yesterday in the pub car park, unlocked and with the tent still on the back seat. The landlord grumbled that the dead man's car remaining there was bad for business. Kenton, with the tent now slung over his shoulder, had placated the man with the promise of a tow truck by the end of the day.

'You promise? 'Ere, where you going?' Kenton had marched off towards a patch of scrub grass with benches that loosely answered the advertised description 'beer garden', where he proceeded to take the tent out of its bag onto yellowed grass.

'You can't put that up there!'

The landlord, in shorts and cardigan, stood agitating as Kenton lay out the components.

'Here,' Gabriel reached inside her shoulder bag and retrieved a pound note, 'how about you fetch us two lime and sodas and keep the change for ground rent.'

The man took the note grudgingly and shuffled off.

'Make mine a cider,' Kenton called out. He stood there, hands on hips. 'Think, think,' he muttered to himself.

'What are you doing?'

'Looking for clues.'

'Are you qualified to do that?'

Kenton flicked his hair back, knelt down. 'I beg your pardon?'

'I mean, what about forensics?'

'It's a tent, Jane. Lowry wants to know the size and any

indication that it was recently erected.' He held a tent pole up close to his face and inspected the metal tip. 'Moist earth, grass and so forth.' He cast the object aside. 'Here, give me a hand spreading this out . . .' He unrolled the groundsheet. 'I reckon it's at least seven by five . . .'

'Eight foot by six,' she read from the label on the bag.

Kenton leapt up. His face was pink. She couldn't determine whether he was embarrassed at being caught out by a woman or he was just hot.

Not wishing to make him cross, she said, 'You know, I don't see any pegs? The metal hooks?'

He stared at her. He had grey eyes, very clear. She'd not noticed that before.

Lowry had realised soon after leaving Sweet Pea Cottage that he was driving in the wrong direction, towards the Silver End Road instead of towards Kelvedon. Having pulled over where he had stopped earlier in the afternoon after spotting Suzanne's Lancia, he then remained there, lost in thought, gazing out across the fields.

Just because Kate Everett had pitched *a* tent in her garden did not mean it was Peter Darnell's tent . . . but Darnell was excited about something and it was not his annual trip to the Italian lakes with his catatonic wife. The wife had never seen the tent: the receipt was only two weeks old. Lowry's money was on a cheeky weekend away with the spinster down the road while the wife was with her sister in Canterbury.

How did they meet, he wondered, doubting Everett's finances complex enough to require an accountant. The hospital and his own wife's infidelity flashed though his mind. Try as he might, he could not distance his own circumstances from the emerging narrative of the case. He saw that his hands held the steering wheel tightly, and released his grip immediately on reflex and groaned. The road and hedgerow ahead abruptly became dull as cloud moved overhead. Just as he made peace with himself, the radio sounded.

Much excitement. Roger Derrick had been picked up for questioning at his home in Feering. The prints on the gun were a match; that was enough to hold him in custody. As he reached to turn on the car's ignition, he saw a yellow-hammer, its bright head animated in song like a beacon on the hedgerow. He switched the radio off. Low sun shone from behind and he wondered if it was the same bird he hadn't been able to identify on the way down to the farm. Lowry sat transfixed, a tingling sense of well-being enveloping him as he listened and for an instant forgot everything else in the world. After a moment, satisfied, he pulled away, leaving the yellowhammer to his song, and returned to Queen Street.

Part 3

THE THIEF

Fifteen Days Later

23

8.30 a.m., Wednesday 10th August, Queen Street HQ

He snatched up the phone. 'Sparks here.'

Sparks and Lowry had a 9.30 meeting at County HQ with Merrydown and the chief was brushing up in preparation. He'd asked not to be disturbed, except for one call, this one, from the warden of Hollesley Bay Borstal in Suffolk.

'You asked me to call when we released Edward Hoare. I can confirm he was safely deposited at Woodbridge station this morning for an Ipswich-bound train.'

'Thank you.'

'I hope the boy keeps his nose clean.'

'Me too,' Sparks replied insincerely. They had toyed with the idea of putting a covert tail on the lad, but decided against it. They didn't want to spook him. From Ipswich, Hoare could go direct on to Colchester and Kelvedon. It was only a matter of time. Sparks pulled out an Embassy, and returned to the file in front of him.

On returning from her holiday abroad, Merrydown had

requested an appraisal of what had gone down over the past two weeks in both the Cliff and Darnell cases. Darnell, at least, was clean-cut and sorted. Sparks read hastily through Kate Everett's confession again. It was extraordinary. Even more so for being so very, very mundane. A man dead and it all boiled down to a lovers' tiff and a tent. He had the cassette recording of the interview before him. He pressed the play button.

'Two weeks ago, Peter arrived at the cottage with a tent, excited as a schoolboy.' (A heavy sigh.) 'He's not a practical man, you understand . . .'

The lovers had had the trip planned for some time but that day they had argued over what time they were going to set off the following weekend. Darnell's wife was due to go to Canterbury. Kate wanted to leave Friday morning, but Elizabeth's sister wasn't collecting her until Friday afternoon and Peter did not wish to leave her alone – he wanted to wait until they were on their way and then set off.

'I pleaded with him to set off earlier. She has her problems but she's perfectly capable of managing – she spends entire days alone when he's at work . . . but no, Pete was adamant. That was the moment I knew for sure: he still loved her. Of course he did.'

This was their first disagreement that day; prompting Darnell to drive away from Everett's cottage in a sulk, taking the tent with him (minus the pegs, which, in his haste, he'd left on the lawn). Ordinarily a man of mild temperament, he was clearly stressed: this was to be their first weekend away and his conscience was troubling him, is what she thought, making her in turn annoyed. Nevertheless he had stopped in the car park at the Angel pub to simmer down before returning home to his sedated wife.

Everett, willing to forgive him and distraught that their weekend was seemingly ruined, had decided to drive after him. Spying his Volvo from the road, she had approached and tried to salvage the situation. Finding Darnell calmer, she had managed to convince him to let her drive him back to the cottage in her car, leaving the Volvo to collect later. But once home, things had deteriorated quickly. Again they had argued. Uncontrollable humiliation had risen up within her; she felt pitiful running after him and deep down, she knew she'd always be second place. Peter taking the tent for fear of discovery was proof of that. In her bitterness, she lashed out. 'I don't mind you taking the tent back, anyway; it's not as is if dear Elizabeth would manage to get it up.' Unsurprisingly, he completely lost it then.

This time without a vehicle, he had stormed off towards the railway track in a rage. He knew the track led in to Kelvedon. This time, his pettiness made her furious. It was to be Peter Darnell's final departure.

The two-person tent, an innocent enough article, had rapidly changed from being a symbol of freedom and fun into being an embodiment of resentments; a canvas structure representing all that was flimsy about their relationship. It had stood in Kate's garden for a couple of days (Kate herself spending a night in it, to try it out), until last Friday when the school term finished and Darnell whisked it back, worried that Suzanne's kids might see it and ask questions.

Sparks was fascinated with this confession. Many of the emotions involved were beyond his understanding. Why would anyone continue with a relationship like this? It came across as an exhausting endeavour, and not for the reasons one would wish. When Darnell had charged off for the second time, Kate Everett had become incensed, hurling tent pegs at his back.

'He turned his back on me. Just walked away. There's nothing quite as infuriating between lovers.' (Inhales cigarette.) 'It's hard to explain, but it's like it is the flip side of the heat of passion – this, this pure hatred *that flairs up as rejection. It is every bit as powerful as the sex that drives it . . .'*

Sparks winced. Her voice by this stage was calm, and her manner that of one analysing another's predicament.

Sparks had taken a special interest in the Darnell case once the arrest was made, and had witnessed the confession himself alongside Lowry. His afternoon meeting with Jacqui Lowry was much on his mind the evening they had arrested Kate Everett. Sparks would swerve uncomfortable emotional entanglements at all cost, even if it meant more work for him in the long run, but he did worry about the parallels with Lowry's own life. Justly so; Lowry responded cynically and unhelpfully to this confession, saying things like 'this doesn't stack up', 'Darnell would not behave like that', which only confirmed the chief's fears that the case was close to the bone.

'Looking at him marching off down the track; the back of his head – egg-shaped, aloof and uncaring. I guess I should say I tripped on a sleeper and fell on him, plunged the peg into his body by accident. But I won't. I did stumble several times – I was wearing a tight skirt which made it difficult to chase along the embankment . . . but not impossible. I caught up to him gripping that tent peg so tight in my fist and then I . . . Then I drove it into him. Hard.' (Pause to light another cigarette.) 'That stopped him. He turned round very slowly and stared at me. He was in shock, but then I saw his eyes spark, as if he was hungry, and I knew if I didn't do something first he would kill me. So I reached behind him and pulled the peg out of his back. He raised his hands and came at me with his teeth bared. Suddenly I found my senses and was very scared. I ran as fast as I could home.'

The tent peg had been recovered not far from her cottage, Everett having flung it away angrily as she neared home.

'I had no idea what state he was in. I certainly didn't think . . . I assumed he was back with his wife. I had no way to contact him. I went home and drank half a bottle of vodka. Next thing I know it's the Monday morning and it's Lucy on the phone to say her dad had shot himself.'

That was all well and good. Except they had made two arrests that Tuesday two weeks ago, and the other had not proved to be as straightforward. At almost exactly the same time Lowry was at Sweet Pea Cottage arresting Kate Everett for Darnell's murder, Sparks himself was in town arresting Roger Derrick on suspicion of murdering Cliff.

Immediately on hearing of Everett's arrest, Sparks panicked.

Could Everett have killed both men? From the outset Lowry had argued the killings were not linked and in truth the evidence strongly supported him. Everett would not have been able to kill Cliff *and* get back to the cottage in time to receive the eldest girl's telephone call. She presently lacked a motive. And in any case why would she confess to one murder but not the other? However, the certainty of Everett's case cast doubt in Sparks's mind, and the case against Derrick stalled as swiftly as it had started.

The fingerprints on the barrel and stock alone did not prove Derrick had fired the gun, only that he had held it, which indeed he may have done in the course of his evaluations. The case could be chucked out; they needed more, either a motive or a witness – so far they had found nothing ... Irritated, Sparks pushed the tape recorder to one side.

He would not give up. That Derrick had failed to mention that he had handled the gun when first questioned remained a superior indication of guilt to Sparks's mind, even if the man's solicitor had defended his client's reticence (his 'threatening behaviour' had forced the man to say anything just to get out, apparently. Well, if tipping a chair back constituted police brutality, they were indeed entering the era of the wimp). It was all very unsatisfactory.

Lowry had urged the chief to hold off the thumbscrews where Derrick was concerned, just for a while, until Edward Hoare had been released. He felt that Suzanne Cliff's son was in some way a missing link. Well, today was the day. He would see where the boy led them . . . he just hoped that Merrydown wouldn't lay it on too thick in the meantime, before they got hold of the juvenile.

The floorboards creaked and Sparks looked up from the case notes. Lowry stood before him, as neatly turned out as ever in a pale grey suit, white shirt, black tie and Brylcreemed hair swept back. 'Ah. There you are.'

24

10.30 a.m., Essex Police HQ, Sandford Road, Chelmsford

'Two weeks on and you're still dithering over whether an antiques dealer is Christopher Cliff's killer?' Merrydown's eyes darted from Sparks to Lowry. Her holiday in the Algarve may have given her the hue of a hardened walnut but it had done nothing to soften her temperament. Her dark tan struck a sharp contrast to the white lacquered surfaces in her Chelmsford office. It was modern. It was clean to the point of clinical. It reminded Sparks of a dentist's surgery (and by extension Merrydown's caustic comments were a sharp instrument scraping a tooth).

'Lack of evidence and motive, ma'am,' Lowry interjected. 'He may have been near the house at the time of death but for now that's all circumstantial – we still lack any tangible motive.'

'What about the two thousand pounds Cliff withdrew from his bank account three days before?'

'No trace of it,' Sparks spoke clearly. 'If Derrick had it,

he wouldn't leave it lying around – him or one of his goons would have stashed it or spent it long since. Besides, that's not motive enough: two grand isn't much of a haul for a man who owns half a dozen properties.'

'Maybe he took it for that very reason, to throw us off-track, make us think it must have been another, more desperate thief ... Good heavens, his fingerprints were on the gun!' Her fabled lack of patience was shining through. 'That is evidence, is it not?'

'Cliff was sizing it up for the start of the season in the Highlands and showed it off to Derrick, a man he knew enjoyed taking pot shots himself,' said Sparks.

'The glorious twelfth,' said Merrydown.

'Exactly; the start of the grouse season, which was last week.'

'Which also transpired to be the day of Christopher's funeral.' Merrydown sounded glum. 'Carry on.'

'Right, so the morning of his murder, Cliff had the gun out in readiness for the shoot, was dusting it off and asked Derrick for an opinion on its value since he happened to be there to assess the Welsh dresser. The firearm is worth a grand, apparently.'

'So where are you at now, hmm? Nowhere it seems.' Merrydown sighed. 'What about the woman. Everett. She's been processed by now, I understand. That at least has been wrapped up?'

'The murder weapon, a tent peg, has since been found in the scrub below the railway embankment. Ironically, it was her wish to be helpful and look after the Ward boys that led to her capture – nobody knew of her affair with Darnell, they had been scrupulously careful, and had she not inserted herself into things with the Cliffs she may have escaped our detection – at least for a while longer.'

'How did they meet?'

'She had a bike puncture on the roadside near her house. Darnell spotted her as he was leaving Fox Farm, having gone round to look through the accounts. He stopped to help . . . one thing led to another.'

'Perhaps Cliff found out. He confronts her, she panics.' Merrydown's eyebrows converged in an attitude of aggression. 'How far would she go to ensure his silence?'

Inwardly Sparks groaned; they'd covered this ground themselves already. Lowry shook his head, and replied calmly.

'Darnell's murder was a crime of passion. There would be no reason for Everett to kill Cliff; she was all for blowing the affair wide open. The tensions rose over his refusal to leave his wife. Besides it's technically impossible – she was at home to receive the call from the Cliffs' eldest girl on discovering her father's body, which she did shortly after the shot was fired.'

'Why didn't she then?' pressed Merrydown. 'Let the cat out of the bag, I mean?'

Sparks was now at his limit. He flexed his fingers. Why all these dumb questions – did she not think they'd bloody well gone through all of this already? And the bottom line was they had her for murder. End of. Who the hell gave a damn what was going through the crazy spinster's head?

'Perhaps she wasn't confident she'd get her man,' Lowry said.

Merrydown sniffed. 'It seems to me, gentlemen, that there's far more to be done.' She smiled that power smile of hers that Sparks loathed. 'Get a psychiatric evaluation of the women, process the data, assemble an evaluation before the end of the week.'

'Both of them?'

'Yes; Katherine Everett and Suzanne Cliff.'

'Always the bloody same – as soon as she pokes her beak in, it means more bloody work. And all of it a complete waste of time.' Sparks shoved the revolving glass door to exit the building. 'Why "evaluate" Suzanne Cliff, for Christ's sake? Everett's confessed to murder – so clearly she's not exactly the full toolbox – there's no need us wasting time dicking around with shrinks . . .'

They stopped on the steps outside County HQ. It had not been a pleasant meeting. Lowry shared his chief's uneasiness on a number of questions. Sparks abruptly turned and squared up to the hexagonal oyster-coloured building. For a split second, Lowry thought he was about to storm back inside to confront Merrydown. But instead he hunched to light a cigarette away from the wind. They'd glimpsed a different world in there. Spic-and-span offices, neatly ordered paperwork, the hum of computers under bright fluorescent tube lights. The future.

Modern it may be, but they both preferred their own Colchester nick.

'Ugly fucking building.' Sparks moved on back to the car, proffering a cigarette.

'What d'you reckon then?' Lowry took the smoke. He was keen to make tracks back east, and see where Edward Hoare resurfaced.

'Touch of the tar brush.' Sparks adjusted his aviators.

'You what?'

'Merrydown's colour. No Brit goes that shade of brown, without a dip from Johnny Arab in the family.'

Lowry inhaled. 'I meant, what do you reckon about Suzanne Cliff's son Edward – aren't you keen to see where he shows his face?'

'I've a man watching the Derrick house. If you're right and there's a connection with this whole rotten business, he'll show there first. If he does, then we will know Derrick is involved.'

That Suzanne Cliff's son had once worked for Derrick added to the complexity of the case, that was without doubt. Especially given that neither Mrs Cliff nor Derrick himself had offered up the information freely and unprompted ... It was easy to understand in the case of Mrs Cliff – a mother protecting her son. As for Derrick, well, a man with his reputation, why *would* he bother telling them?

'My money's on Derrick playing two tunes,' Lowry said. 'He'd taken a shine to the boy, but at the same time, he had

no qualms making the stepfather pay for the lad's thieving . . .
I think Eddie will tap Derrick up for cash.'

They both thought Derrick had the missing two grand –
Christopher Cliff's repayment of the debt Edward owed – not
that they'd share that with Merrydown. Yet.

'I hope you're right. Instead of kicking our heels in the
meantime, why not let's have another chat with Miss Everett?
Two weeks in remand will have given her time to adjust to
her circumstances . . .'

'Are you proposing we act on Merrydown's advice?' Lowry
said, surprised.

'Ha! Very droll. No, I bloody well am not – merely suggesting we pop in as we're in the vicinity. She was the Cliffs'
neighbour, after all. Process, my arse. Sick of that word every
other sentence.'

'If Merrydown heard this conversation she'd have your arse
processed in a Kenwood Chef.'

Sparks took a long drag on his cigarette. 'She'd have to catch
it first. Right, let's "evaluate" Miss Everett ourselves, seeing as
we're here – see how she's managing *her* process. Get hold of
Kenton on the bugle and tell him to mind the fort.'

Lowry lit his cigarette. 'He has the day off.'

'Day off? Just because the sun's out does not mean he can
take his foot off the pedal.'

'Done more than take his foot off the pedal,' said Lowry,
observing the traffic through a puff of smoke. The police
station was not the only shiny new thing in Chelmsford; the

town was full of gleaming motors. 1982 had seen the end of the Y suffix and from the 1st of the month they'd started again at A. In Colchester he'd not noticed the change, but here it was awash with new plates; never before had he noticed how markedly affluent the place was. 'He's climbed out of the car and gone for a dip in sea.'

25

10.45 a.m., Fox Farm

Suzanne hung out the sheets with care and precision, making sure they were not bunched. She reached across, running a thumb and forefinger along the line, before removing a wooden peg from her mouth. She stood back to check her handiwork; the whiteness of the cotton made the sun glare back, causing her to squint. It was over two weeks since she had changed the bedroom laundry. She had held out as long as she could, clinging to the last scent of her husband. There was a breeze today, the first movement of air in a week or so. As she raised the line the wind caused the linen to billow, carrying with it any remaining trace of Christopher. They would dry in no time.

Clutching the laundry basket to her hip, she watched the sheets fill against the deep blue sky, where gulls cruised high against streaked wisps of clouds. Caught off her guard, her senses transported her to sailing on the Blackwater with Christopher last summer . . . She blinked, eyes sore. They began to mist. Two weeks after his death, the drama had subsided. The police had gone and all that remained was a pleasing Christopher-shaped hole in her life, which was larger than she had expected. Her brute of a husband really had dominated her existence; the freedom just to breathe now was exhilarating. With the funeral out of the way, there was no need for pretence; she could start to rebuild her life with the children.

The police had eventually returned, only this time to arrest Kate. The bed sheets lifted and Sweet Pea Cottage was revealed, nestled across the field, small and inconsequential against the vast Essex sky. For a week the police were to and fro – they had the idea that Kate might have killed Christopher as well as her lover. *He might have seen them together*, was the theory. Suzanne had sat there nodding dumbly, as the young one, Kenton, explained the possibilities – but sadly for them she didn't have an opinion. How could she? *Kate and Darnell?* Suzanne would never have paired those two in a million years. An unlikely coupling if ever there was one. Christopher's accountant was – on the rare occasion she'd had contact – as meek as a lamb. There must have been more to him than met the eye, and she obviously didn't know Kate half as well as she thought. Her friend had not so much as hinted at a romance with Peter ... and then to kill him? If she could kill such a harmless fellow as that, it was at least possible she possessed the kind of anger that would drive her to kill again, especially such a pig as Christopher, but her lawyers maintained that, no, this was 'a crime of passion'. Comparisons to Ruth Ellis were drawn. In the end, the police were in agreement; the children had called Kate immediately on the discovery of their father and she had answered. Unless she was the bionic woman, that ruled her out as a suspect in Christopher's case.

Suzanne had twice called Lowry in the middle of the night in inconsolable sobs. She had no one; with her parents now both dead and her friends all in London, she had never felt more alone. The stuffy pipe-smoking academic friend of Christopher's, Tim Pine, had finally plucked up the courage to call round, and they had sat for three-quarters of an hour in virtual silence. If anything, she now knew how little she knew of Christopher's world. Take that man Derrick they'd questioned. How could someone she didn't even know turn out to play such a part in their lives – and deaths?

She felt the hem of her dress being tugged. Emma.

'Mummy, Mummy, look.'

Suzanne followed her six-year-old's tiny pointing finger to the figure outside the house. She dropped the basket.

11 a.m., HMP Chelmsford

'She won't be here much longer,' the guard said snottily. 'Doesn't do to keep women in here.' The door clanged behind them.

'Chippy fuck,' said Sparks. 'They made a bloody movie here. That was all right, wasn't it?'

'I don't remember there being any women in *Porridge*,' Lowry said as they walked abreast down the green corridor. They ventured deeper within the prison without exchanging a further word, their footsteps' echo accompanying them as they went. They'd had no contact with Kate Everett since she'd pleaded guilty. Manslaughter, diminished responsibility.

They reached the end of the corridor and waited for another door to be opened.

'Anyway,' said Sparks to break the silence, 'it's not like she'll be sharing the soap in the showers, for Christ's sake.' He paused and cleared his throat. 'Antonia is having a baby.'

The guard appeared.

'Congratulations,' said Lowry and waited until they were through the gate before adding quietly, 'That explains a lot.'

Sparks shot him a sideways glance. 'What?'

'Nothing. I just said that's wonderful news.'

They followed the guard through to a meeting room. Only Sparks would make an announcement of that magnitude in the sanctity of a prison, seconds before interviewing a woman who had murdered her lover. Suddenly all became clear: the chief's ratty and unpredictable behaviour. He had been distracted for weeks. Antonia, pregnant – that would have taken some digesting. A father for the first time at age fifty-four. Lowry could imagine the turmoil taking over in that steadfast, straightforward male mind. A newborn baby was going to make one hell of an impact on the man's life. Lowry was expected at Sparks's Lexden townhouse for a drink this evening; this sudden divulgence of his was less a sign of friendship than an unfortunate necessity.

Kate Everett was remarkably composed for a woman who could be looking at the rest of her life behind bars. Sparks thought her crazy; Lowry maintained she was too clever for that and upgraded her state of mind to obsessive. Privately, though, he believed her manipulative, too, thinking of how he himself was charmed. He was surprised at what led to Darnell's death as described in her confession; he thought her too calculating to allow emotion to get the better of her. He had nothing to hang this theory on, though, and at times if he thought about it too much, he came full circle: concluding that, as he himself had been fooled, he was perhaps searching for something that wasn't there. And consequently, apart from the odd remark to Sparks about the confession, he'd said nothing further.

In light-blue overalls, she sat languidly, drawing on a cigarette in the pastel mint interview room. It struck Lowry that her attire was the same pale blue of her dead lover's Volvo. Even now, caged in this sterility, far from the countryside she loved, there was something captivating about her. Though perhaps in her eyes, green under heavy lids, he read sorrow rather than mischief. Sparks started the ball rolling. 'Thing is, Miss Everett, there's a case to say you murdered Christopher Cliff.'

She raised her eyebrows nonchalantly, inhaled on her cigarette and blew out a plume of smoke, aiming it deliberately
at both men. Lowry glanced at Sparks before speaking: 'There
are some who would find it convenient, if it were pinned on
you. Though it's not a view we hold ourselves.'

'No? Why you here then?'

'Just passing through,' Sparks said, crossing his legs, positioning an ankle on his thigh to remove fluff from the tassels
on his suede loafer. 'Anything helpful that you might offer
could sway the judge towards leniency,' he offered cordially.

Unburdening himself of the news of his impending fatherhood had loosened his mood. He had timed it perfectly; on
with the case in hand, no room for further discussion. As he
questioned Everett, all the anxiety brought on by Merrydown
and her pristine Chelmsford offices evaporated.

'It's possible you knew the Cliff family better than anyone.
Had you ever the sense there was difficulty of any kind?
Marital or financial?'

'Not as such. To the outside world they were the perfect
family. Successful, healthy, lovely house ... the only thorn
for Suzanne was Christopher's attitude towards Edward, but
I'm sure you're aware of that. His tolerance of his stepson
was less than generous.'

'How would that manifest itself?'

'Edward was problematic rather than academic, and easily
influenced. He was okay if he was occupied, but once he left
school and started earning, he realised that money brought

him freedom. He'd never liked living there, out in the middle of nowhere. When Suzanne was still married to Edward's father, they lived in London. She and Edward and the girls moved down here when she met Cliff. But whereas Suzanne was originally from Essex and enjoyed being home, it was harder on Edward. The countryside is not for everyone,' she flicked Lowry a sultry glance, 'and he grew desperate to fly the nest. If he didn't have enough money, he stole it . . . As a result, his egomaniac of a stepfather believed Edward was a risk – a threat to his career. Christopher would paint himself as a genial academic, head in the clouds, etcetera, but in truth he was a very ambitious man and nervous that his stepson's antics would in some way scupper him professionally and personally. It was a miracle that he managed to bundle Edward off to Suffolk without the papers getting hold of it. He was filming for BBC2 at the time, a programme on British classical music, and was ironically up the road from Hollesley Bay at Aldeburgh – covering Britten.'

'Are you saying Christopher was complicit in his stepson's arrest?'

Everett regarded Sparks with curiosity. 'Is that not something you would know?'

'I'm Colchester's Chief of Police, Miss Everett, and cannot know the ins and outs of every juvenile delinquent in the county,' Sparks said indignantly.

'Wait a minute,' Lowry interrupted. 'Just to confirm, Edward was arrested for stealing in the village, right?'

'Yes, purportedly from an off-licence where that old booze-hound Christopher spent a fortune on vintage port; I'm sure they could have overlooked the odd bottle of Woodpecker cider,' she said wryly.

'And how did Edward feel towards Cliff?' Lowry said. He was unconcerned with Suzanne's apparent ignorance – her attention to detail he had come to realise left a lot to be desired – but this animosity in his mind just levered the thieving lad ever closer to Derrick.

'I have no idea.' Everett shifted in her seat. 'He was aloof.'

'What, not even when he realised his own family colluded with his arrest?'

'Hardly his "family". I'm sure Suzanne didn't know.'

'How do you know?' Sparks asked.

She raised an eyebrow.

'Pillow talk,' Lowry guessed. 'Christopher must have shared his worries with his accountant. Safe pair of hands, trustworthy; surely not the sort to blab to all and sundry.'

Everett did not disagree. 'I hardly ever saw Teddy myself; he went straight from hiding in a bedroom filled with melancholy pop music to working in one of the antique shops in the village, and then one day he just vanished altogether and nobody said a word.'

Lowry remembered the records he'd found in the attic; they must have bundled the son's stuff up there when he got put away, to free his room up for one of the girls.

Sparks rose and so did Lowry. They met each other's eye.

'As you can imagine, we're interested in Edward Hoare's known associates. People that were close to him at the time of his arrest,' Lowry said, not finishing what he was thinking: *someone that might exact revenge on his behalf.*

Sparks had no such filter. 'It's not as though he'd be able to get out and bump the old man off himself.'

Everett watched Sparks as he moved about the room. 'It's not a prison, you know,' she said, 'they're loosening them up there all the time now.'

'How would you know that?' Lowry asked.

'Look, Inspector, you pick things up in places like this. The demise of the borstal system is all the younger inmates, and many of the guards, talk about. Apparently it is being phased out – "youth custody" is much less severe.'

'Think you're a bit past that yourself, Miss Everett; you'll be lucky to be kept out of Broadmoor.'

'Thank you, Superintendent, you're all heart.'

'Don't mention it.' Sparks helped himself to one of her cigarettes lying on the table. 'Come on, Nick, we've learnt all we can.'

'Wait. Miss Everett – that morning, before the girl called you, was there anything, is there anything at all you can recall? Anything.'

She sunk her head dramatically, then raised it sharply. 'My mind was elsewhere, Inspector, as I'm sure you can imagine. Before the telephone call I couldn't think straight ... And as I told you, I'd downed a lot of vodka the previous night.

After the phone call – to be honest that is a blur too. Hard for you to believe it but I'm quite squeamish and I just couldn't face looking at the body.' Sparks rolled his eyes. 'But, but I couldn't avoid the terrible smell of blood and cordite hanging in the kitchen . . .'

Sparks cut in. 'He turned back, you know. Peter, I mean.'

She lifted her pale eyes towards him.

'We found blood just beyond the Cliffs' woods. Had he carried on to Kelvedon, he probably would have been found and maybe he would have lived. Must have been the real thing, eh?'

Lowry watched for her reaction. Sparks's assertion was unfounded and therefore perhaps cruel.

Not taking the bait, she regained herself. 'Christopher did not deserve to die,' she said coldly, 'and if I remember anything, you will hear from me.'

26

Lowry was alone in CID. Many were taking holiday, and those that weren't were making excuses to be outside in the sun. The Uniform section of the floor was empty. Sparks was upstairs, but not for long – the athletics trials were this afternoon. The summer was busy, competitively speaking.

Before him lay Derrick's statement of two weeks before. Derrick was unwise to have withheld information, but Lowry had some sympathy for him. Sparks's manner was aggressive at the best of times, hardly likely to put anyone at ease, and in Derrick's case Sparks was prejudiced – he held a singular kind of hostility towards gay men.

To be fair, Derrick had eventually come clean, admitting to handling the gun and confessing to being a 'dab hand' with a rifle. He stated that he had chatted with Cliff on the phone to fix an appointment to value the dresser. The pair had discussed shooting, Cliff telling Derrick that he had just unlocked his gun cabinet in anticipation of the forthcoming season, Derrick telling Cliff how he was eagerly awaiting the 'glorious twelfth' and a trip to the Scottish Highlands.

As a result, Cliff had asked Derrick to value the gun at the same time as the dresser, and agreed on an appointed time. Derrick had put it at £1,000. Lowry did not think Derrick the sort to engage in a tussle over a firearm, no matter how rare or valuable ... but given the animosity between Edward and Cliff, he did think he was involved somehow, either directly or indirectly. Derrick claimed to know the boy 'vaguely' and said that he had stolen from him on several occasions. Most small-time villains would not tolerate thieving in their firm, but Derrick was rumoured to have a soft spot for young boys.

Lowry had two theories. The first was that Derrick had exploited Cliff's vanity – his fear of his stepson's delinquent behaviour ruining his reputation. The prospect of Edward's imminent release had brought the problem to the surface yet again ... and having been instrumental in the boy's incarceration, Cliff had good reason to be concerned: he was terrified Derrick would encourage Edward to revert to his old habits and start stealing again. Perhaps he had tried to buy Derrick off with two thousand quid but Derrick had refused the cash. He wanted the dresser and the gun. Perhaps a fight ensued and – bang.

Lowry's second theory was that Derrick might have an even greater hold over Cliff than just an association with the historian's stepson. Something Edward had done, perhaps. Was Cliff being blackmailed? Suzanne's haziness over the finer details of her precious boy's arrest did not fill Lowry with optimism at the prospect of further questions regarding the husband's private life. Still, he had to give it go, and reached for the receiver.

The phone rang several times, and he was on the verge of giving up when eventually he heard a faint 'hello'.

'Mrs Cliff?' Lowry asked, uncertain as to the ownership of the voice.

'Yes . . .' she was hesitant.

'Everything okay?'

'Yes, everything's fine.' Her voice, though now bolder, carried reservation. And nothing had ever been *fine*, in any circumstances to date.

'I have just one or two questions for you on Christopher.'

'Very well, ask away.'

'No, I thought I might drive over if it's not too much bother. I may need you to dig around his study.'

'We're going out,' she said firmly, 'to the beach in an hour or so.'

He had not experienced this sort of resistance from her before. 'It really is important. I can be there in twenty minutes, and gone in another twenty.' Intuition told him all was not right, so he patched a call through to the local man watching Derrick's place to get over to watch Fox Farm.

12.20 p.m., Rowhedge village, east of Colchester

Kenton discovered he didn't know the area as well as he thought.

Rowhedge was a small fishing port three miles outside Colchester, perched on the edge of the west bank of the River Colne. He was due to pick up Jane Gabriel at midday, but had deliberately cut it fine so as not to turn up early, or worse, exactly on time. He had not, however, considered the possibility that he would get lost trying to find her road. As turned out to be the case.

Two weeks ago she had joined him at lunch and during the conversation he'd let slip about his new sport. To his amazement, she had floated the suggestion of a trip to the beach together sometime over the summer. At the time his heart had soared but outwardly he'd accepted her proposal as coolly as possible. He was determined to keep his feelings for her hidden after last year's rocky start, but this casualness was easier said than done. Now he found himself stressed at the possibility of turning up late, or God forbid, not at all . . .

According to the sign attached to the white-painted public house, which ran parallel with the river, he was on Rowhedge High Street already. He must have missed the turning for Rectory Road, but no sooner had he entered the village than he was seeing it recede in his rear view. To his left ran the narrow river channel, on the other side of which lay Wivenhoe, set back between an expanse of trees. The road straight ahead led directly into a boatyard. He leant out of the open car window and called out to a rough hewn man in a sleeveless T-shirt.

'You won't launch that here, mate,' the man said before he had a chance to speak.

'What?'

'That board on yer roof – ain't no room for it.' Kenton looked up at the windsurf board protruding out over the Capri windscreen.

'Yes, yes. I know . . . Rectory Road, where is it?'

'Passed it; back there, second on the left.'

Kenton expressed his gratitude overzealously and looked for somewhere to turn the car around; a feat easier said than done. The Capri had a turning circle that at times felt like that of an oil tanker. He scanned behind him; people milling around in the street – more of a market thoroughfare, really: prams, wicker baskets full of produce on display outside shop fronts, fishing paraphernalia. He pushed the car into reverse and edged back at a snail's pace, growing acutely aware of how impractical it was to load a board reaching nearly four metres in length on the roof of a sports coupe. The rear overhang was way more than he thought; pedestrians made a song and dance of ducking out of his way. He felt embarrassment pulse his cheeks as he checked his trajectory via the dreadful visibility afforded by the Capri rear window. He was hot, he was uncomfortable, his glasses were forever sliding down the bridge of his nose and his blood pressure was rising through the roof.

By the time he'd found the correct address, sweat was pouring into his eyes. He reached for a towel on the back seat and gave himself a thirty-second breather and a bit of a pep talk before gently tooting on the horn.

Gabriel descended the steps moments later, her feet as light as the summer dress she wore.

Her broad smile faded as she climbed in next to him. 'Are you all right?'

12.30 p.m., Fox Farm

Edward brushed past Suzanne walking downstairs as she hurried up. She halted midway, gazing back at the broad shoulders of her son moving through into the kitchen. But the whimpering on the first floor pulled her on to continue. Seconds later Emma shot past her after her brother with such fury that Suzanne pressed herself against the wall.

Alice sat on the bedroom floor in tears. Lucy stood by the window, her red face fixed in defiance.

'What on earth . . . ?' Suzanne spluttered.

'He went to hit me,' Alice blubbed.

'*Hit* you?' She glared in disbelief at Lucy, who remained silent and unmoved. 'No, I don't believe that! He's your brother – he missed you terribly. What on earth . . .'

Suzanne ran back down the stairs. Edward was rummaging in the kitchen drawers frantically.

'Edward!' she cried with as much authority as she could muster, 'What on earth is going on?!'

'It was a mistake to come home first, I need to . . .' an array of batteries and light bulbs littered the work surface.

'Did you hit your sister? Tell me.'

He stopped searching. 'Of course I bloody didn't.'

'Don't use that sort of language the moment you arrive home,' she snapped.

'No, I did nothing of the sort. Who was on the phone? Was it for me?'

She walked past him and lifted the motorcycle key from an ashtray.

'Give me those, Mother.'

'You can't just come here and throw your weight around.' She was powerless, and he knew it. He came up close to her – he was much taller than her now. 'Where are you going?'

'Out.'

'Where?' she insisted.

'Just out. I've been locked up for a year. '

She loved him very much, and would forgive her son anything, but maybe unwittingly, Christopher was right, Edward was too big to manage. She could not protect him any more than she could control him. And as he wrested the motorbike keys from her grip, Suzanne acknowledged she had no alternative. The police would be here imminently. Lowry had said they didn't think Teddy involved, but there were sufficient gaps in her knowledge and uncertainty in her heart; enough to warrant wishing Teddy out of reach until some resolve was reached over Christopher's death, if only for a short while.

He bowed to kiss her and exited the house without saying a word.

27

12.45 p.m., Fox Farm

Lowry arrived at the farm as fast as the roads would allow. A breeze swayed through the large trees behind the barn where they'd held the investigation HQ. He left the Saab door open, aware of how quiet the farm was. The soft whirr of the trees highlighted the absence of all other sound. He removed his wrap-arounds and placed them in the top pocket of his suit jacket. To his left the garage door was open; the sleek Lancia glinted dully from inside. A sturdy policeman's bicycle was propped up against the wall – Sparks's man from Kelvedon station, a part-time local outpost. Of course he was on a bike. Sure enough, the constable emerged from the house, looking glum.

'Young fella. High-tailed out of here on a motorbike, sir, nearly had me off the bike.'

Edward. As he had suspected from Suzanne's tone.

Lowry wondered exactly how effective the local bobby's surveillance of Derrick's place was. Bicycle shoved in the bushes and hiding behind a tree. The writing was on the wall for these smaller district stations, Lowry was sure.

'Thank you, Constable, you may return to your duties.'

The constable gave him a knowing wink and wheeled the bicycle beyond the gate.

An anxious face was peering at the ground-floor window. Suzanne Cliff stood behind the door, allowing him to enter without a word.

'I hear I missed him.' They entered the kitchen.

One of her daughters appeared at her side. The youngest.

'Hello, Mister Policeman, have you come to find our brother?' The child had hot cheeks, as though from some recent physical exertion, but she was calm.

'Go and play, Emma.' Her mother nudged her towards the open stable door. The child hovered on the threshold, then disappeared into the sunlight. Lowry detected tension in the air; it felt as if the absent son had left an atmosphere behind him. Suzanne stood still by the sink, nervously tugging at her thumbnail. It was the first time Lowry had been with her alone in the room that had witnessed her husband's last breath.

'I'm sorry, I couldn't tell you he was here,' she pleaded. 'He'd only just been released. You understand?'

'Of course, but as I said, we only wish to speak.'

'I wished he'd not rushed out like that, honestly.' Suzanne bowed her head in contrition.

'Never mind, how are you?'

'Bearing up, thank you.' She lifted her worn face, and smiled faintly.

'And how was he, your son?'

'He was agitated ... I'm mean, he was fine, but he flared up and lashed out at the girls.'

'Do you know why?'

'I have no idea. They hadn't seen each other in a year.'

Lowry handled Suzanne Cliff with delicacy. There was no point in punishing her; a mother's instinct is to protect her children.

'Did he know of his stepfather's death?'

'Yes. The warden informed him that Christopher had taken his own life. And it was in the papers, obviously.' The muscles in her face relaxed. 'But we didn't get as far as having a proper talk about, well, everything, before he flared up with the girls ... funny, he'd not seen them for a year.'

'Tell me what happened from the beginning.'

She pulled out a kitchen chair, and he did likewise.

'I was hanging out the washing, and there he was, like a vision ... just standing there.'

'You sound surprised?'

'I was ...'

'But why? This is his home, where would you expect him to go?'

'He'd more or less moved out by the time he was remanded, spent most of his time in a squat in Colchester, much to Christopher's shame.'

'Even though he'd worked in Kelvedon, he dossed down in Colchester?' Lowry said blankly.

'Yes. He has the motorbike. The allure of the town was too much, I'm sure it would only have been a matter of time before he'd have left.'

Lowry dimly remembered his own teens, his mother moving them away from rural Fingringhoe to the housing estate of Greenstead after his father left. Age fifteen and he was held responsible for the upheaval. *You spend all your time in Colchester; at least out there I'll not be awake all night worrying whether you'll make it home across the fields.* The countryside was a place for the start and end of life, not for trying to find it. He cleared his throat.

'Where was his bedroom? I've seen the upstairs layout, and don't recall . . .'

'Alice's room. Lucy and Alice used to share. He'd scribbled graffiti all over the walls – we painted it when he left and she moved in. We'd no option. I wouldn't want Alice reading that. Christopher moved all Edward's stuff up to the attic room.' She clutched herself as if suddenly cold, though it was north of twenty degrees in the kitchen.

'What sort of graffiti?'

'Depressing adolescent drivel: song lyrics, death and suffering. One band he played over and over sounded like a funeral procession. The singer did in fact hang himself. I remember it, Edward would have been fourteen.' Joy Division. Lowry remembered the LP sleeve in the record box. Kenton went on about them at length; saw them live when he was at university – deep and meaningful, apparently. 'It all happened so fast, Inspector: one minute he's scrawling lyrics all over his bedroom wall, the next he's in the company of thieves.'

She rose abruptly and moved about the room. 'You had some other questions? When you telephoned?'

'Those can wait,' he said firmly. 'Where do you think Edward went?'

'If it were open, that huge pub with the television screens on Crouch Street spread over different levels; not that I frequent it – but it's hard to miss. We buy our meat from the butcher there, when we're in town.'

The Colne Lodge. It was the heart of the scene for the young folks in Colchester and a mecca for drugs and all manner of naughtiness.

'Did he have any money on him?'

'I don't know.' If Edward Hoare had gone to Derrick's, the PC should have had time to cycle over there to witness it. But the Colne Lodge seemed a good bet if he had indeed spent most of his time in Colchester; it was the obvious place to reconnect with old acquaintances.

'Does he have friends in Colchester still? Those he lived at the squat with? Any names he has mentioned in the past?'

'No, he never mentions them.' She put on a brave smile. 'There is one other possibility; he may be with his cousin. He's a soldier, just returned from Northern Ireland . . .'

'In the town?'

She nodded.

'Michael. Michael Hoare, my father's name, my maiden name. My father was in the army too.' She paused, anxious now. 'I hope Edward doesn't get into trouble. He can be a hothead.'

'I'm sure we'll find him,' he smiled and made to go; 'he can't just disappear.'

'Funny you say that, though. He did – disappear – the morning Christopher was shot . . .' Her voice trailed as she realised what she was saying.

'I beg your pardon?'

'Edward was unaccounted for the morning Christopher was shot.'

'Unaccounted for?'

'I mean he wasn't at Hollesely Bay at morning roll-call. The warden didn't want to make a thing of it – so close to his release . . .'

'Did Kate Everett know this?' Lowry was rewinding to the conversation this morning at Chelmsford prison, about the lax security.

'No, why?'

'Nothing, doesn't matter. Where was he?'

'I . . . I don't know. The warden didn't think it a big deal . . .'

Lowry had difficulty holding back his surprise. 'That's somewhat of a coincidence.' He muttered, 'No wonder you didn't tell me. The warden may not be so relaxed about it had he known the situation now.'

'Oh come, Inspector, that's miles away.'

This much was true – close to fifty. But not wishing to deviate right now, he continued. 'Mrs Cliff,' he said, biting the bullet, 'it was your husband who had Edward arrested.'

28

4 p.m., West Mersea beach

The water sparkled in the late sun.

'C'mon in!' Kenton called from the water's edge.

'I'm fine here!' Gabriel called back. And she was right; it was a beautiful place to come on a day like today. She sat back, elbows digging into the sand. The breeze was fresh coming in off the sea. He toppled into the water again with a splash. This 'boardsailing' looked very unappealing. She didn't think it was for her. Pulling that heavy triangular sail out of the water time and time again, only to plunge back into the sea a second later. The board weighed a ton too. She returned to her book, lying on her stomach away from the water.

There could only be one man who would appear on a crowded beach in August in a light grey suit and dark tie. Lowry trudged across the sand towards her. Of more interest was how he could possibly have picked her out amongst the frenzy of children and young mums enjoying the sun; there wasn't a patch of beach free – she felt incognito in floppy hat, shades and loose dress. Daniel went in again, narrowly missing an inflatable dinghy.

Eventually Lowry stood over her.

'Afternoon,' she offered up, as he faced the shore.

'What on earth is he doing?'

'Learning to windsurf . . .'

'He's going to be had up for drowning children.' Lowry loped off over the shingle towards the hapless sailor, hands in pockets. Gabriel jumped up and followed him, one hand holding her sun hat. The breeze had got up – she hadn't noticed before. Maybe the wind was too much for him?

'What's going on?' she called out after Lowry. It was their day off, after all.

'Edward Hoare is out and about.'

'Oh.' She winced, catching her toe on the shells. Lowry was obsessed with the Cliff case; he couldn't let it go. Roger Derrick slipping through the noose had riled him and Sparks alike. 'I thought he was in Suffolk?'

'He got out today. New information has come to light.'

'Ohhh! Look, he's off! That's the first time.' Gabriel pointed excitedly towards Kenton, not only upright on the board but rapidly accelerating. 'Gosh, he's moving fast . . .' She shielded her eyes; the glare off the water was blinding. The breeze had strengthened, turning chilly.

'Can he turn round?'

'I don't know . . . but this is progress, the best he's done.' She squinted.

'The wind has swung offshore – it's carrying him out to sea.'

'Oh well, in that case – might we have time for an ice lolly?' she said.

Gabriel turned to face the inspector. His Brylcreemed hair had loosened in the gust, and flickered across his forehead. He was lightly tanned, or weathered. His years had removed the sheen off his face.

'I suppose so,' he eventually said.

Jacqui lay back on the towel. The cool breeze was perfect. Who needed a Greek island when you had this on your doorstep? Apart from Trish, that is. Trish was oiled up and sprawled out next to her, to the delight of every randy young local man in sight. Trish had yesterday returned from Crete, where she'd spent a week systematically working through the tavernas in Malia (and their unsuspecting, but grateful, teenage waiters).

'I mean, why the hell would I? We've been apart nearly two years.' Trish was pontificating over whether to meet her ex-husband. Andy, an accountant who drove a yellow TR7, had run off with his secretary.

'Don't then.' The secretary had since found someone her own age with a Porsche.

'I wonder if I'd fall for him over again?'

Jacqui opened her eyes and turned her head to see Trish roll over and finger a foreign cigarette out of a soft pack.

'Why would that happen?' It made a change to be talking about Trish's love life and not Jacqui's. Strangely, since Jacqui's recent interaction with Sparks – which she'd kept from Trish – she had no wish to discuss her own situation. This she put down to her growing unrest at living with Trish herself.

'Isn't the attraction always there? I don't just mean the obvious; he is cute . . . I mean . . .'

'I don't get that at all – you've moved on?'

'You know when you *really know* someone?' Trish elaborated, in her own way, about a connection above and beyond the aesthetic or physical. They had had this conversation before but Andy seldom featured.

'What brought this up?'

'I dunno. Guess we've both had our bit of fun, maybe it's out of the system.'

'"Bit" of fun? You've had more than a bit by anyone's standard. You're divorced, for Christ's sake; would you really go back after all the expense and hassle?'

Andy, cute to her friend, was a short-arse, borderline dwarf to everyone else. Trish had hooked up with him for security. She clearly had no recollection of how she went off the rails when she caught him at it with the office bimbo.

'Oh, I don't know. Just thinking aloud, none of us are getting any younger . . . wait. Jacqui! Jacqui!' Trish hissed in her ear. 'Look!' Jacqui propped herself up on her elbows, put her book down on her beach towel and lifted her head towards the water. There, undoubtedly, was her husband.

'Go on, go talk to him.'

'He's working, he's hardly going to appreciate me hassling him on the beach, is he?' Though what was he doing? More to the point, who was the woman who certainly was not in work clothes?

'He'll hardly have a barney with you on the beach. It's ideal!'

'Leave it.' Her eyes were on the tall blonde woman. 'What are you doing?'

Trish was standing, hands behind on her rear, running her fingers under her bikini bottoms preparing to move.

'Going to say hello?'

'No, you are bloody well not. Sit down!' she spat.

'One day you will have to. Eight months is a long time.'

Lowry sat on the terrace while Gabriel went inside to buy ice creams. The Two Sugars Café was formerly a World War Two coastal artillery emplacement and commanded an excellent view of the Blackwater estuary, perched above rows of the multicoloured huts that lined West Mersea beach like peaked slices of Battenberg cake.

The wind had more than a slice of northerly in it now and he received the cool air gladly. The bombshell that Suzanne Cliff had delivered had left him hot under the collar. Edward Hoare was 'unaccounted for' at the time of his stepfather's death. Containing his surprise as best he could, he had left Suzanne Cliff with blanket reassurances that it was nothing more than coincidence. Nevertheless, he hammered it back to Queen Street and immediately called Hollesely Bay. The warden was recalcitrant; Edward had not escaped – there was no transport in the vicinity; no one made it past the screws stationed at Wilford Bridge, which was the only way across the Deben and off the peninsula. (More often than not a farmer would find boys passed out in a barn after raiding his scrumpy.) The warden was unmoved by the news that Christopher Cliff's death had escalated to a murder enquiry.

The boy may not have made it out under his own steam, but with the aid of an accomplice ... but to what end? He took in the view and breathed the sea air. They didn't have Edward's dabs anywhere; it was Derrick's manicured hand that had been up and down the gun.

Still, the case festered within him; why had Suzanne Cliff sat on this detail until today? He could only assume she did not link the two events, even though the timing seemed so stark.

He was now calm enough to take stock of the situation and allow Edward Hoare to surface naturally rather than go old-school and take a sledgehammer to the town looking for him, Sparks-style. It would not have done them any favours with Derrick. No, continued surveillance was required, for which he needed bodies. And thanks to Brixton there were none spare.

Gabriel handed him a rocket lolly. 'I haven't had one of these in years.' She sat opposite in a very short floral skirt with a 99 flake.

'Do you think Edward murdered his stepfather?'

Lowry tore off the bottom of the wrapper, and brought the lolly to his lips to inflate and free the ice from the packet. 'It's technically possible – he could get from Kelvedon to Woodbridge in under an hour, which is the timeframe we'd be considering.'

'How would he have travelled there and back?'

'That's the question. He shot off from the farm on a motor-bike so maybe he stole one, or had an accomplice. It's unlikely, but a remarkable coincidence nevertheless.'

'We can ask Edward where he was when we catch up with him,' Gabriel said simply. To which he could think of nothing to say.

They both attended to their ices in silence, and Lowry found himself considering his colleague's legs, which were bare and in close proximity to his own. He wasn't looking in a lascivious way – he had noticed they were uncommonly pale. He was observant, this he knew, and sometimes caught himself staring at a person, or an aspect of their attire. An eye for detail, he liked to think. Gabriel adjusted her chair to get a better view of the estuary, leaving her bare foot inches from his shin. When he caught very fine hairs low down her shin, beyond a razor's reach perhaps, he averted his gaze to follow her eyeline.

'Aren't you worried?'

He bit the purple top off the lolly. 'No, I've requested Traffic to be on lookout for a blue Yamaha Fizzy . . . but I don't think he'll get far on a jacked-up moped.'

'No, not about Hoare – about Daniel.' She stood and stepped to the terrace edge. 'I can't see him anywhere.'

Lowry rose and stood next to her. There was a soft haze over the estuary which from his vantage point gave the illusion of calm, cloaking the wind whipping across the water – only further out did flecks of white hint at the strength of the north-easterly.

'The tide is on the turn,' he said. 'If Kenton can keep up wind he'll be fine; if not, the North Sea and Holland await him.'

29

5.15 p.m., RMP Police HQ, Abbey Fields, Colchester

The military police commander sat at his antique desk and added the finishing touches to his report. A Mozart piano sonata flittered away softly on the turntable at the far end of the tastefully decorated room. Captain James Oldham enjoyed the summer months. Military personnel, he believed, benefited from fine weather, as it kept them out of trouble. The rank and file were less inclined to grumble during such periods; manoeuvres were less irksome and therefore more likely problem-free. The flip side of course was that they drank whenever the opportunity presented itself; exercise in the heat produced an undeniable thirst. So if he was to provide a balanced opinion, as he was required to do for the forthcoming Discipline Review Board, he would attest that less trouble in camp outweighed one or two punch-ups in the town. He signed the report and replaced his fountain pen in its holder. A small and neat man, he believed in order, as determinedly as the sun rising every morning.

There came a light rap at the door.

'Enter.' He was expecting the piano tuner, and automatically looked towards the instrument bathed in sunlight from the French windows.

'Civilian police to see you, sir.'

'Oh, how very disappointing.'

'Should I say you're otherwise engaged?'

'No, show them in, they don't tend to go away.' Oldham rose from behind his desk, tapped the watermarked paper square on the leather desk inlay and moved to open the French doors. A tall orange orchid rose from a small octagonal table.

'Ah, Inspector Lowry.' The captain's spirits rose on seeing the CID officer, for whom he had great respect. 'No loosening of the tie, eh?' He himself was in open neck, olive-green shirtsleeves.

'A matter of habit.' Lowry touched the slender black material consciously.

'Please,' Oldham gestured to the Chesterfield, 'can we offer any refreshments?' The inspector had a sheen, unsurprisingly; it was twenty-five in the shade.

'What's on offer?'

'You name it, the RMP can provide.'

'Gin and tonic?'

'Wise choice. Make that two.' He dispatched the orderly. The two men had at one time bordered on becoming friends. Since an incident that January, they had at the very least forged an understanding and mutual respect that invited the opportunity for informal drinks once, maybe twice, a month, to discuss the town and its inhabitants. The line that neither man had crossed was that of personal circumstances. It had been a while since their last meeting and the captain sensed a hardness around the inspector. One thing he did know about the brawny policeman was that he loved to box.

'I hear you have been lured back into the ring? Why?'

'I miss it.'

The captain, an expert in the field of duplicity, knew this to be a hollow remark.

'Good for you then.' He slapped the side of the armchair as the drinks trolley was wheeled through. 'Now, how can I help?'

'Does the name Hoare mean anything to you?'

'Why yes, do you mean Colonel Hoare?'

'What can you tell me about him – or to be more precise, his family?'

'Dead for a start; very distinguished fellow when alive. Army family through and through, runs back generations – anywhere the Brits have been in a scrap, there's been a Hoare in the midst of it: Waterloo, India, Crimea, Normandy – our man was in Suez, and Aden in the 1960s.'

'Has several daughters?'

'Three.' He sucked his teeth. The G&T hit the spot. 'Ah . . . I know where this is heading: the husband of one daughter shot himself last month, correct?'

Lowry hesitated, and helped himself to an olive from the silver trolley. 'Yes, he's dead. But it's not the daughter I'm interested in – it's his grandsons. One in particular we'd like to talk to is Edward, Suzanne Cliff's boy. He has just been released from borstal and uses the family name Edward Hoare. The other is here somewhere, I believe. Michael Hoare.'

'When you say here, you mean here, here.' He pointed at the Persian carpet.

'Yes, recently completed a tour of Northern Ireland. Can you help me find him?'

Oldham propelled himself out of the chair to grab a note pad. 'Of course.' The orderly appeared as he approached the desk, to say the piano tuner had arrived. Lowry took this as his cue to leave. 'Stay, if you've time, we can step onto the veranda to admire my roses.'

'I've left a colleague in the car. Some other time, maybe.'

'I do hope so.' The inspector's reticence made him an appealing companion, rather than the jaunty surface banter he was usually subjected to consorting with those whom he had no choice. The garrison commander, for instance, Brigadier Lane. Lane arranged the boxing bouts between the police and the army, and had told him of Lowry's return.

'It's tomorrow evening, I gather?'

'What is?'

'Your fight?'

A faint smile. 'Yep, it is.'

'I might stop by. That is,' he gestured with the crystal glass, 'if you're okay with a supporter from the other side?'

'I didn't think you approved?'

'Oh, nothing as strong as disapproval, rather on the noisy side for my taste, but good to support a friend, eh?'

Lowry nodded, 'I'll look out for you, thank you, Captain.'

5.45 p.m., Creffield Road, Lexden

Sparks watched his wife knock up a potent cocktail, grunted, then slipped down to the basement where newly installed gym equipment awaited him. The possibility that a teenage borstal inmate could slip out, travel thirty miles, murder a man then saunter back in took some swallowing. 'And people think we're shoddy.' He'd had word from Lowry. The boy was in Colchester. Having briefly returned home to upset his family, Edward Hoare had bolted off into town on a moped. They were confident they'd find him tonight. Sparks was relieved at this news; he hated uncertainty and loose ends, and the sooner he could get Merrydown off his back the better. Then, if things quietened down, he might slip away for a week himself. The police chief rubbed his hands and eyed the rowing machine. It was sweltering down here, he hadn't calculated on the ventilation when having the basement converted – it had always been cold and damp even in the height of summer. He stripped to the waist, tossing the Lycra top onto the wooden floor – he'd be sweating buckets in a matter of minutes. Derrick was mixed up in all this he was sure, some tawdry liaison with the boy. Much as he'd like to think the prison authorities were at fault in letting the lad slip away, he couldn't see it. He buckled his feet and reached for the bar and then pulled back with great exertion. *Christ*, he cursed through gritted teeth. It was the regatta next week, and as usual he would front the police rowing team on the Blackwater sprint. How many years he could keep this up, he didn't know. What with a kid on the way his days were numbered . . .

'Don't be down here puffing and panting too long, dear.' Antonia appeared with a tall glass of colourful liquid.

'Only half an hour.'

'The sweat just pours off you, long after you've showered, you know that.' He wished she wouldn't stand there while he was exercising, it wasn't right.

'It's only Nick, for Christ's sake, not a bloody inspection.'

She twisted her left foot in that coquettish way he used to love but had noticed latterly heralded the arrival of bad news. 'Actually, there's something I've been meaning to tell you, I don't know why I didn't mention it sooner . . .'

7.15 p.m., Crouch Street, Colchester

'How long will we sit here – all night?' Gabriel asked, breaking the silence. She didn't want to lose the evening on top of the afternoon.

'Not much longer, give it until it gets dark. I'm expected elsewhere soon, but you'll have company.' Lowry stared across the road at the Colne Lodge where they'd sat without speaking since it opened at six. The silence was enforced; they were listening out for sightings of either of the Hoare boys on the police airwaves, or watching for either to enter the place opposite. With the windows down they'd been subjected to the music from across the way. So far they'd heard 'Relax' three times already. It appeared the inspector's concentration was limited to a maximum of two tasks at any one time. Since he'd picked Gabriel up at five-thirty she'd barely even had the chance to enquire as to Kenton's whereabouts (he'd been dragged to safety on a waterski line by a passing speedboat), as every time she spoke the radio crackled into life with a possible sighting of Hoare. But now she was bored. If this was to be her future in CID, as Sparks had said, forget it.

She sighed audibly. 'Going anywhere nice?'

'Err . . . no.' The usual one-word answer; maybe he was bored too.

A souped-up black Vauxhall drove slowly past, stereo blaring, arms lolling out of windows. It occurred to her that he was doing this on purpose to teach her a lesson.

'Inspector, forgive me speaking . . . may I?'

He flicked another cigarette out of the window and turned to face her, his expression now one of curiosity, as though they hadn't sat for an hour and a half without exchanging a word.

'Fire away.'

'I hope you don't think this rude, but I'm not pushing to work in CID, I wanted to make that clear.'

He frowned. 'Sure. It's not for everyone.' He flexed his knuckles on the steering wheel.

And that was all there was to say, apparently. His head moved, following a crowd of boys and girls with brightly coloured hair and make-up, heavy on the blusher, making for the pub.

'It's just . . .'

'You're doing fine,' he said, in a softer tone. 'Sparks has a point. It's getting harder to tell them apart.' From the opposite direction, four skinheads in bomber jackets approached the door at the same time. Curiously there was no animosity.

'Have you been in there?' Lowry asked.

'No, should I have?'

He shrugged. 'I don't know; no, probably not . . .'

A finger tapped on the glass, making her jump, followed by a sun-scorched face at the window.

'Oh my,' she exclaimed, raising her fingertips to her bottom lip. Lowry leant over.

'The shift change.'

30

8 p.m., Creffield Road, Lexden

Lowry parked the Saab on Creffield Road and grimaced at the Sparks's residence before him. He was expected for cocktails. Until this evening he'd put them off and off, and could delay no further. Initially Sparks himself was dissatisfied that Antonia had invited him, grumbling quietly that his wife ought to check with him first, but a little while later Lowry sensed his commander taking umbrage after he'd cancelled yet again at the beginning of the month.

He pushed the car door shut. Having left Kenton and Gabriel to it, he might as well try to enjoy himself. They knew where he was if they needed him, and, as he framed it to Kenton, it was the lesser of the two evils – if Edward Hoare showed, they were to follow him until he bedded down for the night. He'd hoped Kenton had taken that on board. He didn't want 'initiative' displayed this evening; all he wanted to know was where the boy spent the night. They would get him in the morning – there were to be no public scenes.

Lowry knew Gabriel thought his apparent lack of worry for Kenton earlier was rather cold. But he'd deliberately downplayed it. If the boot were on the other foot, and he were hauled out of the sea before all and sundry, he'd not want a big discussion about it. The experience was a formative one, and Kenton would learn from it. The sea was not to be trifled with, not even on an idyllic day like today. Still, he couldn't help but smile recalling the boy's sorrowful, sunburnt face. He rang the doorbell on Sparks's bright green door.

8.25 p.m., Crouch Street, Colchester

Kenton slumped awkwardly inside the Capri. The sunburn at least disguised his embarrassment, though his face was hot all the time, like a constant burning shame. He consulted the welts on his fingers. How differently the afternoon had started out, with the pair of them sitting here in his car, off for a fun day at the beach. He really fancied a cigarette, anything to take his mind off –

'Are you okay?' she asked. 'You look sore.'

'I'll live,' he said, dodging her blue eyes.

'It must have been scary.'

He heard genuine concern in her voice. He wasn't familiar with the tone; kindness was new, a little uncomfortable even. Still, he'd never really been in peril before . . . had he been in real danger then? He hadn't thought beyond the embarrassment of the tow back in to the beach.

'When did you realise you were in trouble?'

He glanced across the street at the Colne Lodge.

'When the wind stopped. It just disappeared. But the board didn't, the current or whatever pulled me out . . . I could see the beach growing further away.'

'Yes, you probably shouldn't go out in offshore winds. Certainly not when the tide's on the turn. You did just vanish.'

He stared at her in astonishment. Since when did she know about such things? She'd made out she'd not so much as been on a pedalo. 'Come, let's have a look in there.' He nodded towards the bar, preferring not to be reminded of his ignorance of the sea.

'Aren't we best off watching from here? What if we miss a sighting reported on the radio?' Gabriel protested, but he was already on the pavement.

The Colne Lodge was a melting pot of colour and noise with numerous bars catering for every permutation of youth culture imaginable. On the ground floor, two bars were separated by a glass wall so that people in one bar could see what was going on in the other. It felt like an overcrowded aquarium. There were additional levels to the building, and each had its own tribe – different dress codes and hair codes – and each had a large wall-mounted screen flashing out pop videos. The only tune Gabriel recognised was David Bowie's 'Let's Dance', pounding out for a sea of punters with hairspray-enforced quiffs and white jackets. If Edward Hoare were in here, he would spot them before they clocked him; Gabriel and Kenton may as well have a siren strapped to their heads. Not that they were in uniform, of course, but their age gave them away; she doubted if more than one in ten were over eighteen.

Upstairs there was louder, harsher music, but less lighting and make-up; covert goings-on in darkened corners. After ten minutes of looking, they reached the conclusion their man wasn't here and Kenton indicated they ought to return to the car.

The radio was alive. He grabbed the handset roughly before Gabriel was even in the car. They'd received a tip-off: Mike Hoare was at the snooker club. He cursed to himself; he'd wasted precious minutes.

'C'mon,' Kenton snapped crossly, knowing it was his fault if the scent was cold, 'we've a lead. George Street, behind the high street, smack in the middle of town.' They could be there in under two minutes.

8.30 p.m., Creffield Road, Lexden

Sparks was in khaki. Another attempt by Antonia to suave him up. Sparks's loathing to spend money on things he didn't understand – such as fashion – produced a result neither of them were happy with.

'I think our boy will rear his head in town tonight, and

when he does, Kenton will be there to observe. They know to contact me here,' Lowry said.

'Observe? I want more than observation, Nick. You're not birdwatching now,' the chief said jocularly.

Lowry loosened his tie as the chief ushered him into the lounge to be affronted by loud music and Antonia clapping and singing.

'You told me she wasn't drinking?'

'That was two weeks ago, at the beginning. Didn't last.' Sparks's wife was swaying enthusiastically to 'Sooliamon'. He lamented every time she cracked open the Pimm's – his prize Wharfedales took a caning from Neil Diamond. 'Turn the damn music down, Antonia! Jesus.'

Antonia made a play of pretending not to hear him. God, that was annoying. If she blew the speakers again, he'd –

'So you'll be converting that new basement gym into a nursery, then.'

'Trying to be funny?' Sparks didn't mind the jibe, now he'd shared the news of his impending fatherhood. 'That's not a bad idea; move her downstairs with the sprog . . . C'mon, let's sit on the patio. You'll be impressed.'

He led the way outside, where on the white, wrought-iron table lay the source of Antonia's merriment. A jug of Pimm's, already half-empty – a fortified Pimm's; Antonia had left the vodka bottle out. 'Check that out!' He pointed proudly to a bird feeder hanging off a lower branch of a eucalyptus.

'Never thought I'd see that.' Lowry smiled. 'What do you get?'

'Don't ask me. Sparrows? And a little blue and yellow one. Putting seed out is one thing, knowing what they are is something else.'

Sparks was pleased with Lowry's reaction. He wanted the man in a good mood; Antonia had asked a female friend over, an invitation she had kept from him until the last minute. Inwardly Sparks was still furious – he would certainly never have agreed to any ridiculous notion of matchmaking. He had absolutely no interest in other people's love lives, let alone trying to make introductions. The situation was exacerbated by guilt over his recent contact with Jacqui, which he felt no better about with time. Lowry himself never spoke about his current situation, and all that existed was a tacit understanding that he lived apart from his wife – whether he was dating, Sparks had no idea and he'd no reason to ask. For now though, if he was to survive this torturous evening, he needed to blot out all that had gone on before and turn his attention to Lowry, chatting away about blue tits and how they were endangered.

'Is that so? How interesting,' he grinned.

Sparks had zero interest in birds, and thought it bizarre that a man such as Nick could take up such a pursuit. Still, the man was boxing tomorrow, his first this year: feathers couldn't be all that bloody interesting, after all. The doorbell rang. Sparks looked gloomily into his gin and tonic. Lowry stopped talking abruptly.

'Let me get you a top-up?' Sparks offered, downing his

own and taking the other's glass before receiving an answer. 'Don't go anywhere.'

Lowry should have questioned his boss's uncharacteristic cordiality right away. Instead he was lulled in. He'd been amused by Sparks's almost-comic wardrobe; the chief would be less out of place on the set of *Daktari*. It had softened him towards the man. Little did Lowry think that three were to become four. He heard an unfamiliar female voice enter the house and froze. Cogs ticked. He was effectively single. Here was a woman alone. Oh God . . .

Now Jaccqui was gone, he lived the life of a bachelor, a fact that only recently became real to him at night alone in bed. It was true that since Kate Everett had crossed his path, a stoic calm had been unbalanced slightly. But that had been contained, and by day, his situation was never spoken of. To be confronted by his circumstances openly here, in a social situation with Sparks of all people, was hard to compute. He would just have to front it out, as though handling a case interview – no emotional display was required.

In they came, Antonia and a woman in her early thirties with Sparks himself bringing up the rear, fidgeting and posturing, not knowing what to do with his hands (Lowry had seen him like this before, often in Merrydown's company). It was clearly Antonia's idea, obviously not something Sparks would sign up to – Lowry could at least take comfort in that. Usually the dynamics between them were such that an unease in one of them prompted calm in the other but Sparks's disquiet did not prevent Lowry bowing slightly too formally when introduced to the new arrival.

Becky Adams was not what he would have expected of a friend of Antonia's, had he given the matter any thought. The woman had mousy-coloured hair, which she wore in a half-hearted loose perm, and introduced herself in a low husky voice that one would expect of a seasoned smoker of twice her years. She couldn't have been more different from their hostess, with her polished blonde bob and high clipped tones. She did have blue eyes like her friend, a sharper blue than Antonia's, standing out against clean skin and outlined needlessly by heavy mascara. As she smiled between puffs on a cigarette, absorbing news of Antonia's pregnancy, he noticed she wore no make-up apart from underneath her eyes, and that her hair was damp. Just out of the shower? Running late? The detective in him was switched on, if not yet the male.

31

8.40 p.m., High Street, Colchester

The high street was quiet. The town centre rarely roused itself on weekday nights before Thursday. Parking the car on the lip of George Street, they made their way casually down the cobbled street towards the snooker club. They might strike passers-by as a couple on a date; he in Levi's and a white T-shirt and her in an orange and yellow dress and sandals. Perhaps returning from a week on the Costa Brava, judging by the sun-kissed faces (even Gabriel had some colour; Kenton thought her glowing).

Kenton pushed open the door to allow his colleague in first. She pulled her ID out of her handbag. The man behind the desk shook his head. He had a small black-and-white portable TV on in the entrance booth from which his interest did not stray. Still light outside, it was taking Kenton several seconds to adjust to the dingy club interior; his eyes were dry after the hour floating around on his board at Mersea, sore with salt water. Apart from the lights hung over the table, there were sporadic wall lights, whose sole purpose was to illuminate the *'Please Do Not Smoke Over The Table'* signs.

He'd been here before, during the day, where players on the dole managed to drag out a single game all afternoon. The evening had a different vibe altogether, serious young players striding around the tables purposefully.

'There.' Gabriel led the way. Four men in T-shirts, lean but toned, had clocked them for police. Nobody moved as they waited for a player to take his shot. A blond man in his twenties sized up the white ball, cigarette pursed between lips, eyes tight, cue sliding back and forth under his chin, then a white blur across the table. The pink smacked across the corner pocket.

The man rose from the table, and removed his cigarette from his lips. 'Tch, tch.' He shook his head. 'You made me miss that shot. Could lose me the game. Gonna cost you.' He motioned towards Gabriel with the cue.

She took a step forward into the rectangle of light. 'Maybe if you took your cigarette out before taking a shot, you might see clearer what you're trying to–'

He moved into her personal space. He was shorter than her but only just. 'What do you want, copper?'

'We're keen to have a word with Edward Hoare. Might that be you?' The cotton of Kenton's shoulder brushed her bare arm as he asserted himself into the situation. The man's head inclined to the left, where his pals loitered in the dark behind the side of the snooker table.

'Might be, might not. Don't you know who you're after?'

'Name, rank, serial number, Mike,' said a voice.

The light over the table then went off and she couldn't see Kenton. She turned, and the next second an elbow was in her shoulder blade and she was on the ground. She pushed up quickly from the viscous carpet but felt the butt of a cue in the small of her neck.

Now outside, Kenton had the man pinned to the wall, but only just. The well-rounded army shoulders were proudly defiant; trim though the man was, Kenton had the weight.

'Why'd you run?'

'Police never bring you luck. Or are you gonna ask me on a date?'

'Michael Hoare.'

'How do you know that?' the soldier's jokiness evaporated.

'Small town. Seen your cousin?'

'What cousin?'

'You could end up in trouble if you don't cooperate.'

'Really? What, stick me under a sun lamp until I talk? I'll end up like you!' he laughed. Anger surged through Kenton. No matter how hard he tried, he couldn't inflect any menace in his voice and people took the piss. He glanced away briefly, sighed, then punched the soldier hard in the gut, winding him. As the man crumpled against the wall, he moved away and noticed a blue motorbike stashed down the side alley, alongside a large steel bin, as though left for the dustmen, with helmet dangling from the handlebars. Hoare had quickly regained himself, and straightening his T-shirt, said loudly, 'Maybe I was wrong, policemen are getting better looking.' Gabriel had emerged from the club doorway. 'You're a bit of all right in the daylight, luv.'

Kenton swallowed. They should have waited in the car, they'd not have lost him then.

'That his bike?' Kenton said, pulling his attention away from Gabriel.

'He's gone.' Hoare lit a cigarette, the punch all but forgotten. The army made them tough, Kenton thought. 'Had a few sherberts, 'adn't he. Be crazy to hit the road on that death trap . . . What do you want with Eddie, anyway – he's not been out a day, yet? Even for him it's going some to get in trouble *that* quick.'

8.45 p.m., Creffield Road, Lexden

'I love the summer, such a lovely garden,' Becky proclaimed confidently as they all stepped out onto the patio. Lowry waited for more; with her dark jeans and black long-sleeved top, he wouldn't mark her down as a sun-worshipper. She moved to the trellis fixed to the garden wall, as if to smell the roses, but retreated as though their fragrance was off-putting. She returned with a crooked smile, looking beseechingly towards their hostess. She was nervous. The brave announcement had no substance.

'Glorious, isn't it?' Antonia swept to the rescue, examining her own handiwork as if for the first time. 'Shame we don't get the sun at this time.'

'It's perfectly fine,' Sparks said sharply. 'Maybe if you had more clothes on you'd be more comfortable.'

'Don't be such a bore – come help me with the fondue.' She tapped his khakied rump, motioning him inward, giving Lowry a playful wink. Lowry placed his empty glass on the table. He shook his head in amusement. He'd forgotten how fast Antonia neutralised the station chief.

'She's adorable,' Becky said quietly.

'Yes, she is. Where did you two meet?'

'Antonia plays netball for the Lexden ladies ... You look surprised?'

'Not at all, what she lacks in height she makes up for in energy. I know her to be a first-class sailor, but netball is a new one on me. So you're a neighbour?'

She shook her head. 'Teach at the girl's school round the corner. But live in town, on Roman Road.' There was a lilt of an accent he couldn't place.

'I know it, at the back of the castle. Very nice. There's a second-hand bookshop just opened near there, on East Hill.' He'd picked up *The Peregrine* there only last week.

'And you?'

'Great Tey.'

'Where's that?'

'A parish village five miles west of here.'

She considered this, then asked why there. He told her about his boyhood in Fingringhoe and the move later into town when he was a teenager. He did not say this was due to his father's departure or that it was to a council estate.

'And as an adult I moved back out of town; a bit of distance between me and work – '

'Is that a good thing?'

'For me, yes.'

He realised he was repeating what he'd told Kate Everett and suddenly stopped feeling self-conscious. Nevertheless, she seemed satisfied and proceeded to explain that she herself was from the south coast, a place called Rye, and asked whether he had heard of it – he had. The harbour was popular for birdwatchers, but he drew the line at going into his hobbies. She went on, describing the place and the connection to the writer Henry James; she taught English, not P.E. as he had imagined. Sparks reappeared laughing with Antonia, evidently relaxed now. The pressure off, Lowry sunk into the evening and allowed himself to unwind too. Had he known this was on the cards he would have refused outright, but he was pleasantly surprised to find he was enjoying himself and Becky Adams's company.

32

9 a.m., Thursday, Queen Street HQ

Edward Hoare's evasion of the police the previous night was having its full repercussions today. Sparks was incensed, and Kenton was taking the wrath of the chief's disappointment solo. Lowry had yet to appear this morning. Sparks paused to take his tea. Kenton thought him impossible at times, for a man so senior – he leapt to conclusions, and had not a pragmatic bone in his body. How did he ever rise to the level of station chief?

Sparks, as of this morning, was utterly convinced that Hoare shot Christopher Cliff. The fact that they had not been able to find the man on his first day of freedom did not mean he was guilty; it's not as if he'd made off to the Continent. Kenton had been warned by Granger on his way up that the chief was hungover, meaning he had a shorter fuse than usual and was even less susceptible to reason.

'How could you lose him? I mean, how? He's just a kid.' He

banged the desk so hard Kenton wondered if Sparks might not crack the ancient floorboards and send them both thundering to the floor below.

'We were only to watch him, not frighten him, so we've not lost him as such,' Kenton said evenly.

'Oh, no?' Sparks said, eyebrows raised to heights previously unwitnessed – his forehead concertinaed so tight it looked like it might rupture. 'Where is he then, under here?' He ducked dramatically to peer under his desk, white shirt riding up, revealing unsightly sprouts of dark hair from his trousers' waistband.

'He won't have gone far on a 50cc moped.' This was Lowry's belief, at least. 'These unrestricted bikes are quick but you'd not want to go much further than Chelmsford or Ipswich –'

'What is the matter with you? I mean *really*?'

'I'm sorry, sir?'

'Why aren't you . . . I don't know,' he gesticulated airily, 'an engineer or in the civil service. No, not even they'd tolerate hair like that . . .'

'There's no need to get personal,' Kenton said, touching the curls at the back of his head on reflex. 'I'm not sure what your problem is, when I was simply trying . . .'

Sparks leant forward, knuckles resting on the desk. 'My problem is you. You and your pointless observations; *these unrestricted bikes*,' he mimicked in a plummy tone. 'I don't give a frog's fanny whether you can get to fucking Timbuktu on a lawnmower.'

Kenton remained silent.

'The *point* is, you don't know a thing, not one single thing that's going through that young man's head. Do you?'

Kenton opened his mouth to speak, then wisely chose not to and instead shook his head.

'Exactly. So listen.' The chief eyeballed him menacingly. 'See, there's a very big difference between some posh twat just out of university whose biggest worry is what gay-colour sports car Mummy is going to buy him, and the kind of stuff in the mind of some thieving git just out of borstal. Now I don't know what's in the kid's head either, but I'd imagine his thoughts might be on getting pissed up, getting his leg over, or maybe robbing a bank. Who knows?' He appeared to relax, sitting back in his chair, fingers forming a rooftop. 'But what I do know is that the very last thing on his mind is the level of comfort afforded by a Yamaha Fizzy. If he's got a bird out in bloody Ipswich, and he's not had a shag in a year, he might just be prepared to live with a sore arse for thirty miles. See what I mean?'

'Sir.' The jibe about the car was unfair; he'd sold the orange Spitfire . . .

'And if you hadn't lost him, then we might very well have asked, eh? And you're also overlooking the possibility that he might have ditched the bike in favour of some other mode of transport.'

'Sir?'

'The bike was left behind by the bins, correct?'

'Yes, his army chums said he'd had a few drinks and . . .'

Sparks shook his head. 'We'll gloss over whether you're a gullible prat allowing yourself to be fobbed off by a bunch of squaddies for now and focus on the possibility that Edward Hoare murdered Cliff. Now, if the bike was in the barn at Fox Farm, he'd have had to use some other means of getting from borstal to Suffolk and back?'

They were talking at cross purposes.

'Was the bike there, by the snooker hall, this morning?' he asked.

'Err . . .'

'Err what?'

'I don't know . . .'

'Might it be worth checking? Or shall we continue having the whole division on the lookout for a bike that as far as we know is no longer operative, eh?'

'Sir.'

'And don't listen to any old claptrap that squaddies tell you in the street. They are allergic to helping the civilian police.'

'Inspector Lowry paid a call to Captain Oldham; he's the one who tipped us off where to find Hoare in the first place.'

'The garrison's Himmler is hardly your run-of-the-mill soldier, is he? Glad he at least is playing ball. Talking of which, what are you like at chucking a javelin?'

The leap was an unusual one. 'Not since school, sir. There's not much call for any prowess in the sports of ancient Greece in today's world.'

'That, my boy, is where you are very much mistaken.'
'Sir?'

Sparks was sharp on the lad, but how else was he to impress on him the importance of thinking? Thinking in the right way – not in the fannying-around way that Kenton did. But the lad was fit and that was an asset. In a little over a week it was the force's county athletics tournament, a fundraising affair – with a competitive edge, of course. This year, at the last minute, it had been proposed they add a decathlon to the programme. The organisers had felt it needed livening up; watching a bunch of servicemen belt round a running track afforded the casual spectator limited amusement, so why not jazz it up with some discus, shot-put and javelin. Sparks was all for this as his side usually lost at running; the police team were by and large brawn and muscle and no match for the army whippets – this would redress the balance. That was in ten days' time. For now his immediate concern was the boxing match. This evening's fixture lay on his desk. He lifted the foolscap, dislodging cigarette ash he'd scattered there minutes before.

The police team was two points down; it all hung on the middleweight bout tonight, Lowry's return to the ring. Nick had had a few causal spars in the spring but this was the big one and he'd been in training. The army man's stats were laid out before him. He squinted at Granger's barely legible scrawl. Where the Dickens were his reading glasses? He had reached the stage where he needed them for everything, but lost his specs – both pairs – constantly. They can't both be at home . . . he slid open the desk drawer, knowing they wouldn't be there, as the phone rang.

'All right, Sparko.' A familiar north Essex accent greeted his ear.

Tony Pond, car dealer, minor thug. 'Pond, what joy can you add to my day?'

'The doc you wanted me to put the frighteners up.'

'Yeah.'

'Job done.'

Ah, yes, he'd forgotten about that. Good. That was one less thing to worry about. It then occurred to him that he could squeeze something out of this encounter.

'Tony, your standing in the community, as a businessman, how do you feel about that? Always room for improvement, eh? We're holding a meet-and-greet at Abbey Fields, some hobnobbing for bigwigs at the county athletics day. For a small donation, I might be able to squeeze you in, what do you say?'

'What, kneecapping doctors is on the up?'

Lowry was late into the Queen Street office.

He nodded to the PC on reception as he entered the building.

'Sir, a lady has called for you. A Mrs Bowles,' the officer called out as he hurried upstairs. He would call her back, but not right yet. The evening at Sparks's had been a surprisingly pleasant one. However, he had not slept until the small hours;

from the moment he left Lexden at gone eleven, his mind had been churning over the many thoughts and questions he'd avoided for months. He'd tossed and turned long into the night.

There was no denying Becky Adams was the catalyst. Antonia's friend had taken his thoughts and the evening in directions he hadn't anticipated. He'd settled on a grin-and-bear-it attitude. Sparks and he may go way back, drinking their way round town on more than one occasion, but it was just the two of them on the streets. Visits to each other's homes, with spouses in tow, was a different affair altogether. It happened rarely, and when it did, they kept it brief and softly formal. Lowry had factored in an hour or so to congratulate the couple on the news of their first child and gossip with the chief's gregarious wife, before bidding a polite farewell, getting out of there and picking up a curry on the way home. Instead the hours flew by, mostly in conversation with a woman he'd been set up with. Following his encounter with Kate Everett, he recognised he was in need of company, but when an opportunity presented itself he froze. As the dawn chorus sounded he still couldn't decide whether to see Becky Adams again or not. Yes then no then yes – and so it went.

He seated himself at his desk. Before him lay the usual paperwork, but such was the degree of his agitation he felt quite detached from it all. He lifted the first of two notes. From Kenton. 'WE LOST HIM.' Him? Of course; Hoare. Only then did it strike . . . he'd completely forgotten about the events of yesterday. What was in that punch? But he wasn't drunk last night – or not that bad, at least he managed to drive home. He moved the various notebooks and files abstractly about the wooden surface as if reordering his mind, before rising to fetch a coffee. The second note was illegible and written in Sparks's scrawl, but he made out 'last night' – and judging from the exclamation marks was a reference to Kenton's failings, rather than his own success as a host. The chief had not suffered the same blackout as him – which ruled the punch out. Obviously the combination of lack of sleep and sudden self-awareness had disorientated him completely. He realised abruptly he had company.

'How was your evening?' Gabriel ventured.

'My evening? What about it?' Lowry said sharply. His desk was a mess. She had not picked the right moment to approach him. She noticed he hadn't shaved and his hair was askew. She must be bold if she was to get on in the world, not wilt at the first hint of opposition.

'You had to dash, missed all the excitement,' she persisted.

'Oh?' He placed a cigarette between his lips and rummaged in a drawer for matches, unaware that a bic lighter lay in front of his eyes on the desk.

His disorganisation goaded her curiosity. 'Did you have a nice time?'

'Fine, just fine,' he said, brushing away her question. Clearly he didn't want to talk about it. He picked up a pen to indicate the conversation was at a close.

She decided to change the subject. 'Can I ask you a question? Remember when we were in Coggeshall and I mentioned I'd been on a call there, the morning of the Fox Farm deaths?' She suddenly lost her nerve. 'No, no, you're too busy.' She rubbed her wrist; it really did hurt where she'd fallen yesterday and the feeling hadn't properly returned to her little finger.

Lowry took a long drag then lay the cigarette in an ashtray. He put down his pen and brought his hands to his face as though in prayer. After several seconds had elapsed, he resumed smoking. He had regained his equanimity; the shift was palpable. She was relieved but at the same time wondered what was troubling him.

'Fire away . . .' he said.

'The old lady that was spooked, she called again and asked for me in person. I'm not sure what to do. Fletcher thinks it's a job for social services . . . but I disagree. I certainly don't think the lady is batty.'

They stared at each other briefly, before Kenton entered the office.

'We'll pay her a call now,' Lowry said.

'Are you sure?' She was surprised.

'Coggeshall is round the corner from Derrick. Edward Hoare's release justifies a visit, given he's not rolled up there so far and we can't keep a constable in the bushes for ever. If

Hoare is in town he may be there for some time. You never know, perhaps he has severed all ties with ol' Roger . . .'

'*If*,' Daniel grunted to himself. She turned to see him arrive and flump behind his desk, a face like thunder. Lowry ignored his colleague's dark mood and instead asked him to continue enquiring in the centre of town for any information on Hoare. They had to pick up the trail from last night. Kenton grumbled assent.

'What's up with your hand?' Lowry said to Gabriel, getting up from the desk. He intended they leave at once.

'Oh, I fell yesterday in the snooker hall – or was pushed over, to be more precise.'

She had his full attention now. 'All did not go according to plan? Right, you can tell me what happened in the car.'

33

10.15 a.m., Thursday, Coggeshall Road, Feering

Seeing that Gabriel had hurt her hand had jolted Lowry back to the here and now. As the Saab hummed along the tight green country lane he listened to her recount the sequence of events that followed his departure last night. They – or to be precise, *Kenton* – had been impatient and had them wasting time traipsing through the Lodge, all the while Edward was playing snooker. When they finally followed up on the tip-off, they encountered some agro with a bunch of off-duty soldiers – among them, an abrasive Michael Hoare.

'These things happen. If he's not gone to ground, we'll find him,' Lowry remarked. The fresh air of the countryside had allowed him to regain his grip. The warm breeze blowing through the Saab window had softened the edges of his tiredness. Essex summers always could catch him out with their unexpected beauty.

And the home of one of the county's most notorious characters, Roger Derrick, slipped unobtrusively into that landscape.

The long tree-lined driveway to Derrick's place was on a gradual slope. The contour of the land dipped away from the road and most of the houses were hidden from view as a result. The Blackwater River ran silent and unseen behind them. How Derrick had made this much money was a mystery, but whatever it was, it was certainly more than laundering Bejam bags full of banknotes through dodgy antiques. The house was sizeable but not ostentatious and the pale stonework acted as camouflage in the willows, like a big cat blending with the Savannah. If it weren't for the pink Rolls-Royce parked out front they'd not have seen the house until they were standing on the doorstep.

Lowry had persuaded Sparks to ease up on Derrick until they had a handle on Edward's role in all this. Sparks's bullying for an arrest over the past weeks had pushed the man to the brink; his lawyers were primed for a harassment charge. Lowry had received word that the constable watching Derrick's place was to be repatriated to the village station – they could not afford to have him out there another day on the off-chance – so it was time to bite the bullet. After all, he could justifiably make enquiries in Feering as to Edward Hoare's whereabouts, given the kid had worked at one of Derrick's outlets. According to the local bobby, the antiques dealer was a benevolent uncle figure for the young village lads. Of course, this led to darker places when squared with his reputation round Colchester.

*

'Crikey, I heard them call him Lady Penelope at the station, now I see why,' Gabriel murmured, acknowledging the pink vehicle.

'Yep, the fairy is in situ.' Lowry pulled on the handbrake. Gabriel didn't like the way straight men referred to homosexuals; it struck her as base, unnecessary and a sign of fragile egos. She was surprised at Lowry; he did not strike her as that sort of policeman. Her aunt had warned her there were certain aspects to policing that were unpleasant. Some were what she labelled 'old-school affectations' deeply ingrained in the force – 'black or gay, no way' – which she had made her mission to stamp out. Likewise, she was determined to further the careers of female officers, who too often got stuck in the role of secretary or emotional mopper-upper. Perhaps Lowry was unconscious of what he was saying?

'Is it necessary to call him that?' she said.

Lowry paused opening the car door, which stopped mid-groan, like an animal being put down. 'We never say that to his face.'

'Oh, then I guess that makes it all right.'

And there he was, right on the doorstep.

'He doesn't look too pleased to see us,' she remarked.

'Sick to death of us, I'm sure.'

Derrick was upon them before the car door was shut, in yellow trousers, plaid waistcoat, and what appeared to be a mauve kimono and flip-flops.

'Now listen here! You simply can't harangue me all summer.'

Two men in denims appeared as if from nowhere; the one with a ponytail Lowry recognised from the shop in the village.

Lowry held up his hands.'Whoa. This is not about you.'

Derrick's round face sagged a little, perhaps in disappointment.

'We are here about Edward Hoare.'

'Ahhh . . . he must be out then.'

'You knew, of course.'

'That was his stepfather's doing, locking him up, not mine.'

'How much more do you know?'

Derrick signalled for his men to leave. 'Come inside.'

He led them through a spacious hallway punctuated with a large ornate clock, into an exotic drawing room – a large open space, with polished floor and huge bay windows looking out on a deep, verdant garden. Gabriel thought the room was charming. The walls were painted in an unobtrusive lime and tastefully adorned with artwork. A small piece was given plenty of space over the fireplace. She stepped closer: a beautifully lush still life – the glistening grapes and raspberrys had a hyperreal texture; the peaches made her blush.

'The country's foremost painter of fruit, my dear.'

'I'm sorry?' She was ignorant, but intrigued.

'Edward Ladell, 1821-66, and an Essex man to boot; born in Colchester. Mouth-watering, isn't it? There's another over here, see; this features taxidermy: a bird in a glass bubble. One could not strive for a more diametric study of still life, and yet the colours –' He left the sentence unfinished, and watched Lowry move to the bay window, unimpressed, considering what lay beyond. 'Of course I know Eddie, I know the family,' Derrick continued, effortlessly switching conversation. 'Christopher himself was a fan of taxidermy –' he nodded towards the painting while fixing a filterless cigarette to a long holder – 'the house contains several moth-eaten Victorian examples. I'm sure you're aware of the sort.' Lowry remained silent, waiting. 'If your brute of a commander could ease off, I might be able to explain, and be of help.'

'Do. If you know the family, how come Mrs Cliff has no recollection of you?'

'I know the menfolk, Inspector.' Derrick then proceeded to pace the room theatrically, while Lowry remained at the window, hands in pockets, weak light catching on the sheen of his pale grey suit.

'She's an artist herself. Are you sure you've not met her, given your own proclivity?'

'Pah, those abominable daubings of hers do not constitute anything close to satisfying my *proclivity*, Inspector.'

'So you *do* know her?'

'I know *of* her. Although I understand that your limited vocabulary might prevent your appreciating the difference.' Gabriel was impressed at Lowry's ability not to be goaded. After lighting his cigarette, Derrick continued, 'I met Christopher thirteen years ago, when he was filming in Suffolk. I have a gallery in Dedham, and he strolled in . . .'

'An art gallery.'

'Correct. At the time I had come into possession of a Gainsborough sketch of Borley Church and Christopher was keen to see it; a black-and-white chalk drawing – a rarity that will occasionally pop up around Sudbury. An American obsessed with the place paid a small fortune for it.' He paused for a languid toke on the cigarette. 'This was before the wife came on the scene.'

'When was that?'

'Oh, I don't know the exact date, '75? '76? This was an early location scout, wandering around Constable's Suffolk haunts; Flatford Mill, Dedham Lock, Willy's Cottage –'

'When did *you* meet Suzanne?'

'As I've said, I've never met her as such . . .'

'But you've been to the house on more than one occasion?'

'Twice briefly; had the wife been there?' He sighed. 'Who knows? Maybe? Inspector, you must understand Mrs Cliff is absorbed in her own world as much as the dearly departed was in his. The lady of the house is consumed with her own artistic talent, such as it is. Anyhow, after that first meeting I did not see Cliff again for many months, until they came back to film, but it was over very quickly and then he moved on to the university to do background research, and there met his lovely wife.'

'This last meeting, to view the dresser, when was that appointment made?' Lowry asked.

'As I have said a great many times, I bumped into Cliff in Coggeshall, by the clock tower the week before.'

'And that was it?'

'I called in the evening to confirm the time, he was out, so I left a message with one of the girls ... Forgive me, but aren't you here to discuss Edward?' Composed as he was, talk of that morning clearly rankled.

Lowry was still at the window. 'Yes, we are. How did you happen to come across him?'

'I have a number of boys that run errands for me.'

'What sort of errands?'

'We're a bit removed out here on this road, and it's easier to get a lad on a bike to pedal to the shops for ciggies than it is get the Rolls out ... Coggeshall's not a big place, Inspector, and the boys are grateful to earn a few pennies.'

'I'm sure,' Lowry said, without sarcasm. This was what he expected.

'Edward had done this for a number of years. I trusted him and so once he left school, I offered him a job in the Kelvedon shop.'

'What about the Cliff girls?' Gabriel asked.

He shook his head. 'I can't say I've seen them in the village; they never leave the farm for all I know.'

'You didn't see them the morning you called, though?'

'No, but I heard them, caterwauling outside playing, as I've said to Chief Sparks more than once ... I spoke to one yesterday, as it happens.'

'Oh, regarding?'

'Having left it a suitable time and thinking myself no longer a suspect, I telephoned to ask whether Mrs Cliff would like me to alleviate her of the furniture her husband asked me to value.'

'And?'

'Very much so. The lady would be appreciative.' Odd that Suzanne Cliff had not mentioned this. 'I haven't seen Edward, however, if that's what you are after.'

'How do things stand between you and he?'

'He's been otherwise engaged, as you well know.'

'Yes, but are you still friends?' Lowry used the word lightly. 'Would he call on you now, for instance.'

'I'd like to think so. There is no animosity. I do believe, however, he wishes to spread his wings. Coggeshall, and what I have to offer, is not enough any more.'

Outgrown you, Lowry thought, but – was there a tie, still?

'Be a dear,' Lowry said straight, 'and let us know if Edward drops by; we're keen that he keeps his nose clean, that's all.'

'I shall make a note to do so, Inspector.' He moved towards the hallway. 'Will that be all? I am frightfully busy.'

Lowry, still at the window, eventually said in response, 'Do you have kingfishers out there on the river?'

34

10.15 a.m., Stockwell Street, Colchester town centre

'Some coppers were sniffing about last night, did they find you?' he heard Michael say. Eddie poked his head above the duvet to see Mike pulling on a white T-shirt on his way to the fridge. He felt the other side of the bed – Carole had slipped away at some stage in the night. 'The Red Caps must have put the police onto me.'

'Oh, sorry, no, I didn't notice . . .' Though of course he had – news that plain clothes had entered the Colne Lodge spread up the floors of the building like wildfire. He'd ducked out the back with Carole and headed for the squaddie boozer, the Bull. She worked there and got them both free drinks. 'Where did you end up?'

'In the Lodge trying to find you.' Mike swigged from a milk bottle and placed it heavily down on the tiny breakfast bar.

'I didn't stay long; it was a bit much – all that noise and video screens everywhere. That's all new.' He pushed himself up off the low bed, or futon. Whatever it was called, it was incredibly uncomfortable; a cheap version of a sofa bed. At least the borstal beds had springs. First night of freedom and it was his worst night's sleep in months. Mike placed slices of bread on the grill to make toast. Eddie had rolled up at the flat yesterday afternoon. Having quickly grown bored after a couple of games of snooker, he had left to find somewhere a bit livelier in the shape of the Colne Lodge.

'You're not supposed to register, or check in with them, are you?'

'Nah.'

'Then what would the Old Bill want?'

'I guess my mum must have panicked and called them?' he said, scratching his head. It was the only explanation he could think of.

'Christ, you've only been out half a day; what shit could you possibly have got up to?' He wouldn't let it go so easily.

'Are you signing up again?' Eddie was keen to switch subject. 'The army; are you going back?'

'Signing up? I never "signed out".'

'But you finished, and . . .'

'Finished a tour, and six years. But in two weeks, open service.'

'Meaning?'

'Meaning, I'm not tied, like before.'

'My mother is on at me incessantly to join,' he said, pulling out a stool from the breakfast bar.

Eddie had telephoned Michael the morning of his release.

His cousin had said he'd be playing snooker that afternoon. The pair had not really spoken since Eddie had rolled up yesterday evening and proceeded to go on a bender. He'd tried to pace himself; no alcohol in a year meant he felt fuzzy and dehydrated all at the same time. He was certain he'd kept his own counsel and said nothing of what had occurred at Fox Farm.

'Sorry about your stepdad, man,' Mike said, 'must be hard, weeks before getting out. I know you didn't get on, but all the same. How're your sisters taking it?'

'Tough.' He shook his head, remembering the row yesterday. 'I don't wanna talk about it now . . . Look, I need to get straight. Will be easier on the old dear if I'm in employment, know what I mean? Less for her to worry about. I like the idea of seeing the world . . . a bit further afield than Londonderry, but if you think it's a good idea, mate, then that's what I'll do.' He watched Mike butter the toast then slide a piece over in Eddie's direction.

'You can't pick and choose, matey – if they say Northern Ireland, then off you go –' Mike bit into his toast – 'and it'll be a bit more than a tussle in a snooker hall to contend with,' he said reflectively. 'The micks are a different ballgame altogether.'

Eddie wondered what exactly had elapsed after he left the snooker hall last night. And if the Red Caps put the police onto Mike in the first place, they'd certainly find out about a 'bit of a tussle' no matter how lightly his cousin dismissed it.

Eddie thought he better skedaddle. Besides, he was boracic – he'd spent what little money he had and sponged the rest off Carole. Much as he'd rather not, he'd have to see Roger ... If the police knew about Mike, then what else? Did they know the connection between Roger and his father? What had his mother said? Fuck it, he'd have to chance it, he may as well be back inside than be skint outside ...

10.45 a.m, East Street, Coggeshall

'You didn't warm to Roger Derrick?' Gabriel said. In fact, she thought Lowry rude, if one could levy that criticism at a policeman investigating a possible suspect, that is.

Lowry rounded the Saab up out of Derrick's property into Feering Road. 'You did, evidently.'

'He was quite charming.' This was not what he wanted to hear. 'I thought he gave a reasonable account of his relationship with the family, yes.'

'Flannel.'

'That's just his manner.'

'He didn't amass a small fortune cavorting through life like that. It's all a facade, like his shop.'

'He invited us into his house, and seemed eager to help.'

'All the sooner to get shot of us. Well, at least you can understand how Cliff was taken in by him so easily.'

'I suppose, though he did seem to have a pretty well-informed impression of the Cliffs.'

'You mean criticising the mother? He'll have a good idea how things stand from the boy.'

She wouldn't press it any further; he'd always have all the answers. As the road narrowed, the fields disappeared and the trees arched above them to give a tunnel effect.

'You'll probably think we're wasting our time visiting Mrs Harris,' she said sourly. 'Some dotty old woman who hears things that go bump in the night.' The road abruptly forked into a junction ahead. She hadn't seen it, but he clearly knew the area; she remembered his village was not far from here.

'The situation with Derrick isn't clear-cut,' he said. They proceeded to trundle slowly down into Coggeshall itself. A park stretched up beyond an old red-brick wall. Vast yew trees reached skywards and children playing underneath were dwarfed by comparison, darting around like spirits from a fairy tale. 'CID is different from Uniform, the same job but different.'

'Really.'

She readied herself. She was well used to his condescending lectures by now, and bowed her head to consult her nails. Had he forgotten that she was the one who had linked Edward to Derrick in the first place?

'On the beat, by and large, things are as they seem. A bag snatch, an assault, fighting on the terraces; and likewise, an officer is visibly identified by a uniform. But behind the scenes, off the street, nothing is obvious. Nothing need conform to the outside world's perception. Don't be lulled by the surroundings. Fine art does not necessarily make a fine man.'

Lowry stopped the car in a garage forecourt.

'I agree,' said Gabriel eventually, knowing she couldn't win. 'And I've heard the case against this Derrick for weeks, not least from Chief Sparks; the man could well be rotten to the core. The paintings were beautiful, though, and I was pleased to have seen them –' she lowered her voice – 'and that's something I wouldn't have seen on the beat as a policewoman.'

'Sorry, am I being patronising?'

'No, I know I'm still green.' She sighed. 'What are we doing here?' A large man in a vest with hairy shoulders approached the vehicle.

'Getting the door seen to. I don't hear it myself but I know you do – you wince every time.' He smiled broadly. 'And I agree, one must enjoy beauty where one can; it's not on tap in this line of work.' He smiled long enough for her to note his uneven teeth; she'd not noticed before. She remembered him losing a tooth back at the start of the year, and it occurred to her he never opened his mouth more than absolutely necessary.

Gabriel waited by the car while he consulted with the mechanic, feeling awkward that he was fixing the car on her account. Having been short with him before, she decided to refrain from judging or weighing up every remark, and focus on the situation at hand. He'd done nothing untoward to her, didn't leer like those oafs in the station and was only trying to do the job. So what if his manner was condescending – that she could deal with.

*

Lowry was surprised by Gabriel's take on Derrick. He thought her sharper and expected her to see beyond the end of her nose. She was clever by all accounts, but intelligence and perspicuity did not necessarily go hand in hand any more than sophistication and clean living, as evidenced by Roger. These facts seemed obvious to Lowry, who was afflicted with none of these qualities.

Eventually they arrived at the terraced house on East Street. It was cool inside, the ancient brickwork and the lack of windows shielding it from the sun. Lowry listened to Mrs Harris's story of disturbing noises. He wasn't superstitious but many who lived in this area were. The elderly lady went on, explaining again about the moving ornaments; there were several china owls and woodland statues on the bookshelves, but as he reached for a small fox she shooed him away and pointed towards the top shelf. Lowry reached for the wooden figurine up there – a laughing Buddha.

'Where on your travels did you pick this cheeky fellow up? India?'

'Lawd no, just down the road.'

There were a handful of antiques shops on East Street – including Derrick's.

'Unusual-looking, isn't it?'

'Mischievous, I'd say,' Gabriel said behind him.

'Quite.' He replaced the item, thinking the grin on it less cheeky and more a malevolent leer.

'You've moved him, Mrs Harris?' said Gabriel. 'He was lower down when we visited before.'

'Told you; sick of him following me around.'

'What attracted you to it in the first place? It's not in keeping with your other trinkets – the owls and horse brasses and so forth. If it gives you the willies, why not toss it out?'

'My daughter gave it to me for my birthday. I've never liked it but you know how it is, I didn't want to offend her.'

'How do you know she got it on East Street then?' Gabriel asked.

'Her fella was working there; they live a few doors down.'

Lowry took in the room. The place was authentically very old; the chimney breast said it all – irregular handmade bricks and cement inset with oyster shell. He noticed deep scratch marks on the thick Tudor beam above the hearth. Short vertical scars, as if made by a prisoner striking off the days. He ran his fingers lightly across them; from his childhood in Fingringhoe he knew these to be witches' marks, carved there by the dwellers to ward off evil spirits. He caught Mrs Harris's eyes, alive with worry in her shrivelled face. Again, he brushed his hand over the beam.

'A lovely chimney, all original, I bet. Now, let's have a look upstairs, shall we?' He led the way.

Lowry stepped up on the foot stool and peered into the loft. The entrance to the roof was clear and free of cobwebs.

'When was the last time you were up here?'

'Nobody's been up in years; my son-in-law put the records up there, as I said to the young lady here before.'

'Would you have a torch?'

'I've—' Gabriel made to go, but Lowry silenced her with a light touch to the shoulder. The woman shuffled off down the stairs. 'What? she hissed.

'Someone's been up there.'

'Yes, me.'

'You'd expect to find cobwebs and fragments of roof timbers falling out when lifting the hatch. Trust me, someone has been up here more than just once in five years.'

'Oh.'

'Mind out.' Lowry levered himself up. Once in the roof cavity, he realised how cramped it was, with the water tank and low support timbers taking up most of the space. His eyes adjusted slowly. Gabriel reached through the opening and offered him the torch. The roof beams were not boarded, so he was mindful of his step as he reached down. Mrs Harris believed she heard noises emanating from above her bedroom, which was at the back of the house and behind the chimney. With the torch beam on, he lurched from one roof truss to the next, steadying himself with his free hand on the overhead beams as he moved towards the rear of the house. Once there, he found nothing other than insulation material. Instinct told him that someone had been here probably within the last five days, a sense that the otherwise-dormant space had been disturbed, more than the lack of trailing cobwebs (there were a few) . . . he wasn't sure how, though. He spun the beam round; her roof space was not separated from the roof space of her neighbours. Evidently it stretched across at least two other properties. Though he couldn't see the end of the wall, his beam did catch some fibre, hanging from a splinter where some material had snagged. Cobwebs lacked the artificial presence of man-made fluff such as polyester. If a person were up here during the day, anything more than a T-shirt would be sweltering, but at night maybe an extra layer was necessary, if they were up here for any length of time.

'Do you think she's loopy?' Gabriel asked once outside in the street again, shielding her eyes from the sun's glare.

'Nope. But I think someone's put the frighteners on her.'

35

11 a.m., Feering Road

'Tsk, tsk, Edward, you have only just missed the constabulary.'
Derrick stepped back, allowing him into the house. 'So you're
aware they'd like a word.'

Eddie removed the helmet. 'What the bloody hell do they
want with me?' he said angrily.

Derrick made his way through to the drawing room and
Edward followed. What the devil was he wearing; something akin to a woman's Japanese dressing gown. Roger's
bare feet slapped across the wooden floor. Eddie placed his
helmet on the hall clock table, and in doing so a sparkle
under the enormous Russian timepiece caught his eagle
eye.

'Anyway,' he said loudly. 'I know they're looking. A friend
told me last night.' Roger was resting one hand on the door
frame, his silk sleeve sliding down, revealing a thin, lily-white
arm at odds with the fleshy puce ball that was his head.
'Believe me, I have no idea what they want,' he continued

apologetically. 'I've not been out five minutes – if they were that keen, might as well stop me at the prison gate.'

'Well, quite.' Roger turned and continued into the drawing room, offering Edward a cigarette, which he declined. 'Have you been to your mother's?'

'Yes, but . . .'

'Did you perhaps give her cause to telephone the police?'

'I was quite upset.'

'About what?' he said with feigned alarm.

'That's a bit bloody callous – I might not have liked Christopher but I wouldn't wish him dead . . .'

Derrick studied him carefully. 'No? The police haven't left me alone since the old boy topped himself.'

That was rich; Roger had five years on Christopher easily. He cleared his throat. 'Why? What do they want with you?'

'Your father wished to sell some furniture – that wormy timber in the kitchen that clashed with all the German steel your mother had installed. We'd arranged I'd drop in at eight on Monday morning.'

Eddie sighed and paced the room; they'd been doing the house up for ever – they were replastering the walls when he was sent away.

'Go on.'

'Christopher had an ancient Polish deer rifle out, cleaning it in preparation for a trip to the Highlands. I believe your stepfather was dead minutes after I departed.'

Eddie swallowed hard and stared at the two men humping

a stone statue across the back garden, a figure with wings. An angel.

'They think you did it?'

'Undoubtedly. My fingerprints are on the gun, they've every reason to be suspicious.'

'So why are you still here?' As the men adjusted the figure on a plinth, he saw it was in fact some sort of imp.

'They don't have a motive and the brute of a superintendent bungled it – my solicitor made a harassment plea.' Eddie smelt Roger's sickly cologne before he felt the man's manicured fingers on his shoulder. 'Beautiful, isn't he? Mephistopheles.'

'Yeah, cute. My sisters told me you did it too.'

'Hmph. The three little witches,' he said snidely, attention on the statue. Eddie had not once heard Roger make a remark about a woman that wasn't derogatory or unpleasant.

'Did you?'

Roger didn't answer. Edward's head still felt heavy, and his throat was dry. He moved away and turned to face the old queen. 'Roger, can you lend me a couple of quid?' Derrick's hand remained in mid-air. 'Just until I get my feet back on the ground . . .'

'And what's the plan to get your "feet on the ground"?'

'I'm joining the army,' he said, surprising himself. That was it, the decision made.

Derrick let out a small laugh. 'How vulgar. And you were such a delicate child before you went to that zoo . . . No, I refuse to believe it.'

'Straight up. Meeting Carole after her shift ends at three.'

'You won't be needing any more money from me, if you're in the services.'

'Can I have a glass of water? I'm really thirsty.'

Derrick huffed in resignation. 'Too much to drink last night?'

'Just a quiet few in the Bull, with Carole.'

'How sweet,' he said, sounding bitter. 'Come into the parlour.'

'I don't have time, I need to . . .' Do what, prepare? Now he had said it out loud, the army felt real – he was signing up. He needed to get out of here, away from Roger, Feering, Kelvedon. All that was the past. He'd even settle for Northern Ireland. He didn't need Roger's handouts.

'I have something for you, something you'll find useful.'

Edward grudgingly followed Derrick into the kitchen. As they passed the marble table in the hall, he pocketed the sparkling object that lay underneath the onyx plinth of the Romanov carriage clock. He caught his reflection in a gilt-edged mirror and that of Roger's back as he passed through into the kitchen.

'Here.' Roger picked up a large brown envelope from the table and handed it to him.

'What's this?'

'Your stepfather wanted you to have it.'

Inside was an inch of bank notes. He didn't believe it. The short fat bastard must have felt guilty for having him sent down.

'Wha . . . ?'

'Christopher gave it to me the morning he shot himself. He knew a belligerent, stubborn, resentful young soul like you would not take it from him, and he realised you'd come sniffing round here when you ran short on cash.' Roger poured iced water into a tumbler. 'As, apparently, did the police,' he said wearily.

Eddie couldn't believe his luck. 'But what if the police had seen it?'

'What of it? We've nothing to hide, have we?'

1 p.m., Crouch Street, Colchester

Kenton had scoured all the pubs from the snooker club to the Colne Lodge and back again, which was near double figures, and nobody had seen Edward Hoare the previous night. All were adamant he'd not been in. How they could be so certain, he didn't know.

By the time he'd returned to Crouch Street where he had started, the door to the Bull was invitingly open and he decided to stop and have a quick pint. The surly landlord who'd reluctantly answered him an hour ago was nowhere to be seen. Two barmaids were now installed behind the beer pumps. He pulled up a stool; he never drank in here. He'd made a pig's ear of things. If only he'd listened to Gabriel last night they'd know exactly where Hoare was now. At least she was not judgemental; in fact, he and Jane were getting on rather well. Even though he'd failed to impress her with his prowess on the water, the windsurfing incident had pulled them closer together, although he worried it was because she felt sorry for him. He'd been out on the water the previous weekend, but there hadn't been a breath of wind and the tide had carried him nearly up to the port. It had taken two hours to lug that aircraft carrier of a board back. His face was tight with sunburn and his palms raw from pulling the uphaul rope to lift the blasted sail out of the water. He tried to clench his fists now and grimaced in pain; blisters stung every time he closed his hands. No doubt about it: this was the most grueling activity he'd ever tried his hand at. The guy in the shop had said the sport had a steep learning curve; little did he realise he'd need to be Spider-Man to climb the first level. He was still shattered; every muscle in his body twinged. The worst of it was, he was fighting tonight. Maybe if he bound them up? He lay both hands palms up on the beer mat.

'You're a picture,' said a plump barmaid in a fifties-style pinafore dress and beehive hairstyle, sauntering up to the beer pumps. 'Why so glum, eh? Look like you've been away; you've a lovely tan.'

The girl must have been nineteen. She had bright red lipstick to match her check dress and hairband. She gave her name as Carole. He reached in his pocket for his spectacles, but abruptly refrained as his fingers made contact with the plastic rim – glasses revealed him as the nerdy policeman.

'Hard-earned,' he forced a smile. 'I'm teaching myself to windsurf, but it's like forced labour; catch a healthy colour without really trying. Just a bugger it hurts so much.'

'Where'd you do that? Sounds fun. Like sailing but standing up, innit?'

He tried to explain the rudiments, using gestures. The barmaid was curious, or at least made a show of being interested. He ordered a pint of Olde English, which slipped down without notice. Cider combined with the banter released the tension of the past few days.

'You wanna try wearing suncream and then in the evening rub some aftersun in; you'll soon go a lovely colour. My fella's just come back burnt to a crisp like you. He didn't have none neither.'

'In the forces, is he?' It was, after all, a forces' public house.

Carole leant forward, hands on the pumps, and whispered, '*Nah – borstal.*'

Kenton hoped his surprise didn't show. They can't be that many released on a Wednesday in August surely. 'Oh I see, outside a lot, was he?'

'Pickin' fruit,' she rolled her eyes, and rocked back on her heels, 'in Suffolk, like. Can I getcha another?'

'Please.' He slyly checked the bar; a woman in her mid-fifties down the far end was drying glasses on autopilot. The landlord was nowhere to be seen – though Kenton didn't drink here he was sure he could be clocked as a copper by an experienced eye.

'I'm a bit older than 'im but it really toughened 'im up, ya know.'

'Where's your fella now?'

'He's gone to sort some business. We were in 'ere last night. Celebrating.'

He counted the sixty pence as slowly as possible, trying to think what he could possibly say without giving the game away. 'Nice,' was all he could think.

'He wants to join the army, like his cousin. 'Ere, what do you do?'

'I . . . Actually, funny you ask, I was thinking of joining up too.' The lie was instantaneous, flowing out as quick as the cider went in. 'I've been in a spot of bother myself.'

'Hey, maybe you could go with Eddie! Be lovely to go with a friend.'

'That's a fabulous idea, when can I meet him?'

'Later today? He's picking me up when we shut at three.'

Kenton nodded in agreement and the girl bobbed off to serve another customer. After three pints, Kenton thought he'd drawn as much info as he'd get. Returning from a visit to the gents, he thought he recognised two of the men from the snooker hall. He pulled out his glasses. Yes, it was them talking to the barmaid. Excitedly he slipped out the back door to wait until three.

36

1.35 p.m., Colchester General Hospital

Staff Nurse Jacqui Lowry entered the hospital to start a late shift. She was late. The summer was turning out to be a drag. She was unable to lie in at Trish's place when given the opportunity. She was woken at the crack of dawn by milk floats followed by a succession of trucks and lorries squeezing down the backstreets that constituted the Dutch Quarter. It may well be picturesque – the house was sixteenth-century, Flanders style – but the sound ricocheted through the narrow, cobbled streets, and the walls offered no noise protection.

Still, as things in her life went, this was no big hassle. Until last week, she thought she was going to lose her job when her lunatic ex-lover threatened to complain about her 'professional misconduct'. Jacqui assumed Chief Sparks had swung into action; how, she didn't care to know. That her job was secure was all that mattered.

'Bugger.' She consulted the ward rota: she was in theatre.

2.30 p.m., Skye Green Fields near Feering

Eddie had stopped for a breather in a nearby farmer's field, to clear his head and get Roger's cologne out of his nostrils. He chucked his lid on the grass and sat down. Roger's care-free attitude was unnerving – he must be safe from the long arm of the law; had he paid them off? That's what he heard from boys in Hollesley Bay. Those that had fallen into the hands of a perv. If he had learnt one thing in there, it was just how widespread that sort of stuff was. More so than he ever imagined, and some abused boys had been driven to do crazier things than just stealing. At least no one could get to him in the army, and Michael would look after him. Eddie lay in the field gazing up at skylarks ascending. The reasons he'd be safer in the army were the same reasons he couldn't risk any nonsense getting there – the slightest whiff of an association with Derrick would screw his chances. It was one thing being in borstal – that would at least give him credit among the lads – and another being a pet to a known homo and God knows what else.

He'd make a fresh start, just as his mother wished. She'd be over the moon. The only thing that did trouble him were his sisters. They were blaming Roger for shooting Christopher, and that it served him right, the only mistake was Roger should have turned the gun on himself. Eddie had lost his rag, defending Roger. Roger didn't have it in him to shoot Christopher. Eddie believed his stepfather killed himself, and guessed his mother had stopped loving him. Not that Alice and Lucy would understand that. They were not in the real world, all that gobbledygook they messed around with. Roger always said they needed to get out more . . .

Out. Here he was. The warden was a kind man. He'd given him a glowing report. He even turned a blind eye to the night out in Woodbridge. That was before he was certain of what path to take, rebelling against authority. How lucky he'd been. Imagine being stuck in there again. He was straight – almost straight, anyway; some things were hard to resist. He reached inside his jeans pocket and pulled out the brooch he'd knicked off Roger's side table. The diamonds glinted in the sun. He reckoned it was worth a few quid. He nearly felt bad lifting it, after Roger gave him the envelope of cash – he didn't have to do that, after the old man croaked it . . . He shut his eyes, and the sound of skylarks took him back to when they first moved here. Things were different then. He wanted to give the country a go. It was the summer when they moved, the fields were alive with life. It was only in the long dark winter that resentment grew, and he longed for the city and his friends. He fell into Roger's clutches out of boredom.

As a boy on the farm, he found the skylarks mesmerising. Their trills reminded him of his grandfather's old wireless seeking a signal, and the way they rose vertically, they were nature's equivalent of a Harrier Jump Jet. He thought his childish wonder stupid now – a glaring invitation to every predator to come get them, taken out by a sparrowhawk, which

he'd witnessed once . . . He propped himself up on his elbows.
That was the last time he'd taken an interest in birds. And
birds reminded him of his crazy sisters, remembering the nests
he'd flung off the bedroom shelf yesterday. He didn't want to
think about any of that now. He had a fresh start, what with
the cash and the brooch. The piece of jewellery was an ugly
thing from the twenties, art deco or nouveau, he wasn't in
the game long enough to distinguish the period, but he was
savvy enough to spot a row of rose diamonds when he saw
one. As he had cash, he could afford to give it to Carole as a
present, in celebration, after he'd signed up . . .

2.55 p.m., Crouch Street, Colchester

Lowry, having picked up Kenton's message, had stopped at
Darnell's practice first before waiting outside the butcher's
shop beneath the accountancy firm, watching the Bull. Gabriel
remained at Queen Street wading through the telephone direc-
tory to pull out Wendy Harris's immediate neighbours. Lowry
strongly suspected someone had been crawling along the roof
cavity – there was no partitioning – to spook her; though
why, he couldn't even guess at this stage. He ground out his
cigarette; Kenton was nowhere to be seen at his own sting.
About to light another, he saw the young detective crossing the
street towards him, darting conspicuous glances left and right.

'Jesus, at least try to act normal,' Lowry muttered under his
breath, then, louder, 'Where the bloody hell have you been?'

'Boots, for some aftersun,' he beamed.

Lowry shook his head in disbelief. 'Incredible. How are we going to play this?' There was a whiff of alcohol on the younger man's breath.

'Shall I nip in just before they close?'

'No, you wait here. There's no need to blow your cover,' he said in mock seriousness. Suzanne had granted him access to the books; indeed urged him to go through them. He'd been through bank statements searching for anomalies and disappointedly drawn a blank. There were no irregular, large cash withdrawals. They also had access to banked cheques. Again nothing untoward, and nothing close to Derrick. The two thousand pounds, it seemed, was a one-off.

'Aha.' The noise of a motorbike heralded an imminent arrival before it rounded the corner into view. The time for surveillance was over. He'd tell the lad to check in at Queen Street and register his address; they'd present it as condition of his release.

The rider was in the process of loosening his helmet as Lowry tapped him on the shoulder.

'Couple of words, sunshine, if that's all right.' He flashed his badge. 'As a recent release from Hollesley Bay, we'd like you to drop by the station.'

Edward slumped back on his bike. He had his mother's features.

'Is that a matter for plain clothes?' the boy asked, sharply.

'It is if their father is shot shortly before their release.'

'Can't you question me here, then?'

Lowry saw people noticing. 'All right. Roger Derrick, know him?'

'Sort of.'

'Have you seen him since you were released?'

'No.' Anger flashed across the boy's features. He was lying.

'Are you sure?'

Edward Hoare sat on the bike, not uttering a word.

Lowry moved closer; this was not the best place to have this conversation. 'Please, it would be much easier if you could drop by the station. The street is not the place to discuss your father's death.'

Eddie wasn't listening. Bloody Roger had stitched him up. He must have noticed the brooch had gone and grassed him up to the Old Bill. Eddie should have kept his big gob shut; never told him about the army – he'd see that as rejection . . . shit, shit. This could go pear-shaped in a matter of seconds.

'Everything all right, Eddie?' Mike and his pals had emerged from the Bull.

'I'm being hassled by the police,' he said plaintively.

'Oh yeah?' Mike was an aggressive so-and-so, and easily wound up.

'I ain't dun' nothing. It ain't fair.' Eddie milked it; he needed to make a break and lose the brooch.

*

Across the street Kenton dithered. The three soldiers rounded on his boss. He was sure they wouldn't try anything in broad daylight, but then they'd been drinking for the best part of the afternoon. He decided to go over. He recognised Hoare's cousin immediately – the one they'd confronted in the snooker hall; he needed taking down a peg or two.

The broad soldier was in full flow. '. . . just been set free. You can't do this, a bit of compassion – his old man shot himself!'

Lowry calmly advised him to back down, trying to reason with the soldier – inasmuch as one can reason with a drunk – a circular conversation while Edward sat there in the middle. Kenton appeared at his elbow.

'What's your name?' Lowry had suddenly had enough and turned on the older Hoare. 'Name, rank and serial number, come on?'

Mike Hoare opened his mouth in a snarl, but his words were drowned out as the Yamaha kicked into life. The three soldiers rushed the policemen to allow Edward to escape. And escape he did, roaring down the road. Lowry and Kenton had no trouble shucking off the drunken soldiers, who toppled to the ground, but that was enough time for the nifty fifty to disappear from view.

37

3.45 p.m, Feering Road

Roger Derrick sat gently rocking in his swing chair on the veranda. His senses were under assault. Between the fug of insects coming up off the river and the tedium of listening to Kenneth's misgivings, he wasn't sure what was more annoying. His ponytailed henchman had spotted the police in East Street and had concerns they'd been rumbled. Ken had gone home for a break after positioning Roger's statue, only to return half an hour later with news of policemen in the village.

'You saw the police in the street *or* leaving the house? There's a big difference.'

'His motor was out front of the garage on East Street, a black Saab, the same what was here. Lowry and the blonde sort were walking up the street towards Mrs Harris's house around eleven this morning.'

Lowry had been lingering in the vicinity; what on earth for? 'Unless you saw them enter the house then they could have been going anywhere in the village. Why didn't you wait and see for sure?'

'I was in the van, boss. Couldn't stop.'

Hopeless, just one needless worry after another. 'Have you spoken with the old duck?'

'And say what?' Ken was useful muscle but that was about it, probably best he said as little as possible.

'Never mind.'

Roger really had had enough of people for one day, he could do with a break. This was most annoying. Every new endeavour presented a problem. The village was on the cusp of a boom in property prices, double by the end of the year, easily. The bypass meant all the heavy traffic from the Midlands through to Harwich and Felixstowe would finally cease shaking these very desirable listed buildings to their foundations. The village would be a country idyll once again. All he need do was turf out the obstinate old duffers who had been born there and never left, at a quick and tidy price.

'How many nocturnal visits have you made?'

'At least half a dozen. It ain't half cramped up there.'

'And you've not left the tape recorder up there?'

Ken shook his head. In hindsight it was a surprise the great lummox hadn't gone crashing through the ceiling.

'Why the fuss then, Kenneth? Please. I very much doubt the police have time to deal with such pointless complaints. God knows they have their hands full at the moment.'

Ken grinned and chuckled deeply. 'You're right there, boss.'

All the same, Roger wondered whether now might be the time to make an attractive offer via a spot of cold calling, before the new young village estate agent got hold of her. Roger used to have old Riley in his pocket, but he'd been pensioned off just at a time when he could become useful, and this new Flash Harry from Chelmsford was not playing ball at all. Hence the unusual tactics deployed in this instance, when by chance Kenneth's girlfriend lived in one of the now most-desirable streets in the village. The girlfriend's cottage was one of several with a communal roof stretching to her own mother's two doors down. The plan was simply to scare the poor woman into the old peoples' home on the other side of the street. Ken had even purloined a duplicate key, to facilitate a more effective haunting in the house itself by moving objects around. 'I'll have a think. Meanwhile, arrange a time with Mrs Cliff out on Fox Farm to collect the furniture; I've arranged for Christie's to list it in their autumn catalogue.'

'What about the old shooter, boss?'

'If that's your idea of a joke, it is woeful.' The telephone began to trill from somewhere in the house.

'It's the rozzers,' said Ken, emerging once more. 'Edward Hoare has been involved in an accident.'

'And?' There had to be an 'and'.

'They believe he was on his way here, on the London Road. Straight under a truck.'

'And? His mother's house is also out this way – '

'They found a trinket on him they reckon could be yorn.'

'What?'

'A diamond brooch.'

'Hardly a trinket,' Derrick expelled a small sigh. 'Thieving little tyke. Never learns.'

4 p.m., Colchester General Hospital

'What the bloody hell . . .' Jacqui couldn't believe it. There was Paul with his leg hoisted up in a bed on her ward, her bloody bay. She'd been in theatre for two hours, and arrived back to find the ward in pandemonium.

'Funny, ain't it,' Trish called over from the nurses' station, 'best bedside manner at the ready for that one, eh.' One of the student nurses sniggered. The entire ward knew of her affair with Doctor Paul Murphy. The whole hospital.

'What happened?'

'Gardening accident. You can ask him all about it.' Trish was on handover. 'There's another one, young kid, cute, RTA, come off his bike on the new bypass out near you – sorry – where you used to be.'

Jacqui took the clipboard from her flatmate, her eyes still trained on her ex-lover. He hadn't seen her yet. Head propped up, reading a book just like any other patient on the ward.

'– police will be in.'

'Sorry, what was that?' Jacqui hadn't been listening to the

résumé on the motorcycle boy opposite. 'Did you say the police?'

'Wanted for questioning.' The other new addition was in the bed next to Mr Moore. Jacqui sauntered down the aisle. The sedated boy was tanned and Trish was right – finely cut features, almost feminine.

'Over here, Jacqui,' a weak whisper called over to her beseechingly. She veered to Paul's bed.

'What happened to you?' she said, picking up his chart disinterestedly. 'Since when have you been into gardening?'

'I was assaulted,' he hissed.

He was rather pathetic. 'What, while pruning the roses?' She was more curious about the boy across the aisle, and was surprised how little concern she had for the wounded doctor, given how close they once were.

'A bloke jumped out a white transit while I was washing the Maestro. He had gardening equipment in the back. I thought he was after work; instead, though, he said he had come to give me advice.'

Jacqui moved closer, her thighs touching the bed. 'And what was that?'

'That I need to behave and keep quiet, though not in those words . . .' His face contorted slightly as he recalled the incident. 'I asked him what about and he swung a spade at my legs, told me to *keep that cakehole shut* and shattered my kneecap.'

'Jesus, Paul.' A shudder ran through her. 'What are you involved in?'

'And if I said anything, he'd take the other one off.'

She thought he might cry. 'You best not say anything then,' she said disingenuously. The young staff nurse passed them with a trolley, barely hiding a smirk. 'I better go.'

'Did you – did you – I mean, have you . . .' Jacqui watched him squirm. Come on, out with it, you pathetic specimen. 'You know, have you mentioned *us* to anyone, anyone unsavoury?'

'What?' she said indignantly, forcing him to shrink into the bed. 'I'm hardly proud of *that*.'

'Keep your voice down, for Christ's sake. I mean, did you tell anyone what I said about complaining about . . .'

'Oh, did I tell anyone you'd threatened me, you mean? Said you'd get me fired because I wouldn't give you a blow job?' She paused for a second, enjoying it, knowing the builder in the next bed was earwigging. 'Probably, when I was drowning my sorrows in Tramps the other night; God knows who was listening. Maybe someone took pity on me . . . anyway, I have to go.'

He reached and grabbed her hand.

'Don't,' she growled, her voice barely above a whisper. 'Let. Me. Go.'

His hand was cold and clammy.

She bent down. 'Do not expect any sympathy from me,' she spat. '*You* were trying to get *me* fired, remember?'

'Only because . . .'

'Only because nothing. You're pitiful.' And with that, she left to see the bed opposite. She didn't know whether to be cross, annoyed or laugh. Initially she thought it harsh to hospitalise the man, but now she was indignant, beholden to such a wimp. What on earth had she ever seen in him?

38

4.15 p.m., Colchester General Hospital

Lowry waited in the café, smoking one cigarette after another.

If Edward Hoare was innocent as he said, he shouldn't have fled.

Roger had identified the brooch as his possession, and confirmed that the cash found in the kid's bomber jacket was money he'd passed on at the request of the boy's stepfather. That cleared that matter up . . . When pushed as to why Roger failed to tell them of the stepfather's cash gift in the first place, he had not cared to comment. He didn't wish to dig himself a bigger hole.

'You're in it up to your cravat already,' Lowry had told him.

'Would you have believed I was holding onto it for the boy? I had not seen him when you called, remember.'

Suzanne entered the café with her three girls. He wasn't expecting the girls, though where else had he expected them to be but with their mother? Suzanne was ghostly white, nearer to the shade of the cheap, white Formica tables than the healthy glow exhibited by her children.

He watched as she dug out some money from her purse and ushered them off to the Space Invaders machine. This place seemed more like a waiting room than a café.

'Afternoon, Inspector.'

He half rose in greeting. 'Mrs Cliff. How's your son?'

'He'll live.' She sat opposite.

'Good. Can I get you something to drink?'

She shook her head and laced her fingers on the table. Her wedding ring stood out prominently, a jewel providing protection.

'I'm relieved to hear he'll be okay. Motorbikes are dangerous.' The accident had happened due to a negligent truck driver pulling out and failing to see the boy on his tiny motorcycle. 'It's nice to see your daughters here with you.'

'They've taken his injury hard. Much harder than the loss of Christopher; they were very close, so excited that he was coming home . . . and it seems after that initial upset, he was on his way back, hoping to make peace.'

Lowry consulted the green teacup. 'He might not have been, you know, he could have been returning to see Roger Derrick.'

'I know your view of that man. He called this afternoon about the dresser, utterly charming. I find it inconceivable that this man is your prime suspect.'

'As inconceivable as your husband taking his own life?'

Their eyes met. He would not tell her about the diamond brooch that Uniform had recovered.

'Now, what was the cause of the upset, when Eddie first arrived home – did you get to the bottom of it?'

She eyed him warily, perhaps frightened of what he might ask next. A thin layer of trust had built up between the two, stemming from Suzanne's need for support. And she knew he wanted to find Christopher's killer.

'Alice said he'd been clumsy.'

'How?'

'Knocked a bird's nest resting on a bookshelf.' She did not mention Alice's claim that her brother had struck her.

'Seems a bit minor to cause him to storm out of the house, so soon after arriving home?'

'I am sure they had said something to provoke him – not that I'll get it out of them.' Lowry shot a glance at the three girls crowding the arcade game. 'Anyway, does it really matter? Look where he's landed up. Jesus Christ.' Frustration and tired anger were barely contained. 'I'm fragile right now, Inspector.' Instinctively Lowry wanted to reach out and touch her hand. Never had a need to comfort a victim manifested itself like this before. He was caught out by his own emotions and attributed the urge as a sign of his own weakness. He shut down the thought immediately and pulled out a Players.

'Edward will be fine, that's the main thing.'

She nodded sullenly.

'Bolting off like that caused us concern, you understand. If he stopped he could have answered a few questions.'

'It was my fault – that night he was unaccounted for when Christopher was shot.' It was true, she had aroused suspicion by holding back that nugget.

'And is that why he ran?'

'Not at all; the warden had let it go, and that was enough for Eddie. No, his reasons are entirely innocent . . .'

'Mummy, Mummy, can have I ten pee, please? Alice won't give me any.'

Suzanne fumbled with her purse, eventually handing over a pound note. The girl's eyes lit up. 'You'll have to change it.' They watched the youngest girl race to the counter. Suzanne gathered herself.

'Edward's experience in Suffolk has rounded him in ways one could not foresee.' She took one of his cigarettes. 'Suffice to say, he was at last convinced the army was the place for him . . .' She took a breath. 'He just told me. Edward's very determined and once he gets the bit between his teeth, that's that. He doesn't want any trouble. Can't you let him be?' Lowry wondered just how much she knew – or if she was really this naive. Eddie Hoare was a chancer, nicking the brooch after pocketing two grand. A fool. It was plain and simple. Lowry wondered whether accepting the antique dealer's call was her way of drawing a line under all that had gone before.

'He'll still make the army, I'll see to it,' he said – the discipline there was the kid's only hope – 'providing he can account for his whereabouts on the twenty-fourth. I will be frank with you; it is not him we're after. His proximity to Derrick is our only interest. Like it or not, Roger Derrick was the last man to see your husband alive. We really don't want any harm to come to your son.'

She met his eye. 'Edward found the move here difficult. There is a whole side to my son I don't know, and I don't wish to. Not now.' Her mouth was thin and hard. This was as close as he'd get to an admission.

'Don't beat yourself up over it. Everyone has different sides to them, and nowhere does it become more apparent than with parents and their children.' He couldn't imagine what his own son must be thinking, beyond how appalling his parents were behaving. He cleared his throat and said simply, 'If Edward was by chance in Kelvedon the morning your husband was killed, we need to know about it. I'm sure you understand that. The warden is adamant he was not, but I'd like to hear your son's account myself.'

He saw a nurse uniform approaching in his periphery vision. She'd bleached her hair.

4.30 p.m., Colchester General Hospital

Suzanne's heart almost stopped. The nurse stood stock-still, searching for words; eyes flitted from Lowry to her. It could only mean Edward had not come to, that he'd passed away. Bringing her hands to her mouth, she felt a scream well up inside her. Then the nurse said, calmly, 'Mrs Cliff, Inspector, Edward is awake.'

Suzanne followed the inspector and nurse back onto the ward, heart still pounding from the scare. She had witnessed a peculiar moment, of that she was sure.

Edward had been moved from A&E onto a fracture ward, by the look of it; a fellow with a weak ginger beard lay on the bed opposite, one leg hoisted up in the air. He appeared agitated and stared at the three of them as they made their way down the aisle. Did he think her son a menace? She tried to wipe all thoughts from her mind as they settled at her son's bedside. Lowry was in discussion over Edward's positioning in the ward and requested the nurse screen him off.

Lowry was satisfied that Edward Hoare knew nothing. He was high on painkillers and gibbering nonsensically. Instinctively Lowry believed he'd give himself away; something would come out – either about his night away from borstal or Roger or his stepfather – but all he managed to get was rambling on joining the army. He reassured Suzanne Cliff there was nothing to fear, and urged her to rejoin her children.

He rose shortly after she had departed and left the boy talking nonsense to himself. Beyond the curtain the ward was quiet. Most were dozing. Apart from the man in the bed opposite, whose eyes were wide open. Lowry smiled broadly at him. His wife was nowhere to be seen, but he was uncon-cerned at the thought of seeing Jacqui; this was the hospital, he was bound to bump into her. She evidently had more of a problem with it than he did. Curiously, his sleepless nights had anaesthetised him to his wife's presence. He might take a Valium tonight after the fight, as a reward. The fellow with his leg up was staring fixedly in his direction. Did he know him?

'What happened to you?' If Lowry had met the man before it didn't register. The patient's eyes darted left to right, seeking assistance. He was clearly terrified.

'Have we met before?'

The man didn't answer, prompting Lowry to pick up the notes at the foot of the bed. *Dr Paul Murphy.* The name sent a tiny weakness to his legs. He took a deep breath and glanced up and down the ward before moving closer to the bed. The man opened his mouth, a slight tremble.

'You're nothing to write home about, are you?' Lowry said quietly. He calmly pulled out his pocket knife and turned from Murphy's view, increasing his agitation. 'This can be our little secret.' And with that, he strode to the end of the bed and jabbed the exposed foot sharply in the soft instep. Not hard enough to draw blood, but sufficient enough to trigger a reflex and cause a paroxysm of pain. The man gritted his teeth in anguish. Now Lowry understood why Jacqui was so agitated to see him. He jabbed the man again. This time

Murphy could not contain the agony and let out a terrible yelp.

'Let me see if I can fetch you a nurse,' Lowry said to the writhing figure and exited the ward in a better humour than when he had arrived.

39

6 p.m., Queen Street HQ

'That's that, then,' Sparks pronounced, handing over a crumpled pound note to the barmaid. The pair sat in the dingy social bar in the bowels of the building, Lowry on water and Sparks with a Guinness – the latter would not allow him so much as a shandy; the fight was in an hour. It was darker than usual; the main ceiling lights must have blown a fuse.

The boy had not enlightened them any further to Roger, other than that he was connected to him, that much was evident. Had he not come off his motorbike, it would have been interesting to see which direction Edward ran, but they had reached a dead end as far as Cliff was concerned. And the 'connection' was straightforward to Sparks's mind.

'Young Eddie has been letting Roger take 'im up the Aris, that's the fact of the matter. And that is all we've uncovered – much as I'd like it to be so, it does not point to Roger blowing Cliff's brains out.'

'Very eloquent.' Lowry blew a jet of smoke across the beer

pumps and produced two swirling, dirty lightsabers beneath the recessed downlights that poorly illuminated the bar. 'That's your summing up of the case, is it?' Lowry said.

'Well, they may not own up to it, the mother's in denial.'

'I don't think that's fair, she doesn't even know Derrick.'

'People see what they want to see, Nick, you and I both know that.' He knew Lowry would not concede defeat though. 'That Rog handed the cash over from the father says enough for me. Much as I despise the old woofter, I reckon he's off the hook.'

'Unless there's something we can't see . . . right under our noses.'

'Pah, the scent's cold, like this.' He drank deeply from the pint glass. 'Move on.'

'We are missing something.'

'I'm not, and neither are you. There's plenty more trouble to deal with.'

'If we do arrest Derrick –'

'If we do and he's innocent –' he wiped his top lip – 'we create a whole heap of trouble, and if he's guilty, we don't want what he's been up to reaching the limelight.'

'But you hate homosexuals.'

'I don't mind them, if they keep to themselves. Each to their own. Roger is a tart, though. And while the very thought of him gives me the willies, blowing all this stuff out into the open is worse. Okay, we might be a bit grubby round the edges, but it's a nice part of Essex, Coggeshall and Feering, quaint not queer. Start unearthing a ring of vice with teenage boys in the antiques trade and all of a sudden the chocolate box image melts and instead of confectionary, you've a giant brown turd staining your reputation and county.'

'Even if he's guilty?'

'Even if.' He gulped his Guinness. 'But straight up, I don't think he is.'

'And Merrydown?'

'Bollocks to her.'

'Every time you say that, she ends up twisting yours.'

'She wouldn't understand.'

'You've changed your tune from this morning, talk about ants in your pants.'

'That was this morning.' He spied Kenton at the other end of the bar ordering a pint in near darkness. 'Oi! None of that – you've had your quota already today, I heard.' The young policeman was crestfallen. 'Jesus, look at the colour of him.' He clapped his number two on his back. 'Face it, we've reached a dead end; it's not the first time.'

Lowry rose.

'Where you going?'

'Call Darnell's widow – she phoned this morning and I haven't been able to catch her back.'

'What does she want?'

'Haven't a clue. Odd – I didn't think she left the house much.'

'Don't be late.'

Lowry's square jaw caught in the bar light as he turned to

watch Kenton chat to a WPC. According to Antonia, Lowry had been a hit with her pal; his wife had pressed him for feedback. He'd fobbed her off – he didn't want to ask what Lowry had made of her; that would cross a barrier he was not comfortable with (and certainly not here in the smoky police club room).

'Time to move on,' Sparks said, half to himself, 'time to move on.' He was referring to the case, but perhaps in his mind he was also thinking of Lowry's life.

7.45 p.m., Army Gymnasium, Cavalry Barracks

The fight was not going Lowry's way; Kenton cringed as his boss took another pummelling to the ribs. The army man was all over his police opponent, weaving and sidestepping, slipping in deft punches at every opportunity. It was not that the soldier was that much younger, he wasn't – mid-thirties – he was just there, in the zone, and quicker as a result. Build-wise Lowry had the height. His opponent was stockier but to be fair he had phenomenal reach and the man's prowess was accentuated by Lowry's lack of it. He was barely in the fight at all . . .

'I'm no expert, but he doesn't appear to be enjoying himself.' Kenton spun round to see the military police captain, Oldham. Surprisingly Oldham was in mufti, a tan short-sleeved shirt and white cords.

'No, he's not,' Kenton shouted grimly back and returned

his attention to the ring. He didn't quite know how to take the captain, a man of fearsome repute and not known for small talk. At least in uniform, polite respect would suffice, but here in the garrison gym, and he a casual spectator, it was out of context.

'He should stick to birdwatching.' The crowd surged forward as Lowry suffered a blow to the head.

Kenton winced. 'Apparently the summer is not good for birds, so he thought he'd keep his hand in.' Why? To prove that he could? They'd never discussed it. Kenton had vowed that once he made sergeant he'd jack it in. 'Oh my God.' Lowry had gone down.

Sparks walked in the locker room as Lowry was cleaning himself up.

'Appalling,' the chief remarked.

'Thank you.' Lowry spat blood into a flannel. Sympathy was not a quality Sparks had in buckets.

'You should have creamed that fat bastard.' He handed him his Players.

'He's got a punch.'

'Tch. He's a fatty.' Sparks lit up. 'Makes the Michelin man look svelte.'

Lowry's fingers were shaking as he teased the filterless cigarette out of the packet – Sparks hadn't noticed that before, the shakes.

'You could contest the weight,' Lowry said eventually.

Sparks held out his lighter. 'I did – he's the same as you, but six inches shorter.'

Lowry sucked on the cigarette. 'Quite a reach, though.'

'I'll say – surprised his knuckles don't drag on the floor.' Sparks rounded Lowry's sweat-sheened body. 'Like a fucking orang-utan . . .'

A roar went up from the main hall. Sparks recognised his own team's chant. Kenton had delivered. The younger man's success could permit a softening and some clemency, but no – instead he would tell Lowry straight.

'Except the truth of the matter remains – you should have won. You were not match fit, and as a consequence of not training sufficiently, you have wasted six months of everybody's time: going through the motions ain't good enough.'

Lowry didn't comment. Sparks strongly believed the man's personal life was at the root of it, but again he couldn't bring himself to ask a direct question. Fearing he'd been a bit harsh, he changed tack. 'Maybe lighten up a bit, let go of the tension and you'll find the energy to go for it properly – then the boxing will fall into place.' He gestured sweepingly, trailing smoke. 'Maybe give that Becky sort a crack. Probably a bit of a goer under all that hair and mascara . . .'

'Do you mind.' Lowry slipped from the table, and faced him. His eye had practically closed shut. 'If it's all the same, I'd rather not have life coaching from you after I've just been floored.'

Sparks shrugged. 'I best go watch young Kenton. See you in the Britannia after.'

He left Lowry to it; maybe it was a mistake to have him return to the ring, but he hadn't twisted the man's arm. If he was going to get a pasting, there was not much point having him, but he needed that weight . . . where could he find that? He rounded the corner and walked straight into Oldham. The man was in civvies, a sight he'd not seen before.

'Captain. The last person I thought I'd find here; thought you strongly disapproved.' Unusual, Oldham being here – strict disciplinarian that he was, he believed these bouts little more than organised street brawls.

'Quite so, Superintendent, but I thought I'd come view your inspector's return to the ring.'

'As you saw, it was far from spectacular.' The chief grunted and made his way out to the hall. Now he had Kenton to worry about – he could hear the lad bleating about sore hands. The whole bloody division was going soft.

Lowry pulled a strand of tobacco from his swollen lip and considered the blood on the cigarette before re-applying it to his bruised mouth. He was unmoved by defeat. It happened to all but few. The only surprise was how much it hurt, going down like that. He should have seen that punch coming – in fact he did, but his mind wasn't there; he could not block out the hospital and Edward Hoare. Cliff's son was four years older than his own. Four years would pass in a flash. Where would Matthew end up if he landed with a stepfather he hated?

A familiar figure appeared in the changing-room doorway.

'Ah, Captain Oldham, you catch me not at my finest.'

'It would seem not. Have you considered a less physically demanding pastime?'

'I have; I'll tell you about it one of these days.' Lowry moved to pick the towel from the peg.

'Did you find your man?'

'Indeed. Thanks for the tip . . . he's on my mind. He'll need a spot of help, to keep on the straight and narrow.'

'Anything I can assist with?'

'Yes, yes, I think you can.' He tossed the towel aside and picked up a T-shirt. 'Can I buy you a drink?'

Part 4

YELLOWHAMMER

40

10.30 a.m., Sunday 14th August, West Mersea beach

Lowry had driven Edward Hoare to the beach.

Edward was discharged from the hospital after two days, with a fractured arm. Lowry had telephoned Suzanne Cliff on Saturday to see how they were coping and while she was enormously impressive juggling three girls and an injured son single-handedly, she admitted to being unable to get to grips with her husband's affairs. It didn't help that Edward had been mooching around dolefully, distracting her. Lowry seized the opportunity and offered to take Edward out for the morning; having smoothed the kid's way into the army through Oldham, his standing was good with the family and Suzanne readily agreed. If Lowry were duplicitous as to his motives, he had no qualms; kindness could go hand in hand with a little discreet digging around for facts. The heat was off Edward Hoare but the death of his stepfather remained. The isolation of Fox Farm, once its main attraction, was now its curse. The widow had swiftly reached a decision, with Fox

Farm and its three acres soon to be on the market, though Mrs Cliff was well aware the sale would be slow. Who'd want a house where there'd been recent bloodshed?

Lowry and Edward now sat in the same beachfront café where, not so long ago, on the day of Edward's release, Lowry and Jane Gabriel had watched Kenton floating off to the horizon. A young couple in swimming trunks and bikini passed their table and Lowry wondered if Jane and Kenton were down there on the beach below, enjoying the fine weather. He liked to think so.

'Do you think it'll take long for my mother to sell the house?' Edward was wearing a Killing Joke T-shirt and a baseball cap to keep the sun off his eyes.

'It depends whether she's holding out for a good price,' Lowry said.

'She's already been on the phone to the estate agents.'

'Oh.' Lowry was not altogether too surprised. 'What did they have to say?'

'Couldn't get an appointment until next week – that new bypass has created a lot of interest in property round there; people got wise and are selling up . . .'

'Is that so.' Not everyone was 'wise'; some were old and vulnerable. Lowry was thinking of the lady on East Street.

'But that's not really what I mean – more the impact of my stepfather dying there. Would she be able to sell it?'

Lowry shrugged. 'Any place of a certain age has seen its fair share of unpleasantness.'

'Yes, I suppose . . . I doubt he was the first in that place.'

'Not the first, how do you mean – to be killed?'

'It's a very old house. Must've seen many people come and go through the ages. I mean it wouldn't surprise me *if* people had been killed; the house has history. When my parents started renovating the kitchen last year, they even found a mummified cat in the wall.'

'To ward off evil spirits.'

'You know?'

'It's not uncommon, we're a superstitious bunch round here.'

'I guess so,' Edward said non-committally. 'My stepfather knew all about that stuff obviously, being a historian. Anyway, the cat suggested to him that many people had lived and died in the house.'

Wishing to engage the boy further in conversation, Lowry relayed how he'd recently come across witches' marks on a chimney in the house in East Street: superstition was as good an opening as any, and was a subject that had been on his mind since visiting the cottage in Coggeshall. 'My mother was always trying to scare me with her stories.'

Edward turned from the sea, interested.

'I grew up in Fingringhoe, a village not far from here on the mainland. I was badly behaved, and she always threatened me with a ducking in the village pond – just like a witch . . .'

'Why were you badly behaved?' Edward asked.

'My parents argued all the time when I was small, and to

try to stop them I sought attention. By whatever means I could,' Lowry replied, frankly. 'And it did work, though not quite in the way I anticipated. I'd just cop a severe scolding.'

'How old were you?'

'Six or seven.'

'That is brutal.'

'She gave me a choice, though,' Lowry said, 'either the pond or the green; string me up like a pirate.'

'Pirates?'

'A regular occurrence – the Blackwater was riddled with them through the ages. We have an oak tree, there on the green. Six hundred years old like the one in your meadow, a six-metre girth they say sprouted from a pirate buried there, with an acorn his mouth.'

'You were spared that at least.'

'I'm here.'

'I did something similar . . .' he said, then hesitated. 'Just before I got released, I slipped out and missed roll-call the next day. I wanted someone to notice me. I was a problem and I knew my mum and Christopher didn't know what to do with me.'

'And doing a bunk from Hollesley Bay would make them worry less?'

'Huh, no . . . but it's like you say, attention-seeking. But the warden was very good, I don't think he told me mum.'

Lowry said nothing.

'You know I didn't realise I wanted to join the army until

I was out, and there was just trouble in every direction? I'm very grateful.'

'Don't mention it.'

By touching on his own background he'd put the boy at ease. Edward went on to explain he was essentially a townie, coming from south-west London with his mother, but didn't realise it until they got here and there was nothing to occupy his time once the novelty of the place wore off. The only curiosity was Coggeshall itself, where there was all sorts of weird stuff going on.

'Like what?'

'Just stuff.'

Lowry encouraged him gently. Edward had soon outgrown running errands for Derrick and had started getting the train to Colchester to see his cousin Mike and hang out at the snooker hall in the high street. For that, he needed more money than Derrick was paying.

'Don't get me wrong, this place is all right, just there's a lot more in the world than mummified cats to explore.'

'What about the cat?' Lowry asked after a moment's reflection. 'Did you reseal it in the wall?'

'No,' he said grimly, 'my sisters were freaked out and insisted we burn it.'

'Burn it? That seems a bit . . . extreme.'

Edward shrugged. 'What else were we to do?'

'Your stepfather might have offered it to a museum?'

'Who cares? He's dead now.' The boy returned his gaze to the estuary.

'Edward, when you first arrived home there was an altercation with your sisters. What was that about?'

'Ah . . .' He picked at his armcast. 'I dunno. Nuthin'.'

'You hadn't seen them in a year. They had missed you – it must have been something significant to cast such a shadow over your return and cause you to leave so suddenly.'

'I don't remember, I really don't . . . I got off the train at Kelvedon and walked home, it was blisteringly hot. Mum was hanging out the washing. I caught them all by surprise.'

'Was that the intention?'

'I suppose, the prodigal son and all that. No, I didn't want a fuss, that's all. Then I went inside with Emma, my youngest sister, and went upstairs. It was fine to start with, all hugs 'n' kisses then – even tears. They hadn't been allowed to visit, so you know, a year's a long time when you're only twelve. They were overjoyed, if I'm honest. And then the conversation moved on to my stepdad . . . and they were like –' A gull strode boldly along the edge of the terrace.

'Like what?' said Lowry.

'Unconcerned. Not bothered that he was gone, their own dad . . . well, Emma's, anyway. And so I said, you don't seem that upset. And Alice said it was all his own fault.'

'That he was shot?'

'Yeah, I guess. Like you, they think Roger shot him.'

'They have never said.'

'Once they found out that he was round that morning, they leapt to the same conclusion. But Roger is not that sort of bloke, I swear. I mean, he's a far cry from an angel but he's no murderer. Anyway, they kept on and on and then I just lost it. Sounds stupid now.'

'Try me.'

'*They* are into all that superstitious twaddle.'

'Explain.'

He snorted. 'They love magic spells, the green man – you know, country bumpkin nonsense. I told Roger once, he called them "the Weird Sisters".'

'And you argued over that? Why?'

'Lucy said they were *told* it was to happen, like they were told that he was gonna die, which was mental.'

'Told by whom?'

'Oh, I don't know, the trees for all I know. They live in a made-up world stuck out here, too much time with their noses in books; our house is full of all kinds of weird shit . . .' he sighed. 'Look, he was never my dad, just some posh wally Mum hitched up with after my dad did a runner. I'm sad for my mum, but it was wrong coming from them – disrespectful. Emma's only bloody six, filling her head with that crap. So we had a barney. I shouted I don't want to hear any of that shit ever again.'

Lowry considered this for a moment. 'Children need rational explanations for things, and where there aren't any, they sometimes fabricate the most outlandish things imaginable.

Just to make sense of what's happened.' He understood why Edward was upset. He was still only a boy himself and despite a year in a harsh environment, had a lot to learn. 'Don't be too hard on them. Or yourself.'

– 41 –

11 a.m., Wivenhoe House, Wivenhoe

Suzanne arrived at Christopher's university office in good time. Tim Pine was waiting dutifully to let her in. She had picked Sunday deliberately thinking it would be quiet and free of students, forgetting that term had finished over a month ago. Another sign that her mind was not as clear as it should be. However, Inspector Lowry had kindly offered to take Edward to West Mersea for a breath of sea air and she had dropped the girls off in town. She didn't feel comfortable leaving them on their own at the farm, but was happy for them to mooch around the shops.

Tim and Suzanne had only spoken briefly on the phone since his previous, awkward visit and he exuded discomfort when confronted again with the widow of his former colleague. Pushing the door of her husband's office open for her, he pressed himself back against the wall, as if afraid of what they'd find within.

'You know, I have absolutely no idea what he was working

341

on,' she said, more to the empty chair than to Pine. She stood facing piles of paper and books stacked untidily. 'Much as his work was largely done at home.'

'Take whatever you wish. I shall archive the rest.' He parted, gently shutting the door behind him.

The room was organised chaos; the piles of paper, books and ephemera would all have had a place in Christopher's encyclopedic mind but to anyone else, it was just a huge mess. It would have helped if there were shelves in here, as one would expect to find in any academic's study. But he'd taken them down, preferring to hang pictures. The walls were adorned with paintings and prints of various sizes. Many of them were Gainsborough and Constable, the largest being *The Cornfield*. She felt a pang of grief . . . she knew this to be Christopher's favourite, though one that was not received well at the time. Constable himself could not sell it for toffee. The painting of Fen Lane depicted the route the artist as a boy took to school from East Bergholt to Dedham. Constable would refer to it as 'The Drinking Boy' and it was unique in that it was not topographically accurate and depicted artistic insertions (something of a deviation for Constable). She recalled Christopher explaining how the scale was curiously out, and the boy at odds with the scene. 'Like Edward,' those words, simply said. Was the boy the artist himself, an interloper to the scene, or was he with the farmer, perhaps his son?

What made it more painful was that her husband had wished to hang it in the house and she'd flatly refused.

They lived in the middle of the country – why the need for a landscape painting? She had opted to hang her own work instead and only one print – the more decorative Klimt. Christopher sniffly declared the Austrian's *Lady in Gold* indescribably garish, and yet hung it in the bedroom. And here was his choice, consigned to his office. She stepped up closer. She had never really examined it closely. The farmer beyond the stream held the gate into the cornfield, a dog bringing up the rear. Was there symbolism she missed? The boy's tunic was bright red, at odds with the farmer's smock. She thought of Edward and of her first husband, and noticed the farmer wore a red neckerchief. Maybe they were father and son after all.

Underneath the print was a letter rack. Christopher's correspondence; he was an enthusiastic letter writer. Ought she to go through them and reply where appropriate? She picked the two-inch thick wodge from the holder. Her husband's death had been reported in the press and the *Telegraph* ran an obituary, written by their art critic, Sir Patrick Janson-Smith. She spotted Sir Patrick's elegant scrawl as she thumbed through the letters. She also recognised another hand – her mother's. How unusual; unusual that she should write to him – they did not get on – and unusual that she should write to him here, at the university. Her mother had died last November. The envelope was postmarked 10 August 1982. Unfolding the crisp paper, she began to read:

Dear Christopher,

As the opportunity to speak with you seldom occurs, if ever, I feel compelled to write. I'll be blunt: the way you manage your family is deplorable.

I will start with Edward: he may not be your natural son, and heaven knows teenagers can be a trial, but as any responsible adult, you ought to provide a modicum of care. Suzanne is beside herself with worry; to think it has come to this – a grandchild of mine in borstal! Wayward he may be, but nevertheless he loves his sisters and was a guiding hand in settling them to the country life you and Suzanne chose for them. They looked up to him. With him gone, what will they do? It cannot fall on my frail shoulders to nurture them. They grow restless, and you show little or no interest in any of them, even the youngest – your own child!

When you relocated to Essex with Suzanne and took up the farm, I was overjoyed and thought it praiseworthy. What a considerate fellow this is; my daughter's family are dear to her and this man respects that. But as time passed, I grew to realise how foolish my initial impression had been – with such alacrity did you ignore your wife's children. The only reason you chose Essex was thinking it handy for a babysitter! At every opportunity you offloaded them here with me, enabling you to pursue your career unhindered.

Why on earth did you choose to marry a vulnerable divorcee with three children, if you had no intention of loving them as you did her? I warn you – unless you change your attitude, no

good will come. I am only glad my husband is not alive to see
this misery you are causing.

  Margaret

Suzanne saw immediately the truth of this letter. Why then, though? She thought back to last summer, and Edward's trial. Yes, that was a difficult time, and the girls ... the girls, how were they? And then she remembered – they did spend time with her mother, both here and at Bergholt, until Lucy had turned fourteen in May and Suzanne had deemed her old enough to remain at home. Still, she was shocked by her mother's vitriol, she had never aired this view to Suzanne herself. Margaret had died suddenly in November. As Suzanne's gaze drifted to the boy in the Constable painting, she wondered what her mother would have made of Christopher's death.

11.15 a.m., Creffield Road, Lexden

'It's Sunday morning,' Sparks spat down the receiver.

  'I haven't been able to get hold of you,' she replied, calmly. 'Typical policeman – tons of them about making a nuisance of themselves until you need one. Then rare as hen's teeth.'

  'What do you want, your little problem is sorted.'

  'So I see. On my bloody ward too; see more of the blighter now than before.'

  'Hazard of the profession.' Sparks straightened himself. 'Come on, I haven't got all day. My breakfast is getting cold.'

'Nicholas. I want him back.'

'Do you really? Well, get round there and talk to him then.'

'It's not that easy. I don't know what frame of mind he's in.'

'I don't know why you're asking me. As I said before.'

'You're close to him.'

'Nonsense. We work together, that's it.'

'And drink together, box together. You're as close to him as anyone is. Bet he was delighted at your handiwork on Paul.'

Sparks didn't know what to say. But his silence spoke for him.

'Ahh . . . You haven't told him – why would you? Wonder what he'd say, if he knew you were behind this.'

'Just you wait a minute.' Sparks felt his temperature rise.

'Probably best, he might react badly . . .' her voice trailed off. Typical woman – can never fathom whether they're talking to you or themselves. 'It's for Matthew – I worry he is missing the stability of a father figure. Can you just mention that.'

'A father figure? He's got a dad, where's the need for a figure?'

'Not at the moment, he hasn't. A child needs a proper family, especially at his age. Otherwise he'll end up like Nick.'

Antonia wandered in yawning, tapping her increasing belly.

'What does that mean? What's wrong with Nick?' he said, holding the receiver closely. The last thing he wanted was his wife overhearing this.

'His parents split up when he was a boy, and see how he's turned out? Emotionally retarded.'

346

Sparks couldn't help but take umbrage on Lowry's behalf, even though he had no idea what she was on about. 'He's done just fine,' he said stiffly. 'Look, should the opportunity present itself, I will mention your son, but that's the limit of my involvement.' With that he hung up, leaving the receiver off the hook. He had developed a sneaky habit of doing this at the weekends, just for an hour or two, to give him some peace. Antonia's friends had no respect for the sanctity of a Sunday morning and if there was an emergency the station would know where to find him.

Antonia was buttering toast on the work surface, and humming as she did so. He took his place at the kitchen table. Two things were clear – one, Lowry really was unknowable, or friendless, if Jacqui wanted Sparks to be her gopher. And second, at certain points in the conversation Jacqui's voice had waivered. She was intimidated by her husband.

Enough, though, it was the bloody weekend. The paper lay before him. Of course, as a policeman the press was always a source of irritation, but he found himself increasingly less resilient to criticism and triteness, and as such he ignored anything that annoyed him if at all possible.

'These eggs are hard,' he grumbled to himself. He moved the *Daily Mail* to one side, to reveal the newly purchased *Asterix and Son* hardback. Sparks was obsessed with Asterix, and the arrival of a new one in the series was a very special moment. The police chief knew they took the piss out of him at the station – his favourite euphemism for a boxer with spirit was one with 'magic potion', and he often alluded to Colchester as the Gaul village and Chelmsford as Rome – but he didn't care. Now he sat transfixed by the arrival of this latest volume and its startling congruity with his own circumstances: there on the cover was a giant baby being fed from a gourd by a diminutive Asterix, a grown man a fraction of the infant's size. His hero wore an expression of woe and weariness. The symmetry was extraordinary – it was undoubtedly a sign. He dare not open the book, just eyed it with awe and concern, lying there pristine on the table.

'They're fine, you're like a bear with a sore head at the moment.' It was gone eleven. Antonia scraped back the chair opposite and seated herself, still not dressed, dressing gown gaping open. His wife had taken languishing in bed to extraordinary new lengths since falling pregnant. He didn't know how she operated in the week when he was at the station. Maybe she didn't get up at all. If this continued much longer, he'd take to breakfasting on his own.

'Maybe if I didn't have to wait until the middle of the day for breakfast, you might find me more agreeable.'

'Oh, hush.' She reached and pulled the paper towards her. Kate Everett's trial was everywhere, drawing attention to Christopher Cliff's murder and their failure to solve it. Yet strangely, as the publicity had intensified, Merrydown had fallen quiet. Sparks was beginning to wonder whether she really knew the man at all. All that fuss about being at Cambridge together had been forgotten . . .

'Remember what you promised, last night?' Antonia viewed him archly across the breakfast table. He paused prodding a soldier pointlessly into an overdone egg. No, he couldn't remember making any promises last night. 'Remember?'

All he could recall were a couple of bottles of Claret, then . . . yes, some clumsy love-making, but nothing –

'We'd take a run out to Flatford Mill this afternoon?'

The *Arena* arts programme had shown a rerun of Cliff in Suffolk; they'd watched it last night. Bloody hell. He must have let his guard down and made one of those throwaway remarks.

'Are you sure I didn't say one day *soon*? Not literally today.'

'Why not today? For once you're not doing anything with your bumchums.'

'Don't call the sports committee that.'

She poked her tongue out.

'Much of what we do is important for the community –'

'How on earth does boxing help the community? I fail to see how Nick Lowry getting a pummelling provides a service to the people.'

Why this need to justify his activities all the time. 'The boxing is different. That's the army, who we share the town with, it's essential . . . Wait a second, how do you know Lowry took a pasting?'

She tapped the side of her nose in that ever-so-annoying way. He pulled the Asterix book closer. Maybe he should make his own breakfast in future.

Midday, Fox Farm

Shadows fell across the kitchen floor, causing a slight flutter in Suzanne. Her nerves were not settled. The kitchen door was open and the two silhouettes were that of her son and the inspector. In an attempt to keep busy when she returned from the university, she had tried her hand at baking bread – something her mother had always done – but all that had made was a mess. She dusted flour from her hands and beckoned the men in. She offered Lowry a coffee but he shook his head.

'Do you have any plans tomorrow evening?' she asked.

'Monday? Nothing.' He wore the same suit. Even on a Sunday.

'Why don't you join us for supper?' She'd given the idea no thought, but it felt natural to ask. He had, she felt, acted beyond the call of duty, and the invitation would show her gratitude. 'We can eat outside. It will be informal.' She wanted to say *come as a friend* but couldn't in front of her son. Instead she said, 'Dress down, even?'

He didn't rise to this remark, but accepted graciously.

'How was the beach?' she addressed Edward, who grunted affirmatively before leaving the kitchen.

'I think Edward enjoyed the fresh air,' Lowry said.

'It's very kind of you to take him, it gave me a chance to –'

'Make some bread, I see.'

'Yes, rather unsuccessfully. Kate always put me to shame, we used to bake together this time of year.' Really she wanted to tell him about the visit to Christopher's office, but couldn't endure wondering what conclusion he may draw. 'If you don't want a coffee, can I fetch you a cold drink? You must be parched.'

'No, no, I'm fine. I must go.' He nodded slightly. 'I will see you tomorrow, six-thirty?'

'Yes, that would be perfect.'

Lowry was in demand. He had a lunch date today too, though this liaison in his local pub was one he was less enthusiastic about than the proposed evening with the Cliff family. However, first he'd call on Mrs Bowles and her sister at Darnell's place, after giving Jane Gabriel a little errand.

42

1 p.m., Cambridge Road, Lexden

'He won't help you if you're rude to him.'

'Oh, do be quiet, Mother.' She slapped the phone back into the portable cradle that she'd trailed across the living room. Engaged. Jacqui wanted Sparks to fix a meeting between her and Nick. She'd no doubt he'd do it. Sparks was a pushover. He'd have a heart attack if he knew Jacqui was in the next street. Her parents' place was a detached house round the corner in Cambridge Street (and considerably more impressive than that Georgian semi of Sparks's).

The only problem was, Jacqui was not sure exactly what she wanted. Devoid of marital responsibility and free from Paul, she was content for a time. Then, abruptly, she realised she did not have her own space. Freedom, yes, but not space, and she had a son. It would be better to be under her own roof while figuring out what she wanted to do. Now Sparks had dealt with Paul, and her career was no longer under threat, she could focus on pulling her life back together. First though, she had to get an understanding of Nick's state of mind. She'd not clapped eyes on him in months, not until that moment on the beach and then again at the hospital.

'He's not going to make friends being shunted around like this,' her mother said, nodding towards Jacqui's son. Matthew sat at the dining table with his grandfather, who was reading the paper. The boy was a painfully slow eater at the best of times. He wheeled his sprouts around the plate, fruitlessly. Her mother was right. Her son had grown withdrawn since the separation.

'You can leave it, Matty,' she called sweetly.

Nick would have insisted he finish and if not, place the plate in the fridge. A number of times, Matt had been faced with a plate of cold cabbage for breakfast. Not the best way to start the week. Jacqui would remonstrate with her husband only to be told his father had done the same, which did not make it right. But Nick was not here.

'I know, Mum.'

What to do? Sparks was right; she had to confront her husband, she couldn't use an intermediary for ever. Eight months was a long time, but was it long enough for that much polluted water to flow under the bridge?

2.15 p.m., Great Tey, the Chequers Pub

The landlord cautiously placed another cider on the wooden table.

'Can I put the umbrella up for you?' he asked with concern. Lowry, loosening his tie, declined and thanked him for the drink. Three days on from his spectacular defeat and his wounds were in full bloom. Today he would allow himself some rest; there was nothing further to do. Neither Mrs Darnell nor Mrs Bowles were at the Cambridge Road house, he could only assume they'd taken a break after all.

The invite to Fox Farm tomorrow allowed him to pause, if only for the afternoon. Driving Edward home from the beach, he'd been contemplating how he could get a further insight into the family without being invasive; the invite for a meal solved that dilemma. The boy's account of his argument with his sisters was interesting; it may be nothing, a child's way of coping with grief as he'd suggested, but he was intrigued by the family dynamic.

Swallows swooped low and close, picking off insects. They never ceased to dazzle, no matter how often he saw their grace and dark blue sheen. He picked up the pint glass and drank. How he loved to watch birds. If only he'd realised they were there, right under his nose, earlier in his life. It had proved to be a pursuit more absorbing than any of the sports he'd pursued as a younger man. The boxing was now over, once and for all; he may have tried fooling everyone – including himself – that he went down because his mind was locked into the Cliff case, but that didn't ring true. There'd always been murder cases, and there'd always been fights. No, he'd elected to return to the ring purely as a diversionary tactic.

To avoid staring the mess of his marriage in the face. Even in training, he was only going through the motions, jogging effortlessly down the lanes, all the while drinking and smoking like a bastard. He wasn't Kenton's age, Sparks was right – he should have trained harder, with conviction, if he was even remotely serious about winning.

The birds darted off high into the blue above the cottage rooftops. Could Matty appreciate birds, was it something they could do together, maybe? His son, he had to do something about the boy. Soon, once this case was resolved.

On the table lay a tatty paperback copy of J. A. Baker's *The Peregrine*. His head was not in a place to concentrate on reading, so instead he watched the birds and waited patiently for his date to arrive. It was not that he was nervous – though if he gave it any consideration, he probably was – no, he was thinking on his time with Edward Hoare this morning. There was something in the boy's manner that suggested he was holding out on him. A family cycled past, a girl of about eight teased by an older boy. *'I can go faster than you!'* she screamed gaily as they disappeared down the lane. He thought again on the Cliff girls and the hokum that had vexed their brother. Of course they had lost their father, and there was no accounting for how they may react to the news, as he'd put to Edward himself this morning. Except, thinking about it as mere withdrawal was not right: absence was a more accurate description. His mind whirled back to the day of Edward's release: answering Suzanne's call, racing to the house. The mother was upset, but there was no trace of a fierce exchange among the girls – in fact, he didn't even see the oldest two, only Emma – who, come to think of it, was perfectly fine. It took the maxim 'seen and not heard' to a new level entirely . . .

He raised his head to the crunch of gravel as a car made its way slowly down to the pub's rear car park; he was sure it was her. He sipped on the second pint. He must try to put these jumbled thoughts aside, just for one afternoon at least, since he was resolved to give this a try.

'Hello there,' she approached, gaily swinging a cloth bag. 'Am I late?' she said, observing the two pint glasses.

'Not at all.' He rose and held out his hand. 'I live across the way. It's good of you to travel out of town.'

'Nonsense, it's not that far. Crumbs, you have been in the wars. Black and blue.' She dumped her bag on the table and ran her fingers through her hair, tilting her head back as she did so.

'I did warn you I wasn't a pretty sight.'

'Does it hurt? Silly question. Can you see all right with that eye?'

'Well enough to read a menu.'

'I'm starving, what's on offer?' She wore make-up and was paler for it. In the sunlight it struck him as theatrical, like a mask.

'Let me get you a drink while you peruse the menu. The

roast is serviceable if you can turn a blind eye to the tinned carrots.'

'I'm vegetarian . . .' she said the word slowly and, he thought, playfully. He glanced across the forecourt: a couple of local, ruddy rural faces, mixed with some younger weekend crowd. Two women in their twenties whom he caught gawping as Becky sat down. 'Most people think women not eating meat equates to lesbians and Greenham Common,' she continued.

'Great Tey may appear to the casual observer a sleepy parish village – a church with a pub and little else – but I assure you, we're very Right On and the thinking is progressive. Now, what can I get you?'

'A pint of Guinness, please . . .' She smiled, squinting in the sunlight.

'Coming up.'

Lowry entered the cool of the pub. 'Pint of Guinness, please, Terry.'

'For the lady?'

Lowry nodded and turned to observe Becky through the window. She had lit a cigarette and, ignoring the menu, had picked up his paperback. There was something enticing about her – she was both forward and guarded, bold yet brittle. He picked up another menu from the bar.

'What's the vegetarian option?'

'The what?'

'Food that's not meat.'

The burly landlord contemplated the Guinness he'd left

to stand, as if the dark liquid contained an answer. 'There's the vegetables – roast spuds and Yorkshire pud? Peas, carrots and what not . . .'

'Pasta? Macaroni cheese?' Lowry suggested hopefully.

'Nick, this is north Essex, not flamin' Tuscany.'

'Obviously.' He tapped his forehead. 'I was forgetting myself, must be the hot weather.'

One of the two women came to the bar. Removing her sunglasses, he recognised her as one of his wife's friends. Returning his attention to the landlord, he stood expectantly. 'I'll have to consult with my friend, but give me a bag of KP for now, Tel.'

43

3.45 p.m., Saffron Walden, north Essex
on the Cambridgeshire border

Gabriel was running late. Sunday lunch at her aunt's was a strictly observed affair. Aperitifs at three-thirty, sit down at four. It wasn't so much a lunch as an early supper. It was a strange way to go about it; Jane assumed it was an affectation, class-inspired. Regardless, she was starving and she had no excuse not to be punctual – except Lowry had had her drop in at two estate agents on the way, one in Kelvedon and the other in Coggeshall, where at the latter she had discovered something of interest. The property market in this part of Essex was buoyant – particularly in and around Coggeshall, where the region had experienced a burst of private house sales that had nettled the local branch of a Chelmsford estate agent. It was hearsay that one local businessman alone had bought four freehold residences in the last month. Gabriel had asked whether there was any similarity between these sales – were they in the same street, perhaps?

'Not location-wise – a smattering all over the village – but there's a pattern: old codgers with period properties,' the savvy youth had replied, with his shoestring tie and button-down shirt, chewing gum noisily. 'Oldsters that have been holed up in these Grade II places for donkey's years.' *Did he suspect foul play?* she asked. Whereupon he frowned: 'It ain't quite right – it's not they've been out and out swindled – don't get me wrong, one old dear got more than she'd a' had this time last year, but nothing like what I could have got 'er.' He added despairingly, 'City types are coming down on the train and checking the place out – there's no need to sell to some local big shot mincing about in a cravat.' From that point, she need hear no more – there was no doubt in her mind this was Roger Derrick. She gave the estate agent her phone number and continued on to Saffron Walden. That she had been taken in by Derrick's cultural intelligence, as Lowry had insinuated, rankled and made her impatient with other motorists for the remainder of the journey.

There was no accounting for Sunday drivers, and she forgot how the pace of life slowed for many at the weekend: there was still such a thing as a leisurely drive, such as the dawdlers in the mustard Allegro she'd been stuck behind for what seemed like an eternity.

Finally she entered the market square, the familiar Guild Hall standing sentinel. The village must be as old as Colchester, but there was aloofness here. She had long thought class and money preferred inland retreats; coastal towns historically were not for the faint-hearted – the sea brought traders and invaders, why run the risk if you could afford to live up country? Her aunt was a fine example of such elitism.

Merrydown's Jag sat gleaming before the large period house, bordered by evenly spaced rose bushes of a uniform height. Her aunt was widowed three years ago, and being childless, she had always taken a keen interest in her niece. She was the one who had convinced Jane Gabriel to take up the police, having quit her modelling career.

The large, dark table was set for two. The *Telegraph* lay neatly at the far end.

Merrydown caught her spying the front page. 'They're full of it. Kate Everett's trial.' She sipped on a Campari and produced a profile piece, which she must have been reading as they sat down. She slid it across the polished mahogany surface. 'Her compassion towards the Cliff children will lend leniency.'

Gabriel did not comment. The woman had killed her lover; she didn't fancy that emergency child-minding exonerated her actions. Merrydown's housekeeper wheeled in the heated trolley.

'Do you disagree?' said her aunt, noting the silence.

Gabriel peeled open the glossy to see an array of Polaroids reproduced under the banner 'Fatal Farm'.

'I think those children are quite capable of fending for themselves.' There they all were, grinning up at her. And Edward too.

'Hmm. We shall soon see.' Merrydown considered the

matter required no further discussion. 'How are you fitting into barracks?'

'Just fine.' Her aunt always referred to Queen Street as 'barracks'.

'It is very male. Chief Sparks's stance on equality is no more evolved than when Claudius was here. How about the rest of them?'

'There's a couple of women in Uniform that I get on with. I like them.'

'No, I meant in CID. That Lowry is an oddball, but the young chap is educated – how do you find him?'

'Oh, he's okay. Quite young.'

Gabriel was reluctant to discuss her friendships with her aunt, who tended to infantalise her, lapsing into a condescending tone, thinking her naive. More to the point, Jane certainly did not want to discuss Daniel Kenton. She was not sure how she felt about him herself. Her love life had been one disaster after another thus far and she didn't want to leave herself open to criticism until she'd made up her mind. Jane had suffered the way all beautiful people did – being nice to look at, everyone was nice to her face, but ultimately they'd taken advantage of her – as she'd discovered on numerous occasions. Should something develop with Daniel, and she had an inkling it might, her aunt would be the first person she would tell. For now though, she preferred they stuck to police business. But, as often with the ACC, when away from the station and her subordinates, it was as if they never existed.

The attention in the press clearly had no impact on her; if it wasn't on the front pages she would never have mentioned the case. Odd given her connection to Cliff. Though she must have read the profile piece.

'Aunt, you knew Christopher Cliff. What do you really think happened?'

'I think the poor devil shot himself.'

'Really?' She watched Merrydown's tanned jaw move. 'But the evidence suggests otherwise.'

'When a man wishes to end it all, he will stop at nothing.'

'Then why pursue Sparks with such ... determination?' She wanted a stronger word.

'It's called management, Jane. Should I let him off the hook, he'll grow complacent.'

Gabriel was surprised at her frankness.

'They work hard.' A defensive bristle caught her unawares. 'But still – the gun, his reach ...'

Merrydown placed her knife and fork gently at the side of the plate. 'I am not a detective, Jane, I am a manager.'

'But you knew him, Cliff, knew him well?'

Her aunt picked up her glass.

'That was thirty years ago, we hardly knew each other at all at Cambridge. The connection was of value in spurring the team on, that's all.'

This cool businesslike line was as unpalatable as the rich gravy. The conversation then moved towards County and Chelmsford and the future. Gabriel had only herself to blame for the direction of the conversation; by not being willing to talk of her personal life there was little else her aunt could focus on.

At the end of the meal, Gabriel was aware of a dryness in the house. Perhaps it was a taste of loneliness. As she left the village, she thought it polished but soulless, and taking advantage of the clear road accelerated homewards. She'd take Rowhedge and its quirkiness, and much as her aunt wished for her progress through the ranks, she found herself veering in favour of Colchester and its unsavoury commander.

4 p.m., Fox Farm

Edward filled a glass from the cold tap in the kitchen. He soon returned to his subdued state of mind once Lowry had gone. The boxing copper's line of conversation was entertaining, though Edward remained naturally suspicious of the law. Even if Lowry had been influential in getting the army to take him, he still could not trust a rozzer completely, not with the uncertainty of his stepfather's death still hanging over them all. He really hadn't had time to digest it completely; everything happened so quickly. Selfishly he had been pre-occupied with his own freedom and only now was he able to take it on board.

As he made his way up the stairs to reach his attic room, he wondered how it was possible to feel so suffocated in such a spacious house surrounded by fields, as he currently did. Now more than ever, he needed what the policeman had briefly provided – to get out of here. This instinct pained him; he loved his family, but he could not return their affection with any satisfaction. Their need for him was an oppressive weight, like water pressure experienced by a diver, increasing as each day passed. And like a diver, the weight of the water bearing down only becomes a problem if he is not in harmony with his surroundings.

Edward knew he should be able to cope with – even relish – this belonging, this pulling together, but he simply wasn't equipped for it emotionally, or so he assumed. His little fat stepfather had always been pretty bloody useless, and Edward had always been there for his sisters as their big brother, but no more than that. He'd gone from one extreme to another: from the company of men in Suffolk, detached save for their comradeship, to home and his family of women, all making demands – demands he couldn't decipher.

As he neared the first floor, he became aware there was an argument in full flow in his parents' room.

'Why have you done that?' Lucy said indignantly.

'I thought it would be nice.'

'Don't you think we've seen enough of the police this summer?'

'He has helped us, Lucy, with your brother; it's kind of him to help –' his mother's voice was fractious – 'and it was a way of saying thank you.'

'We wouldn't need him if you didn't just go off as usual, for your *art*.'

'Lucy, enough! I have not left your side in days, apart from an hour in your father's office. Come now, you're fifteen, for heaven's sake, time you started to think like a young woman.'

'Motherrrrr . . .'

As he climbed painfully into the attic, the noise reduced to a muffle, and flopping on the bed, he picked up *Melody Maker*. The time since his release had been tumultuous, much of it his own making, it was true. Now, though, he longed for peace, at least until his arm healed and he could get back on his bike. It was important to get riding again as soon as possible. With his future secure in the army, he really was interested in only himself, it seemed. A blonde head popped up through the floor hatch.

'Alice.' He smiled at his sister.

'Don't hide away up here,' she said plaintively.

'There's not a lot I can do with this.' He tapped his broken arm.

'You can give me a hug, that won't hurt.'

He tossed the music paper aside. 'Of course.'

She lay alongside him.

'You can have your old room back, you shouldn't be struggling up here.' He was touched. His poor mother in her anguished state hadn't even noticed his difficulty hauling himself to his room.

'There's no need for you to go to any bother.'

'It wouldn't be any trouble –' she stared lovingly up at

him – 'I would stay with you on the camp bed, in case you need anything.'

'Alice, that is sweet, but I'm okay, really I am. You guys should go easy your mum.'

'Pah, inviting that policeman round for tea, how ridiculous.'

'He's all right, you know.'

'I don't care. He's not wanted.'

He drew back, curious. 'Why? What's your problem, he's done you no harm?'

'He took Kate away,' she said flatly, rising from the bed. 'Be careful with that arm, Edward,' and started to descend the steps. Edward shook his head, not knowing what to think. Kate? What the hell did she have to do with anything? Lowry might be right about them finding unusual ways to cope with Christopher's death. Nevertheless, the podgy sod was getting precious little by way of grieving from his family, from what Edward could see.

44

4.30 p.m., Great Tey

Lowry's house was a few doors down from the pub. Asking Becky in for coffee after lunch had seemed the most natural and polite gesture at the time. But now they were here, it was a profoundly awkward situation.

On many occasions over the years, especially during summer, he and Jacqui had invited folks round after an afternoon in the pub to sober up. This was markedly different. He allowed Becky in before him. The place must smell musty, he thought, even though he had the windows open. He steered her beyond the kitchen through to the living room at the rear of the house. Now, senses alert, he saw his home through the eyes of a stranger – as he would view a crime scene. The patio doors were open to the garden. He had to fight the urge to usher her out there, immediately.

'Make yourself comfortable,' he said instead, smiling. 'Coffee, or something stronger?' The instant he said it, he wished he could take it back.

JAMES HENRY

'Love to,' she said, eyes trying not to pry around the room, 'but I'm driving.' For eight months Lowry had inhabited the house alone, except for every other weekend when Matthew would dutifully cross the threshold. Did it feel like a family home? Or that of a bachelor or divorcee? He felt unable to see himself clearly.

'Come outside, the garden catches the sun at this time.'

She did as he suggested, and he hurried inside to put the kettle on. By the time he'd returned, Becky had settled into a plastic garden chair.

'How would you describe your circumstances?' she asked as he pulled the ring on a can of Holsten Pils.

'Cut to the chase, eh?' He drank from the can, a long, smooth drag. He was vulnerable here, alone in the family home, and should have seen this coming.

'I like you, so I am curious. If you are available . . . or not . . .'

'There's no one here but me,' he said.

Her face fell slightly, seriously. 'I don't want to get hurt.'

He swallowed, uncomfortably. 'No, of course not.'

This seemed to put her at her ease again, and she drank the coffee slowly, staying for half an hour. She left him a telephone number and, after a moment's hesitation on the threshold, she embraced him. Lowry couldn't remember the last time he'd felt any physical contact other than a right hook. She squeezed him tightly, purposefully. Or so he thought; but perhaps he was reading more into it than was really there. Some women were naturally tactile; he didn't trust his own judgement, especially after a drink. For a second he wanted to reach out, take her back inside and lose himself in intimacy, but it was a fleeting moment. No sooner had he shut the door than a wave of exhaustion struck him.

He wandered back to the living room with a bottle of fino from the fridge. The cat followed him. The time with Becky had certainly taken his mind off police work. For a few hours, Fox Farm and the Cliff family were not at the forefront of his mind, and that was no bad thing; a bit of distance would allow some perspective. Obsession with cases happened all too easily; get too close and you couldn't see what was staring you in the face. He decided to write the afternoon off, and carry on drinking. At least he was in his own home. He flicked the television and the hi-fi on, not knowing which he fancied. High on the shelf full of videos a small photo of Jacqui beamed down at him. He'd taken the others down, but had missed that one.

'What have you got to smile about?' he said, and placed the frame face down, as he ran his finger along cassette spines.

4.30 p.m., Creffield Road, Lexden

Sparks surfaced from the basement gym in much the same mood as when he'd descended. Gloomy. Jacqui Lowry's phone call that morning had pushed him to his limit. It couldn't go into another week, and he sensed she would not relent. Should he tell Lowry about the kneecapping . . . ? He was sure he would laugh that off. Sparks felt rotten about having had a pop at Lowry after he'd been put on the canvas. Talk about striking a man when he was down. It was disappointment, that was all . . . nevertheless, got to make that call. Clasping a substantial gin and tonic, he picked up the receiver and cleared his throat.

'Ah Nick, good to catch you at home. Been meaning to have a word.'

'Sparks,' Lowry greeted him. Sparks was momentarily taken aback; Lowry never addressed him like that. There was music in the background. Fleetwood Mac, if he was not mistaken.

'Are you free?' Was he having a barbecue, a spot of entertaining? Now might not be the best time for a chat.

'As a bird.' He didn't sound his usual self.

'Your wife has been on the phone asking after you, thought you should know.'

'Jacqui,' he replied deadpan, barely audible above the music.

'Yes. She, erm . . . had a little problem she asked me to sort out.'

'Problem.' Was he drunk?

'Yes,' he cleared his throat again and took a swig of the G&T, 'just thought you should know.'

'Thanks.'

That was straightforward enough; the bloke didn't seem fussed at all. He decided to switch subjects while he was ahead, shift the emphasis of the call. 'And it's the track and field day tomorrow, so you'll be thin on the ground in the afternoon.'

'I know.'

'Well, just so you know, is what I'm saying – I'll be out of the office but that's no secret. Merrydown was personally invited by the Brigadier.'

'Oh. Good. Have you seen the papers?'

'Saw and avoided.'

'Kate Everett's trial is everywhere; dragging up Cliff's murder ... I suspect we may be in line for a stinging from Merrydown tomorrow.'

'Wouldn't expect less.'

And with that he rang off. Maybe he was over-thinking things; was he going soft in old age? Who cares. His mood considerably lightened, he called out to his wife.

'Antonia,' he hollered, 'grab your gear if you want to go to Suffolk.' The prospect of a quick stroll down the banks of the Stour, followed by a couple of pints in the Sun when it opened, struck him suddenly as a very agreeable prospect.

Lowry let the phone fall to the floor and swallowed the tablet in his hand. He had lost all sense of time. It was still light outside. *Rumours* was on the turntable and *Bad Timing* on the television, paused. The album was hers and the film, a bootleg video, his.

Had they just been speaking about Jacqui? It seemed so unlikely; he was a bit pissed, but the idea of the chief talking about his wife was so remote that, seconds after he'd dropped the phone, he doubted it had taken place. Whether it occurred or not, it hardly mattered – he was jolted back into the world.

He was pleasantly inebriated. Not out of it totally, but comfortably mellow. The bottle of fino on the mantelpiece was empty, so he stumbled into the kitchen to retrieve another bottle of sherry that he had placed in the freezer, but it was almost frozen solid. When did he put it in?

Jacqui's bottle of Valium was on the table, small and innocuous, when he returned to the living room. Had he taken another pill or was he about to with the fresh bottle of sherry? He'd forgotten they had a stash of the drugs in the house until he recognised a user in Mrs Darnell. He had popped one every evening since the fight. Jacqui had them on prescription to help readjust after finishing nights. Lowry had decided that if he were to try a second meet with Becky, he would rule out the possibility of tormenting himself late into the night over his wife – and Valium would see to that. Bird. Birds. The mangy sparrowhawk in glass at the Cliffs' popped into his head as he compressed the bottle cap down. He didn't want to think about it. Valium didn't work with booze, but it did knock you out. One more then he'd sit outside to hear the evensong before watching the end of the film. If he sat there long enough and still enough he might see the barn owl pass over.

He clumsily slid open the patio door. There was something comforting about being out of it in daylight. Birdsong greeted him. He plonked himself in the cheap plastic chair and held the frozen bottle to his head, rolling it gently. There was nothing else to drink. He could go back to the pub, but was switched on enough to realise that that would be a mistake. He stared at the empty seat opposite, where Becky had sat earlier. He did like her, but he was frightened. Of what, he was not sure.

He really *didn't* like Fleetwood Mac though, so he could not fathom why he had put it on. It was her record. He was sure he didn't mind if Jacqui never came back. He was content here in his garden listening to the birds. Wisdom had it that he should grow maudlin with drink, or even angry, given she was having or had had an affair. Yet he felt neither of those things. The emotional sterility must in part be due to the drug, but so what. Enjoy the afternoon in your garden. He took a deep breath, realised he was quite drunk, and tried to focus on the thirty-foot fenced plot. The grass needed cutting, the roses deadheading, and many of the plants were leggy with flowers on the wane: overgrown and uncared for, he sadly acknowledged, and a far cry from Kate Everett's cottage garden. The woman herself then entered his head and the moment beyond her garden, in the field where he'd felt funny. He saw her green eyes, clear as day. He pushed the image out and scanned the sky. High up were the swallows. Beautiful. Ah, he was okay. He reached back to shut the patio door and promptly fell out of the chair. He lay sprawled on the paving slabs, disinclined to move. The concrete against his cheek was soothingly cool. He could see the bottle of sherry nestled on the geraniums. The bottle had not broken at least. Good, he would just lie here a while and watch it thaw.

45

8.15 a.m., Monday, Queen Street HQ

Kenton's weekend had been uneventful. He couldn't contemplate windsurfing after last week, and he ached all over, so he drove back home to Godalming to see his parents, thinking it wise to rest given what Sparks had lined up for him today.

'Won't be a moment, son.' It was as if Sparks could read his mind, detect it straying to matters unconnected with those at hand. Kenton stood in the chief's office, while Sparks conducted a hushed discussion with Granger, the coordinator for the station's many social activities. There was some plotting involved not suitable for his ears, though he couldn't imagine what it was about; today was the track and field day at Abbey Fields.

The telephone rang. The chief stood still and lit a cigarette, meaning for Granger to take the call, which he did, only to replace it seconds later.

'She's not coming,' Granger said.

'Excellent, of course she wouldn't't.' He exhaled a cloud of smoke. 'No mention of Cliff?'

Granger shook his head. 'Though she wished to remind you of the promised visit to the Mersea station, to see how her protégé was coming along.' The desk sergeant took the liberty of grinning slyly.

'Balls to that,' Sparks waved away the smoke and addressed Kenton. 'If you ask one's commanding officer to attend an event of great importance to the community, and she declines, what can you do, eh? Righto, off you scoot. Now then, Kenton, as field captain, you have your day mapped out to the full, as they say.'

'What about the Cliff case?'

'Don't worry about that, it's as dead as he is. Live a little, enjoy the summer – even villains need a break when it gets this hot.' Kenton was surprised at this carefree manner, as his face must have shown. 'We've got lives to live. Cheer up, it's Monday morning, something bad will happen to someone by the end of the week, if not sooner. In the meantime, let's enjoy what we have, eh?'

Kenton guessed this attitude came with age. Sparks was unusual. He wasn't world-weary or cynical like many older cops, and it wasn't due to lack of experience on the front line; he'd seen it all, including being held hostage soaked in petrol, so station rumour had it. This rampant social activity must be what kept him on the line. That and Asterix. Though Asterix at least didn't have to run himself into the ground competing on behalf of his master.

*

Lowry was nose down at his desk when Gabriel entered CID. Feeling slightly embarrassed, she spoke quickly and evenly about Roger Derrick's possible connection to property deals.

'Though in this case, I'm sure it's Mrs Harris's daughter's boyfriend – remember she had a wooden ornament that moved? Her daughter had got it from an antiques place up the road where her boyfriend worked.'

'Good work. That sounds entirely plausible. One of Roger's boys, no doubt. Smart thinking.' Gabriel was pleased, though his attention remained on his work and he spoke the words to the paperwork in front of him. 'We'll get him soon enough. Bear with me. Just running over the notes from the Cliff case one more time . . . we're missing something . . .' He continued running his finger down the paper.

'I had lunch with my aunt yesterday,' Gabriel said, determined to have his attention. 'Kate Everett's trial was all over the papers and the Cliff family was plastered inside the supplements. Here, if you're interested.' She lay the *Telegraph* on the corner of his desk.

Lowry still did not look up. 'Uh-huh.'

'She thinks the jury will show clemency, her helping with the children; says her heart was in the right place – the speed with which she was at Fox Farm. Sounds like guff to me, just because she was there when his gun was still smoking . . .'

Gabriel didn't mention what Merrydown herself thought of the case; it wasn't constructive at all. She noticed he'd stopped what he was writing.

'Oh my God, your face – it's worse! Awful!' She held her hands to her mouth.

'Thank you . . . you know you're not the first person to say that.' He frowned and scratched the back of his head as if it hurt just to think. 'Not about my face – about Kate Everett.'

'Oh, about the leniency?'

He rose and moved to the filing cabinet, ignoring her shock. 'No . . . I meant "the gun still smoking". Where've I heard that . . . was it Everett herself?' He stared at Jane. 'Yes, when Sparks and I went to see Everett in Chelmsford prison. I made a note of it.'

'Where is he, by the way? Haven't heard him bellowing unnecessarily at anyone. It's quiet . . . and no Daniel either.'

'Otherwise engaged for the present. Right . . .' He pushed back his chair, concentration tightly drawn on his face. 'When Sparks and I visited Kate Everett, there was something she said, minutes afterwards,' he reiterated, as if crystallising the moment in his head, and pulled out a folder from a stack of similar ones piled on the desk.

'She said *smell of blood and cordite*. Whether she literally smelt a smoking gun, I doubt it; it's more than likely auto-suggestion – she expected to smell it so she thinks she did. The point is, she was on the scene soon after the gun went off. Too soon, maybe.'

'What do you mean?'

'I don't know yet. But I think you have triggered something.' He smiled at her, revealing uneven teeth. 'Let's start at the beginning: Alan Ward hears the gun go at precisely eight-fifteen. Kate Everett arrived before eight-thirty. That's all we know from this –' he jabbed the case file – 'she was approximate. Now it would take her five minutes, seven maybe, to get there, depending on whether she was able to leave immediately or not . . .'

'What are you –'

'Wait.' He held up a forefinger, and flicked through the file rapidly. 'But we didn't check the time Everett received the telephone call from Fox Farm.'

'That's because there was no need: the time in her statement corresponded with the time Lucy Cliff gave us.'

'Exactly – and after all, at the time we were looking at a suspected suicide, why bother to ratify it? Get on to BT now. Get the precise time.'

'Where are you going?'

'To see Alan Ward.'

Lowry left her and hurried down the stairs. Though sluggish to start, his mind was now perfectly lucid. He could see the attraction of Valium – the morning half-life was negligible and he must have slept a good ten hours.

He'd been re-examining the statements from that first morning at Fox Farm, and weeks on, it read like a different story. The police had approached Cliff's death as a suicide at the start; the situation had not been conducted as a murder inquiry. Had they considered Cliff's death a murder at the time, as they did now, they might have looked at certain aspects, such as the timeline, more closely. Subsequently, they had considered Derrick as the prime suspect, only scrutinising *his* arrival and departure times. Now Lowry realised he should go back to when Kate Everett got the call for help, and the thought of where that may take him was becoming too chilling to contemplate . . .

– 46 –

10.35 a.m., Stanway, Colchester

Alan's mother called him from the bottom of the stairs. Her tone was unfamiliar. It did not suggest that his friends were here, or that she wanted him to do some chore or other. There were low voices at the door and as Alan reached the landing, he knew it was the policeman he'd met at Fox Farm. His mother's expression confirmed it.

Sitting at the dining-room table with a stranger any day but a Sunday mealtime reminded him of the extra maths lessons his father insisted he endured after school. His mother brought the policeman a cup of tea, then closed the door behind her.

'Someone give you a black eye?' He couldn't help it. The policeman's face was a bit like Andrew Chapman's after Julian Brazier had finished with him for writing *'Brazier est un bender'* on the blackboard in French when Miss Green was sick.

'Yep, they have.' The inspector sipped at his tea. He seemed a lot larger and older in the dining room than he had seemed when Alan first saw him out in the meadow at Fox Farm.

381

It was funny to think of a policeman getting hit. 'Was it someone trying to get away?'

He smiled. 'No, it was from a boxing match.' The way he said it was as if it didn't hurt. Alan bet it did, though. The policeman placed the teacup delicately on the saucer. 'Your mother tells me you have been sleeping badly since that day?'

'I'm all right,' he said defensively.

'You wake up in the middle of the night?'

'Only once or twice.'

'What is it you dream?'

'Just the moment I heard the gun, with the fox on the track . . .' This answer satisfied the policeman.

'Alan, I want you to think back to that weekend, from when your parents dropped you off.'

'We were sleeping in the attic, me and Darren. I didn't check what time I woke,' he said apologetically.

'Let's go back a step or two further. When did you first see your cousins, on Sunday evening?'

'I don't remember much about it. Sorry . . .'

His memory of the evening was fuzzy. Everything before finding the body slipped further away as the events of that Monday morning became more dominant, imprinted on his brain since the nightmares. He relived it most nights in some form or another, waking up drenched in sweat from terrifying dreams, many of them featuring a fox with red eyes. The burning eyes, with veins the colour of straw coming nearer and nearer, until Alan thought he'd retch, and then bang – he'd wake up. Never the man, or blood, or screams, or his dead uncle, just the anticipation of a gunshot and a fox with red eyes. In real life, foxes had golden eyes.

'Where were your cousins?' Alan was gently brought back to his mum's pristine dining room and the policeman at the table.

'Upstairs. Upstairs playing a game.'

'See, you can remember. I've a note you said that when we chatted at the time, good boy.' He smiled. 'Were the girls pleased to see you, you and Darren?'

Encouraged, Alan scrunched up his eyes and cast his mind back really hard. To his surprise, it worked. There she was, Emma, glaring at him from behind a book. 'She said we ought to knock first. Before going in a girl's room.'

'Who said that?'

'Emma, she was on the bed reading.'

'So the three of them were in Emma's bedroom reading?'

'No, it was Alice's room. Lucy and Alice were playing a board game on the floor.'

'What were they playing?'

'I don't know, I couldn't really see. Alice had her back to me. There were some letters . . .'

'Scrabble?'

'No, no, the letters were on the board.'

'Did they not invite you to play?'

He shook his head. 'We went outside . . .'

'And did what?'

'Dares.'

'Dares?'

Alan could feel himself begin to colour, 'Alice is quite keen on dares.' He went quiet. 'We went to the pond.'

'Oh, yes, I saw you there before, what's the fascination?'

He winced lightly. It was cruel and didn't show her in a good light. Alice was his favourite, too.

'At this stage, Alan, every tiny bit of information is very important.'

Alan chewed this over before answering. 'Alice ... Alice would dare Darren to swallow a froglet whole and ...'

'What?'

'... and if he did, she would kiss him on the lips.'

Lowry listened to the boy carefully. Underneath these innocent happenings, he was sure there was a vital component to the chain of events leading to the death of Christopher Cliff. Ward described the following morning much as Lowry understood it from the original transcripts, apart from one detail.

'Everything was fine until my aunt left the house. Nobody said a word, no fuss – even Emma was well behaved. Normally she makes a show and kicks off every time Aunt Suzanne leaves the house.' He gave a strange laugh. 'It's as if they were silently pushing her on her way.'

'How do you mean?'

'By not distracting her, like not asking her to make their breakfast; we all got along and sat down quietly ...'

Lowry checked his notebook. Quite clearly he had written: 'fight: cream/milk', meaning over breakfast.

'Are you sure?'

'Positive.'

'What about this argument between the girls?'

'That was after my aunt had left.'

'After?'

'Yes, they quarrelled.'

'Might it have been over you?' That was the other answer on the file, an inconsistency they had overlooked, thinking it immaterial.

'*Me*? Why?'

Lowry raised his eyebrows. 'Winning their affection?'

Alan didn't know what to say to that. 'They only pretend to like me, I'm sure of that . . .' He screwed up his face, wracking his brains. 'Alice was watching out the window, and Lucy told her to stop it and got quite cross.'

'Was she seeing her mother leave?'

'Err . . . no, she'd gone while we were finishing breakfast. She started shouting *out now*.'

'Out, out where? Outside?'

'I don't know, but that was when Uncle raised his voice and told us to play outside.'

'Had it anything to do with Mr Derrick coming?'

'Who? Oh, the visitor.'

'Waiting for him to come?'

'Yes, Uncle said he was expecting someone.'

The policeman sat back and studied him in a way his teachers might. 'Remember I said to you that morning that you were grown-up enough to know the truth?' Alan nodded. 'Well you see, the truth is there, hidden just under the surface, so I need to know every detail leading up to Mr Derrick turning up. Mr Derrick is a man who arrived the moment after you left to play outside.'

'Mr Cliff asked us to play outside, that's all I know of any visitor. Alice was at the window. Maybe Alice was waiting for him, too? He'd see her, too, that bedroom window is above the front door.'

47

11.15 a.m., Abbey Fields, South Colchester

The cricket pavilion was bristling with all manner of stout Colchester dignitaries in linen suits, floral women on their arms sipping Pimm's. The pomp outdid the circumstance by some magnitude. Kenton was uncomfortable in his navy shorts and a white vest, as Sparks wheeled him from one businessman to the next, making bold claims as to the form of the police team. He knew the chief meant well; he was proud of them – the force, too – and what better way to impress the local community than to display your men in full fettle? Kenton was sure this show of strength would provoke doubt in the minds of any would-be white-collar villains in the room. He only wished he wasn't parading around in what amounted to little more than a school PE kit. As the chief stopped to light a cigarette, Kenton took the opportunity to slip away down onto the grass into the full glare of the sun.

Behind him, by the side of the pavilion under the shade of the poplars, was the urgent sound of betting odds being discussed. Two men stopped and looked over at him. He smelt cigarettes.

'You may not entirely approve, but funds are needed for the social club.' Sparks was back at his shoulder, stopwatch resting on the crux of his open-neck shirt.

'Might funds be found for a kit upgrade, sir?' He tugged at the sack-like material of his shorts. 'Steve Ovett wouldn't be caught dead in these.'

'Steve Ovett wouldn't be caught, full stop. You run like him and we'll see.'

He clapped him on the shoulder and the pair made their way towards the track, where men could be seen stretching and warming up. The early heats for the sprinting had been completed. It was then that Kenton spotted the broad forehead of Michael Hoare.

'What you grimacing at?' Sparks halted too.

'That man there,' he nodded towards the army team, 'is Edward Hoare's cousin.'

'He's from a military family. What of it?'

'He's smirking at me.'

'*Smirking* at you? What the fuck does that mean?'

'Smiling smugly.'

'So bloody what?' Sparks's forehead creased in the blazing sun. 'He could blow kisses for all I care.'

'Sorry, sir,' Kenton abruptly remembered his place and that the chief had no truck with vagaries. A man either wanted to punch another man, or shake his hand – there was no in-between. He start to wrap gauze round his hands. 'Just the chap was a bit cocky the other day, when we tried to pull in Edward Hoare. I'm not saying he's responsible for him coming off his bike, but he might not have left in such a hasty fashion . . . might I scrounge a cigarette, sir?'

'Of course. Now's your chance to put him in his place, then . . .' The chief patted his shorts for cigarettes. 'What the fuck are you doing?'

'Binding my hands. They're rather sore and I want as firm a grip as –'

'You're throwing a javelin, man, not feeding a red-hot poker up your jacksy.'

'Yes, but my grip . . .'

'Son, the only grip you need to improve is your grip on yourself.' The chief leant forward, cigarette firmly between his teeth. 'Show me.'

Kenton displayed the unbound palm. The calluses on his fingers had torn yesterday even though he'd been careful with them at his parents; last time he went out, a man on the beach had said he must be gripping the boom inefficiently, using poor technique. Sparks winced. 'Disgusting. What on earth have you been doing? No – forget that, I don't want to know.'

'Windsurfing. At first it was the uphaul . . . but now I've got going, it's even worse hanging on to the wishbone.' He studied the weeping sores. 'I must be holding it wrong –'

'Too many exams have left you with nancy-boy soft hands that wilt at the first contact with real life.' The signal went up for the first event. 'Ah, there's the Beard.'

Kenton followed the chief's eyeline to alight on the garrison commander, a big man standing ramrod-straight dressed in an olive uniform, talking to a tiny woman in a huge hat.

'Why is he nicknamed the Beard, sir? Apart from the obvious, I mean. Hardly imaginative.' Kenton had always puzzled over it.

'Because the army did away with beards in the Crimea and it's against regulations. That pompous twat is the only soldier – apart from the Action Man in your toy cupboard – that has one in the entire country. Now if you'll excuse me, I must go talk with him. And you, focus on winning, you've got your mark.' He nodded towards Hoare limbering up. 'You can do it, son, I know you can.'

7.15 p.m., Fox Farm

They sat in the courtyard. It was a beautiful evening; birdsong and children's laughter. The sun was sinking low, but it still had a powerful glare, which allowed Lowry to keep his sunglasses on and watch the children while appearing to listen to their mother. The girls knew their father was expecting Derrick that fatal morning; Derrick himself had said he'd left a message with one of them. This snippet of information had been overlooked in the quest to nail Derrick himself, and was something Lowry only picked up on last week when they saw the man at home in Feering.

Suzanne was gay, the happiest he'd seen her; elated that Edward's application to join the forces had been successful, thanks largely to Lowry. Oldham had pulled strings. The mother's talk to the children was scattergun, urging them to eat and drink and at the same time projecting excited imaginations about her son seeing the world. It was difficult to gauge whether the girls were listening. The youngest child, Emma, was withdrawn. The more Suzanne spoke of Edward's departure, the more the mood between the girls deepened. Edward himself had eaten hastily, and left the table with a full glass of his mother's wine to go to work on his motorbike.

'Come on, Emma, trifle is your favourite, you too, Alice?' Suzanne had noticed the two bowls were untouched, and made to shoo wasps away.

'I'm not hungry,' Alice said in a flat tone. Her gaze was on her younger sister.

'Come, Emma, let's play a game,' Lucy said; it was a command, not a request.

'Don't want to.'

'I heard from Alan you play a lot of board games,' Lowry said. This wasn't true but it was an opening. Lucy's eyes shot to his, he feigned not to notice.

'Huh, I don't think so.' Suzanne poured herself another glass of wine. 'Once or twice at Christmas. Monopoly usually ends in tears.'

'You were playing at something when Alan arrived, he told me that he interrupted you.'

'Oh really, what was that?' Suzanne gulped her wine merrily.

'He must have been mistaken,' Alice said lightly, her attention still on her younger sister.

'No, he was quite adamant,' Lowry blithely carried on.

'Come on, Emma,' Lucy said again.

'More wine, Inspector?' Suzanne refilled his glass without waiting for an answer. 'I can't say how grateful I am for all you've done for Edward, that morning I saw him, I never envisaged him taking the step and joining up . . .'

'That was *not* supposed to happen,' Emma said, standing bolt upright. Lowry watched for the two other girls to respond. Alice was up immediately, standing behind her mother, young face distorted in the fading sun, casting her eyes deep against her brow. Her mouth twisted slightly and then she emitted a short, rasping hiss, sudden and high. Lowry then saw, in a flash, what he could only describe as pure evil. The cry caused Emma to freeze momentarily and hurry off. The incident was brief, lost seconds later under the wheeze of a nearby greenfinch. So fleeting, in fact, Lowry wasn't entirely sure he heard it, except for a flinch from Suzanne. After the girls left the table, he was in no doubt that he had witnessed something irregular, something more than a trick of the light caught in the evening sun.

Emma Cliff's remark remained with him, and after a suitable pause, he made his apologies to use the bathroom. From the landing window, he could see all three girls out in the pasture, back to becoming three playful schoolgirls. The house was empty. Alice's room was identified by a small floral plaque on the door. Inside he scoured the room; he didn't know what he was searching for but he would when he found it. To the casual observer, it suggested a room occupied by a child with a curiosity for natural history – dried flowers, bird's nests, feathers, rocks. Brightly coloured gemstones sat amid shelves full of books, amethyst and fossils. On the top shelf sat a shoebox with a boss of a smiling green man propped up outside it. They had played a game on the floor. He knelt on the bare boards. There was no sign of a board game, or even a jigsaw. The bed was of modern design with a two-inch gap between it and the floor. He ran his fingers along the gap, where they instantly caught a wooden edge. He forced his hand further in, his knuckle catching on the edge; whatever it was, it was placed where only slender hands might reach. He shifted position to jack the bed up and as soon as it was lifted, he froze. For a moment, he couldn't believe what he was seeing. He gently let the bed down and suddenly felt uneasy in his surroundings. He looked back around the room. What at first he had perceived to be a harmless collection of curiosities now took on an air of foreboding. His eye was again caught by the green man's face, propped up against the shoebox. He saw it now as a sentinel, placed there as protector. He moved to the bookshelf and took down the box. He removed the lid. The contents were quite ordinary . . . apart from one thing.

He frowned. Aware that the minutes had flown, he made a mental note of all he'd seen, then swiftly moved downstairs. He would thank Suzanne kindly for dinner and take his leave. The further away he was from Fox Farm, the easier it would be to consider all that he'd just experienced.

6.25 a.m., Tuesday, Great Tey

Lowry had slept soundly. The windows were open all night and he was woken by a breeze tickling his toes. A faint change in the season was in the air. Summer was on the wane, but only just – the chill would have gone by the time he was dressed. He was alert this morning, and a moderate number of pints at the Chequers had allowed him to sleep well.

As he'd sat at the bar last night, he'd turned things over and over in his mind, assembling what he knew, knocking it down and building it up again. Each time, he arrived at the same outcome. He knew he was right, however absurd it might seem. Lowry was well versed in superstition and folklore. He could see beyond the cosy appeal and its quaint charm. He understood how it could be more troubling, especially with the young and susceptible. There was no stronger imagination than a child's. He thought about his own mother, and the conversation he'd had with Edward that morning at the beach. For a non-believer such as Lowry, paganism was far easier to understand than Christianity; at its root it was nature-worship – and to him, there seemed to be a hell of a lot more verisimilitude in the fact that the sun rose every day than there was in the everlasting wait for the Second Coming. What starts as harmless fun and an appreciation of the natural world could rapidly transform into something far more sinister, if the need for it arose. Lowry could understand the leap from Green Man to Ouija boards, if the need was there, and Christopher had taken their beloved big brother away from them. The house was bursting with antiquated books, a library filled with history, folklore, ancient religion, and English customs. With this sort of information at their fingertips, it was easy to see where the knowledge came from. But they would need more – inspiration, encouragement – to understand the natural world surrounding them, from a cognisant adult. Not the mother, she was too absorbed – like her dead husband – in her own solitary pursuit, art. A teacher, though, one right under his nose: Kate Everett. Wasn't it she that had taught them how to make the corn dolly? That was what the object was called, originally a pagan symbol, subsequently hijacked by the Christian church. A woman who loved nature, and one whose enchantment he himself had felt – imagine the impression made on three resentful young girls in need of attention?

The doorbell went. At this time in the morning, it could only be the postman. He ambled down the stairs. A Littlewoods catalogue delivery, no doubt – eight months on she might at least amend her delivery address. The figure through the glass was indeed wearing pale blue. However, when he opened the door, he was faced with the blue uniform of a State Registered Nurse – it was his wife.

'You've bleached your hair,' he blurted out.

'It was more than just a bottle of peroxide. Anyway, it was this colour when I saw you on the ward last week. Do you like it?'

He shrugged. 'It's fine.' He thought she looked cheap; she was too old to have that shade of platinum white.

'Can I come in? Odd to ring one's own doorbell.' She stood expectantly on the doormat appraising him. 'Or are you off somewhere?'

Standing bare-chested in only running shorts, he edged aside, allowing her into the house.

'I know you are angry with me and have every right to be. But there's Matthew to consider . . . don't you think?'

He said nothing and followed her into the kitchen and filled the kettle on autopilot.

'He can't stay at Mum's every school holiday.'

'It's easier for him to see his old friends in Colchester than being stuck out here,' he said matter-of-factly. That was indeed true. Matt was a weekly boarder at a private school in Chelmsford. Following a period of bullying at the comp at Stanway they'd moved him, and it was of course convenient if he was away during the week, there was no denying that (even if he and Jacqui were together, it was better, given the shift work).

'That's nonsense,' she said dismissively.

'He can come back here, then – it was you who decided he ought to be with your parents.' He passed her a coffee.

'What about me?' She stepped closer, clutching the mug close in beseeching fashion as though needing its warmth, despite it already being above twenty degrees out. He moved back against the kitchen unit. A cupboard door pressed hard against his coccyx.

'What about you?'

'Can I come back?'

'I haven't given it any thought.'

'No? Well, can you give it some now? My name is on the mortgage, too.'

The surprise of her arrival had now been superseded by annoyance. She could not barge her way in and make demands.

'We should probably sell it.'

'Sell it? What about us?' Her eyes took in his bruised face. His own gaze moved to the tiled floor. He hadn't noticed how filthy it was. When was the last time it had seen a mop? Jacqui repeated her entreaty. 'What about us?' What a ridiculous question. So hackneyed – straight off a cheesy soap. What could he say that wasn't equally ridiculous?

'What about us, Nick? Look at me.' She moved closer, he could smell her perfume. And that finally triggered a response.

'If I look at you, I may just knock you unconscious.'

She backed away.

He heard the front door click shut. Her coffee sat unfinished on the empty work surface, the mug rimmed with a faint trace of lipstick. He could never remember the rules about make-up on duty – was it allowed, or had she worn it for him, for effect? He'd always thought her cute in her uniform, and in the old days she could twist him round her finger. He'd often pick her up off a late shift then, before she passed her driving test, and he'd do anything she asked, go to a party or gig, when he would've rather stayed in and watched a film. He was a sucker for her. Yes, there was something about the uniform, not sexual, that got to him. A purity, maybe, ironically. Anyway she'd always known this, hence catching him unawares now, this morning. As he sipped his own drink and slowly savoured a cigarette, he realised that he did not miss her. Sober or drunk, he remained resolutely passive.

He stubbed out the cigarette and went in search of his running vest.

Jacqui was still trembling as she tried to start the car. Cigarette smoke swelled in the XR2 as she held a fag between her lips and fumbled blindly at the steering column. Her eyes began to sting. The key wouldn't go in the ignition. She paused to wind down the window and removed the cigarette with her other hand; he was not, after all, going to rush out here and beat her to within an inch of her life. If Nick was going to punch her he'd have already done so. He was probably taking it out on some unsuspecting light switch.

The car cleared. She inhaled calmly, then turned the ignition key again. The radio came on. 'See You' by Depeche Mode.

She half-choked back a laugh. Jacqui had wanted Nick to take her to see them, the Basildon boys, at the university but he'd refused, saying they were for kids. They'd rowed about it . . . their first big one perhaps, and it was at that very point in time she'd realised she was bored and didn't want to grow old quite yet. Through the windscreen, a dodderer walking a Jack Russell conversed with an equally old, round lady waiting for the Post Office to open. Why did old people get up so early? When she was their age she would lie in until noon every day.

She sighed and adjusted the rear-view mirror. The smoke had caused her mascara to run. Damn. She dropped the clutch and revved the Fiesta, and inadvertently made the wheels screech as she pulled away into the quiet village lane. The terrier barked soundlessly at her. She smiled to herself. All in all, it had not gone as badly as it might have: Nick would never have welcomed her back with open arms; he wasn't that type. That he'd threatened to knock her block off was a good sign. If he was still that angry after so long, then he still cared. Until that moment she wasn't really sure what she wanted – only that she couldn't continue living with Trish – and now she knew she wanted her husband back.

As she sped noisily towards Colchester General, Dave Gahan's plaintive ruminations gave way to Billy Idol's determined 'White Wedding', and she felt similarly energetic. She was not going to lose him – of that she was certain.

48

9.15 a.m., Queen Street HQ

'And what did it contain, the shoebox?' Gabriel asked.

'A bird's nest.'

'Hmmm, but there were several in the room already, right?'

'This one had eggs in it.'

'Eggs?' She pulled a face. 'What sort?'

'I have no idea. The nesting season finished months ago. They had very unusual markings – this is going to sound crazy, but they appeared to be sprayed in blood – reddish streaks, splattered across them like Jackson Pollock had whipped a paintbrush over them.'

Gabriel felt her stomach turn. 'Christ, are you sure?'

He shrugged, 'I don't know. Keep it to yourself for now.'

'Of course . . . Back to the board – are you positive that's what it was?'

'I know a Ouija board when I see it.'

'I'm not sure I've ever seen one.' She hadn't. Other than on the cinema screen.

'Nor should you.'

'What do they do, exactly?'

'Everything or nothing, depending on your susceptibility – spiritualists use them to contact the dead; very popular with the Victorians. You've heard of seances, right?'

'Yes. Are you going to confront Suzanne Cliff? *Your children are talking to dead people.* She's going to love that.'

This case was taking the most bizarre turn. If anyone else spun a tale of Ouija boards and blood-coated eggs, she'd think they were pulling her leg. But she had no doubt in Lowry. He was completely serious and unruffled; in fact his mood was the best she'd seen in a while. She could only assume he'd run this over and over in his mind before letting her in.

'Everything, however wild it may seem, is pointing in that direction. I'm not saying they literally heard voices from a Ouija board ordering them to shoot their father. The point is, the belief is there, driving them to commit murder.'

'You're serious, aren't you?'

'Deadly.'

'Why?'

She listened carefully as he explained his theory's logic. The two older girls had taken grave exception to the way that their new stepfather treated their big brother. They spent long days out at the farm with nothing but fields to play in and books to read. And read they did, picking through Christopher's volumes, discovering all manner of topics – art, nature, magic.

The resentment builds and eventually they plan a revenge, nurtured by Kate Everett.

'Kate Everett?' This came out of the blue.

'Perhaps. They spent a lot of time at Sweet Pea Cottage. It's a hunch. Cliff's books alone are not enough, however precocious the girls are, to spur them on.' He paused, caught in his own thoughts. 'Everett loves children and is alone, and has a gift for inspiring them with the beauty of their natural surroundings. Remember the one person they admire has gone and the parents are preoccupied – one with his own eminent career, the other with her paintings. Both have no idea what's going through the girls' heads, no real sense of the impact Edward's arrest has had on the children.'

'And what? Everett encourages them to kill him?'

'No, no, at least not knowingly, but encourages a thirst for learning and understanding the supernatural.'

'Are you saying she's a witch?'

'I guess I am, yes.' The word crystallised in both their minds. 'A modern-day one, at least. Though she is not present at the time Cliff is killed, we know that from the phone records. But perhaps in the background – not at the shooting . . .'

'And you're confident that one of the girls pulled the trigger. That is a giant leap for me,' Gabriel confessed.

Lowry sat back. 'You've not spent the time around them as I have.' He reached for a cigarette, and scrabbled for matches in the desk drawer. 'The girls knew when Derrick was due to call, so were able to plot around that timescale in order to lay the blame on him. Cliff had the gun out with the intent to show Roger, and willingly hands it over to one of his little angels to inspect.'

'Safety around guns in the house is non-existent,' she added, 'the cabinet wasn't locked, Suzanne wouldn't have a clue where the cartridges were stored. Her daughters steal them on the Sunday night and the next day slip one in. Bang.'

Lowry nodded slowly in agreement.

'Maybe share this with the chief first, in case it goes badly?' she advised, sipping her coffee.

He smiled. 'That's probably a wise idea. But we'll spare him the supernatural angle, practical salt-of-the-earth sort that he is.'

'You're in a very good mood, sir, if you don't mind me saying.'

'It'll pass . . . and we won't get a conviction.'

'Why not?'

'We'll never be able to prove it. Can you imagine the furore? No, our angle with the mother is to lead her to doubt her children, gently squeeze the girls and see what happens. If she hears they are not all they seem to be, she may believe a less brutal outcome.'

'Such as?'

He shrugged. 'An accident? He hands them the gun, and horseplay results in him being shot.'

'Do you think that's possible?' she asked, not without hope.

'Nope. Cliff is an experienced gun-handler, and would not clean the weapon loaded, neither is he likely to hand his stepdaughter a loaded gun in the kitchen, after he'd been shouting at them to get out of the house. It's a tack to take, though – an admission that they were in the room when the gun went off has our foot in the door.'

He rose, his gaze falling on the empty desk opposite. 'Where's Hercules got to, I wonder?'

All was good with the world. Sparks whistled tunelessly as he tidied his office. Yesterday's results glowed within him. To excel in such a public arena lifted morale and furthered the police's standing within the community. The local paper head-line beamed out at him. The fittest, fastest and the strongest. Kenton had done them all proud, and Sparks had also secured donations from local businesses to support the social club. Tony Pond the car dealer had been especially generous. On a darker day he'd have thought him a little too generous, and instinct would have told him that his decision to accept the gift may come back to bite him, but he was not going to allow that to cloud his day. He tapped the Manila files squarely into line. The smudged type of 'Everett' showed in the top corner. He slapped the pile into the tray – that was that finished. He nudged the phone as he did so. That had been mercifully quiet, too, not so much as a murmur from County. Cliff was forgotten, it seemed. Strange, but not his to reason why. No, the only blot on the horizon was Merrydown's

visit to Mersea, which he could not wriggle out of any longer.
A rap on the door.

'Come! Ah, Nick. What gives?' he beamed.

'Suzanne Cliff.'

That was the one name he didn't want to hear. He continued
to shuffle papers.

'Er, where's Kenton?' Lowry asked. 'I thought he was up
here, he's not called in.'

'Chelmsford. Running at the county grounds.'

'Bloody hell, again? In this heat?' said Lowry, surprised.
'What on earth for?'

'You're not his mother, what's up? A scout from the Athletics
Association was impressed with his time for the 1,500m and
asked him if he fancied a trial.'

'And he agreed?'

'I agreed for him. Good for the lad. There won't be a criminal
in the south-east that'll be able to outrun him!' He grinned
unpleasantly at Gabriel, who he'd only just noticed was with
Lowry.

'Glad to hear it, now there's something I need to run by you.'
Lowry then proceeded to tell him he was about to question the
Cliff girls over the death of their stepfather. The commander
took it in like a cup of cold sick.

'That punch you took must have been harder than we
thought. Are you mad?'

'Not at all. You've burnt your forehead, by the way, ought
to be careful in that sun . . .'

'Bollocks to my forehead. Sit the fuck down and explain this lunacy.'

'It's a logical progression, nothing else has come to light,' Lowry said.

'You go accusing that woman's kids of blowing their old man away and there'll be merry hell to pay.'

'We've been through every possibility and we're left with only what appears impossible.'

'Possible, impossible, you're talking about patricide by minors.' Sparks glared across the table. 'All right, you've two minutes. That's all Merrydown'll give you, if that.'

'It's timing. The shotgun went off at eight-fifteen. Derrick was there at eight, and gone before whatever took place – it had to be before eight-fifteen, at any rate.'

'If that fucker didn't do it,' Sparks said dubiously.

Lowry ignored the remark. 'The kids were mucking about in the field by now; they'd have to have exited the house almost simultaneously as he arrived.'

'Are you saying it's planned?'

'Wait.' He lit a cigarette. 'Kate Everett turned up at eight-twenty-five or thereabouts. But most importantly, we know that she picked up the telephone at eight-sixteen according to British Telecom's records.' Lowry waited to make sure he'd heard.

'So?' Sparks grimaced.

'It takes at least two minutes to reach the farmhouse from

the oak tree, the base for their game of hide and seek. Even if they ran back the second they heard the gunshot, they wouldn't get there until at least eight-seventeen.'

'Maybe one of them returned to the house early?'

'*Exactly*. Alice herself says she left the game and went to the kitchen for a snack; that's when she finds Cliff and runs for Lucy.'

'I still don't see how this proves anything. '

Lowry rose. 'The girls would have to have been in close proximity to the house when it occurred. Real close, not game-in-a-meadow-close. Think about it: we know the gun went off at eight-fifteen. If the girls' story is to be believed, Alice discovered Cliff – in what must've been seconds after the shot, its own issue – ran back to the meadow for her sister, and then they both returned to the farmhouse and Lucy made that phone call to the neighbour. All this, *by eight-sixteen*, when Kate picked up the phone. If this is really what happened, we're talking Olympic-level sprinters here. Not to mention that response time shows remarkable presence of mind, don't you think?'

'Yep. Sharp. Too sharp, that's what you're saying?'

'It started me thinking, and it's a line we did not examine. Everett's response time matched exactly what Lucy Cliff said – "I called straight away". We thought nothing of it at the time and didn't consider how close to the time of the shooting the call for help was.'

'Yes, yes, but it doesn't prove anything, does it? You're

second-guessing a child's reaction time. You're going to need a hell of a lot more than that.'

'Then there's the argument between the two youngest girls – the story is inconsistent. I didn't consider it before, what with the general confusion, and they were not suspects at that point. There were two versions: one says they argued over who got the cream on their breakfast cereal and another says they argued over the boy, Alan. It was not until I spoke to him this morning that I realised the timing of this row was inconsistent – it couldn't have been over breakfast, as Alan said they had eaten in silence when the mother was there. The shouting came *after* she'd left.'

'Those girls have been through a lot. They can be forgiven for what is essentially failing to recount child's play. What about a motive? It's got to be more than Daddy kicking them out of the house because he's got a bent antique dealer coming . . .'

'I just want a closer look.'

'How fucking close?'

Lowry rose and paced the room. 'Not breathing down their neck close, just near enough to maybe make them jump – lead the mother to believe they might have witnessed his death, if not actually pulled the trigger. Edward's real twitchy about his sisters, there's a chance with some pressure they may give themselves away . . .'

'He's soft in the head, that one. The widow trusts you. And don't forget Merrydown has gone easy because of that.'

'I know, I was invited round for dinner last night.'

'Well, tread carefully.'

'I will.'

'And I mean carefully.'

After they left, Sparks realised Lowry was not being completely open with him. There was something missing – had to be for him to get the bit between his teeth like this. Probably for the best if he didn't know; delicate situations were not the chief's forte, and if it all went tits up he'd feel better coming down like a ton of bricks if he'd been left in the dark . . .

– 49 –

11.30 a.m., Fox Farm

Suzanne Cliff did not expect to see Lowry back again so soon.
She had a feeling this time it would not be so pleasant.

Lowry, who arrived with Gabriel, asked her whether her
daughters were at home. They were in the house; he asked
if he and she might have a word outside. She agreed and
slipped on some sandals, offering to walk them round the
farm, forgetting for the moment the police were more than
familiar with the layout.

'Mrs Cliff,' Gabriel opened the conversation, which Suzanne
took as a further bad sign. 'Are you aware your children
possess a Ouija board?'

'A what?' Her response was almost angry. 'I don't think so.'
She watched Lowry for an explanation as they slowly rounded
the house, but the inspector walked slightly ahead of them
and gave nothing away. This frightened her.

'We have reason to believe there is one in the house, under
your middle daughter's bed.'

'How on earth would you know that?'

'Forgive me.' Lowry stopped yards outside the barn where her son, against her wishes, was cumbersomely continuing to fix his motorcycle. 'I saw it poking out when in search of the lavatory.'

Her mind was racing; why didn't he mention it then? Yesterday was a lovely evening, the first time she had relaxed in weeks. 'No, I didn't know.' Her heart sank, she felt duped.

'So, it's not something you or your husband had purchased?' His voice was stiff.

'No, whatever for?'

'Some people treat it as a party game when they've had a few.'

'Monopoly is the limit in this house, I told you, Inspector,' she said with as much authority as she could muster. 'Where on earth is this leading?'

'You would agree it's an unusual possession for a child to have?'

She nodded.

'Could they have got it from Kate Everett?'

'Kate?'

'Yes, they spent time with her – that's right, isn't it?'

'I really don't know,' she said. 'It's possible, I suppose.' Her mind was still reeling from such a left-field revelation.

'If your girls are in the habit of keeping secrets, I just wonder if they're being honest about what they saw and heard that morning, and I would like to ask them a few more questions.'

Lowry did not feel great about the situation and was well aware of the distress he was causing Suzanne Cliff, but he saw no other way; he was glad to have Gabriel here as a buffer, to allow him to regain a formality perhaps breeched over recent days. Edward, holding an oily rag, glanced up curiously. Lowry smiled across weakly; he should not feel betrayal in the pit of his stomach but it was there. Suzanne Cliff needed to hear her daughters were lying; this foolery with the occult would at the very least inject doubt in her, and at best trick the girls into implicating themselves.

The three of them entered the house. Lowry would talk to the smallest child first, leaving the older girls until later. If they were questioned first, they may influence their sister. He suggested the front room as suitable for the six-year-old, but would move to the kitchen later, subtly dividing the girls and sowing dissonance. He required Suzanne to be present to witness whatever was to follow, but made a pretense to her that he would only allow her to sit in on the interview if she pledged to remain quiet. He did not want Emma distracted, and of equal importance to him was that the mother listened. The girl had short, untidy hair. Sitting in a huge winged chair, she reminded him of her sister's namesake in Wonderland. He and Gabriel sat apart on the sofa, while Suzanne knelt to the side, Lowry aware of her hand resting close by.

'Tell me about the cat,' he said breezily.

'We don't have a cat?' Suzanne couldn't help but interrupt.

Lowry raised his forefinger to remind her she was there to observe.

'Tell me about the cat,' he repeated.

'The one in the wall?' the girl answered.

'That's right, the one in the wall.'

'We burnt it.'

'Oh? Why?'

'It was bad – needed to go,' she said firmly. Suzanne's jaw visibly dropped.

'But it was there to protect the people who lived here,' he said matter-of-factly.

Her china features narrowed. 'We don't want its protection.'

Lowry was aware of Suzanne's tension: Emma had acknowledged the cat's significance. 'Don't want protection from what?' he continued.

Her small shoulders shrugged nonchalantly, which he read as a sign that she had rumbled his form of questioning and knew he was on to her. Eventually she said 'whatever'.

'Of course you need to believe in it for its powers to be real,' Lowry said, turning to explain to Suzanne, 'To burn a mummified cat is ritualistic. Was it a special fire?'

'I can't remember,' Suzanne mumbled.

'Can you, Emma?'

'Yes, it was the longest day.'

'June twenty-first? Is that significant?'

'The sun begins to fall, and the dark rises.'

The words hung there. Lowry thought she was reciting from memory.

An open admission of witchcraft from a six-year-old child was not what he was after; rather an intimation that her daughters were perhaps not the angels their mother believed them to be. This familiarity with folklore was more than enough. He would not press the child for details of the fatal morning, but rather allow each girl to add detail to a broad picture assembling in the mother's mind. So when Emma asked if there was anything more, he said not for now and let her go, knowing she would have nothing significant to relay to the other two.

Emma left the room. Suzanne had only a vague recollection of something unpleasant discovered in the redecoration of the kitchen last year. A bundle in a swaddling, like a doll from a nativity.

'What on earth that was all about, I have absolutely no idea. How in God's name did she get her head filled with that at six?' Her brave face was slipping; her heart was telling her this was a precursor to something more sinister. Then it came back to her – 'Wait. White smoke everywhere.'

'What's that?' Lowry asked.

'There was a bonfire, I remember now, Lucy and Alice started it too close to the house; white smoke got in the kitchen. I was very cross.' She looked to Lowry for an explanation.

'Midsummer is a pagan festival. The white smoke is from

414

groundsel, a weed – burning it is a form of purification. I've seen it as a boy in Fingringhoe.'

Lowry rose from the sofa.

'What are you going to do?'

'With your permission, I want to search the house.' There was one thing missing.

'But that's been done . . .' She had no strength in her voice.

'No, not properly; at first we thought your husband's death a suicide, and did little more than a cursory examination of the ground floor, with the gun cabinet dusted for prints and so forth. Then our attention was drawn to Derrick, the antiques dealer. Now we are searching closer to home.' He picked up the phone. 'May I?'

She wanted to ask *what for*? But she did not want to hear the answer.

'Of course.' Her throat caught. And what did he mean, 'closer to home'? That her children had been dabbling with magic worried her the more because the police were taking it seriously; it could be put down to silliness otherwise. An overwhelming feeling of inadequacy consumed her – she had no idea what her children had been up to. With considerable effort, she managed to continue.

'Inspector, I'd appreciate it if you'd be frank with me. Where is all this leading? What do you mean "closer to home"?'

Lowry, who had been conversing in a low voice, replaced the receiver.

'The night before your husband was shot, you quarrelled about Edward, yes?'

'I've already said as much.'

'Initially the discussion took place at the Angel pub. It was an unusual move, the night your nephews arrived for the holidays, to abandon them almost immediately, don't you think?'

'Lucy and Alice are teenagers and more than capable, and Alan is on the cusp. They run wild as it is. Would I countenance them up on the railway track, no . . .' Suzanne held his gaze. 'Christopher and I wished to *discuss* Edward. I was to see my son the following morning, as you know and . . . and there was uncertainty over what would happen on his release. Christopher and I did not see eye to eye on Edward, it was he who suggested the pub to talk of my "problem son", as he would say . . .'

'To avoid your daughters overhearing, presumably.'

'They reacted badly to Edward's incarceration. He's their big brother, and they look up to him.'

'Did you reach a conclusion in the Angel?'

'No, we started to argue before even getting there, in the car. You see, Edward is the biggest reminder of my past; it's as if Jon – that's my ex – is materialising before his very eyes, they look so similar. Alice too, has a strong likeness to her father. Christopher would struggle even if Edward behaved perfectly. Anyhow, Edward had been spending a lot of time in Colchester since losing his job; Christopher believed he ought to forge his own path there, but I wanted him back at the farm, at least initially. Christopher refused. Then I wanted to go home, but he sensed his night in the pub was under threat so he said he'd think it over to placate me.'

'There were no raised voices then?'

'Not at first, no. Later, yes. I should probably have known better, the pub was just a ruse to get away from the children; he had no intention of discussing Edward. He proceeded to get pissed and we had an almighty row on the way home.'

'And continued once back?'

'I ceased to argue, aware of my nephews asleep upstairs, but was tipsy myself; perhaps our voices were raised. Christopher could be loud when he'd had a few. Please, Inspector, where is this heading?'

'I wonder, Mrs Cliff, if your daughters may have been in the kitchen when your husband was killed? Perhaps an accident, a tussle with the gun?'

11.45 a.m., Chelmsford Athletics Ground

Kenton lay on the grass almost delirious; the exertion and the ferocity of the sun had combined to sap him dry, albeit in a rather agreeable way. He'd been tried out for the 400 metres first, before getting onto 1,500 metres, the reason he was here. Why, oh why had he mentioned to Sparks that steeplechase was his favourite at boarding school . . .

How much sport was it possible to cram in? He closed his eyes and considered the possibility of taking the afternoon off. He was dehydrated from a session in the Dragoon last night. The station was quiet, there wasn't much going on, he was here on Sparks's orders. He had to draw the line on all this activity, he found he was fast becoming little more than a mascot for the police, an advertisement of their physical capability, which was all well and good but he really wanted to be a detective, and of late that had fallen into second place. He must raise his concerns with the chief . . . A shadow passed overhead. He opened his eyes to see a district official.

'Any water on you, mate, I'm parched?'

'You are required to report to Fox Farm, Kelvedon, immediately.'

12.15 p.m., Fox Farm

Lowry wished to sow a seed of doubt in the mother's mind, but did not wish to cripple her. Suzanne stared at Gabriel, as if expecting her to refute Lowry's explanation. The woman smiled unconvincingly in return.

'I don't believe it. The magic is just a childish prank, a fancy,' Suzanne retorted eventually. She had halted further questioning of her children until she had a clearer idea of where this might take them. She was starting to wonder whether she should have legal assistance, but then that would be an admission that she was worried . . .

'Children will look for guidance in any available quarter when distressed; whatever is to hand,' Lowry said. She did not grasp this at all.

'Where does the magic even come from?' she said finally.

'You moved from a suburban area to an isolated farmhouse deep in the countryside, no children for miles around and long, long days. What is there for them to do other than explore

419

the surrounding area and read? Your husband is a historian, the books in this house hold all kinds of mysteries.'

She regarded him suspiciously.

'Did you not read what was on your parents' shelves?'

'Yes, I did, *Lolita*, *Lady Chatterley's Lover* . . .'

'And did your parents know?'

'I doubt it, too busy with the parade ground . . .'

'Attention is always paid to what kids see on TV or cinema, but not what they read. Books have been around a lot longer.'

'It's one thing to skim a novel to find the juicy bits, and another entirely to read with the intention of learning about witchcraft, which is what I think you are saying.'

'Fair point,' he willingly conceded, 'it may be that books alone are not entirely responsible, but they do provide a good starting point – a springboard into another world. I suspect there was encouragement to be had not far away, but first let's talk to the girls and see how we go? If what we hear gives cause for concern, I promise we will investigate further, beyond your husband's library.'

Lucy, being the eldest, made the obvious ringleader. The Ouija board lay on the oak table in front of them. They sat at the kitchen table, which was light and airy with the windows and door wide open. With flowers on the table and the soft rumble of a washing machine, it would take a vivid imagination to place a death and bloodied floor here weeks earlier, and yet that was what they were here to discuss.

'Can you explain this?' her mother asked sternly.

'Just a bit of fun.' Lucy's no-nonsense appearance – a neat fringe, no make-up, and spectacles – did not lend support to this answer. 'We found it.'

'Found it? Where?'

'In Father's study.'

Lowry found her steely cool too much. Precocity on this level was chilling. Suzanne shrugged faintly, as if to say *maybe*.

'And you know how it works?'

'Works? It moves all by itself.'

'To communicate with dead people.'

'Yes, I know.'

'Who would you have to talk with?' Suzanne cut in.

'Grandma.' She stared fixedly at her mother.

'And what does she say?'

'Just a natter.'

'Don't be ridiculous, Lucy.'

'And you used it the night before your father was killed?' Lowry said evenly.

Lucy placed her forefinger on her bottom finger. 'Did we?'

'Alan saw you.'

'Then it must be so.' Her eyes moved to him.

'What sort of things do you chat about?'

'How we're all doing, are we well. That she misses us all.' He had to hand it to her, chilling or not, she had remarkable composure. After ten minutes they had established that this Ouija practice was a regular occurrence – which explained why

Lucy made light of it. Lowry was not convinced but did not challenge her. He was about to raise the question of Emma's argument with Alice that morning but was interrupted by Suzanne.

'Lucy, I don't know what you're up to but I want you to tell the truth. All this nonsense makes the police think you're fibbing. Are you? Did you see something when Daddy was killed?'

Immediately, as if by the flick of a switch, the girl went red and burst into tears. If he were being cynical, Lowry would have said Suzanne provoked her deliberately to sabotage his efforts to tease information out of her daughter. The interview was, to all intents and purposes, over.

'My mother was not a fan of Christopher,' Suzanne said as the girl hurried out of the room.

'Would your daughters know that?'

She held her head in her hands, elbows on her knees. 'I have no idea. My mother was a soldier's wife and disciplinarian with a strict code of conduct.'

'When did she pass away?'

'Last year. She herself never had a son, only three girls. Oh God, what a family.'

'What is it?'

'She wrote to Christopher after Edward's trial.'

'And?'

Suzanne sighed. 'I left it there, at his office, but the gist was that he was negligent with the children ... and ... and that no good would come of it. That I remember exactly.'

'Do you think she may have poisoned them against him?'

'No. She babysat regularly, and perhaps bemoaned their absent stepfather, but I don't think she cut any sway with them.' She reached for her cigarettes, and glancing at him gravely said, 'Certainly not of a magnitude to reach them from beyond the grave, if that's what you're suggesting.'

Alice was the prettiest of the three, with sun-blond hair, and Lowry now saw the resemblance to Edward. The calm look of one steadfast in belief. Demur, she stood with her back towards the television, hands clasped behind her as if summoned before a teacher. Lowry and Suzanne Cliff remained seated. Gabriel intentionally wasn't in the room. As far as possible he wished to create the air of an informal chat.

'Can you fire a gun?' Lowry asked casually.

'Of course, Father taught us.'

'Oh really? For what purpose?'

'Rabbits. Miss Everett is plagued by them.'

'Not a *Watership Down* fan, then?'

'If I heard a rabbit talking, I would spare it, otherwise they are pests, like rats. But rats move too quick to shoot.'

'Did you go hunting with your father? Pheasants and partridge were his speciality, I believe.'

'No, we were not allowed to point a gun above waist height. For safety reasons.' The girl raised an eyebrow ever so slightly. This middle child was the most precocious of the lot.

'I see.'

The door chime went. 'That'll be your colleagues, no doubt,' Suzanne said, rising. Alice registered this and tilted her head to one side as her mother left the room.

Lowry stood and said softly, 'Why were you at the window, the morning of your stepfather's death? Your cousin, Alan, saw you. Did you know Roger Derrick was coming?'

'You're a clever policeman.' Her tone had changed.

'Thank you.' He heard the door through to the hall click shut. Funny. That can't have been Suzanne –

'But you're not that clever.' Alice stepped closer, her clear, unblemished features and startling bright eyes, green-brown, untainted by the world. He lowered his head to meet her gaze when she screamed so loudly it rang right through him, leaving his ears deep in white noise, whereupon in a blink of an eye she lashed out and tore at his throat with her nails, leaving him with the sensation of water running down his neck.

'He attacked me!' Alice shouted over his shoulder. Stooped and clutching his neck, he saw from Suzanne's face, now at the door, that he must be bleeding. His fingers confirmed this. The girl ran to her mother, who held her tightly.

'What did you do?' she said accusingly.

'Do you think I would?'

'I— What happened . . . ?'

'Mummy, he tried to touch me.' The girl was convincing. Lowry could see Suzanne search for an explanation: she wanted to believe her daughter's words – the alternative was too much to bear. Alice cowered into her mother, covering her mouth, fingers displaying lengthy nails that seconds earlier had transformed into talons of supernatural strength.

'I saw the whole episode from outside.' Gabriel appeared. 'The window is open.' All three adults turned to the window. Alice darted between Gabriel and her mother. Lowry lunged after her, nearly knocking into the two other girls who stood motionless in the hall. For a second he stopped to consider them – why there – then ran through the kitchen, catching his foot on a broom. As he crashed into the work surface the two girls whooshed through and out the door, laughing as if in a game.

'You okay?' Gabriel's hand touched his arm and he nodded, urging her past him as he regained his footing.

'Stop her!' Kenton had never heard Gabriel so much as raise her voice and was more taken aback by the surprising volume than what she had shouted as she ran out of the farmhouse towards him. Before he knew it, a child with long, light blonde hair shot past him towards the meadow. Lowry appeared in the doorway, clutching his neck, ashen-faced. He stared dumbly at his colleague before turning his eyes to the child, now in grass up to her shoulder.

'Catch her, Dan!' Lowry shouted, and with an effort Kenton lumbered off, not waiting for Gabriel, into the meadow, his throat as dry as the grass he waded through.

After a hundred yards of blind pursuit, Kenton realised he'd lost sight of Alice and paused, panting amid the scrape of crickets just beyond the giant oak tree to catch his breath and scan the horizon. There, a movement. She was bobbing along, the sun catching her hair, close to the woods lining the railway embankment. He hadn't any idea what had gone on and why he had to catch the kid. The whole situation felt wrong – a casual observer would see a child at play on a glorious summer afternoon. And a grown man in pursuit. He cursed under his breath and ran on. The girl, knowing the hidden paths and tracks, soon disappeared into the woodland. Kenton had only been out here once, when they had found Darnell, and was soon bamboozled by the landscape. However, he imagined that police backup was on the way. That girl was not dumb enough to try to hide in the undergrowth, so he forged ahead, not sure where he was going, eventually lumbering up the incline of the railway embankment. On reaching the track, he stopped again, hands on his knees. His head throbbed mightily. The combination of this morning's run and the track day had well and truly drained him. Two tiny, plastic cupfuls of water were not enough liquid for a schoolboy on sports day, let alone a man of his build . . . After a moment he stood and glanced to his left then right. Nothing. The girl's knowledge of the terrain had allowed her to give them the slip. Looking back towards the house, he saw the flashing light of a newly arrived police Cortina and a scurry of blue uniforms. God knew where Gabriel was, she hadn't been here before, and was probably lost in the trees below. Off to the other side of the track sat a combine harvester, like a sleeping crocodile in a yellow sea of shorn wheat. Then a darting motion caught his eye. The girl appeared on the embankment to his left, scrambling up and running down the track eastwards, towards Kelvedon. He'd put her in front by fifty yards. Ordinarily he would catch her without breaking a sweat, but as he took up pursuit, his leaden legs didn't have it in them. They both continued east, along the London-bound track, the gap between the man and child growing all the time and the sun's powerful rays on his back adding to his discomfort. He felt increasingly queasy with each laboured breath. Up ahead he saw the horizontal parallel white bars of the level crossing. Surely she wouldn't continue further, and they'd apprehend her in the village. Inwardly he groaned with relief – the chase would soon be over, hopefully before he himself expired. He prayed Lowry had put those blasted binoculars of his to some practical use for once and had clocked the direction in which they were running. If so, he'd head her off rather than continue to hunt her on his own in the village. The girl slipped over the white gate . . . hold on – it was moving. That meant only one thing. An oncoming train. A shiver ran through his dehydrated body. But from which direction? He moved in between the two tracks. He stopped. Behind him he could see nothing. He continued but at a much-reduced pace. The view ahead now stretched away into the distance, unbroken with the gates back, the road halted. He needed to get clear of the line. Then he thought he could hear something, or feel it – running through the track. At the same time, a figure moved out from the right, in front of him, accompanied by a cry of warning some distance off. The girl stood with her back to him in the right-hand track, then with exaggerated moves as in a child's game, she hopped into the Colchester down track to his left. The train was almost upon them, he knew it, but couldn't tear his eyes from the girl standing on the track. He opened his mouth but his throat was arid and his voice gone. As he tried to speak, the thunder of a train's horn shot through him with such force his bladder released. On impulse he glanced to his trousers before lifting his head to see the girl spin round, arms spread and fingers splayed, face alive in mirth, and though the unearthly squeal of metal on metal drowned the immediate world, he swore she mouthed 'BOO!' as she jumped in front of the train and he fell onto the adjacent track.

– 51 –

3.15 p.m., Queen Street HQ

'Hmm, traumatic.' Sparks said the word with a sharp clip, as if he had trod on a tack, barefoot. 'Very traumatic.'

Lowry, sitting opposite, did not look the full ticket either. His appearance was deteriorating on a daily basis. The bandages on his neck did little to improve it. The bottle of Scallywag stood vertically between them on the desk. The mascot terrier on the label staring Sparks in the eye, goading him: why didn't he get a dog instead of a baby?

'Where is he now? Kenton?'

'Home, I guess. He was shaken, but he'll live.'

Sparks nodded. Could the girl have lived, did it have to end like this – those would be the thoughts running through Kenton's head today, tonight, tomorrow night and every night for the foreseeable future. Both he and Lowry had experienced it; every policeman went through it at least once in their career. He reached for the bottle and unscrewed the top. The Cliff girl's death had snagged at an incident from his own past.

'It would have ended badly, for the girl – I mean, if not now then some time in the near future. I doubt she'd have made it through her teens. You should tell him that.'

Lowry took his Scotch and stretched out his legs, his eyes on the corner of the office. Sparks knew that Lowry himself could have let it lie, left the case shrouded but shut. His words for Kenton were as much for Lowry.

'It might not be true,' Sparks continued, 'but that doesn't matter.'

'I'll tell him,' he conceded.

'What of the others?'

'Severalls.'

The asylum up on the Essex plains; a huge sprawling place built by the Edwardians to house the region's nutters. A capacity of two thousand.

'That'll be the last we hear of them for a while.' The place gave him the creeps. 'Well. There's nothing more to do for now, Merrydown has shut you down. No talking to the press until she's signed off on a statement. You understand? It's tricky.'

Lowry nodded.

'You are sure it was Alice that pulled the trigger?' Sparks asked, not wanting Lowry to think there was any doubt in his mind as far as he was concerned.

'Her or Lucy, the youngest wouldn't have the strength to hold the gun accurately. They could easily have squirrelled away the cartridges, he willingly hands over the gun while cleaning it ... just one thing is missing, and that would clinch it.'

'What?'

'Cliff was shot at very close quarters – that we've always known – but I hadn't thought of blood splashback until I guessed the trigger was pulled by someone on the farm.'

'And the clothes must still be there, somewhere?'

'Exactly, that's why I called Kenton in to search the place. Nothing yet but Uniform are going over it with a fine-tooth comb, there has to be a garment hidden somewhere. That's the concrete proof, only then will we get access to the other girl. Otherwise the mother will fight to have the other two out after a period of observation. I'm sure she'll win – they disguise it very well.'

'Tch. What exactly is *it*? "Granny told me to do him in" – through a Ouija board? Madness or religion?'

'I don't have an answer, but can't help but think there's another involved. All right, the grandmother loathed her son-in-law, we have that letter as evidence, but she's been dead since last November. There must be more of an impetus than a bunch of old books to drive these girls to do what they did and become what they became. They can't just be condemned as crazy and that's it; there has to be an explanation. My money is on Kate Everett.'

'Why? On what evidence?'

'She's a teacher. They spent a lot of time together. She has this ...' He searched for a word.

'What?' Sparks said.

'Aura.'

'You'll need more than an "aura" to start meddling with Everett again, I can tell you that for free. Her defence is pushing for diminished responsibility, so don't go poking around; we don't want to give them cause to complain. She's been transferred to Bullwood Hall, by the way.' Lowry was as grounded a policeman as Sparks knew; though calm as ever, something had got under his skin with this case. He needed a break. 'Just find the clothing or let it go.' Sparks continued resolutely, 'Anyway, regardless how these girls ended up like this – in this condition or illness, whatever it is – you don't just shake that off.'

'Perhaps, perhaps not.'

'You're remarkably cool all things considered. How was the mother? You got pretty close there?'

'I'm sure she's not given me a second thought. She's lost a daughter and husband in the space of a month. Her life's in pieces right now.'

Sparks saw a flicker in the nonchalance. 'You did what you had to do. Who knows what mayhem might have transpired had you let sleeping dogs lie.'

Lowry sipped his drink. 'Sleeping dogs. Let dead cats lie would be more accurate.'

The cat buried in the farmhouse wall. Sparks did not want to go there. He noticed blood had started to seep from the plaster on Lowry's neck. 'Get that seen to.'

'It's fine, I can't feel it.'

'Don't be a twat, get it cleaned up. There's no point risking an infection. And take a day off tomorrow.'

Lowry smiled, 'I'm touched.'

'If I didn't know better, I'd think you're feeling sorry for yourself – I mean, you're practically falling apart.' Lowry lit a cigarette. 'You've not had a day off all summer. It doesn't do not to take a break. Go shut yourself in a bird hide somewhere.'

'Maybe you're right . . .' He blew smoke into the room and rose to go.

'About what?'

'The girl, about the girl, Alice.' Lowry left the office without finishing his thought. They all wanted to believe on some level that what had happened was unavoidable. It made the job easier.

Sparks reached for the Scallywag. The situation was far from satisfactory. He didn't doubt Lowry's account of what had gone on, but the wider world might take some convincing; all this weirdness without any concrete evidence. Not to put too fine a point on it, if they could find the kids' clothing marked with Cliff's blood, it would make the whole episode a heck of a lot easier to swallow. Otherwise he foresaw the Fox Farm murder dragging on for months, reaching an unsatisfactory conclusion. He tipped the Scotch down his throat in one go. How unsatisfactory, he couldn't yet countenance, although his years in the force nudged his conscious towards an ignominious stain on the department: *'Remember that hot spell in the country when a young detective chased a girl under a train?'*

3.25 p.m., West Mersea beach

Kenton sat on the beach.

'I know it's useless to say this, but it comes with the job.' He flinched as Jane placed her hand lightly on his shoulder. Gabriel withdrew it, and the second she'd done so he wished she'd let it remain: eager for contact, but too raw at the same time. He turned and caught her eye, though was unable to look at her for more than a matter of seconds and returned to squinting at the sea and the yachts keeling over in the estuary.

'I'm not sure I'm cut out for this,' he said, moving his heels into the sand. 'This job.'

To this she did not reply either, for there was no answer. Not right now, at any rate.

'Call me this evening?' she said finally.

She left him be, upset to see him so shaken, visibly transformed, the bright, laughing boy she spent time with on the beach gone. Unsure of how she felt herself, she craved company, and decided to see how the land lay with Lowry.

4 p.m., Queen Street HQ

With his feet up on the sash window, Lowry nursed a tumbler of Scotch in his lap, allowing the breeze and the noise of the street to wash over him. The telephone continued to ring. Whoever it was, he didn't want to speak to them. Sparks had not told him anything he did not know. And he knew well enough not to question whether he could have played it any differently; there lay the route to madness. As far as police work went, to maintain objectivity was key; for an even keel in the future you had to live by your decisions. His was a mind that would turn in on itself, if he allowed it; he only had to think back to when he met Becky Adams. Confronted with his own predicament, by a situation not of his making, he'd spent a dark night of the soul, unable to fathom what to do. His work could not be like that. Besides, there were plenty of others in life who would question your decisions for you. This case, however bizarre, was clear-cut. Kenton would learn this too one day. Lowry drank from the tumbler and shut his eyes. He thought of Suzanne Cliff. She blamed herself, as any mother would. The girl's suicide had frozen the case. Merrydown had closed them down. If it was Alice that pulled the trigger, the general public would be none the wiser, unless they found supporting evidence. He now thought he could do with a distraction to clear the woman and her family from his mind. And that went for Kate Everett, too – he shouldn't muddy the waters there without good reason. He should try to relax. Oldham had offered to take him sailing, cruise up the Blackwater, overnight in Maldon. Drink rum and listen to music. It had its appeal, even if the music had to be classical. It would put him out of reach of his wife, and defer any decision over Becky. If only Uniform would uncover the garment that must exist somewhere on the farm. Meantime, he would go to the hospital – Sparks's suggestion of martyrdom had rattled him enough to go even if it was pointless – then he'd head to Mersea in time to make the evening tide. On his desk sat a brown paper parcel delivered by his second-hand bookseller. Lowry had expressed a great urgency for the contents, hence the personal service; he reached over for the parcel.

'Sir . . . excuse me, sir.' He spun round on the chair to see a young uniformed officer. 'On the telephone, it's a Mrs Darnell?'

'Jesus, yes, put her through,' Lowry said. Since dismissing Peter Darnell's wife as on holiday, he hadn't given the poor widow another thought. 'Hello, Lowry speaking,' he said hurriedly; 'my apologies, Mrs Darnell, I did try to call you back but assumed you'd gone away with your sister after all.'

'Inspector Lowry, this is Sarah Bowles, Elizabeth's sister.'

Something was wrong. He waited.

'My sister is dead.'

Elizabeth Darnell had been to see her doctor several times the previous week before being admitted to hospital, where she died within hours. The cause of death was judged to be respiratory complications. The consultant under whose brief care Elizabeth had been placed, having requested a list of all prescribed medicines, soon arrived at a verdict of Valium overdose. 'My sister wasn't the type to do that, Mr Lowry.'

'I'm very sorry,' Lowry said, not commenting on the hospital's judgement.

'There was something else in the medicine cabinet.' She stopped speaking long enough for him to take in the hum of the phone line, then said, 'Something unprescribed.'

'Go on.'

'An unlabelled brown jar. The hospital said it was possibly a herbal remedy, harmless, but I wanted to tell someone as I have no idea where Elizabeth would have got such a syrup.' Again a pause. 'She wouldn't kill herself – I know her, no matter how bad things got.'

This time the silence was from Lowry's end.

'Thank you for telling me this, I'm glad you called.' He swallowed, and tried to think of a helpful remark, while his mind was racing. 'Your sister has experienced a lot of pain, and the doctor, hard though it is to hear, is probably right. But let me check for you. Leave me your number and I will call back, would that be okay?'

Lowry was in no doubt where this 'syrup' came from. He asked for the consultant's name and then hung up. He needed to make two telephone calls, first to the hospital, then to the scene-of-crime's doctor, Sutton, a keen amateur botanist.

5.30 p.m., Sweet Pea Cottage, Fox Lane

'Doctor Sutton, thank you for agreeing to meet me at short notice.' The doctor's Morris Traveller was parked in the tiny driveway, forcing Lowry to leave his car in the road.

'I must say, Lowry, this is most irregular.' The man's bald dome shone with perspiration in the late afternoon sun.

'I'm appealing to your inquistive nature.'

Dr Sutton, wearing a navy linen suit, sniffed in affirmation. 'I am curious, that much is true. Tell me again.'

'A woman in her mid-forties has died of unknown causes. The consultant who examined her said her death was consistent with poisoning, administered gradually over a period of time, say two weeks. The only item in the deceased's possession that has aroused suspicion is a herbal remedy.' Lowry, to engage the doctor, readily exchanged the hospital assessment with his own theory.

'That originated here?' The doctor eyed the cottage dubiously.

'I think so, yes. The occupant was a keen, but unorthodox,

gardener, who perhaps kept plants for reasons other than their beauty,' Lowry said, vocalising for the first time his suspicion that Kate Everett may be a double murderer. 'This way, round the back.'

'The house of the woman that killed the accountant, eh?'

Sutton, once through the arbour, stood tutting. 'Nice, very nice.' Together they strolled around the flower beds. Lowry pressed keenly for a result, pointing out plants he thought the doctor had missed, but the man took in all and would not be hurried, and considered the various specimens, whether thought to be harmful or not, with equal precision.

On the verge of giving up as they neared the end, Sutton suddenly exclaimed, 'Aha! There at the back, sticking up behind those marigolds, with the purple tubular flowers.'

'What is it?'

'Foxgloves.'

'Poisonous?'

'Lethal.' The doctor stood back, satisfied. 'But only if ingested in very large quantities. Contains digitalin, which is actually used to treat heart conditions, to moderate heart rate. Too much is very bad.'

Lowry considered the tall spikes of the admittedly beautiful purple flowers. 'But the flower looks to be very much intact?'

They both moved closer. 'Yes,' the doctor noted, 'that cluster is.'

Lowry was not convinced. What did he really expect, after

all, a witch's cauldron? He looked to the cottage. This wasn't going to be as straightforward as he had hoped. He needed to get in, but not with Sutton present.

'Thanks, doc.'

'Smashing garden.' The man was unsurprisingly far more cheerful in a garden filled with beautiful plants than on a railway embankment examining a corpse. 'That what you're after?' he said.

'Inconclusive,' Lowry smiled dryly leaving the garden, 'but thanks all the same.' He'd see Sutton away, then try to get in. Lowry waited by the doctor's Morris.

'Hold on a sec,' Sutton called out. 'Here, we've not examined the front garden.'

'There's nothing there, it's overgrown with weeds.'

'Exactly.'

Lowry retraced his steps, as Sutton pushed past the black-thorn and waded into the garden. 'Well, well.' He grinned.

'What have you found?'

'Nightshade, recently cut too.'

6.30 p.m., HM Prison Bullwood Hall, Hockley, Essex

Lowry telephoned Gabriel at Queen Street asking her to meet him in an hour at Sweet Pea Cottage with the forensics team currently at Fox Farm. He should, he knew, spearhead the search of Everett's cottage himself for toxic substances, but he was impatient, and could not resist a final encounter with

Everett herself. The south Essex women's prison was fifty minutes drive due south, close to Southend.

Kate Everett was impartial to Lowry's arrival. Wearing the same pale blue overalls allocated her in Chelmsford, she struck him as just as relaxed as on their previous encounter. He pulled up a chair in the box interview room.

'Alice Cliff is dead,' he said bluntly.

Lowry watched very closely for a reaction.

'I don't believe you.'

He shrugged, 'Up to you, it will be in the newspapers tomorrow, if not this evening's news.'

'How?'

'Dreadful. Especially difficult for me: I was the last person she spoke to. See this?' He pointed to his neck. 'She did it' – her eyes moved from his eyes to his throat, as he continued – 'before throwing herself in front of a train, rather than face a few questions over the shooting of her father.'

Everett closed her eyes then slowly opened them, betraying nothing, and said, 'Why are you here?'

'I thought you'd like to know, given your close relationship.'

He held out his cigarettes. She thanked him politely and said, 'Inspector, that is devastating. Poor child, and poor Suzanne, as if that family has not suffered enough.' The insincerity was thinly veiled. 'You don't really think Alice shot Christopher?'

'I do and I think you are involved.' He struck a match and held it out.

'Involved? How so?'

'Pulling the Cliff girls into whatever pagan rites you preach. Seducing them while neglected by their parents.'

'They were "Pagan rites",' she laughed mockingly, 'what do you know of "pagan rites"?'

'I know they exist, always have, passed on from generation to generation. The girls burnt a mummified cat – I doubt that was at the suggestion of their mother; more likely a teacher familiar with folklore?'

'Ridiculous.' Her green eyes, once alluring, flashed hard, angry emerald. He pictured now how she had lashed out at the mild-mannered Peter Darnell. And that was what had troubled Lowry all along – why did this gentle man storm off? Over what, an argument about a tent? A departure time for a weekend away? No, Peter Darnell had discovered his lover was slowly poisoning his wife, and he himself was the one administering it, naive enough to think it a herbal remedy – until it dawned on him his wife was getting worse, not better.

'Why is it ridiculous? You taught them to make a corn dolly, and they wouldn't know to burn groundsel – the only reason Suzanne remembers the fire, from its white smoke.'

'They needed love –' Everett's mouth fell – 'that's all I offered. That, and the love I have of the earth we live on.'

'Perhaps.'

She remained silent, staring into space. And he would not be drawn.

Lowry had as close to a confession as he was likely to get. He realised now that he had been strangely compelled to come here. There was no real reason to see Kate Everett; she would tell him nothing new in this sterile place. The answers lay in the cottage.

'Did you know they planned to kill Christopher?' he said finally. 'You were round there, at the farm, in record time. That's something we will never know, I guess. Unlike the poisoning of Elizabeth Darnell.'

'Elizabeth's dead, isn't she?' It was her turn to be blunt. 'That's the reason you're here.'

He nodded, and rose. 'Did you know the symptoms of nightshade poisoning are very similar to that of overdosing on Valium?'

7.45 p.m., Sweet Pea Cottage, Fox Lane

'Hello.' She leant down to the car window. Gabriel's appearance in the road surprised Lowry. Even though he'd asked her to meet him, at the back of his mind he thought she would be comforting the stricken Kenton.

'They've not found anything, sorry.'

'That's okay.'

She didn't ask him where he'd been, instead she nodded towards the brown paper parcel on the seat. 'What's that you've got there?'

'Oh yes, I forgot about that.'

On the drive back from Bullwood he'd been preoccupied thinking how Everett's defence of diminished responsibility would be drastically compromised – surely the poison originating from the cottage alone would do damage there, before they even arrived at the complexities of who gave Elizabeth Darnell the damn stuff.

'Come quickly,' a young forensics man called out to them, 'the woodburner.'

Inside the kitchen, on the table, lay what appeared to be a dirty blackened rag, but on closer inspection was a girl's dress. The officer having led them in, stepped back and uttered, 'Around the neck.'

There, on the material, was unmistakably dried blood. 'Alice's dress?' Gabriel said.

Lowry thanked them all. It was a relief – maybe he didn't realise how much right then – but if the blood tested, then they were clear. They had a case. He stepped out into the garden.

'You don't seem that pleased,' Gabriel said, misreading his thoughts.

'Just need some air.'

'Oh.'

'Hello, what's he doing here still?' He gestured towards a figure in navy moving about beyond the gate at the bottom of the garden.

'Sutton, the scene-of-crime doctor?' Lowry didn't have the energy to explain Elizabeth Darnell's poisoning.

'Excuse me a moment, Jane.'

*

'Ah Lowry, there you are. See here, a red ribbon, tied in the thorn.'

'What of it?'

'There for a reason, I think.' He scoured the rest of the hedge, which as it stretched further along the field blended with brambles, sprouting fronds of young blackberries. The bridleway itself, running between the field and the hedge, was pocked with the yellow flower heads of the weed ragwort. Lowry reached to touch the ribbon. As he stepped closer, he noticed below the weeds the earth was a dusty grey. Except it wasn't earth, it was ash.

Lowry knelt down, pulling out his Swiss army knife. 'The earth has been disturbed among this ragwort.'

'So it has.'

'Someone has been digging here,' Lowry said. The soil underneath gave easily to his blade, revealing sheared twigs arranged over an eight-inch circumference. 'Why bury hedge cuttings?'

'Good question, but the hedge up here is blackthorn, while this,' he said, holding up a specimen, 'is whitethorn.' Sutton pulled the rest out. 'There's something underneath it.' The doctor scrabbled away excitedly. 'It's a jar,' and he yanked the object from the ground. Dusting it off, the brown jar was of a similar variety to the ones that lined the cottage kitchen. 'Wonder what's in it. Shall I?'

Lowry gave his assent. He was uneasy; it would have to be unpleasant.

Sutton loosened the lid, and peered inside. 'Oh, how boring.'

'What is it?'

'A bloody cigarette lighter.' The familiar object tumbled onto the doctor's palm. Lowry believed he had misplaced his Ronson some time ago.

'As we're in the area, shall we pay a call on Roger or check in on Wendy Harris?' Gabriel said. They sat in his Saab, watching as the last forensics man left the cottage. Lowry was impressed with her enthusiasm, but didn't share it.

'That's enough excitement for one day, but don't worry, we'll sort that out,' Lowry said, with more sincerity than he'd wished. Gabriel secured her seat belt and placed the brown paper parcel on her lap.

'What did you find in the field?' she asked. He had, as yet, not commented on what he and Sutton were up to.

'Oh, nothing, just some old jar.' He could sense her eyes on him, but would say no more. If he revealed it was his lighter tucked away, it would only lead to more questions, none of which he had an answer for.

The one fact that had leapt out at him, though, was that the day he'd experienced the nausea, he'd been standing on the exact spot they'd found the jar. The logical answer was she'd put something funny in his coffee, but the feeling had passed as swiftly as it had risen. What else could it possibly be? *Was he under a spell?*

'What have we here?' She tapped a fingernail on the package. 'May I?'

'Be my guest.'

She tore at the paper. 'Can I ask just one question? How did you know it was the daughter, Alice, that shot Cliff?'

'I didn't.'

'But you were right.'

'Take birds,' he said, seeing her reveal his books, 'raptors are difficult to identify; if not far away, then they'll be moving very quickly, so you have to assess size, outline, colour, the way they fly. I don't mean to bore you. Simply put, one has to rule what a bird isn't before one can discover what it could be ... and then by elimination, what you have must be the answer, however unlikely.'

'It's not boring. That sounds like Sherlock Holmes to me.'

'Exactly. Birds, murderers, same difference.'

She was sweet; nobody wanted to hear a trite bird analogy. He was aware he was sweating and needed a drink. He felt a crushing urge to be away from here; take a break as Sparks advised. 'The way we see things – people, objects, situations – often depends on circumstance. We see what we want to see, or expect to see. In this case we saw right past those girls until they were all that was left.'

'Here,' she said, pulling out the *Observer's Guide to British Bird Eggs*, 'this is for identifying the nest in the bedroom?' She flicked through the pages, then passed it over. He ruled out the obvious ones, robin, blackbird, sparrow, and turned to farmland birds. At first he speculated on raptor eggs. And then there it was. Yellowhammer.

He uttered a small sigh, 'Well, well.'

'What's that?'

'It's a yellowhammer.' He held the book out for her to see.

'What does that mean?'

'I don't know, maybe nothing. Let's see. Hand the other over.' The second book was grubby and without a dust jacket. Written in the thirties, this was a book on superstition and the natural world, and to his surprise there was an entry in the index for the brightly coloured bunting:

> The bird is often thought to be evil and bearer of the Devil's blood, as it holds a drop on its tongue and eggs. These latter markings are thought to be occult, conveying a demonic message, leading to the old name 'scribble lark'.

He passed the old book over. She bent her head forward curiously towards the page. 'Is it an evil bird?'

'No, it's beautiful, a beacon of the summer, with a mesmerising song.'

Lowry thought back to that moment when he saw a bird on the hawthorn on the road to Fox Farm and how then he was unable to identify it, the creature appearing only as a silhouette in the sunlight; but when leaving the farm and approaching the hedgerow from the opposite direction with the sun behind him, he fancied he saw the same bird, a yellowhammer, in all its glory. The shift in light altered one's perception just as he'd described to Gabriel – the same was true when applied to the Cliff girls. When they'd first met in the wake of their stepfather's death, they appeared bereft; at the hospital visiting Edward, they were radiant in health, as if wearing a sheen as form of protection; and finally, Alice ablaze in her fury with her sister, was caught in the late sun, where he saw her features deformed like a malevolent spirit.

'I'd like to see one,' Gabriel said, drawing his attention to the present, 'a yellowhammer.'

He turned to face her and smiled, starting the car. 'Let's see if we can find you one then; they are very much here.'

Don't miss out on the latest thriller
in the DI Nick Lowry series,

WHITETHROAT

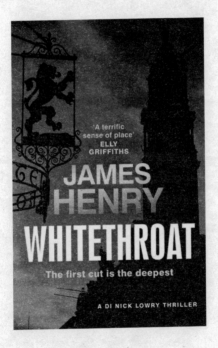

'A terrific
sense of place'
ELLY
GRIFFITHS

JAMES
HENRY

WHITETHROAT

The first cut is the deepest

A DI NICK LOWRY THRILLER

Coming July 2020 . . .

ACKNOWLEDGEMENTS

Thanks to Jon Riley, Sarah Castleton, Felicity Blunt, Richard Arcus, Sharona Selby, David Shelley, Olivia Hutchings, Dave Murphy, Ron Beard, Bob Mackenzie, Dominic Smith, Patrick Carpenter, Keith Bambury, Andrew Smith, Georgina Difford, Richard Beswick, Alan Munson, Sarah Neal, Katie Gurbutt, Henry Sutton.